A Broken Vessel

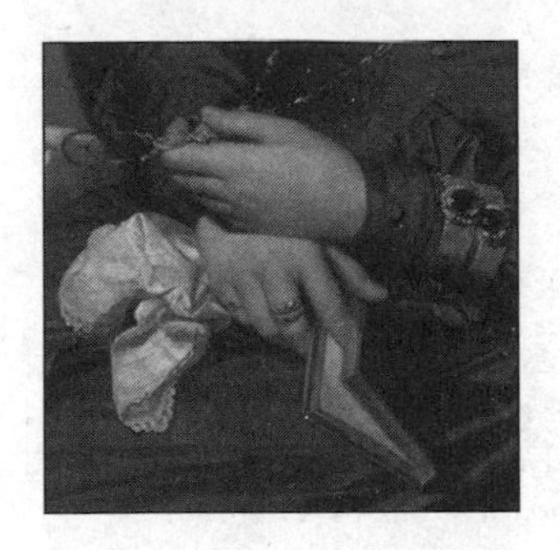

A Broken Vessel

Kate Ross

Felony & Mayhem Press • New York

The characters in this novel are fictitious, with the exception of Sir Richard Birnie, who was Chief Magistrate at Bow Street at the time the book takes place. Stark Street is an imaginary locale; the other streets mentioned by name are authentic.

A BROKEN VESSEL

A Felony & Mayhem mystery

PRINTING HISTORY
First edition (Viking Penguin): 1994
Felony & Mayhem edition: 2011

ISBN: 978-1-934609-71-2

Manufactured in the United States of America

Printed on 100% recycled paper.

Library of Congress Cataloging-in-Publication Data

Ross, Kate.
A broken vessel / Kate Ross.
p. cm.
Originally published: New York, N.Y., U.S.A.: Viking, 1994.
"A Felony & Mayhem mystery" --T.p. verso.
ISBN 978-1-934609-71-2
1. Kestrel, Julian (Fictitious character)--Fiction. 2. Police--England--London--Fiction. 3. London (England)--History--1800-1950--Fiction. I. Title.
PS3568.O843494B76 2011
813'.54--dc22

2011000748

To Dana Young, who is too modest
about her abilities as a critic

I would like to thank Richard Sharp and Ken Stone, of Scotland Yard's Metropolitan Police Museum, for their considerate assistance with my research. I would also like to thank the following people for their help, advice, and moral support: Edward A. Ross, Louis A. Rodriques, Mark J. Poerio, Mark L. Levine, Christina Ward, and Al Silverman.

Contents

The icon above says you're holding a copy of a book in the Felony & Mayhem "Historical" category, which ranges from the ancient world up through the 1940s. If you enjoy this book, you may well like other "Historical" titles from Felony & Mayhem Press.

For more about these books, and other Felony & Mayhem titles, or to place an order, please visit our website at:

www.FelonyAndMayhem.com

or contact us at:

Felony and Mayhem Press
156 Waverly Place
New York, NY 10014

Other "Historical" titles from

FELONY & MAYHEM

TONY BROADBENT
The Smoke
Spectres in the Smoke

DAVID STUART DAVIES
Forests of the Night

ANTON GILL
City of the Horizon
City of Dreams
City of the Dead

KEITH HELLER
Man's Illegal Life

PETER LOVESEY
Bertie and the Seven Bodies
Bertie and the Crime of Passion

FIDELIS MORGAN
Unnatural Fire

KATE ROSS
Cut to the Quick

CATHERINE SHAW
The Library Paradox
The Riddle of the River

DAVID WISHART
Ovid
Germanicus

A Broken Vessel

The Luck of the Draw

The man trudged along the pavement with his hands clasped behind him and his eyes on the ground. The night life of the Haymarket swirled around him. Lights winked in coffee-house windows. Laughter, song, and abuse boomed from public houses. Carriages thronged the street, blocking one another's way and setting off shouting matches between the drivers. Street-sellers hawked fruit, nuts, oysters, or gingerbread and kidney pies served hot from little portable stoves. A one-man band performed on one corner, a lantern-lit puppet show on another. Ragged boys circled the spectators, on the watch for something to steal.

The man plodded on, starting nervously whenever a raucous barker tried to lure him into a theatre or shop. Gaudily dressed girls angled for his attention, but he hurried past them, shaking his head.

Sally watched him approach, undaunted by those other girls' lack of success. He was just the kind of flat she liked:

middle-aged, respectable, timid. His sort were clean, and apt to be grateful, and they treated a girl decent. Of course, picking up a flat was always the luck of the draw: you could never be quite sure what you were getting. But this one looked like a square cove, right enough. She wondered what he was doing in the Haymarket at this time of night.

She waited by a gaslamp till he came near, then stepped straight into his path, so that he had no choice but to stop and look at her in the murky, yellowish light. Her cloak hung open to reveal her favourite gown, made of Turkey red silk. It was not so clean as it once was, and too flimsy for the October night, but it showed off her figure to advantage: short and slim, but with the right curves in the right places.

"Evening, sweetheart." She gave him her melting, mischievous, take-me-and-do-what-you-like-with-me smile. "Long day in the shop?"

"How did you know I kept a shop?"

"I've got me ways. Now, don't take on," she added, seeing him start. "I can tell by your duds—neat as ninepence, and a bit formal-like."

"Oh. Well—er—goodnight—"

He moved to pass her. She stepped with him, blocking his way.

"I—I can't stay—" he faltered.

"Not even if I was to ask you nice?" She touched his cheek. "Stubbly, ain't you? I'll have to call you Bristles." Because of course you never asked a flat his name, but you had to call him something.

He hesitated, glancing guiltily around him. Married, probably, Sally thought. Some men seemed to think their wives had eyes all over London.

"I know a crib we can go to, private-like," she coaxed. "Just down that street. Only a bob for the room. Wha'd'ye say?"

"I—I don't think I should—"

"Come on now. You have some'ut better to do?"

He closed his eyes. She thought she saw him shudder. "No."

"Come on, then."

She bore him off to the Cockerel, a little dark public house tucked away in a little dark street. Toby, the owner, was a former boxer, short and stocky, his sinews running to fat. He had a neck like a bulldog's, and a nose broken in at least three places. He said very little and never smiled. Nothing much, good or bad, impressed him.

Toby lived on the first floor above the public house and let out the second-floor rooms to ladybirds and their flats. There was not much danger that the authorities would take notice: the parish constables were too indolent, and the Bow Street Runners preferred bigger game. Slip them a bottle of spirits now and again, and they would turn a blind eye. God knew, such accommodation houses were common enough round the Haymarket, where girls like Sally were as numerous as the paving-stones they trod each night.

Sally brought Bristles into the taproom and up to the bar. "Evening, Toby. You have a room free?"

"Second floor back," he grunted.

She dug an elbow into Bristles, who put a shilling on the counter. Toby whisked it away and replaced it with a key. Sally took it, winking at him by way of thanks.

Lighting a tallow candle, she led Bristles into a dim, cobwebby hall behind the taproom. There was a door to the little-used back parlour, and a rear street door that was always barred. Through it, they could smell rubbish congealing in the alley behind the Cockerel, and hear the noise of skittering, squabbling rats.

They climbed four flights of uncarpeted stairs round a murky well. "Go careful," Sally warned, for the steps were slippery and uneven. "And don't lean on them banisters, they're rotted through. A good shove'd just about do for 'em."

The second-floor back room had nothing in it but a scantily covered bed hardly big enough for two, a cracked washbasin and pitcher on a wooden stand, and a chair with one leg missing. Everything was thickly coated with dirt, and the rusted grate had not seen a fire for some time.

Sally put her candle on the washstand and hung up her wide-brimmed bonnet on a peg. Its yellow flowers and bobbing canary birds made a splash of sunshine in the gloom. She pulled the pins out of her hair and put them on the washstand for safe-keeping; she was always losing hairpins. Her nut-brown hair tumbled over her shoulders: long at the back, but curling at the front and sides in imitation of the fashion plates in shop windows. Not that she would ever look like one of them, with their fair skins, straight noses, and daintily pursed lips. She had a brown complexion, a snub nose, and a wide mouth, with a missing tooth just visible when she smiled. Still, she was satisfied with her face. There was not much an enterprising girl could not do with a little cunning and a pair of liquid brown eyes.

Turning to Bristles, she found him shuffling uncertainly toward the door. She hauled him back. "What's to pay, Bristles? Don'cha like me?"

"I—yes, but—" He swallowed. "It's been a long time—"

"Then it's *high* time, and no mistake." She smiled, and came up on her toes to kiss him.

He was hard to bring on at first. She did her best with him, if only to cheer him up—he looked as if he needed it. Finally his body awakened, and he fell on her ravenously. If he had a wife, she certainly wasn't doing her duty by him. It amazed Sally how some wives stinted their husbands, then rang them a peal for going with girls like her. She did not think much of respectable women, but, then, she hardly knew any, so she would have admitted she was no judge.

While he was least likely to notice, she reached behind him and felt in the tail pocket of his coat. She liked to steal a little something from each flat she picked up. It was a kind of game to her; besides, it kept things business-like. Once in a while, especially if she did not like the man, she tried for something valuable, like a watch or a cravat-pin. But that was risky: if he found out, he might have her up before a magistrate, in spite of the embarrassment to himself. So she usually contented herself with a handkerchief, which could be counted on to fetch a few pence at the Field Lane handkerchief market.

She found Bristles's handkerchief and teased it out of his pocket. This was a bit of a challenge, lying on her back with him on top of her, but she had had plenty of practice. She rolled it up swiftly and tucked it behind her back until he was finished.

Afterward, he was tongue-tied, embarrassed, and awkwardly grateful. While he tidied himself, she furtively ran her teeth over the coins he had given her. He did not seem the sort to put the fun upon her, but you could not be too careful. Satisfied, she stowed the money away in a secret pocket under her skirt and, while he was not looking, stuffed the handkerchief in with it. Then she smoothed down her dress, put her bonnet on, and went to unlock the door.

As she turned the key, she heard quick, light footsteps in the hall outside. She knew what that meant: some cove had tipped Toby a shilling to let him spy on them through the keyhole. She looked down the hall, but he had gotten clean away. She shrugged. She was used to peepers: they were a hazard of her trade. She did not say anything about it to Bristles—he would only get into a fret.

She saw him to the door of the Cockerel. "Goodbye," he muttered shyly.

She kissed him lightly. "Keep out of trouble."

He flinched, shut his eyes for a moment, and walked rapidly away.

He's a rum 'un, she thought. She looked after him, watching him fend off the advances of other ladybirds. Hard luck, gals, she grinned, I seen him first.

She set her bonnet at a jaunty angle and sauntered outside. A cart piled high with some theatre's scenery was blocking the street, forcing a hackney coach to pull up behind it. The occupant of the hackney, a young man, let down the side-glass to see what the trouble was. Catching sight of Sally, he smiled.

She looked up airily, as though wondering if it might rain. The bold ones liked you to resist a bit—it gave them a sense of conquest.

"Come over here," he called.

"Was you talking to me?"

"You know I was."

"Me ma told me never to talk to a gentleman till we been introduced."

"Come over here, and I'll introduce us."

She strolled up to the hackney, curious to get a better look at him. He spoke like a gentry-cove, and she did not hook many of those. The carriage lamps showed her a man of about five-and-twenty, dressed in a blue evening coat, a white shirt and neckcloth, and a waistcoat of white silk embroidered with silver flowers. Anyone could see he had more blunt than he knew what to do with—just the cost of keeping all that white clean would pay Sally's rent for a year. And on top of everything else, he was handsome—Lord! He looked like the prince in a pantomime.

"Come in and have a ride." He opened the carriage door.

"Where'll you take me?"

"What's the odds? I wasn't planning you should look out the windows."

"Oh, it's like that, is it?" She looked in, wrinkling her nose. "There ain't much room in here."

"We won't need much." He held out his hand to help her in, with a smile that could light up Drury Lane Theatre.

"You're a charmer, *you* are. Anybody ever say no to you?"

His smile went a little awry. "You'd be surprised."

"Say, what's your racket, anyhow? I ain't your sort. You ought to be picking up one of them high-fliers as ride in the park in carriages, and taking her to some swell crib for supper and dancing."

"I don't want lights and people and witty conversation."

"What *do* you want, then?"

His charm fell away for a moment. His dark blue eyes were earnest, almost desperate. "I want you to stop me from thinking."

She looked at him for a short time. "Move over, Blue Eyes."

He called out to the driver to keep going round the neighbourhood till he told him to stop. The driver did not blink an eye; hackney coachmen had seen everything.

Sally resigned herself to a cramped, uncomfortable bout. The ride was bumpy: who ever heard of a hackney coach with four wheels all the same size? The torn seat cover scratched her bottom, and her beloved bonnet with the canaries got kicked about on the muddy floor. At least Blue Eyes wore armour—a sheath of sheep's gut tied with a ribbon at the open end. She was always glad when her flats protected, themselves, since they were protecting her, too. No law said a gentry-cove couldn't give you the Covent Garden ague, same as anyone else.

It was a lark to go with a gentry-cove now and again. They smelled so nice, and their hair was soft with care and cleanliness. Otherwise, they were pretty much the same as other flats. If they had better manners, they did not waste them on the likes of her. Blue Eyes was a bit of an odd fish, though. His heart was not in it. He might be a hundred miles away.

Just as well: it was all the easier to lift his handkerchief without his knowing. It was made of first-rate cambric—she could tell by the feel. She did not steal anything else, though she would dearly have liked to have the ring he wore on his little finger. It was square, with a jewel at each corner, and in the centre an ivory carving of a skull.

Afterward, he was glum and heavy-eyed, like a tired child. He did not ask how much he owed her, but forked out two crown pieces as if they were nothing. She hid them in the secret pocket under her skirt—quickly, before he could come to his senses and ask for change. While he leaned back against the seat, eyes closed, she slipped his handkerchief in after them.

He let her out not far from where he had found her. She decided to go back to the Cockerel and see if she could get some cove to stand her a drop. Of course, she had plenty of blunt now—she wriggled with pleasure, feeling the pocketful of coins and handkerchiefs bump against her knee as she walked—but that was no reason to buy herself a drink, if she could get a man to buy it for her.

She strolled around the taproom, exchanging greetings with people she knew. Many of Toby's patrons were former boxers like himself, come down in the world and given to the drink. The rest were common enough types in this neighbourhood: street performers, brothels' bullies, thieves. Some brought their wives; the other female customers were whores, though some preferred to call themselves actresses or dancers.

One woman was making a scene, tugging at a man's coat and railing at him to come home. In the crook of her free arm, she held a baby about six months old. Sally stared, and a lump came into her throat. Becky would have been just about that age.

She tore herself away and went up to the bar. "Give me a drain of pale," she muttered to Toby. Seeing him look at her narrowly, she added, "I have the blunt!" While he poured her drink, she leaned on the bar, her chin propped on her hands. What was the matter with her? Almost nineteen years old, and as fly to the game as a girl ever was—and here she was ready to burst out blubbering over a baby that died six months ago! Why, some girls had a kid every other year, and buried them all, and they didn't take on like this!

Toby clapped her brandy on the counter. She started to fish out a coin, but he shook his head. "That cove there paid for it."

He jerked his thumb at a young man standing a little way down the bar. He was soberly dressed, like a clerk or shop assistant, in a black frock coat and trousers, a grey waistcoat, and a black cravat. He carried a sturdy black umbrella with a handle shaped like a ram's head.

She lifted her glass to him, with a broad smile. That's the ticket, she told herself—business'll drive the mulligrubs away. Blue Eyes was right: it's as good a way as any to stop yourself from thinking.

The man came closer and leaned an elbow on the bar, watching her drink. He had a thin face, thin body, thin nose and lips. His hair and eyes were a lacklustre brown. He wore round, goldrimmed spectacles, so Sally decided to call him Blinkers. Those spectacles were the only vivid thing about him. They shone when the candlelight hit them, and threw the light back again, as though defying anyone to get a good look into his eyes.

His fingers were stained with ink, she noticed—most likely he was a clerk. He was certainly a sight too respectable for this place. She wondered what he was doing here.

"You don't want nothing?" she asked.

"I don't want a drink," he amended.

"It's a bob for the room if we stay here."

"I can afford it."

The conversation lapsed.

"Talkative, ain't you?" she remarked.

"When there's anything worth talking about."

She shrugged. If that was how he wanted things—strictly business—it made no odds to her. She finished her drink and asked Toby for a room. Blinkers took the key and led the way upstairs. He must have been here before.

They had the same room she and Bristles had used. Blinkers locked the door behind them and put the key in his pocket. He hung his umbrella on the doorknob, took off his spectacles, and laid them down carefully. Then he turned to her and smiled. In that moment, she knew she had made a terrible mistake.

Screaming would do no good. Nobody would hear her in the taproom two stories below—and anyway, who would want to get mixed up in a row between a doxy and her flat? She was on her own, and she knew it.

She edged toward the door, giving Blinkers a wide berth. He watched her as a cat watches a mouse. All at once he sprang. He grabbed her by the shoulders and flung her against the wall. Her head banged, and she almost fell. He was coming at her again. She dodged and ran for the door. He laughed. After all, the door was locked, and the key was in his pocket.

But it was not escape she was seeking—it was the umbrella he had left hanging on the doorknob. She seized it by the pointed end and swung it at his head. The handle smashed against his left temple.

"You damned bitch!" he cried.

She tried to hit him again, but he caught at the umbrella and wrenched it away. The oil-cloth tore; the ribs broke with a sickening crack. He started beating her with the umbrella. She dropped to the floor and curled up protectively, letting the blows rain down on her back.

At last he threw the umbrella aside. He dragged her up, kicking and flailing, and shoved her against the wall. Very deliberately, he punched her in the left temple, just where she had hit him with the umbrella. The pain exploded through her head; the candlelight splintered into stars.

His hands moved to her throat. He pushed her down on the bed, his grip on her neck tightening. She beat on his arms with her fists and tried to bite him. Her eyes bulged, she gasped for air, and clawed at his hands. A red mist came up in front of her eyes, she groped in her mind for a prayer—

He laughed and let her go. She gulped the air, wailing with relief and pain. He pulled up her skirt. She was past resisting. But after a while, out of sheer instinct, she felt in the tail pocket of his coat.

There was nothing to steal but a handkerchief—a poor revenge, but better than nothing.

He got up, tossed some coins on the bed, and left her. She sat up dizzily. Her stomach heaved. She groped her way to the washstand and retched. Finding water in the pitcher, she splashed some on her face. Her rouge ran down in little pink rivulets.

She burst into tears. "Bastard!" she sobbed. "Pox take you, you stinking sod, you frigging son of a whore!"

She pounded on the washstand. She felt so helpless. It was not as if the like of her could go and complain to a watchman. It was only at times like this that she wished she had a fancy-man to look after her. But she knew she could never have borne that: giving some man control of her money, accounting to him for her comings and goings, keeping house for him by day and walking the streets for him by night.

She cried and cursed for a long time, wiping her eyes and nose on her sleeve. No sense soiling any of the handkerchiefs: they were worth money. She stuffed Blinkers's in with the others.

It was of grey silk, plain and nondescript like everything about him—till you knew him better.

She rose, stiff and aching, and examined her red dress. The bodice was badly torn at the neck, but the skirt could be saved. At least her bonnet was all right. She put it on, wrapped her cloak around her, and hobbled downstairs, stopping at each landing to rest and hold her sore back and sides.

She went into the taproom and moved slowly to the bar. "Give us a drop of warm flannel," she said to Toby.

He looked her briefly up and down. Then he poured her a glass of hot gin and beer, flavoured with sugar and nutmeg. "Keep your money," he said curtly, when she would have paid him.

For Toby, it was an extravagant gesture. "Thanks," she said huskily.

She sipped her drink slowly, letting the heat and comfort flow through her. She had had enough for one night. She was fit for nothing now but to go home to her lodging in the labyrinth of dirty streets and squares known as Seven Dials. There she could rest and lick her wounds—

And use up her small supply of coal, she reminded herself. And sit in the dark all alone, and throw her shoes at the mice to drive them back in their holes, and listen to the couple upstairs curse and knock their children about, then tumble into bed to make more. No: she must have been off her head even to think about going home. Anything, even picking up another flat, would be better than that. At least then she would have company, warmth, someone to snuggle with for a while.

She went out again, back to the Haymarket. The night was colder than before, or perhaps it was only that her bruises made her feel it more. She searched among the game girls for a friend she could have a gossip with, but there was nobody she knew. So she cast an eye over the men. Coves is mostly all right, she told herself firmly—there ain't many like Blinkers. She must not let him make her afraid. That was one victory she was damned if she'd give him.

But she would be careful whom she approached. That boy, for instance—the one walking just ahead, with a light, springy step. He was small and slender; she should be able to fight him off if he cut up rusty. She summoned all her courage, caught up to him, and slipped her arm through his. "Hullo, sweetheart! How about a bit of a lark?"

He stopped, stared, took her by the shoulders. She started to jerk away—then she stared, too. With one accord, they stepped under a gaslamp to see each other better.

"Is that you, Sal?" he breathed.

"Well, I'll be blowed!" She flung her arms around him, laughing and crying at once. "Dipper!"

Handkerchiefs

They hugged, drew apart, drank in the sight of each other, hugged again. Several bystanders cheered lewdly, not realizing they were brother and sister.

"I can't hardly believe it's you, Sal! How long's it been? Two years?"

"I dunno. *Too* long!—that's all I knows about it!"

He peered at her more closely in the lamplight. "You're in half-mourning!"

She lifted a hand to her left eye and tried to smile. "I picked up a curst cull as tipped me a facer."

"You all right?"

"It ain't nothing. Pa served me worse sometimes, when he was lushy." She stood back, gazing at him in wonder. "Look at you, Dip! You look so nobby, I'd never've knowed you! Where'd you get them duds?"

"I'm in service."

"Go on!"

"It's true, Sal—God strike me blind if it ain't. I'm valet to a gentry-cove."

"Some gentry-cove's spider-brusher? And you the best fingersmith as ever picked a pocket?"

"Not no more, Sal. I'm on the square."

"What for?"

"'Coz I want to be. I never had me heart in the old life, Sal—you knows that. But I couldn't get no reg'lar work, on account of I didn't know how to do nothing, and there was nobody to give me a character."

"How'd you get this job, then?"

"I met up with this gentry-cove. I lifted his ticker, and he had me up before a beak. But then he changed his mind and let me off, and we talked awhile, and he asked, did I want to have a try at being his slavey, and I said yes."

"He must be off his head."

"He ain't, then. He's Mr. Julian Kestrel, and he's a very great swell."

"Bender! Your master's Mr. Julian Kestrel? Cor, everybody knows who *he* is. I seen a drawing of him in the window of a tailor's shop."

"He's a go among the goes, is Mr. Kestrel. He's only got to sport a new kind of topper, or tie his crumpler a new way, and every gentry-cove in town does just the same. But what about you, Sal? Where you been? I was always asking after you, but I couldn't hear nothing about you nowhere."

"I knapped a quarter stretch in a bridewell—that must be how we lost touch." She was matter-of-fact about it. Any game girl got sent to a house of correction now and again. "Then I went and lived in Ratcliff Highway. I liked it there. Sailors is bob culls, and their women was dolly pals to me. But in the end I piked back here." She stopped abruptly. She could not bring herself to talk about Becky.

"I'm that glad I found you, Sal! Come on, we'll find some snug crib where we can have a drop and talk."

He drew her arm through his. But after a few steps he stopped in dismay. "Oh, Sal. You can't walk."

"'Course I can! See?" But her back and sides cried out in protest. Hobbling was the best she could do.

"Stow faking, Sal. We'll take a hack." He thought for a moment. "You'd best come home with me. You has to be looked after."

"To Mr. Kestrel's? That'd be something like! I never seen inside a gentry-cove's ken before!"

Dipper considered. "I expect it'll be all right. Mr. Kestrel's out to dinner with some of his pals, and he 'most never comes home till lightmans."

"Suits me. Then I can have a good look round."

"I can't let you pinch nothing."

"Who says I would?"

"I knows you," he said reasonably.

"Oh, all right!" she grumbled. "You'd think we was going to bloody Carlton House while King was out."

"The King's things ain't my look-out. Mr. Kestrel's is."

"I don't care *that!* for Mr. Kestrel."

"You ain't met him," Dipper said.

The hackney let them out in front of a grey brick house in Clarges Street. Blocks of white Coade stone formed a striped pattern round the archway of the door. Just above the fanlight was a white moulding of a woman's face, framed by snake-like hair.

Dipper unlocked the street door, putting a finger to his lips. "I don't want to wake up Mrs. M."

"Who's that?" whispered Sally.

"Mrs. Mabbitt—her as owns the house. She lives on the ground and kitchen floors, and lets out the first floor to Mr. Kestrel. 'Cept they hardly ever sees each other, 'coz she's al'ays up at lightmans, which is mostly when he goes to bed, and when he gets up it's after mid-day, and she's gone out. So then he goes off to one of his clubs, and by the time he comes home to put on his evening togs, she's 'most ready for bed. A very nice lady, is Mrs. M., and a deep 'un, too—knows what's what, and no mistake."

They tiptoed past Mrs. Mabbitt's door and up the stairs to the first-floor flat. A hallway ran between the front and back rooms.

"That's the parlour," said Dipper, jerking his thumb at the front room on the left, "and the one opposite is Mr. Kestrel's bedroom, and the bandboxical room further down on the right's his study."

He took out a tinder box and a candle from a marble-topped cabinet. While he struck a light, Sally went into the front parlour and looked around eagerly. She could see fairly well by the gaslight from the street, thanks to three elegant French windows opening on a narrow balcony.

"Cor, this is lummy!" she called to Dipper. "Only it ain't so flash as I expected. I thought there'd be lots of ginger-work, and silks all different colours, and that."

"Mr. Kestrel don't like nothing gaudy."

"He wouldn't like me much, then," she said cheerfully.

She explored the room more closely. It was full of wonders: crossed swords hanging over the mantelpiece, a pianoforte of polished inlaid wood, a gilt clock showing the phases of the moon, and a painted fire-screen of a woman with a lion's feet and wings. When Dipper came in with the candles, she was gazing, starry-eyed, at a decanter ringed by little gold-rimmed glasses. She picked one up. "Lord, ain't that fine! It's like something a king'd drink out of!"

"Stow your forks, Sal."

"Dip, he'd never miss one—he's got five more."

"Yes, but you see, they're a matched set," said an amused voice. "Perhaps you could relieve me of that clock instead. I've never much cared for it—it has such a disapproving expression."

Sally and Dipper spun around.

"I thought you was out, sir," Dipper stammered.

"Evidently." The gentleman in the doorway smiled. "I ought to come home early more often—I've obviously been missing a good deal."

"This ain't what it looks like, sir," said Dipper.

The gentleman looked at Sally more closely. "No, I see it isn't. I beg your pardon."

"What for?" she demanded.

"Because I can see this is a family party. You and Dipper are as like as you can stare."

"Sally's me sister, sir. We met up in the street tonight. We hadn't seed each other in more than two years. And I saw as how some cove had darkened her daylights, and she seemed pretty down pin, so I brought her back here."

Mr. Kestrel's face changed. He crossed quickly to Sally, holding up his candle to look at the black eye she half tried to conceal. "Dipper, go and knock up Dr. MacGregor and tell him we need him."

"I ain't having no doctor!" Sally exclaimed. "He'll send me off to hospital, and shut me up with folks as has the pox and the influenzy! I'd as lief be in the stone jug as there!"

"Dr. MacGregor would be the last person to send you to hospital. He's from the country, and I believe he thinks there's never been a patient so ill that a London hospital couldn't make him worse." Mr. Kestrel put down his candle and pushed a plush scroll sofa nearer to the hearth. "Please sit down, Miss Stokes."

Sally guffawed. "You hear that, Dip? He called me Miss!"

Dipper shifted from one foot to the other. "Shall I make up the fire before I goes, sir?"

"All it needs is a bit of nudging back to life, and I think I'm equal to that. Go, for God's sake! Your sister will be safe enough till you get back."

"It ain't me he's worried about," said Sally, grinning.

Mr. Kestrel's brows shot up. "You don't mean to say you're afraid to leave us alone on *my* account? What in the devil's name do you suppose she's likely to do to me?"

Dipper waved his hands, as if to say, it boggled the mind. But he gave it up and went off to fetch Dr. MacGregor.

"Won't you sit down?" Mr. Kestrel repeated, indicating the sofa.

"I don't mind." She sauntered over, keeping an eye on him all the while. She could not make him out. Why was he trotting out all these airs and graces, just for her? It made her want to be rude and provoke him, just to scratch his surface and see what he was really thinking.

She looked him boldly up and down. He was about Blue Eyes's age: five- or six-and-twenty. His hair was dark brown, his eyes lighter, with a greenish glint. He was not handsome. He did not need to be, to make you want to look at him twice. He had keen, alert eyes, arresting brows, and a wry smile always at the ready. He was not tall; he did not need to be that, either. His figure was proportioned just right: slender but solid, masculine but graceful. He wore a frilled white evening shirt, a dressing-gown of bottlegreen silk brocade, and black trousers in the style called eelskin, fitting closely as a glove. Well, he had the legs for them—no doubt about that.

She lowered herself onto the sofa—carefully, for her back and sides felt like one large, smarting bruise. He watched her, his brow creasing with concern. Why? What was she to him? Just his servant's sister. She said, with deliberate impertinence, "I could do with some'ut to sluice me ivories."

"Of course. Brandy and water?"

"Leave out the water, and it'll be something like."

He fetched a bottle and two glasses. But after an instant's thought, he poured her brandy into one of the little gold-rimmed glasses she had admired. That small gesture touched her; she forgot to be saucy. She clinked glasses with him and took a swig. "That's bang-up, that is!"

"I'm glad you like it."

He went to the hearth and began to stir the coals. She drained her glass, took off her bonnet, and hung it on a nearby chair. Her hair, which had come unpinned in her struggle with Blinkers, spilled over her shoulders. Her skirt was twisted uncomfortably round her legs, so she gave it a vigorous shake.

The secret pocket, overburdened with coins, came loose, flew off, and hit Mr. Kestrel right between the shoulder blades. He looked around, brows raised. She bubbled into laughter, her hands to her mouth. At the same time, she was a little frightened. What would he do when he found the stolen handkerchiefs?

He picked up the gaping pocket. "You appear to have lost something."

"And you wants to know what it is, I expect."

"It's quite evident what it is—some coins, and a few handkerchiefs that you found before they were lost."

"How do you know they ain't mine?" she said challengingly.

"Three men's handkerchiefs?—one of them with a monogram, *CFA*?" He pointed out the neatly stitched letters in the corner of Blue Eyes's fine cambric handkerchief.

"Well—the coins is mine, anyhow. I earned 'em meself. I expect you can guess how."

"I have an idea."

"So you might give 'em back to me."

He restored the money, but not the handkerchiefs. She eyed him resentfully. "You going to call a watchman?"

"Why? Do you want one?"

"You knows what I mean. If you ain't going to peach on me, why won't you give me back the wipes? You going to keep 'em?"

"My dear girl!" He looked shocked. "Russet calico?" He held up the handkerchief that must have been Bristles's; Blinkers's was made of coarse silk.

"Well, what you going to do with 'em, then?"

He considered. "I'll ask Dipper to find some worthy charity—a society for interfering in the lives of contented Africans, or some such thing." He started to tuck the three handkerchiefs into his pocket—then he looked at them more closely. "Here." He took out a folded paper from among them and handed it to her. "I didn't see this before."

"What is it?"

"Isn't it yours?"

She unfolded it and frowned at the writing inside. She could not read very well. "I never seen this before. You sure it come out of me pocket?"

"It was here, among the handkerchiefs."

She looked up, suddenly enlightened. "I must've pinched it from one of them coves along with his wipe! I wonder which?" She held out the paper. "What's it say?"

A Remedy for Boredom

Mr. Kestrel read the letter aloud:

October 1824
Saturday evening

I hardly know what to say to you, how to tell you where I am, or how I came to be here. It's just as well I'm obliged to write it: how could I speak to you or look you in the eyes, even if I were permitted to leave this place and had the means to find my way home? I do not think I could face anyone I know, ever again—not you, nor anyone else in our family, nor him I once thought I loved. Please forgive me! I've been punished so much! I am punished again every day—not so much by the miserable life I lead, as by the memories I can't banish: of my happiness, my hopes, my innocence—and of the stupid, stubborn, ungrateful rashness that swept them all away!

My ruin has not been all my fault. I can't write about that—I can only say that I never knew there was such evil in the world as I've known since I left you.

When you know where I am and what has happened to me, you may not ever wish to see me again. I will understand. You can't despise me, reject me, hate me, any more bitterly than I hate myself. But if you wish to know once and for all what has become of me, come to No. 9, Stark Street. You need not come in, or speak to me. I will never seek you out, or force you to support or acknowledge the thing I have become.

I have not told anyone here my name, or put into this letter anything that might reveal who I am. People spy on me in this place—I'm afraid they may take this from me and read it before I can send it. Thank heaven, there's someone I think I can trust to post it for me secretly, so that no one will see your direction on the outer sheet. So if you choose not to answer it, no one will ever know what has become of me. I shall be forgotten as one dead, like the broken vessel in the Psalm.

I love you dearly. Pray for me.

Sally stared. "Well, carry me out and bury me decent!"

"You know nothing about this at all?"

"No, I told you, I must've lifted it off one of them flats I picked up. There was three of 'em: I called 'em Bristles, Blue Eyes, and Blinkers."

He was momentarily diverted. "Why do they all begin with 'B'?"

"I dunno. They just do. I al'ays gives me flats names. I'll think of one for you, maybe."

"I don't see any need," he said lightly. "I wasn't planning we should enter into a business relationship." He ran his eyes over the letter. "No signature, no direction. She mentions an outer sheet—I suppose she used another sheet of paper as an envelope. *Saturday evening*—that must have been the day before yesterday.

There hasn't been another Saturday in October so far. If she sent the letter by the twopenny post, it could have arrived today. Have you any idea at all which man you got it from?"

"I couldn't, could I? Soon as I nicked them wipes, I stowed 'em away double-quick, in that pocket under me skirt. I could've pinched that letter along with any of 'em, and not knowed a thing about it."

"I wonder if the man you got it from is the person she was writing to?"

"Must've been. How else would he get it?"

"I don't know." He frowned at the letter. "What sort of place do you suppose it is—this place where she says she's being held against her will? A house of correction?"

"A knocking-house, more like."

He grimaced. "I think Stark Street is in a fairly respectable neighbourhood, near Russell Square. But God knows, there are discreet 'houses' tucked away all over London. It's curious, though. This letter is from an educated woman—the penmanship alone shows that. Some governess taught her to write like this, all curlicues and feminine flourishes. And the language is literate, eloquent. She sounds young, though, don't you think? Naive, bewildered. How did she ever come to this?—ruined, shut up and spied upon, afraid to see her family again?"

Sally shrugged. "I expect some cove made up to her, and next thing she knew, she was seeing stars lying on her back."

"It does sound as if she'd been seduced. Her shame, her self-disgust, her regret for some rash act, all point to that. *My ruin has not been all my fault.* That could be a reference to her seducer. *I do not think I could face anyone I know, ever again—not you, nor anyone else in our family.* So the person she wrote to was a relative. Perhaps even her husband—no, it must be a blood relation. Because she next speaks of *him I once thought I loved*—that could be a husband, though it sounds more like a suitor. Perhaps she turned from him to another man, who compromised her. And after that false step, she could all too easily have gone on sliding downward."

"It's the end of the world to a lady, ain't it?" marvelled Sally. "Losing her character, and all?"

"Because there's no going back from it—not if it becomes known. Casting the first stone being a favourite recreation in this Christian land." He added, "How are you feeling?"

"I'm all right. 'Cept I've got a cobweb in me throat."

He refilled her glass. As she drank, her eyes fell on the handkerchiefs, which he had laid on a nearby table. She suddenly snatched one up. "It was him, I'll take me oath on it!"

"I beg your pardon?"

"See this wipe? I lifted it off the cove I called Blue Eyes. He was a real gentry-cove, togged out to the nines, very swell in his speech. Now, if this gal was a lady, it's him she would have wrote to, not one of them others."

"What were they like, the other two men?"

"This here is Bristles." She held up the russet calico handkerchief, as if introducing the man it came from. "He kept a shop, I could tell by his duds. He was very natty—wore a clean white crumpler, with his gills standing up all straight and neat." She held up her forefingers, imitating the corners of a turned-up collar. "He had on a plain brown frock coat, and his waistcoat and trousers was buff. He must've been about fifty, dark hair going grey, brown eyes, and his chin was stubbly, like his beard growed faster than he had time to shave it."

"You're very observant."

"You has to be, if you goes with a lot of coves like I does. You learns to drop down to 'em slap off, so you don't pick up none of the wrong kind. 'Cept sometimes you guesses wrong."

Her lips twisted. She took up the third handkerchief, a square of cheap, nondescript grey silk. "This is Blinkers. I called him that on account of he wears specs. He was young—younger than you, most like—and rigged out in rusty black, like a clerk. Which I expect he was—his forks was stained with ink. He was skinny, his hair was brown, and so was his eyes, but you couldn't see into 'em very well, on account of his specs. I don't think he wanted nobody to know what he was thinking: he was muffin-faced, never flashed his ivories, never showed no feelings at all—till we got upstairs, that is. Then he pitched into me. Some coves is like that—it brings 'em on, hurting a gal."

"I'm sorry."

He was looking at her with that concern in his eyes again. She could not bear it. She leaned toward him, smiling, letting her torn gown gape at the neck. His eyes dropped briefly—so he was human, after all—then returned to her face. "The third man was a gentleman, you say?"

"Well, he was the second, really. He come in between. He took me into a hack with him. He give me a ride, and I give *him* one, if you get me drift."

"Quite."

"He was a dimber cove, he was! Dark gold hair; blue eyes you could dive into and drown, and a figure as could warm up a dead gal. He was rigged out in a blue tailcoat, with white trousers and shiny black stampers, and miles of white frill on his shirt front. He flashed a gold ticker and a bunch of seals, and a ring that was an out-and-out slasher: gold, with a skull in the middle, and a sparkler in every comer."

"Good God." Mr. Kestrel caught up the white cambric handkerchief. "*CFA*. Sally, I know who that man was. He was the Honourable Charles Avondale, Lord Carbury's younger son."

"Cor! He really was a nob, then! And you knows him?"

"Not well, but we cross paths from time to time. The ring you described is a family heirloom—he wears it all the time. The initials fit, and so does your description. I'll lay you any odds, Avondale is the man you call Blue Eyes."

"And it's him I pinched the letter from, don'cha think? He's the only one as'd have a real lady in his family—one who'd write a letter like this."

He shook his head. "If Blue Eyes is Avondale, it's very unlikely the letter was written by a relative of his. His father is a peer, and the whole family is prominent in society. A lady couldn't very well go missing in that family without attracting a good deal of attention. And as far as I know, all the Carbury ladies are accounted for."

"All right, you're such a downy one, *you* guess which of them three coves she wrote to."

"Perhaps none of them. If you think about it, there are all kinds of other explanations. The man you stole the letter from may have been entrusted with it by a friend, or had it sent to him by mistake, or even found it in the street. Or else—"

"Or else what?"

"This woman says she's being spied upon, and she's afraid someone may take the letter from her before she can post it. That may be what happened: the man from whom you stole it may have stolen it from *her*."

"My, ain't you twistical, though!" she said admiringly. "S'pose you're right, and somebody pinched her letter? That means whoever she wrote it to never got it, and don't know where she is. And she'll think he don't want her and don't forgive her, and maybe she'll never get out of that place she's shut up in."

"Of course, it could all be some sort of joke. Or an exercise by some high-strung would-be novelist."

"What if it ain't? What if it's on the square?"

He smiled quizzically. "Then we'll have to do something about it, won't we?"

There was a bustle in the hallway. Julian went out and found Dr. MacGregor and Dipper just arrived. It had begun raining, and MacGregor's hair and beard stuck out in little wet points. "You look like Neptune on a fountain," Julian greeted him.

MacGregor gave Dipper his hat, shook off his capacious old greatcoat, and rounded on Julian. "How you can live in this city, year in and year out, is beyond me! The streets are never quiet for a blessed instant! Even at this time of night, there are carriages rattling by as loud as cannons, people out shouting and singing and fighting, and I don't like to think what else! We were almost run over by a coal-heaver's wagon—Lord knows what it was doing out at this hour—and then a group of scurvy drunken louts stole my hat and carried it halfway down the street before Dipper got it back. Yes, all right, you can smile, but there was nothing funny about it! Where's my patient?"

"She's in the parlour. Thank you for coming out so late."

"I'm used to it. If you want to get a good night's sleep, don't become a surgeon."

"How is Dr. Greeley?"

Dr. Greeley was an elderly surgeon who had been MacGregor's teacher many years before. MacGregor was in London to help look after his patients while he recovered from an illness. "He's well enough. Trying to take back too much of the work before he's ready. Truth is, he's getting too old for it, but he's too blessed stubborn to think about retiring." He picked up his medical bag. "All right, let's have a look at her."

"I should warn you, she's a bit nervous of doctors."

"Quite right, too. Some of 'em don't know a kidney stone from a peach-pit. I'll manage her all right."

He disappeared into the parlour, as calm and practical as he had been irascible a moment before. He might give the rough side of his tongue to everyone else, but Julian had never seen him show his temper to a patient.

"He'll be wanting tea, I imagine," he said to Dipper, for MacGregor rarely took spirits.

"Yes, sir. Sir?"

"Yes?"

"I want to thank you, sir, for having Sally here, and that."

"I don't know what there is to thank me for. Did you expect I should throw her into the street?"

"No, sir, I knew you'd treat her uncommon fine. That's why I sneaked her in when I thought you was out—so as not to take advantage."

"What rubbish. Hadn't you better put the water on to boil? Dr. MacGregor should be finished examining her shortly. If she cooperates," he added, with a wry smile.

"Yes, sir." Dipper turned to go.

"Just a moment. Have you and Sally any family besides each other?"

"No, sir, not as I knows on."

"I see. All right, you may go."

Dipper left to get the tea ready. Julian went into his study, frowning. He was more than willing to take Sally in and see that she got any medical care she needed. The question was, what on earth were they to do with her afterward?

"Nothing wrong with her that a little rest and good nourishment won't cure," pronounced MacGregor, plumping down in a chair by the study fire.

"I'm glad to hear it, thank you, sir." Dipper gave him a cup of tea.

"She's badly bruised, mind you." MacGregor's face darkened. "That man's a brute, whoever he was."

"Yes, sir," Dipper said quietly.

Julian could see that Blinkers would be in a very bad way if Dipper ever ran across him. "She'll stay here for the present, of course. She can have your room, if she's able to walk up to the attic, and you can sleep on the sofa in the parlour."

"Thank you, sir."

MacGregor's thick, grizzled brows shot up, but he said nothing until Dipper had gone. "You think that's wise? Keeping her here, I mean."

"What else can we do? She can't go out again at this time of night, injured as she is."

"No, I suppose not. But I don't like it above half."

"My dear fellow, what is this all about?"

MacGregor set down his tea-cup with a clank and leaned forward, hands propped on his knees. "Do you know what she wanted to talk about the whole time I was in there?"

"I have no idea. Repeal of the Corn Laws?"

"No—you! How did I meet you, what did I know about you, what did I make of you—"

"You must have found the deuce and all to talk about," said Julian, eyes dancing. "Just making a catalogue of my faults could have occupied you an hour or more."

"She'll make trouble for you, Kestrel, mark my words."

"What sort of trouble?"

"What sort do you think?"

"Oh, really, my dear fellow!"

"You can laugh, but if you're shut up, long enough with her, it could lead to anything: She's a taking little thing, and you're a young man, with a young man's weaknesses."

"I think I can manage to spend a night or two under the same roof with her without my passions overcoming me. For God's sake, she's Dipper's sister. I should as soon think of dangling after my venerable landlady."

"Hmph! I still say there's trouble in store for you, one way or another."

"I shouldn't mind a little trouble. I'm frightfully bored."

"I can't understand that," MacGregor said tartly. "You change your clothes at least three times a day. That ought to be occupation enough for anybody."

"I know you think my life is somewhat lacking in purpose."

"I think you fritter away your time, if that's what you mean."

"I liked the way I put it better."

"Yes, well, fine words butter no parsnips." He added more quietly, "I've seen what you can do when you're roused to a purpose. That's something I'd like to see again."

"But not another purpose like the last one, surely?"

"If you mean, would I like to see another murder—no, I could get on very well without that!"

Julian said nothing for a time. He had conflicting feelings about the Bellegarde murder. The hunt for the killer had been fascinating—hardly any experience he had ever known could match it. But his solution to the crime had caused so much grief that he had felt more guilt than triumph. At least it was over and done with, he had told himself when he returned to London. His unlikely career as a Bow Street Runner was closed.

It was not so simple—he understood that now, three or four months later. He glanced ruefully around his study. Well-thumbed editions of the Newgate Calendar, with its lives of famous criminals, mixed themselves in with the history and music books on his shelves. Today's *Morning Chronicle* was tossed aside to make room for Bow Street's police gazette, the *Hue and Cry*. Like it or not, he was developing a consuming interest in crime—its motives and methods, and the clues that brought them to light. Perhaps he had always been drawn in that direction; that might be one reason he had taken on a pickpocket as his servant. Then, too, the Bellegarde murder had made him vividly aware of the anomaly of a bustling, modem nation with almost no professional police. Of course, the English were jealous of their liberties, and convinced that a large, ubiquitous police force like France's would undermine them. But to Julian, who had lived in France, it seemed that one of the foremost liberties any subject ought to enjoy was the freedom to walk in the streets without fearing for his pocketbook, or his life.

"I do have what you might call a purpose just now," he said, "though it may not turn out to be any great matter. I should like to know who wrote this letter, and what it means."

He took the letter from his pocket and gave it to MacGregor to read, first explaining how Sally had come by it. "It conjures up a vivid picture," he finished. "A lady of good breeding and education, writing secretly at night, on cheap paper, without an India rubber or a penknife, squinting to see by the light of a farthing dip."

"Aren't you getting a bit fanciful?" said MacGregor.

"I don't think so. You can tell all that from looking at the letter. We know she hadn't an India rubber, because she had to cross out her mistakes. And she had nothing to sharpen her pencil, so the point got duller as she wrote, till she had to bear down quite hard to make an impression. She used a tallow candle and held the paper very close to it—you can see where the tallow dripped on it, here, and here."

"You've given this a lot of thought."

"Well, it's devilish disturbing. I don't think I can simply let it drop. At the very least, I should like to see what's at Number 9, Stark Street. That might throw light on what sort of trouble this woman is in."

"You say you've identified one of those three men. You could sound him about it."

"I could, but at present there's only a one-in-three chance that Sally got the letter from him. And the woman who wrote it is so intent on secrecy that I don't like to let anyone know about her plight if I can avoid it. Perhaps I can return the letter to her discreetly, or find out what she wants done with it. If she isn't at that address anymore, or I'm not able to get near her, that will be time enough to approach Charles Avondale."

"What sort of fellow is he?"

"He's the comely and charming scion of a very comely and charming family. His sister Lady Gayheart is a famous beauty; so was her mother before her. His elder brother, the heir to the Carbury title, is rather a lumpish sort. I believe he's away in Scotland just now on a shooting trip. I'm surprised Avondale is still in town. Perhaps he's another victim of the Braxton disaster."

"The what?"

"Didn't I mention that to you? It's the reason I'm in town at this unfashionable time of year. Lord Braxton, who has several daughters to marry off, was planning a large country house party, and a good part of society's *corps élite* was invited. But then one of the daughters ran off to France to marry an undesirable suitor, and Lord Braxton is in such a temper, he called off the whole affair and shut himself up in his castle in Shropshire. So a good many of us who thought we had an engagement for October are thrown on our own scant resources. Avondale may be one of the casualties."

"Sounds like a lot of flummery to me. If you and your set did something useful, instead of flitting from one entertainment to another like will-o'-the-wisps, you wouldn't be bored all the time."

Julian looked thoughtfully at the letter. "Perhaps I shall do something useful now."

The Honourable Charles

Next morning, Ada Grantham sat by her drawing-room fireplace, sorting yarn. The weather was so mild, she needed no fire, which was a mercy, since Mama badly needed to save coal. Ada even had the window open, letting in the clatter of carriages up and down Green Street, and the singsong cries of the street-sellers making their rounds.

She hardly noticed the sound of a carriage pulling up outside the house. But she could not miss her little brother James's ecstatic cry: "It's Charles!"

Ada put down her work and sat very still for a moment. Then she rose and went to the window, standing to the side so that she could look out without being seen. Her cousin, the Honourable Charles Avondale, was just springing down from the driver's seat of his smart cabriolet. His tiger—the little groom who rode at the back of the carriage—stood holding the horse's head.

James came running out of the house. Mama followed with Emma and Lydia, aged fifteen and thirteen. They were all dressed to go out. Mama, who was a martyr to colds, was wrapped in a rather worn pelisse, with an immense poke bonnet stuck atop her cap.

Charles came forward, took Mrs. Grantham's hands, and kissed her cheek. "Good morning, Aunt Dot! I'm glad to see you out and about. Do I take it your cold is better?"

"Oh, rather, yes, but I'm afraid it won't be long till the next one. How is your mother?" Mrs. Grantham and Charles's mother, Lady Carbury, were sisters.

Charles chatted about his parents, who were at their house in the country. Emma and Lydia hung back awkwardly, shy of their magnificent cousin, but Charles talked to them with such ease and grace that their stiffness soon melted away.

James jumped up and down. "Oh, Charles, will you take me up in your carriage?"

"Now, James—" Mrs. Grantham began.

"Please, Mama, I want to go for a ride with Charles. Can't I go shopping for trousers some other day?"

"You mustn't say that word in front of ladies, James, it's vulgar. Say 'inexpressibles.'"

"Oh, very well, mayn't I go shopping for inexpressibles some other day?"

"Better go today, old man, and have it over," Charles advised. "I'll take you round the park next time I come." He paused, then asked offhandedly, "Is Ada at home?"

"I—I'm not certain—" Mrs. Grantham faltered.

"Why, Mama, you know she's in the drawing room," said James.

"Splendid!" cried Charles. "I'll just go up and say good morning to her, shall I? You needn't walk in with me; I don't want to keep you. Shall I have Jake fetch you a hack?" He indicated the tiger.

"Oh, no, we'll walk, it isn't far. Well, good day, Charles." Mama looked at him doubtfully, then shepherded her children off down the street, James craning his neck to look wistfully back at Charles and the cabriolet.

Ada hastened from the window back to her seat and took up her work again. Brisk footsteps sounded on the stairs. The next moment, Charles appeared in the doorway. "Hullo, angel."

"Hullo, devil." She looked up, smiling.

He came in and perched on the arm of the sofa, his hands thrust into his trouser pockets, his coat-tails flung over his arms. "What are you doing?"

"Sorting yarn for darning. Somehow the colours have all got into a tangle."

"Must you sort it? Why not let it all run together like a rainbow?"

"Do you want us to look like a pantomime troupe?"

"Why not? I think you'd all look monstrous fetching in stockings all different colours, like harlequins." He swung his heel against the sofa for a short time, then looked up. "Your suitor's back in London. I saw him today at my club."

"You mean Major Thorndike?"

"Why," he said gaily, "is there another one?"

Try as she might, she could not keep the question out of her eyes: *I don't know, Charles—is there?*

He got up abruptly, took a turn about the room, then stood at the window with his back to her. "Look here, I don't mean to pry. But I'm the nearest thing you have to a father or older brother. I can't but take an interest—want to know if everything's all right. What I mean to say is—do you mean to take the fellow?"

She put down the yarn she was sorting and clasped her hands. "If Major Thorndike offers for me," she said steadily, "I've made up my mind to accept him."

"Do you think he will?"

"I'm almost certain. He's been writing to me all the while he's been on duty in Ireland. His most recent letter was very clear about his intentions. Of course, he's not a man to do anything suddenly, without careful thought. He takes a long time coming to a decision, but stands by it firmly once it's been made."

"A regular rock of Gibraltar, in fact. Well, I'm sure I wish you happy. I'm told he bends at the knees, though I've never seen it. And he smiles at least once a year, at Christmas, between eleven o'clock and noon."

"I know he hasn't much humour." She smiled ruefully. "I shan't be marrying him for that."

"Don't tell me you're marrying him for love, because I've known you since you were on leading-strings, and you couldn't love an old stick like that."

"I don't love him. But I respect him. He's honourable and good. He'll make a fine husband and father."

Charles winced.

"Please, Charles, try to understand. I'm the oldest of six children. Mama's annuity barely keeps us in coal and candles. Today she's had to take the children shopping for clothes, and we were up half the night thinking how we should pay for them. Mama's worried that Edward will have to leave university, because we can't afford to keep him there any longer, and there are Richard and James and the girls to provide for. How can I refuse a man who has so much money, and who I know would be generous with it and help us all? If Major Thorndike were a wicked man, or repulsive to me, I wouldn't think of accepting him. But I can't refuse him simply because he isn't—isn't everything I should dream of in a husband."

"But why be in such a hurry to settle yourself? There are plenty of fellows in London with a little money, and a character that's up to the mark."

"I can't refuse him in the hope that a better man might come along. This may be my only chance to marry well. I'm twenty-two years old, and I haven't a dowry, and I know I'm not a beauty."

"You're well enough," was all he said. But his eyes conveyed much more.

She felt a rush of hurt and frustration. Why was he putting them both through this? "Charles, I hear your brother is shooting in Scotland. Why don't you go and join him? It might be easier—"

"Don't talk to me of Scotland—that gloomy, mist-ridden, barbarous, nightmare of a place! I'd rather be in hell!"

She blinked at him in amazement.

"Oh, confound it, I'm sorry, Ada! I didn't mean to pitch into you like that. I shouldn't have come here today, God knows it was pointless, I just couldn't help it—"

"Come here, Charles," she said gently.

He pulled up a chair beside hers and sat down, hunched forward, arms resting on his knees. His dark gold hair curled softly on the nape of his neck. Ada longed to stroke it ever so gently. Her throat tightened. Her heart seemed to swell in her breast.

She drew a long breath. "I think perhaps you feel guilty, Charles, on account of my having to marry Major Thorndike. You mustn't, you know. Just because you and I paired off as children, that doesn't mean I expect we should do so, now we're grown up. It never occurred to me that—that—" She tried again. "I know you're a younger son. There's only so much your father can do for you, what with the estate being entailed to your brother. If you're to go on living in the style you do now, you have to marry money. I've always understood that—"

"No!" He clasped his head distractedly. "Oh, God, you don't understand at all—"

"What?" she pleaded. "What don't I understand?"

He froze, his eyes wary, shuttered against her. "I'd better go. I'm not doing any good here. If you need me, just dash off a note. I'll come like a shot."

"I know. Thank you. But I don't think you ought to come again—not for a while, not till—everything's settled. It worries Mama. She doesn't know what you mean by it. And you're right—it doesn't do any good."

He stood looking down at her. For one terrible moment, she thought he might kiss her goodbye. There was only so much she could bear. Her self-control was strong, but not invincible. How could it be? He was Charles, who had taught her to dance, to ride, to play piquet. Charles, with his boyish charm and his grown-up vices, his bursts of generosity and his core of selfishness. She knew him better than she knew herself. After all, she had been in love with him all her life.

He did not kiss her. He said, "Well, goodbye," thrust his hands in his pockets, and walked out, as if he did not much care where he went or what became of him.

She was glad he was gone, yet, perversely, she went to the window to catch a last glimpse of him. He was just coming out of the house. His tiger, who had been ogling a maidservant across the street, ran back to the cabriolet. It was raining lightly, so he lifted the small folding hood over the driver's seat. Then he stepped back, staring.

There were three large slashes in the leather hood. They formed a big, bold letter *R*.

"How the plague did that get there?" Charles exclaimed.

"I dunno, sir. Knocks me acock, it does!"

"Hell and damnation!" Charles sputtered. "Is this how you look after my property? By God, I ought to thrash you within an inch of your life—"

Two respectable-looking elderly ladies were coming along the pavement. Charles choked down his rage and muttered something to the tiger, who let down the hood again. Charles leaped into the driver's seat, the tiger clambered up behind him, and the cabriolet dashed off in a cloud of dust.

Ada turned away from the window, knitting her brows. She was not surprised Charles was so angry. He hated to find a dent or a scratch on his swift little sporting carriage. She supposed one of his friends must be playing a prank on him. Still, it was very odd. Who would do something so destructive? And why the letter *R*?

Getting Past the Dragon

On the morning after Sally arrived, Julian was up bright and early by his standards—which is to say that he was shaved, dressed, and breakfasted before noon. Dipper summoned a hackney coach from the nearest stand, and he set off for No. 9, Stark Street, to find out what was at the address in the unknown woman's letter.

Stark Street was a cul-de-sac in a drearily respectable neighbourhood, south of the Foundling Hospital and east of Russell Square. Julian got out of his hackney coach at the corner, so that he could walk down the street and have a look around. He passed several nondescript houses, a chandler's shop, a stationer's, and a shabby-genteel boarding house with a sign in the window announcing that one of the lodgers taught French and another gave lessons on the pianoforte. The next house was No. 9.

It actually consisted of two adjacent houses, loosely cobbled together. They were of the design used for houses all over London for more than a hundred years: narrow but deep, with two or three rooms to a floor. These were debased examples of the type, built of a sickly yellow brick that was probably only a veneer for cheaper materials. The front door of the right-hand house was the formal entrance; it had a bell-pull and a dignified brass plate, too small to read from the street. The left-hand house looked meek and self-effacing. The knocker had been taken off the door, there was no bell, the shutters were closed, and for good measure there were iron gratings on all the windows.

Julian did not like the look of the place at all. The right-hand house had an air of rigour, stinginess, distrust. He would have liked to cut the two houses apart and set the left one free. He went up to the front door of the right-hand house to read the brass plate. It said: "Reclamation Society."

Reclamation of what? he wondered. Stolen goods? The American colonies? People's lost buttons and boots? In reality, this must be one of those associations for improving the public morals. There were a good many of them springing up in London these days.

He rang the bell. The door opened a crack, and a woman looked out. She had a small, square face, the skin drawn tightly across it, like fabric stretched on an embroidery frame. Her eyes were black and beady, her hair a salt-and-pepper grey. Her mouth seemed set in a perpetual grim line. "Yes?"

"Good morning." He doffed his hat. "I was just passing and saw the sign on your door. Would you be good enough to tell me what the Reclamation Society is?"

"We reclaim lost women. We turn them from their evil paths, and make them into humble, repentant, useful members of society. Perhaps you've heard of our founder," she added proudly, "the Reverend Mr. Harcourt."

He had, now he thought of it. Harcourt was a clergyman from some country parish, who had made a minor stir in London lately with his sermons on the evils of prostitution. This had brought him a devoted following of respectable women, who were apt to be much harder on their fallen sisters than men were. Julian vaguely recalled that Harcourt had opened a refuge for prostitutes. This, obviously, was the place.

"Whom do I have the honour of addressing?" he asked.

"I'm Mrs. Fiske, one of the matrons." Not that it's any of your business, her tone implied.

If there was a Mr. Fiske, he had all Julian's sympathies. "It sounds a formidable endeavour—reforming these women, making them humble and useful. How do you go about it?"

"We require them to confess their sins, as the first step toward repentance. Then they must submit to a regimen of hard work, prayer, and penitence. We impose the strictest discipline. Only by learning to conquer their wicked appetites and impulses can they regain some shred of the character they've thrown away."

"What if they don't—take to it?"

She drew herself up. "If they are too depraved to profit by the example we set and the chance we give them, they are free to leave. This isn't a prison. But any of the creatures who leaves us is barred from ever coming back again. Otherwise we should have them crowding on our doorstep whenever they're hungry or their landlords have very properly thrown them out, then returning to their vile habits after they've been fed and housed at our expense!"

"I should have thought that was charity."

"Charity for the body—perdition for the soul! Who are you, sir? Are you a journalist?"

She would never believe him if he said he was—not the way he was dressed. The question had been rhetorical, a tart comment on his inquisitiveness.

She was starting to close the door.

"Just a moment—" he began.

"Good day to you, sir. I've no time for idle and curious people. Too many young men hang about this place as it is."

He thought quickly. "I might wish to make a donation."

The door stopped an inch from the jamb, and came grudgingly open again. "I'm sure we should be very grateful, sir," she said stiffly.

"Of course I should like to know a little more about your work. What sort of women do you take in? Are they all English? Are they any particular age? What sort of families do they come from?"

"I can give you a pamphlet to read that describes our work. Mr. Harcourt wrote it himself. He isn't here at present, but perhaps if you come back another day, he might find time to see you." She spoke as a cardinal might of an audience with the Pope.

"I should like to read it. Thank you."

"I'll get it. I must ask you to wait outside. Gentlemen aren't permitted in unless they have an appointment with Mr. Harcourt, or can prove they're an inmate's father or brother. Don't think we haven't had their fancy-men coming here pretending to be relatives, trying to get them out!" She pressed her lips together, her little eyes glinting.

She went inside. Julian admitted ruefully that he had not accomplished very much. True, he knew now what was at No. 9, Stark Street. And it seemed very likely that the woman he sought was an inmate of this place—or had been three days ago, when she wrote the letter. The shame and regret she expressed certainly fit the character of a repentant Magdalene. And he understood why she might feel a need to keep her identity a secret: the insistence on confession and public abasement in this place could easily make a woman shrink from laying bare her true name and history. Especially if she came of a respectable family, as this woman apparently did, and did not want them to share in her disgrace.

The question was, what should he do now? He had no means of identifying, much less speaking with, the woman who had written the letter. He could not hope to pass for a relative, since he did not know the writer's name, how old she was, or what she looked like. He could show the letter to Mrs. Fiske, but he did not trust her not to browbeat the writer, force her to reveal the letter's destination, perhaps even cast her out of the refuge. It was hard to see how leaving this place could be anything but a blessing, but perhaps the writer had nowhere else to go.

If he could only speak to her for a few minutes, he could explain how he came by her letter, and offer to make sure it reached whomever it was meant for. He did not know why he wanted so much to help her. Sheer boredom, perhaps, or his confounded chivalry. And then again, it might be that Mrs. Fiske, with her narrow, crabbed religious views, reminded him of his mother's family, with whom he had spent several wretched years as a boy after his father died.

All at once he had an idea. When Mrs. Fiske returned with the pamphlet, he asked, "How many inmates do you have at present?"

"Four-and-twenty."

"Are you accepting any more?"

"Mr. Harcourt thinks we might accommodate as many as thirty. Of course, we're careful whom we accept. No papists, no known felons. And if they're diseased, we send them to hospital."

"How do you find them?"

"They find us. They hear of our work and come to us here. We interview them, and if we're satisfied they're truly repentant, we take them in. Some don't stay more than a few days. They're too soft and self-indulgent. They think to find an easy life here. We soon set them right on that score!"

"I've no doubt you do," he said, with wry conviction. He thought for a moment. "Do they relapse very frequently?"

"How do you mean, frequently?"

"Well—have any left the refuge in the past few days?"

"No." She eyed him, puzzled and suspicious.

"Thank you, Mrs. Fiske. You've been extraordinarily kind. Good afternoon."

"Good afternoon, Mr.—?"

But Julian was already walking away.

He read the pamphlet on his way home. It was not very enlightening. It consisted largely of rhetoric about prostitution—"the stain upon our national soul," as Harcourt called it—rather than any practical information about the refuge or its inmates.

Not that it was foolish or facile. Harcourt wrote with force and grace, and without the pomposity that made so many reformers seem comical just when they were most sincere. But was all this eloquence in earnest? Julian felt he would like to know more about the Reverend Gideon Harcourt.

He let himself in at the street door of his lodging and went upstairs. As he was laying his hat and stick on the hall table, Sally came running out of the parlour. Her nut-brown hair hung damp and loose. Her bare feet made little wet marks on the floor. She was wearing his green silk dressing-gown (and nothing else, that he could perceive). The sash was loosely tied, the sleeves pushed up to her elbows. She kicked the hem from under her feet as she rushed toward him.

"Did you find her? What did she say about the letter? What kind of place is she shut up in? Is it a knocking-house?"

"Aren't you afraid of catching cold?"

"Pox on that! Who *is* she? What's it all about?"

"I don't know who she is, but she seems to be an inmate of a refuge for fallen women. That's what's at Number 9, Stark Street."

"Oh, one of them places." She wrinkled her nose. "Did you see her?"

"I couldn't. There was a dragon guarding the door." He described his encounter with Mrs. Fiske. "At least we know the woman who wrote the letter is still there, assuming she really is an inmate. Mrs. Fiske says no inmates have left in the past few days."

"What'll we do now?"

"We could find you something warmer to wear than my dressing-gown."

"I don't want nothing else. This is plummy, this is. Feels like heaven next me skin!"

"Where did you get it?"

"Out of your wardrobe." She shrugged, as if to say, where else? "Suits me, don'cha think?"

"Yes. It does."

A slow smile spread over her face. "You fancies me, Mr. Julian Kestrel."

"I think you're very fetching," he said politely.

"Bender! I know when a cove has the itch. You likes me in this here dressing-robe of yours, but you'd like me a sight better out of it. Wouldn't you, now?"

He began drawing off his gloves. "What's become of Dipper?"

"He went to fetch me traps from me lodging in Seven Dials. But first he brought me up a tub of hot water, and I washed meself all over. Even me hair and under me nails! I never done that afore."

Julian looked rather blank.

"Scrubbed meself raw, I did. On account of, Dip's so swell now, I has to live up to him. And you—! Cor, I never seed a cove so splash. Dip says you changes your linen every day. I'm glad it ain't me as does your washing, that's all!"

He suddenly realized he had not yet asked how she was. She seemed so gay and lively, he had all but forgotten what she had gone through last night. He wondered how much of her cockiness was pure, stubborn courage. In all the time she had been here, he had never heard her complain, though she still hobbled a little, and there was a mottled bruise over her left eye.

She saw him look at it. "Regular rainbow, ain't it? Looks worse nor it is, though."

"I'm sorry, Sally."

"It ain't nothing." She gave a little wriggle, as if to shake off his concern. "You ain't said what we was going to do about that letter. You mean to ask Blue Eyes about it?"

"I'd rather not. It may have nothing to do with him—and if it does, it's probably a personal matter he wouldn't relish my knowing about." After the Bellegarde murder, Julian was not anxious to receive any more forced confidences from the erring aristocracy. "I still think the most tactful and sensible course is to find the writer, and see what she wants done with the letter."

"But you said you can't get in that place."

"*I* can't, no."

"Then how—Oh, I'm down upon you! You wants *me* to have a try!"

He did not answer at once. It was true he had meant to ask her to go to the refuge, and he sensed that she would do it without hesitation—whether to keep on his good side or because she was curious herself, he could not say. But the realization that he had this power over her made him think twice about using it.

"If you're willing," he said at last. "It's a grisly place—I wouldn't blame you for avoiding it like the plague. But Mrs. Fiske told me they had room for a few more inmates. And if you could once get inside, I shouldn't think it would be difficult to find the writer. There can't be many women like her there—educated and gently bred. You've only to tell her we have the letter and ask her what she wants done with it, and then you can take yourself off."

"It might be a lark, at that! I'll do it. I'll go slap off!"

"I didn't mean you should dash off this instant. Wait till you feel more the thing."

"I'm in high gig now."

"I can see that. But wait till tomorrow, for God's sake. A day won't make any difference."

"Oh, all right, Mr. High and Mighty. You do order a gal about!" She cocked her head at him appraisingly. "I been wondering: have you got a woman? I asked Dip, but he wouldn't tell me."

"How inconveniently discreet of him."

"Well, have you or haven't you?"

"I'm not married."

"I knows *that*," she said impatiently. "I mean women—any kind."

"As with racehorses, I lose money on them from time to time, but I haven't one of my own."

"You're enough to make a cat laugh, *you* are."

"A cat? You mean, like the one curiosity killed?"

She grinned. "All right, Lightning, I get your drift."

"Lightning?"

"That's what I've a mind to call you. 'Coz why, 'coz you're so flash. You know what 'flash' means?"

"Showy, stylish, having something to do with thieves—"

She shook her head. "That ain't what a game gal means when she says 'flash.' You see, for us there's two kinds of coves, 'flash' and 'foolish.' 'Foolish' means a cove as has to pay. 'Flash' means you'd give it all to him for nothing."

Their eyes met and held.

All at once there were footsteps on the stairs below. Julian's landlady, Mrs. Mabbitt, came bustling in, her white hair tucked under a big checked cap, her sleeves pushed up to her elbows. Her cheeks glowed with health and hard work. Mrs. Mabbitt was so full of vigour that sometimes the very sight of her made Julian want to take to his bed for a month. Dipper came in after her, bearing a bundle of clothes in one hand, and a large bonnet with a draggled red plume in the other

"I ran into Dipper downstairs, sir, and—" Mrs. Mabbitt broke off, staring at Sally's attire.

"I've just had me very first bath," Sally announced.

"And I've just come home," added Julian hastily, "and heard all about it."

"As I was saying, sir, I ran into Dipper, and he told me his sister's come to visit. Now, I'm sure it's quite all right, seeing as she *is* his sister—" She looked keenly from Dipper to Sally, verifying the resemblance. "But still, in the strictest sense, it ain't proper, a young woman staying with two men. You must see that, sir."

"Quite, yes."

"I'll tell you what, sir. I have that little back room where the maid sleeps, when I've got one." Mrs. Mabbitt took on maidservants from time to time, but few could live up to her standards of cleanliness for long. Julian suspected she was really much happier doing all the work herself. "How will it be if I let Miss Sally stay there, while she visits her brother and—er—gets her affairs in order?"

"That's very kind of you, Mrs. Mabbitt. Of course you'll make an appropriate adjustment in the rent."

"That's my look-out, sir," said Dipper.

"Stuff and nonsense," said Mrs. Mabbitt cheerfully. "Nobody needn't pay anything. Miss Sally's to be my guest. I shall like having her about."

"I don't want to be no trouble," broke in Sally, not liking this arrangement one bit.

"You won't be, my girl. I like to have a visitor now and again. Come with me, and I'll show you your room. Are those your shoes in there by the fire? Here, put them on at once, we can't have you catching cold padding about on your poor bare feet. Once you're settled, we'll see about getting you some proper clothes." She clucked her tongue at the red-feather hat. "And you haven't washed properly behind your ears. You've a good deal to learn about bathing, my girl."

She got a firm grip on Sally's hand and led her away. Sally looked back, mutely appealing for rescue. Julian and Dipper smiled and shrugged, in a stunning display of male helplessness.

After they had gone, Julian said, smiling, "I think Sally may have met her match." He added, "How much does Queen Mab know about her?"

"I didn't tell her much, sir, but I think she dropped down to a good deal on her own. She's up to snuff, is Mrs. M., and a pinch or two above it. Caught me tracking up the dancers with Sally's togs, so I had to put down to her that she was here. There wasn't no hiding this." He waved the red-feather bonnet.

Julian explained his plan to send Sally to the refuge. "She seemed very keen on the idea."

"It's a first-rate dodge, sir. Might keep her out of trouble for a bit, too."

"Are you worried about her?

"'Course I am, sir. It ain't no kind of life she's got now."

"You know, I could help her find work. One of my friends could give her a character."

"That's good of you, sir, but I don't think she'd stick it. Why, sir, she can earn more blunt in a night, seeing company like she does, than she could in a month as a moll-slavey, or in one of them factories. And the work ain't so hard, and she's got more liberty, like. What's being on the square got to offer, compared to that?"

"Self-respect," suggested Julian doubtfully.

"Self-respect's a fine thing, sir, but you can't eat it, nor drink it, nor put a red feather on it and tie it under the chin."

Julian had no answer to this. There's a poser for you, Mr. Harcourt, he thought. Write us a pamphlet solving that, and we'll hail you as the genius of this age.

Sally was up before dawn next morning. She could not sleep any later, with Mrs. Mabbitt bustling about the house, clattering saucepans and raking out grates. By half past six, she was on her way to Stark Street. She supposed they would be up and about at the refuge—she had an idea that reformers did not waste time lolling in bed when there was God's work to be done.

She took a hackney coach to Stark Street, which made her feel very grand. She had never had a hackney to herself before. But she got out at the corner, thinking it would not fit the character of a penitent whore to arrive in a coach. The driver let down the steps, and she swept out with her nose in the air, pretending she was a lady, and this was her very own carriage. Then she spoilt it with a giggle. Tipping the driver, she sent him on his way.

She walked up to No. 9. It was just as Mr. Kestrel had described it: two houses joined together, with the formal entrance on the right-hand side. She went up to the door, put on what she hoped was a doleful, repentant face, and rang the bell.

The door opened a little way, and a woman looked out. Sally guessed at once that she was Mr. Kestrel's dragon. "What's your business?"

"If you please, ma'am, I've come to be showed the error of me ways, and save me soul."

The dragon looked her scathingly up and down. "Very well, you may come in. But no one can see you now. We're about to have morning prayers and breakfast. Mr. Harcourt may find time to speak with you afterward, or he may not. We're very busy this morning. We're expecting the trustees."

She opened the door just wide enough for Sally to enter. Sally found herself in a sparely furnished hallway, with stairs leading down to the kitchen level, and up to the floors above. The walls were painted a sedate, leaden grey. An incongruous door was cut into the left-hand wall. Sally realized this must have been added when the two houses became one, to make a passage between them.

"What's your name?" the dragon demanded.

"Sally Stokes, ma'am."

"Sally isn't a proper Christian name."

If you're a proper Christian, Sally thought, I'd as lief be in the other place. "It's short for Sarah, ma'am."

"If Sarah is the name you were christened with, then Sarah you must be called. I'm Mrs. Fiske, the matron on duty today. Come with me. Not there," she added sharply, as Sally turned toward the elegantly furnished front parlour. "That room is reserved for trustees and patrons."

She led Sally to a well-scrubbed back parlour. It had no furniture but a rectangular deal table and four bare, armless chairs. There was a view of the back garden: a couple of stunted trees, some pinched, precise flower-beds, and a gravel walk. Around the garden ran a high brick wall, with iron spikes along the top.

"Wait here," said Mrs. Fiske. "After breakfast, I'll inform you whether Mr. Harcourt has time to see you. He interviews all the women who come here, to determine whether they're suitable candidates for reclamation."

She went out. Sally wondered what to do now. Being pent up in here was no way to find the writer of the letter. Why shouldn't she venture out and have a look around? The worst they could do if they caught her was to chuck her out. And it was not as if she really wanted to stay.

She opened the door a little way and looked out. There was no one in sight. All the activity in the place seemed to be in the basement below, where Sally could hear footsteps, the scraping of chairs, and the clanking of pots and pans.

She tiptoed downstairs. The front room here was the kitchen; she peeked in, but saw no one there. All the noise was coming from the back room. Sally crept toward it and hid behind the open door, looking in through the narrow gap between it and the wall.

This was the communal eating room. There were two long tables, each with about a dozen women seated at it. The women varied in age from perhaps fifteen to thirty. Some were fresh and pretty, others withered and losing what looks they ever had. They were all dressed alike, in stiff grey gowns with white collars, aprons, and caps. Sally scanned their ranks, wondering if one of them had written the letter. If so, how was she to single her out from the rest?

Mrs. Fiske stood stiffly before one of the tables. Beside her was a young woman Sally felt sure must be Irish: no English girl had such porcelain skin, or such delicate features. Her hair was black, her figure straight and trim, her age perhaps five-and-twenty. She was dressed in the same grey and white uniform as the inmates. Perhaps she was to serve breakfast—she was standing by a large tureen, with a pile of wooden bowls and a ladle ready to hand.

At the head of the room stood a man holding a venerable-looking book—a Bible, Sally supposed. He was dressed soberly, yet with a dash of elegance. His skin was very pale and smooth, more like wax than human flesh. He had straw-coloured hair, thin lips, and disdainfully flaring nostrils.

Some of the inmates were talking among themselves. Mrs. Fiske clapped her hands, and at once there was a dead silence. "We are fortunate to have Mr. Harcourt here to lead us in prayer this morning," she announced. "As you know, the trustees are coming today, and Mr. Harcourt was obliged to remain here all night, preparing to meet with them—"

She broke off, staring across the room. Sally followed her gaze, and saw a small, forlorn table pushed into a corner. There was a chair before it, empty.

"Where is Mary?" thundered Mrs. Fiske.

The inmates exchanged glances and shifted about in their chairs.

"Has anyone seen her this morning?" Mr. Harcourt's voice was as smooth as velvet, and seemed to fill the room without his raising it.

There was a tense silence. At last one of the inmates stood up hesitantly. She was in her early twenties, plump and pretty, with a few flaxen curls stealing out from under her cap. Her bosom and hips strained against the stiff, straight lines of her gown. "If you please, sir, I did look in on her, very quick, just before we come down to breakfast."

"And what was she doing?"

"She was sleeping, sir. I said to her, 'Sst! Mary! It's almost seven o'clock!' But she was sleeping so sound, she didn't stir. Then Peg—Margaret, I mean"—she bobbed her head at the Irish girl standing beside Mrs. Fiske—"come looking for me, and I had to shirry along to breakfast."

"Lazing in bed at this hour!" exclaimed Mrs. Fiske.

The Irish girl dropped a meek curtsey. "Shall I be after fetching her, ma'am?"

"You ought to have done so, before. Mr. Harcourt's put you in charge of making sure the inmates are prompt at meals and prayers."

"I think we needn't blame Margaret overmuch," Mr. Harcourt interposed. "I'm afraid this is merely another instance of poor Mary's intransigence. Margaret, go and bring her here for prayers. As she is late to breakfast, she will have none this morning."

"Yes, Mr. Harcourt." The Irish girl darted off. Sally stood very still behind the door, hardly daring to breathe until she had passed.

The flaxen-haired girl had not sat down. Mr. Harcourt looked at her, brows lifted. "Have you something else to say, Florence?"

"W-well, sir, it's only that—" Florence swallowed hard. "I don't think Mary meant to sleep so late, sir. I was thinking, happen it might be her medicine as made her sleep so sound. I seen the bottle on the table by her bed, and—"

"What bottle?" said Mrs. Fiske impatiently. "She doesn't take her medicine from a bottle. I give it to her in a glass."

"But I seen a bottle—"

"You may sit down now, Florence," said Mr. Harcourt.

"Yes, sir."

"While we wait for Mary," he said, "this seems an opportune time to read the lesson of the wise and foolish bridesmaids." He opened his Bible.

Suddenly Margaret came running down the stairs and into the room. She stopped still in the doorway, hands clasped. Every head turned toward her.

"Oh, Mr. Harcourt, Mrs. Fiske, it's a grievous thing I've seen! Sure, we knew Mary had an unrepentant heart, but I never thought she'd stoop to such wickedness!"

"What do you mean?" demanded Harcourt. "Has she left us?"

"Aye, sir!" wailed Margaret. "And I shudder to think of her where she is now!"

"What are you saying?" cried Mrs. Fiske. "Where is she?"

"Where no hope nor help can ever reach her! She's dead, ma'am—and by her own hand!"

The Wages of Sin

The inmates broke into gasps, exclamations, shrieks. "Quiet, all of you!" Harcourt commanded, his voice ringing clearly through the din. Margaret strode in among them, enforcing silence by shaking their shoulders and boxing their ears.

Mrs. Fiske stood clenching and unclenching her fists. Her face was contorted with passion, but Sally—her eyes glued in fascination to the gap in the door—could not tell what passion it was. "Are you sure of this?" she pressed Margaret. "If you've caused all this row to no purpose—"

"It's true, ma'am, I swear it! Bad luck to me if I lie! I saw her as clear as I see you now—stretched out on her bed, cold as ice! And there was a bottle of laudanum, almost empty, on the table by her bed, and a bit of laudanum left in the glass she takes her medicine in. Sure as Shrove-tide, she's used the laudanum to put an end to her miserable life—"

"Don't blaspheme, Margaret," said Harcourt curtly. "Come, we must go to her at once. Mrs. Fiske, will you be so good as to come with me? And Margaret, I'll need you as well. The rest of you are to have breakfast as usual. Bess, you may serve the porridge and bread, and Nancy, lead the others in saying grace."

He went out, Mrs. Fiske and Margaret with him. Sally hid behind the door till she heard them go up the stairs, then crept quickly after them. She reached the top of the stairs just in time to see them disappear through the door that connected this house with the one adjacent. To her disappointment, she heard a key scrape in the lock. She tried the door, but, as she expected, it would not budge.

What should she do now? Mrs. Fiske seemed to have forgotten all about her. She did not want to leave yet—she still had not found the writer of the letter, and besides, she was curious about this girl Mary. Perhaps she should go downstairs and talk to the inmates while they were left free of supervision.

The key turned in the lock again. Sally fled a little way down the stairs and stood pressed against the wall. The light was dim enough here for her to look up into the front hallway without much chance of being seen herself.

Mrs. Fiske came through the connecting door, locked it behind her, and hastened upstairs. Sally started to follow her, then scurried back into cover. For Mrs. Fiske came quickly down again, wrapped in a shawl and tying a drab bonnet under her chin. She went out by the street door.

Now, where are you off to, you old cat? Sally mused. To fetch a doctor, p'raps, or a constable—

Suddenly she was struck from behind. She stumbled on the stairs and scrambled around to face her enemy.

It was only the flaxen-haired girl, Florence, looking as dazed as herself. "Who are you?"

"Me name's Sally. I come here to be reformed, only it seems like it ain't a good day for it."

"No, it ain't." Florence giggled nervously. "I'm sorry I run right into you like that. I'm in such a pucker, I didn't see you. We're all at sixes and sevens—Red Jane's spilled her porridge down the front of my apron. Just look!"

"I heard a gal laid hands on herself last night."

"Hush!" Florence put a finger to her lips and looked about warily. "Mr. Harcourt'll cut up rough if he hears us talking about it."

"He won't hear nothing—he's too far off." All the same, Sally sank her voice. "This gal Mary—who was she?"

"Nobody knowed, really. She wasn't like the rest of us. She was a lady."

"A lady?" Sally pricked up her ears.

"Certain sure. You could tell by the way she talked—*when* she talked, which wasn't often. Mr. Harcourt was that cross with her, on account of she'd never say nothing about herself, or where she come from, or who her people was. He wanted to know all about her, you see, because anybody could tell she'd been brung up respectable, and he thought if he could send her home, reformed and right as a trivet, her people'd be ever so grateful. Leastways that's what Peg says, and Peg always knows his mind."

It must've been this gal Mary as wrote the letter! Sally thought. A lady, and one as wouldn't talk about herself.

"It's mortal sad, ain't it?" said Florence, "her drinking down that poison in the dead of night, all alone. If she hadn't been in the Black Hole, she couldn't have done it. Somebody would have stopped her."

"What's the Black Hole?"

"It's a little room—hardly more nor a closet, really. We call it the Black Hole on account of it has no windows or hearth, so it's always dark and cold. It's for punishing an inmate as is *in-tracktable*. Mr. Harcourt put poor Mary in it directly she come, because she wouldn't confess her sins or tell where she come from, or even give her true name. Just called herself Mary—and when she was asked her surname, she'd say 'Magdalene.' She was plucky, in her way, was Mary. So Mr. Harcourt was in a bad skin with her from the first. He made her sleep all alone in the Black Hole—not like the rest of us, we sleeps four or five to a room—and in the daytime she had to take her meals at a little table by herself, and wear a sign round her neck that said

'Unrepentant.' I don't know why he let her stay at all—he's put many a gal over the door for much less. I s'pose it's as Peg says: he thought her people might be swells, and do something for him." She cocked her head thoughtfully. " 'Cept, that's not all there was to it. He wanted to break her."

"Bugger his eyes!" said Sally. "That ain't no way to treat a dog, let alone a poor gal as is gently bred, and lost her character!"

Florence nodded sadly. "She felt it, did Mary. Very low, she was. Though it's queer—"

"What?" Sally prompted.

"She seemed better the last few days—not so green about the gills as she was before. And she'd smile to herself sometimes, like she was hugging a secret to her heart. Mr. Harcourt didn't like that above half, I can tell you! But p'raps it was just her medicine put her a bit more in form. She was taking a cordial—'Summerson's Strengthening Elixir,' it's called. You wouldn't think she'd want to make away with herself, just when she was on her pins again, now would you?"

The door that connected the two houses suddenly opened, and Harcourt swept in, Margaret hurrying after him. "I'll be in my office," he said, without so much as breaking his stride or looking back to see if she was listening. "Tell Mrs. Fiske when she returns that I can't see anyone—unless one of the trustees should come early. And remember, on no account is anyone to speak to any journalist, on *any* subject, until I give leave."

"Yes, Mr. Harcourt," the Irish girl said soulfully.

Harcourt suddenly stopped and peered down the basement stairs. He must have especially keen eyes, or perhaps the light was growing brighter. "What are you doing there, Florence?"

"Please you, sir, I come up to change my apron. It has porridge spilled on it."

"Change it at once, and go back to breakfast. Who is that with you?"

Sally had no choice but to come upstairs. Harcourt raked her with his pale blue eyes. It gave her the shivers. Men often looked at her as if they could see through her clothes, but Mr. Harcourt's gaze seemed to pierce her very skin.

"Who are you?" he said. "What do you want?"

For once Sally's tongue was tied. Florence stepped into the breach. "She's come to be an inmate, sir."

"You had no business speaking with her. You know you're forbidden to talk to strangers."

"Yes, sir. But there wasn't nobody to look after her, and I—I—"

"Never mind. I'll overlook it this once, seeing that things are somewhat—irregular—today."

Irregular? thought Sally. Is that what you calls it when a poor gal hops the twig right under your own roof? But she held her tongue, thinking she might get Florence into trouble by revealing she had talked to her about Mary's death. One thing was certain: she was not going to breathe a word about Mary's letter to these people. Mr. Harcourt was a cold fish; she did not trust him. And the inmates seemed completely under his sway.

Harcourt turned to Margaret. "As Mrs. Fiske is absent, I'm relying on you to keep order among the inmates. Have them go on with their work as usual. The trustees will be here in a few hours, and I wish them to see that our normal routines are unshaken. Not that we're not greatly saddened and sobered by this event, of course."

"It breaks me heart, Mr. Harcourt!" Margaret pressed her hands to her breast. "Sure, if she'd only listened to you, and repented of her evil ways—! It's a lesson to us all, a bitter lesson! The wages of sin is death!"

"I'm glad to see you've profited by her example. I hope you will encourage the other inmates to do likewise."

"There's never a day goes by when I don't strive to shine on me fellow sinners a bit of the light that's fallen upon me."

"I perceive that, Margaret. Be assured, your efforts do not go unappreciated." He started up the stairs, waving his hand dismissively at Sally. "Send this young woman away."

"Yes, Mr. Harcourt."

The Irish girl stood looking after him till he was out of sight. Then she turned to Sally, with a smile that transformed her face. Her long eyes turned up at the corners, her chin and cheekbones sharpened, till she looked just like a fox. "Well, you heard what Himself said. You'll have to go. Come back another day, if you can stomach this place after seeing him—the great bloody ass!"

"Well, I'll be blowed!" marvelled Sally. "You're a reg'lar out-and-outer, you are."

Margaret tossed her head complacently. "I know a trick or two. Faith, isn't it Wideawake Peg they call me? I should live to see the day when I couldn't bamboozle a stiff romped pulpit-thumper like Himself! And lucky for you I do, Florrie Ames," she added, rounding on Florence. "Where would you and the other girls be if I didn't play up to Himself, and piss down his back, and make meself out to be the greatest penitent since St. Mary Magdalene kissed the cross?"

"It's true," Florrie confirmed. "Peg's got Mr. Harcourt's ear more nor any of us, and she can go 'most anywhere she likes here, even his office. If we wants something—extra food or candles, or anything at all—it's Peg can get it for us."

"You makes 'em fork out for it, I expect," said Sally to Peg.

"And why not?" Peg was unruffled. "Isn't it meself that takes all the risks? I'm not a public charity, now, am I? If I do a favour for one of me friends, I expect a favour back. Off with you, now. Himself won't like it if he finds you still here."

Sally went. She had a good deal to tell Mr. Kestrel and Dipper. And yet, it was simple enough when you came right down to it. She had found the writer of the letter—and found her too late.

"And then Peg shooed me out, and I come back here," Sally finished. "And that's all about it." She threw herself down on the sofa. "Now, you might give me some'ut to wet me whistle, seeing as how I've talked so long."

"Give her a drink," said Julian, without looking around from the window where he stood.

"Yes, sir." Dipper poured her some ale.

Julian gazed out at the street, unseeing. The rattle of carriage wheels and the clangour of hooves rang in his ears, but could not drown out the voice in his head—his own voice, speaking to Sally yesterday. *I didn't mean you should dash off to the refuge this instant. Wait till tomorrow, for God's sake. A day can't make any difference.*

He turned abruptly. "There'll have to be an inquest. Dipper, go and find out when and where it is."

"Now, sir?"

Julian's brows shot up. Dipper ran for his hat, and was gone. Sally looked at Julian more closely. "What's wrong? You disappointed we couldn't ask Mary about the letter?"

"Rather."

"Can't be helped, I s'pose."

"No."

He went to the table, where his breakfast lay untouched. "Would you like some coffee?"

"Catch me drinking that stuff!" She wrinkled her nose and took another swig of ale.

He would have poured some coffee for himself, but she jumped up and did it for him. Then she studied him, her head on one side. All at once she asked, "Did Dip ever tell you how he come to be called Dipper?"

He looked up in surprise.

"It all started when we was kids. Our pa, he was a bricklayer's labourer, but he took to drink, and kept missing work. And when he did go, he'd have the staggers, like as not, and finally he got the kick-out, and he couldn't get honest work no more. So he took up with some burglars as taught him their trade, and George, our brother, as is older than Dip, went in with him."

Julian sat down opposite her, stretching out his legs. He already knew Dipper's story, but he was willing to hear it again. It was better than listening to those words reverberate endlessly in his mind: *A day won't make any difference.* What had he been thinking of? How could he have miscalculated so disastrously?

She chattered on, "Our ma was a good soul, and straight as a pound of candles, but she couldn't do nothing with Pa, and besides, she was sick of a consumption, so she was too weak to blow him up proper. Dip, he was little and limber, so Pa used to take him along on a job and hoist him through the window, so he could unlock the door and let in Pa and his pals. But later on Pa 'prenticed him to a pickpocket. Dip was tip-top at that lay. That's why he was called Dipper—'coz he had such a knack for dipping his forks into other coves' pockets.

" 'Course, he was never easy in his mind about being on the cross. He knew it grieved Ma—and the worst of it was, it was mostly on her account he had to do it. She was took so ill, and Pa never did nothing for her—all the blunt he got, he spent on gin and fancy women. And finally Ma died, and Pa got nabbed and kicked the clouds" —she made a gesture eloquent of hanging— "and George, he was sent to Botany Bay. And I didn't know what become of Dip, till I run into him t'other night."

"What about you? What were you doing all this time?"

"Oh, there ain't much to tell about me. When I was a kid, I picked pockets like Dip, but I never had the gift for it he had. Mostly I was a stall: I'd play up to a cove while me pal did him over. I give that up—I likes being on me own hook, and not having to answer to nobody. 'Sides, thieves is al'ays getting took up on account of the reward, and I can't stick being locked up. So I went on the grind. Nobody bothers a honest whore, as is just trying to make her way in the world. 'Course, I lifts handkerchiefs off me flats, but that ain't nothing. It's mostly for sport of it, and to keep me forks in form."

"How did you and Dipper get separated?"

"I got in a kick-up with another gal, and we was both sent to the house of correction. When I got out, I went to live in Ratcliff and married a sailor. I don't mean married legal, in a church—just temporary, like sailors does when they comes ashore. I fancied him uncommon. He was a first-rater—sent me blunt for months after he went back to sea, and he didn't even know I was full in the belly—"

She broke off, biting her lip.

He asked gently, "Do you have a child, Sally?"

"I did have. Becky, I called her. She only lived for about a fortnight. She wasn't strong—right from the beginning, everybody told me she'd never stick it. I didn't want to believe 'em. When she went, I cut up something mortal. Even now, I thinks about her sometimes, and I—" She swallowed hard, "I miss her."

She wiped her nose on her sleeve. He gave her his handkerchief. She blew into it, then slipped it into her pocket. He pretended not to notice.

"It's over and done," she said. "I've put it behind me, mostly I'd like to have another one, though. I dunno why. If it was a boy, I couldn't do nothing for him, and if it was a gal, she'd only end up like me."

"You might marry."

"Not likely!" she laughed

"Of course, I realize—" He broke off uncertainly.

"That I ain't just what every mother'd like her son to bring home?" She grinned. "I expect there's coves as'd marry rite all the same. But I ain't so soft as that comes to! A friend of mine married her fancy-man, and she never had a farthing to call her own again—he took all she earned and turned it into drink. So she went to a parson and said, What'll I do? and he said there wasn't no help for it, 'coz why, 'coz the bastard was her husband, and everything she had in the world—everything she got by her own hard work—belonged to him. He said that's the *law*. Is that true?"

"I believe so. The law doesn't recognize a married woman as a person separate from her husband."

"Well, with a law like that, what gal'd be so dicked in the nob as to get spliced? Not me, I can tell you!"

He regarded her thoughtfully. "Why have you been telling me all this?"

" 'Coz you was blue-deviled, and I wanted to cheer you up. If you was any other cove, I'd've found better ways to do it than by talking, but you al'ays stalls me off when I makes up to you. So I thought I'd talk about Dip, 'coz he's somebody you and me has in common, see?"

"Yes, I see. That was very kind of you, Sally."

"There ain't much I wouldn't do for you, Lightning—if you'd let me."

"You've done more than enough. Would you think me rude if I asked to be alone for a while?"

She glared at him and got up. "Some folks," she said darkly, "wouldn't know a good thing if it was to bite 'em in the cods!"

"The inquest is at two o'clock, sir, at the Rose and Thorn, in Guilford Street."

"What, today? How the devil did Harcourt arrange for it so quickly?"

"I talked to some of the neighbours, sir—them as lives around the refuge. They says Mr. Harcourt wants to get it over slap off, afore the leers takes too much interest."

"The newspapers will be one too many for Mr. Harcourt. This is the kind of story they flock to—a fallen woman, a tragic death, a mystery surrounding the woman's identity."

"I dunno, sir. The neighbours says Mr. Harcourt has some great guns for patrons: well-breeched tradesmen, parsons, even a gentry-cove or two. He's counting on them to clap a stopper on the hurly-burly about Mary's death."

"Is he?" But there may be rather more hurly-burly than you expected, Mr. Harcourt, Julian thought. "Dipper, I mean to go to the inquest, and I want you and Sally to come with me."

"You going to hand over the letter, sir?"

"I can't see that I have any choice. It will be rather awkward explaining how we came by it, but still, it's evidence that might throw light on Mary's death. We can't in all conscience keep it back. All the same—"

"Sir?"

Julian shook his head. "There are things about Mary's death that don't make sense to me. They may all be explained at the inquest, but if they're not—Well, never mind that now. The reason I want Sally to come is that I should like to know if whichever of those three men she stole the letter from is there, and, unless he turns out to be Avondale, she's the only one who'll recognize him. But tell her to wear a veil. It's just possible we may have reasons for not wanting *him* to recognize *her*."

Mr. Harcourt Pours Oil on the Waters

The Rose and Thorn was a neat, respectable eating-house near the refuge. The inquest was to be held in its large back parlour. Tables had been cleared away to make room for the coroner and jury. The numerous spectators sat on chairs and benches, or in booths along the sides of the room. Julian, Dipper, and Sally found a corner booth and sat down, looking about them.

Harcourt was there, moving suavely among the crowd, with a becoming mixture of sorrow and disapproval. *I regret that poor young woman's death, but I am shocked and repelled by the manner of it,* he conveyed. A group of dowdy matrons trailed after him, hanging on his every word. Julian recognized Mrs. Fiske among them. Many of the other spectators were stout, important-looking business or professional men and members of the clergy. These must be the wealthy and influential patrons Dipper had heard about.

A couple of journalists stood by, idly kicking the wainscotting or cleaning their nails with penknives. Julian identified them by their expressions of mixed cynicism and curiosity, and by their evident habit of mistaking their trousers for blotting-paper. On the whole, though, Harcourt seemed to have been remarkably successful at keeping this business out of the newspapers.

"Do you see any of your three men?" Julian whispered to Sally, who had been peeking out from under her veil.

"No, none of 'em," she whispered back. "If one of 'em comes in, I'll tip you the nod."

There was a small stir as the coroner and jury entered. But to Julian's surprise, the reporters were not looking that way. They were nudging each other and glancing toward the other end of the room, where a corpulent elderly man had just hobbled in on crutches. He had one foot bandaged, as if with gout. His head was bald and shiny on top, with tufts of white hair at the sides. His clothes were very plain, but, to Julian's practised eye, impeccably tailored and costly. He wore an immense, old-fashioned gold watch and a gold-rimmed pince-nez.

Julian had great faith in the instinct of journalists for knowing what was really important. While the coroner fussed over some papers and made a pontifical speech to the jury, he sent Dipper to find out from the reporters who the man on crutches was.

Dipper conferred with them briefly and returned. "He's Mr. Samuel Digby, sir. He's a very warm cove, and a beak, and lives in Highgate."

Julian had heard of him. He was a retired wool merchant, very plump in the pocket, who had made a name for himself as a shrewd magistrate, severe but just. He was also renowned as a philanthropist, although he was selective in his charities. Julian wondered what could have brought him all the way from Highgate, with a gouty foot that sent spasms of pain across his face whenever he moved. Was he one of Harcourt's patrons? If so, he showed no inclination to mingle with the others.

There was a short recess, while a parish officer took the jury into another room to view the body. They filed back in again, much sobered, and the coroner called the first witness.

This proved to be Margaret Muldoon, otherwise known as Wideawake Peg. She had been kept in another room, perhaps in compliance with Harcourt's rule against the inmates of the refuge mixing with strangers. She described how she had found Mary cold and dead at about seven o'clock that morning, with the empty laudanum bottle on her night-table. The coroner found her Irish sense of drama a little overwhelming and kept her testimony as short as he could.

Florrie Ames's testimony was even shorter. She recounted how she had looked in briefly on Mary and tried to wake her, and how she had noticed the laudanum bottle on the night-table but thought it was only Mary's medicine. The journalists had to be admonished for winking at her during her testimony. She stole a smile at them as she and Peg were ushered out.

The next witness proved to be a very dignified and supercilious doctor, a prominent member of the Royal College of Physicians, who had examined Mary soon after her death. He made clear that, but for his high regard for Mr. Harcourt, he would not dream of lending his name and expertise to such a sordid proceeding. The coroner was duly awed, and treated him with great deference. No doubt about it, wealthy and powerful patrons had their uses.

The deceased was a female between the ages of sixteen and twenty, the Great Doctor testified. She was somewhat thin, but otherwise showed no sign of ill health. He had examined her body at about ten o'clock this morning, which he understood was some three hours after she was found dead.

Julian looked up sharply at this. Why had it taken the people at the refuge three hours to call in a doctor? And what were they doing in the meantime?

As the Great Doctor understood it, nothing in Mary's room had been moved since her body was discovered. She was lying on her bed, dressed in a coarse woolen nightgown, with the blanket drawn up to her shoulders. She had no wounds, and there was no sign she had suffered a seizure or sudden illness. To judge by the onset of rigor mortis and the extent and pattern of lividity, she had lain dead in that position for anywhere from six to twelve hours.

He gave a brief description of her room. It was some ten feet square, without any window or fireplace. The only furniture was a small bedstead, a wooden chest, and a bedside table with a porcelain basin for washing. The basin was clean and empty. Beside it stood a jug half full of water, and an almost empty bottle.

The Great Doctor took the bottle out of his medical bag and held it up. It was about six inches high, made of clear glass, with a label attached to the cork. There were traces of a ruby-coloured liquid at the bottom. The coroner scrutinized it closely, then showed it to the jury. "You see, gentlemen," he pointed out, "the bottle was clearly labelled 'Laudanum.' The deceased can have been under no misapprehension about what was in it. I'm sure most of you have had occasion to take laudanum at one time or another; all the same, will you be good enough, Doctor, to explain briefly to the jury what it is?"

"Laudanum is tincture of opium dissolved in alcohol. It's prescribed for relieving pain caused by various ailments—toothache, rheumatism, and other more serious complaints. The average dose is twenty-five drops."

There was a glass beside the bottle on Mary's night-table, the Great Doctor said. It contained traces of laudanum, water, and a substance he believed to be Summerson's Strengthening Elixir, a cordial Mary had been taking.

What exactly was this cordial? the coroner asked. The Great Doctor explained that it was a concoction of sugar syrup, herbs, and a dash of spirits, designed to raise a weak patient. It was very popular, he believed, and was sold at shops all over London. It had a distinctive label, with a sun in the corner, shedding healing rays. He had no personal knowledge of why Mary was taking it, since she had never been his patient. He was told she had not been seriously ill, but merely weak and in low spirits—perhaps a debilitating effect of the depraved life she had led before she came to the refuge.

Here the coroner cautioned the jury that there was no evidence as yet regarding Mary's past life, so they could not draw conclusions about it. The Great Doctor stifled a yawn and looked at his watch.

The coroner asked him if he had an opinion about the cause of death. The Great Doctor cleared his throat. "In my view, death resulted from respiratory failure brought on by the deceased's deliberate ingestion of an overdose of laudanum."

"How can you be certain it was deliberate?"

"At Mr. Harcourt's request, I boiled down a small amount of the laudanum left in the bottle, to determine how high a concentration of opium it contained. Most druggists have their own preparations, and the amount of opium they use may vary. This was not a strong preparation. A female of Mary's age, in moderately good health, would have had to take an exceedingly large dose to end her life. No young woman of even minimal intelligence would swallow such a dose by mistake."

"Habitual opium-eaters are often reckless in the amount they take," the coroner suggested.

"This young woman was not a habitual opium-eater. Had she been, she would have needed constant doses of the drug. Deprivation would bring on severe physical symptoms—chills, aches, vomiting. I have been assured that she, like the other inmates of the refuge, was watched carefully, and her room frequently searched. There is no evidence that she was secretly taking opium in any form. Therefore I conclude she was not accustomed to opium, and that she knowingly took an excessive dose on this occasion, with fatal intent."

The coroner thanked the Great Doctor and dismissed him. The reporters wrote furiously in little notebooks. The jury exchanged grave looks.

Mrs. Fiske was called next. She sat down stiffly in the witness's seat. She was Mrs. Matthew Fiske—Christian name, Ellen. She was a member of the Reclamation Society, and one of the three matrons in charge of the refuge. The other two were Mrs. Jessop—she pointed to a stout, red-faced woman seated beside Harcourt—and Miss Nettleton, a thin, fluttery woman on Harcourt's other side.

The three matrons took turns on duty at the refuge, Mrs. Fiske explained. Mrs. Jessop presided on Mondays and Thursdays, Miss Nettleton on Wednesdays and Saturdays, and Mrs. Fiske on Tuesdays and Fridays. They each took every third Sunday. The matron on duty was responsible for keeping the refuge running smoothly: dealing with tradespeople, answering enquiries about the Reclamation Society's work, and maintaining adequate stocks of food, coal, candles, and such things. In addition, the presiding matron kept her eye on the inmates, and made sure they attended to their work and their prayers. If there were any serious infractions of discipline, she reported them to Mr. Harcourt. He visited the refuge at least once a day, and always held services there on Sundays.

Yesterday, following her usual practice, Mrs. Fiske relieved Mrs. Jessop in the morning and remained at the refuge all day. In the evening, the inmates had their supper in the refectory as usual. They finished at about half past eight. Then they went upstairs to the chapel for prayers and Bible readings until nearly ten.

"Was the deceased present at supper and evening prayers?" the coroner asked

"Yes."

"Are you certain?"

Mrs. Fiske bridled. "She wouldn't have been excused from them unless I gave her leave, which I should only have done if she were ill. Which she wasn't."

"Did you observe what frame of mind she was in?"

"There was a deal too much fuss about Mary and her moods, in my opinion, sir. She was always hipped about something—mooning and making a great drama of things, as if her speaking like a lady and being what some might call pretty made her different from the other girls. Which it didn't—they were all the same in God's eyes, all sinners in need of chastisement."

"But on this particular evening, Mrs. Fiske?"

"She seemed much as usual. I didn't especially notice. Though Mr. Harcourt has observed since that she seemed troubled in her mind, and I feel sure he must be right. He has a great understanding of character."

"So Mr. Harcourt was there yesterday evening?"

"Y-es." She eyed him warily.

"How long did he remain?"

"He—well, he was there all night, sir."

"Was that unusual?"

"Very. As a rule, Mr. Harcourt is scrupulous about observing the proprieties, and doesn't remain under the same roof with the inmates after they've gone to bed. But on this occasion we were expecting the trustees the next day Mr. Harcourt was to make an important presentation to them regarding the progress of our work. There was a great deal of preparation to be done, and Mr. Harcourt asked me to go over the accounts with him. We worked together the entire night."

"When did you last see the deceased alive?"

"I suppose it must have been at about ten o'clock. I gave her her dose of cordial after evening prayers."

"That was the cordial called Summerson's Strengthening Elixir?"

"Yes. She took a glass of it to bed with her every night—about a finger's length." She held up her forefinger to illustrate. "She was a bit thin and wan. The cordial was supposed to raise her," She pursed her lips skeptically.

"Did she say anything to you when you gave her the cordial?"

"Just, 'Thank you, Mrs. Fiske,' and bobbed a curtsey. She was a great one for little airs and graces."

"How long had she been taking this cordial?"

"About ten days."

"Was anyone else at the refuge taking it?"

"No, sir."

After Mary and the rest of the inmates had gone to bed, Mrs. Fiske worked with Mr. Harcourt in his office. From time to time, she went down to the kitchen to make tea. At about three o'clock in the morning, she went to the inmates' house to see that they were all in bed and behaving themselves.

"What do you mean by 'the inmates' house'?" asked the coroner.

"The refuge consists of two houses, joined together by a passage on the ground floor. The inmates sleep in the house on the left, so we speak of it as the inmates' house. The house on the right contains Mr. Harcourt's office, some reception rooms and work rooms, and the chapel."

"Did Mr. Harcourt go with you to look in on the inmates?"

"Mr. Harcourt go to the inmates' rooms while they were in bed? Certainly not! He would never do such a thing!"

The coroner coughed. "Hm—well—did you see anything out of the ordinary in the inmates' house?"

"No, sir. A few of the inmates were sitting up whispering, but I soon put a stop to that."

"Did you look in on the deceased?"

"I did, briefly. She was lying on her bed, and seemed to be asleep."

"Was she alone?"

"Yes, of course. She slept in a small room by herself, as she was in disgrace."

"Why was that?"

"That was Mr. Harcourt's decision. I wouldn't presume to speak for him on matters of discipline."

"Very well. Did you notice the empty laudanum bottle on the table by her bed?"

"No. It may have been there—I couldn't say. It was quite dark, and I wasn't looking around for such a thing. I just put my head in long enough to see that she was in bed, and then I moved on."

She had heard of Mary's death from Margaret Muldoon, at the same time as the others did. She went at once to the inmates' house with Mr. Harcourt, who summoned the doctor and ordered that nothing in Mary's room be touched. "And I can't say of my own knowledge what went on after that, because Miss Nettleton came to relieve me and had an attack of the vapours when she heard what had happened to Mary. So I had to take charge of her." She glared at Miss Nettleton, who shrank down in her chair.

Sally tugged on Julian's coat. "She didn't say where she piked off to in such a hurry in her bonnet and shawl, right after she come back from seeing Mary."

Before he could reply, the coroner asked, "Was laudanum readily available to the inmates?"

"It certainly was not. We keep some in the stillroom in case there's a need for it, but the door to that room is always locked. We keep spirits there, too, for medicinal use, and we can't have the creatures sneaking in looking for drink."

"Could the deceased have gotten laudanum from that room somehow?"

"I suppose she might have, sir, but the fact is, she didn't. I looked, and no laudanum had gone missing."

"Have you any idea at all how she might have gotten the laudanum?"

"Not the least, sir. But these women are sly enough for anything. Whenever I'm on duty I watch them closely and search their rooms, to make sure they haven't got hold of anything they shouldn't, but I wouldn't put it past them to find a way of smuggling things in from outside. That certainly isn't my fault, nor Mr. Harcourt's! We do everything we can to control them. We can't help it if—"

"Yes, yes, Mrs. Fiske, I'm sure you did all that was proper. Thank you. You are excused. And now"—he cleared his throat portentously—"I should like to hear from Mr. Harcourt."

The jury craned their necks and murmured to each other as Harcourt took the stand. They had been looking troubled by some of the evidence, especially about the harsh treatment Mary had undergone at the refuge. But if Harcourt sensed their mood, he gave no sign. He was grave and serene—respectful to the coroner and jury, but a little remote, as if a spiritual gulf set him apart from the law and its Pharisees.

At the coroner's behest, he gave a little information about himself. His name was Gideon Harcourt. He was an ordained minister of the Church of England, and the rector of a parish in Norfolk, which was now in the care of a curate. (Julian pricked up his ears at the mention of Norfolk, but no one else seemed struck by it.) On a visit to London some months ago, he had been shocked by the number of abandoned women on the streets, and by the shameful profligacy, at all levels of society, that fostered this trade in vice. He began to lecture on the subject, and found that there were many like-minded people eager to remove these baneful influences—these chancres in human form—from the streets. He resolved to dedicate himself to reclaiming as many castaways as he could, first helping them to repent and reform, and then either restoring them to their families or training them to earn their living at some virtuous, respectable trade.

The jury nodded approvingly, but they were not yet won over. Harcourt described his founding of the Reclamation Society and praised the hard work of its members, many of whom, he said, were kind enough to express their support by appearing here today. The women in his coterie beamed. The prosperous-looking men puffed out their chests, as if confident that their patronage was support enough for anyone. The journalists rolled their eyes at each other and shook their heads.

The refuge had opened about three months ago, Harcourt testified. Inmates had come and gone during that time. A few, he regretted to say, were unable to profit by the regimen of work and prayer laid down for them, and by the sterling example the matrons set. Those unfortunates were permitted to go their ways; the refuge held no one against her will.

"But there have been many more successes—women who came to us hardened, their moral sense deadened by vice—just as hearing is deadened by constant noise or taste by over-indulgence. Those women have learned to repent: to cleanse their souls by confession, and weep for their sins like children before a stern but loving father. I refer, of course, to God, not to myself, who only strives to do God's work in man's imperfect fashion."

The coroner was impressed, but seemed to feel they were wandering a bit from the subject. "When did the deceased come to the refuge?"

"About a fortnight ago. I believe it was late in the afternoon, on a Tuesday. She arrived alone, dressed in the tawdry finery of her calling. She seemed distraught, but said very little. I happened to be at the refuge, and interviewed her myself. Mrs. Fiske was also present, for propriety's sake. In my work, I cannot afford even the faintest appearance of unseemliness."

"Of course not," said the coroner.

"I was struck from the first by the young woman's speech and manners. She was clearly from a higher sphere of life than most of the women we see. Her fall seemed to me all the more unfortunate, given her advantages of breeding and education, she ought to have set a better example to her more ignorant sisters. I must confess, I was torn two ways in deciding whether to take her in. Her tears, her remorse, her clear understanding of her fault, boded well for her salvation. On the other hand, there was a want of openness—an unwillingness to acknowledge and confess her wrongdoing—that showed she could not yet humble herself sufficiently to repent with all her heart. She would say nothing of her family, her past life, or how she fell from grace. She steadfastly refused to tell us her surname—and even the Christian name she gave, that of the Mother of our Lord, I fear may have been invented.

"Gentlemen, what was I to do?" He appealed to the jury, who looked fascinated. "To cast her out would have forced her back upon the wretched course she was trying to abandon. Yet her stubborn silence, for which she would give no explanation, showed that her mind and heart were too filled with pride to make room for penitence. I could think of no better solution than to admit her to the refuge, while drawing a stem distinction between her and the other inmates, who had placed their trust in us and fully embraced our teachings.

"To open Mary's eyes to the incompleteness of her repentance, I was obliged to take certain painful but necessary measures. As she had isolated herself in spirit, so I isolated her in body. I ordered that she should sleep alone, in a room barren of luxuries and distractions, and that she should take her meals at a table separate from the other inmates. A father must chastise as well as comfort, and so must a man of my cloth make felt his displeasure when an ailing soul spurns the only medicine that can save her. That Mary did not leave us—though at all times she was free to do so—suggests to me that in her heart of hearts she understood my motives, and would have submitted herself to the consolations of religion and repentance, if only her faith had been greater, or her vanity less."

He paused. The jury waited, spellbound.

"Her death of course came as a terrible shock—I grieve for it with all my heart. That she should rush into the presence of her Maker, with her own blood upon her hands, is of all fates the one I should have wished most to spare her. Self-murder is a wicked act; I do not and cannot condone it. But I pray for her, and hope she may find mercy and peace where she is now. In spite of her obduracy, and her criminal despair—for who has the right to lose all hope, while we are in the hands of a just God, and redeemed by his Son's grace?—even so, I would like to think it was not impiety that prompted her desperate deed, but a burden of guilt so great that it turned her mind. Gentlemen, I hope that in reaching your verdict, you will take into account her mental imbalance, and deal gently with her memory, as you would wish to be judged yourselves."

The women spectators sniffed. One of them buried her face in her handkerchief. The jury lowered their eyes, humbled and moved, as if they were in church.

Julian marvelled at Harcourt. He had turned Mary's death while under his care into a source of acclaim for himself and the refuge. No one dreamed of asking how he could have let such a thing happen. No one cared about the facts anymore, but only about the lovely, tragic tale he had woven around them. To Julian, the evidence was full of holes—some of them large enough to drive a coach-and-four through. But anyone attempting to point that out here would be a voice crying in the wilderness.

"Just a few last questions, Mr. Harcourt." The coroner was practically purring. "Mere formalities, nothing more. I am sure none of us wishes to distract you any longer from your valuable work."

Harcourt inclined his head graciously. Julian wondered if the coroner would become the newest subscriber to the Reclamation Society. Perhaps the jury would all join as well.

"Was there any evidence of forcible entry into the refuge after the deceased was found dead?"

"No. There were no broken windows, and no locks had been tampered with."

"Have you any idea how the deceased might have obtained laudanum?"

"There, I blame myself." (Protests and shaking of heads among the jury and the spectators.) "Yes, I feel the fault is primarily mine. These young women are self-indulgent by nature, and skilled in evading the law. They are not permitted to leave the refuge during their rehabilitation, or to have contact with anyone from outside except under close supervision, but even so, Mary may have been clever enough to smuggle in the laudanum without our knowledge. I fear I have been too trusting with the inmates, believing that their desire to reform is sincere, and that they can therefore slough off the deceitful habits inculcated over many years. I can only assure you all that I will redouble my watchfulness over them, and do everything in my power to guard them against the treacherous promptings of their own natures."

Julian gazed at Harcourt almost in wonder. The man was grotesque but fascinating, like a figure at Mme. Tussaud's—which, with his white, waxen skin, he rather resembled. Julian felt sure he was a fraud; there was nothing behind his rhetoric but vanity and ambition. Yet there was no denying he was eloquent. And once again he had completely diverted attention from the facts. Instead of thinking about how Mary had gotten the laudanum, the coroner and jury were caught up in his personal dismay and regret, and his resolve to surmount this misfortune and persevere in his cause.

Julian knew the time had come for him and Sally to produce the letter. He also knew he had no intention of doing so, if he could think of any justification for keeping it back. He did not believe anyone here would give it serious attention. Harcourt would dismiss it as further proof of poor Mary's stubborn pride—for why should she be so secretive, if she were truly humbled and repentant? The coroner and jury would sigh sympathetically, and that would be the end of the matter. Julian looked around the room, but there did not seem to be one person immune from Harcourt's spell, who could take a cold, unsentimental look at the facts.

All at once his eyes fell on Samuel Digby. He was leaning back with his gouty foot propped on a chair, his arms folded, and an expression of cynical amusement on his face. Thank God, thought Julian, I'm not mad, I'm not alone—here's someone else who sees Harcourt for what he is.

And Digby was a magistrate, Julian recalled. He might have a duty to come forward with the letter, but surely he could choose which of the authorities he would approach. He had a good idea now who his choice would be.

The Waters Stirred Up Again

What he needed above all, Julian thought, was to talk this whole business over with Dr. MacGregor. That evening, he called on MacGregor at Dr. Greeley's and gave him an account of Mary's death and the inquest. Dr. Greeley was settled for the night, leaving MacGregor free to talk with Julian in the snug, dark-panelled library.

"The verdict was a foregone conclusion," Julian finished. "The coroner summed up briefly to the jury, making it clear what he thought had happened. An almost empty laudanum bottle was found by Mary's bed, next to the glass that had contained her dose of cordial. Traces of cordial, laudanum, and water were found in the glass, *ergo*, she must have poured the laudanum from the bottle into the glass, diluted it with water from her water jug, and drunk it. The doctor's evidence ruled out accidental death, but it didn't necessarily follow that Mary was rational enough to be held accountable for her act. The jury understood what was expected of them and obligingly brought in a verdict of suicide while the balance of her mind was disturbed. So the enquiry is over, Mary can be buried in sanctified ground, and Harcourt left the inquest with a few more strands of gold added to his halo."

MacGregor shook his head sadly. "Poor little soul. This city's got a good deal to answer for—taking a nice, respectable girl and turning her into the most abandoned thing in nature. You can't wonder she couldn't live with the idea of what she'd been once, and what she'd sunk to now. But it's a terrible thing she did, to put herself beyond hope or help that way. I won't believe there's a human soul that can't be saved, if you can just bring to bear the right influence at the right time. Those Reclamation Society people were too harsh with her, that's all. No point in beating a broken reed. Of course she was a sinner, but I wouldn't punish a soul as frail and tender as hers, any more than I'd bleed and purge a body that's weak with disease—though I know there's many a medical man who'd disagree with me about that! Oh, well, it's a pity you didn't reach her in time. Something might have been done to help her."

"Yes, it *is* a pity," said Julian quietly.

MacGregor looked at him very hard, then exclaimed, "I see why you're in such a fret about this! You young lunatic, you think it's your fault she's dead!"

"I don't think it's my fault, exactly. I didn't pour the laudanum down her throat. But still—I can't forget that Sally wanted to go to the refuge yesterday, and I told her there was no hurry. A day can't make any difference, I said—"

"For God's sake, man, you couldn't have known! You had every right to assume that, of all places the girl could be, a refuge run by a clergyman would be the safest. And who would have thought she'd put hands on herself just now? She'd only just written that letter—it was dated this past Saturday evening, wasn't it? So she couldn't have sent it more than three days ago. You'd think she'd have waited long enough to give whomever she wrote to a fair chance to come and find her—"

He broke off. Julian was leaning toward him, his greenish eyes strangely alight. "So that's struck you, too?"

"What are you getting at? Dash it, man, what's this all about?"

"You're exactly right: why should she kill herself when she'd only just sent her letter? It may have miscarried somehow—it's hard to believe she intended it for any of those three men. But she must have thought she'd posted it successfully: Florrie Ames told Sally she'd been in better spirits the past few days. This was no time to kill herself. If weeks had gone by, and there'd been no response, she might have given up hope and determined to die. But this was too soon."

"Perhaps she did get an answer, in some way we don't know about. Whomever she wrote to may have got a message to her last night, saying he wanted nothing more to do with her."

"He would have had to be remarkably intrepid, to smuggle a message to her at the refuge. The place seems little better than a prison. But here's another question: why didn't she leave a note?"

"Not all suicides do."

"No. But not all suicides are as articulate as this one was. After writing an eloquent letter like this"—he took it out of his pocket and held it up—"can you conceive she would take her own life without leaving a note of explanation or regret—some expression of her feelings?"

"It's happening again—the same confounded thing as that business at Bellegarde! Here's a perfectly cut-and-dried affair—a straightforward suicide—and you stir up a hornets' nest of complications!"

"Wasn't that how we solved the Bellegarde murder?" Julian asked mildly.

"But that was obviously a murder!"

"This is, at the very least, a highly unconvincing suicide. How did Mary get the laudanum? Harcourt and Mrs. Fiske both said, with magnificent vagueness, that the inmates are so corrupt and clever, they could have found some means or other of spiriting laudanum into the refuge. But it appears the matrons watch them like hawks, searching their rooms and looking in on them at all hours of the night. It's all very well to say that since Mary had the laudanum, she must have had some means of obtaining it. One could equally say that if she had no means, she must *not* have obtained it."

"What are you saying? Somebody sneaked into Mary's room last night and forced her to drink the stuff?"

"Well, she did have a room to herself. Florrie told Sally she was the only one of the inmates who slept alone."

"Heavens above, man, think about what you're saying!" MacGregor paced back and forth, waving his hands. "Anybody meaning to kill Mary that way would have had to pour out a whacking great dose of laudanum, mix it with water or spirits—you can't drink laudanum neat—and then force her to drink it down. It seems like a pretty clumsy and dangerous way to commit a murder."

"People do commit murder by opium poisoning."

"Once in a month of Sundays, yes. But they do it by adding opium to the victim's food or drink by stealth. In this case, an empty laudanum bottle was left by Mary's bed. That's a funny thing for a poisoner to do."

"It's a very natural thing, if the poisoner wants the death to look like a suicide."

'But wouldn't it be much simpler if Mary drank the laudanum herself?"

"No, Doctor, it would be much more complicated. For one thing, what happened to the cordial?"

"What are you talking about?"

"The dose of cordial Mrs. Fiske gave her before she went to bed."

"She drank it, I suppose, then used the empty glass to take the laudanum, just as the coroner said."

"But, my dear fellow, think how preposterous that is! Why would anyone take a strengthening cordial just before committing suicide?"

"Well—she probably wasn't thinking clearly. When a despairing young girl sets out to end her life, you can't expect her to go about it rationally."

"Nobody who saw her that evening thinks she looked despairing or irrational. Even Mrs. Fiske said she seemed more or less as usual. Anyway, this isn't a question of rationality—it's intuition." He pressed a hand to his heart "You don't tale a medicine to fortify your body just before taking a poison to destroy it. Nobody would do such a thing. No, the natural thing would have been for her to pour out the cordial into the washbasin by her bed. But that was found clean and dry. And apparently the cordial wasn't poured out anywhere else. I've seen Summerson's Strengthening Elixir—it's a gruesome-looking, purplish-brown syrup. It would have left a devil of a stain."

"Why should she have had to take them one right after the other? Maybe she drank the cordial at bedtime, then later felt despondent and turned to the laudanum."

Julian shook his head. "That cock won't fight. The doctor testified that she'd been dead for at least six hours when he examined her at ten in the morning. That means four in the morning is the latest she could have died, and she might well have died much earlier. Laudanum poisoning wouldn't have killed her immediately, would it?"

"No, it would probably have taken several hours."

"Well, there you are. If she took an overdose of laudanum, it must have been at or very shortly after ten in the evening, when she went to bed."

"I don't know how you do it!" MacGregor started pacing again. "There's nothing under the sun so straightforward that you can't tease enigmas out of it. If you found a chimney-sweep up a chimney, you'd think of a dozen ingenious theories about what he was doing there. All right: if Mary didn't commit suicide, how did she die? A very reputable physician testified that her death was caused by opium poisoning. You can't think he was wrong about a thing like that?"

"I'm not expert enough to say. But let's suppose he was right. Isn't opium sold in all sorts of forms, some of them much stronger than laudanum?"

"Yes. There's Kendal Black Drop, for instance—that's about four times stronger than the average laudanum preparation. And you can get opium pills and lozenges from apothecaries, grocers' shops—public houses, even."

Julian considered. "Mrs. Fiske says the inmates finished supper at half past eight last night, then had prayers and Bible readings until nearly ten. Suppose a fatal dose of opium had been put into Mary's food at supper: would she have shown the effects of it by the time she went to bed?"

"An hour and a half later? No doubt about it, yes."

"Then, assuming she was poisoned with opium—or some other drug with a like effect—the only other possibility is that it was put into that cordial she took to bed with her. It was Mrs. Fiske who gave her the cordial, and Mrs. Fiske didn't like her—hated her, even. That was clear from her testimony at the inquest."

"If Mrs. Fiske killed her, wouldn't she have taken care to hide the way she felt about her?"

"I don't think she was capable of hiding it. She tried to testify calmly and succinctly, but her bitterness and anger kept breaking out. She's a very angry woman. It's my impression she hates all the inmates."

"Then why is she working so hard for their salvation?"

"I don't believe she cares a damn about their salvation. She works with them, first, because she's infatuated with Harcourt, like the rest of that little coven he gathers around him. And second, she enjoys lording it over the inmates, crushing their spirit, flaunting her own respectability in front of them. There's no charity in her—only hatred and fanaticism and resentment. Hers is the kind of spirit that drove the Inquisition."

"None of that explains why she would go so far as to kill an inmate."

"No. But I think she had a peculiar hatred for Mary, perhaps because she was young and pretty and genteel. And, of course, Harcourt took a particular interest in her. He'd become quite obsessed with breaking through her silence, and finding out who she was."

"You're not suggesting there's anything between Harcourt and Mrs. Fiske?"

"What, in the way of a love affair? Good God, no. If you'd seen her, you wouldn't ask. But she could still have been jealous on his account. A woman doesn't have to possess a man to be possessive of him. If Mary's dose of cordial was poisoned, it was most likely Mrs. Fiske who poisoned it, since she gave it to her. But there's another possibility."

"I might have known there would be."

"I'll overlook that rather unencouraging response. Mrs. Fiske said Mary was the only person at the refuge taking the cordial. A really bold murderer might have poisoned the entire bottle, so that Mrs. Fiske poured out a fatal dose without knowing it."

"But the murderer couldn't have known for sure nobody else would take it."

"No. That's why he or she would have had to be exceptionally daring and cold-blooded. Now, Mr. Harcourt is both those things."

"Harcourt? Why would *he* have wanted Mary dead?"

Julian made a rueful face. "Frankly—I have no idea. He seems to have had every reason to want her alive. Florrie said he hoped to ingratiate himself with Mary's family by restoring her to them. He must also have thought it would add lustre to his name to rescue and reform a well-bred young woman. All the same, his handling of her death is devilish odd. Why did it take him three hours to bring in a doctor to examine her body? And why was he in such a rush to have the inquest over?"

"That's only to be expected. The death of an inmate under circumstances like that can't do his refuge any good."

"No, that's true. But why not air the matter thoroughly, and prove there was nothing amiss about her death? To shroud it in mystery only invites puzzlement and suspicion. Here's one more curious fact: Harcourt's home parish is in Norfolk. You know, opium use is rampant in the Fen Country there. Families grow poppies in their gardens, and make their own concoctions of the thing."

"And you think Harcourt's an amateur distiller? Even if he is, that doesn't explain why he'd want to kill Mary."

"No. I'm afraid I'm awash in theories, with very few facts to support them."

"Look here: are you going to fret yourself into a fever about this business, burn your fingers meddling in what's not your concern, and get yourself and everybody around you into a parcel of trouble?"

"Those were more or less my plans."

"Oh, well—I know better than to try and hold you back, once you've got the bit between your teeth. I just have one thing to say to you: if you want to get to the bottom of what happened to Mary out of curiosity, or a regard for truth, or a sense of justice—well and good. But don't do it out of guilt. Whatever happened to her, you're not to blame. You did as much as could have been expected of you, and a dashed sight more than most people would have done."

"But if I hadn't been so concerned to respect her privacy—if I'd come right out and shown her letter to Mrs. Fiske yesterday, instead of trying to be clever and communicate with her through Sally—"

"Then you might have made things worse instead of better. There's no second-guessing what's past, or knowing what might have made a difference. It's arrogant, it's a waste of time, and there's an end of it."

Julian smiled and said quietly, "My dear fellow, thank you for that lecture. You've proved that not all strengthening elixirs come out of bottles."

"Hmph—well—what are you going to do now?"

"I'm going to call on Samuel Digby. He's a magistrate, he seems interested in this affair, and his attitude toward Harcourt is something less than reverent. If he seems disposed to be fair and openminded, I'll show him Mary's letter and ask him how he thinks I ought to proceed."

He rose to depart. Then he paused and glanced around at the bookshelves lining the walls. "Do you have a Bible ready to hand?"

"A Bible?"

"Yes. I just remembered one more thing I wanted to tell you."

MacGregor found a Bible and handed it to him. Julian leafed through it. "Do you remember, Mary said in her letter that if the person she wrote to never answered, she would be forgotten as one dead, like the broken vessel in the Psalm? I've found that Psalm—it's Number 31. Listen:

> *I was a reproach among all mine enemies, but especially among my neighbours, and a fear to mine acquaintance: they that did see me without fled from me.*
>
> *I am forgotten as a dead man out of mind: I am like a broken vessel.*
>
> *For I have heard the slander of many: fear was on every side: while they took counsel against me, they devised to take away my life."*

MacGregor stared. "But—but that doesn't prove anything."

"No. But it sent a chill through my blood all the same."

Mr. Digby's Investment

Samuel Digby lived in a stately red-brick house on Highgate Hill. There was a big brass knocker on the front door: the head of a smiling, satisfied lion. Julian knocked, and gave his card to a stooped old retainer. The man withdrew, then returned and said Mr. Digby would see him.

He led Julian to a cosy back parlour, with a cherry-coloured carpet and fine old mahogany furnishings. Digby sat in an easy chair by the fire, his gouty foot propped on an ottoman, and a table piled with books, newspapers, and medicines close by. Across from him sat a rosy old lady, with a work-table at her elbow, and her hands clasped expectantly in her lap.

"My dear," said Digby, eyes twinkling, "this is Mr. Julian Kestrel, the famous man of fashion. Mr. Kestrel, it's an honour to have you under our roof. I hear you have only to visit a house once, to make it the pink of fashion. I'll be much disappointed if dukes and duchesses don't throng our gates after this. You'll forgive my not rising."

"Of course." Julian turned to the lady and bowed over her hand. "How do you do, Mrs. Digby?"

"It's lovely to meet you, Mr. Kestrel. Heavens, you look so like that engraving we saw in the stationer's shop—oh, dear, perhaps that wasn't a tactful thing to say."

"You mean Mr. Cruikshank's caricature?" Julian smiled. "It's very good, isn't it? I had it framed."

"It doesn't half do you justice." Her voice was warm with relief at not having given offence.

"Thank you, Mrs. Digby. You're very kind." He turned to Digby and shook hands. "How do you do, sir?"

"How d'ye do? It's a pleasure. I've been wanting to meet you for some months."

"I'm flattered," said Julian. But he was more surprised.

Digby nodded. "I've taken an interest in you ever since I heard how you solved the Bellegarde murder. A very pretty piece of unriddling, that. When I saw you at the inquest yesterday, I thought: He's on the scent again. He thinks there's something wrong about this business, and knows I do, too. In short, Mr. Kestrel, I've been expecting you. Sit down."

"Thank you, sir," said Julian, more surprised than ever, and now much impressed.

"Take my chair," proposed Mrs. Digby. "No, please, I shan't stay. I never intrude on Sam when he's talking business."

She took her workbox and bustled off. Julian opened the door for her, then returned and sat down. Digby offered him some first-rate Madeira, which he accepted. "Now then," the old man said, "what is there about that fine and upright man, Mr. Harcourt, to set your teeth on edge?"

"Perhaps it's the same thing that brought you to town for the inquest—ordeal though that must have been." He glanced at Digby's bandaged foot.

"Perhaps. But we're not talking about me just yet. Be plain with me, and I'll return the favour. What is it about this young woman's death that's troubling you?"

Julian told him. He did not mention Mary's letter yet, but he explained his other grounds for suspicion: the lack of a suicide note, the mystery of where Mary had gotten the laudanum, her inexplicable drinking of the cordial just before her apparent suicide, and Harcourt's efforts to hush up her death. He pointed out that she had been the only inmate who had a room to herself, that Harcourt had been strangely obsessed with her, and that Mrs. Fiske could barely conceal her rancour toward her even now.

Digby listened attentively, asking a trenchant question now and then. "Well," he said at last, "you've posed some ticklish questions. But there's not one shred of proof that any crime's been committed. Without that, what do you expect me or anyone else to do for you?"

"An enquiry has to begin somewhere."

"This one is going to end where it began, if you can't show me any better proof than this. I don't mean to be harsh with you, young man, but you know as well as I do how justice in this country works. Without some direct evidence of foul play, the authorities aren't going to interest themselves in this affair. Bow Street won't act because there's no money in it, and higher officials know there's nothing but trouble to be gained by meddling with Harcourt. The man has powerful patrons: evangelical clergymen, lawyers, merchants like myself. Or rather, he has their wives' support, which comes to the same thing. He's a great one for making up to the women, is Harcourt. Nothing improper, you understand—just flattery and wheedling and silver-tongued speeches. Why do you think he's gone into the business of reforming prostitutes? It gets the women behind him. There isn't a respectable female in London who doesn't loathe those creatures who come between her and her husband or sweetheart. Though Harcourt's cause has broader appeal—we've all got a sneaking interest in that particular vice, whether we admit it or not. Lately, he's even made inroads into the Quality. He's got some titled patrons—Lord Carbury, for one."

"Lord Carbury?" said Julian quickly.

"Seems unlikely, doesn't it?—Carbury being such a wild fellow when he was young. But Harcourt makes some surprising converts. He approached me, you know. I do a little in the charity way."

"Rather more than a little, I've heard."

"That's as may be. The fact is, I didn't like him, and nor did Mrs. Digby. To be more precise, I didn't trust him. I thought he was driven by ambition—you could smell it on him, like a whiff of brimstone round the devil. I said to Mrs. Digby, there's a man who'd stick at nothing to advance his own interest. I expect he's in high feather about bringing Carbury up to scratch. He's a great tuft-hunter, is Harcourt, for all his seeming other-worldliness."

"No doubt you're right. But to me, the most remarkable thing about Lord Carbury's being Harcourt's patron is that he's Charles Avondale's father."

"Charles Avondale? What's he got to do with this?"

"I think it's time I told you how I got interested in the Reclamation Society, and Mary's death."

He recounted how Sally had stolen the letter, and how they had traced it back to Mary. He pointed out the strangeness of Mary's committing suicide so soon after writing it, without even waiting for an answer. Finally, he handed the letter to Digby, who read it, then sat back, shaking his head.

"You've certainly saved your best card for last. This is very disturbing—very. But I don't think, frankly, it would move Bow Street to take any action. In fact, if Charles Avondale is mixed up in this business, it's all the more likely to be hushed up. I'm not without influence in government myself, but even I know better than to take on the Carbury interest."

"What if I could find concrete proof that Mary didn't commit suicide—that she was murdered?"

"Well, that would put a different complexion on things. There is some justice in this land. Even Harcourt and his patrons couldn't choke off an enquiry, if there were a sound basis for thinking somebody'd killed the girl. I for one wouldn't let the matter rest till justice was done. But how are you proposing to get this proof you talk about? Harcourt won't cooperate with you. As much as he wanted to find out about Mary while she was alive, he'll be equally anxious to squelch any enquiries about her now she's dead. God forbid anybody should identify her now, and bring her relatives down on him, holding him responsible for her death!"

"We had a devil of a time identifying the victim of the Bellegarde murder, and finding out who killed her, but we did in the end."

"*You* did, you mean. And you think you can do it again?"

"I should like to try."

"And I should like to help you. I'll tell you what: how will it be if I pay the expenses of your investigation?"

"I couldn't possibly—"

"Now, don't turn squeamish. I have more money than I know what to do with, and laid up as I am, there's nothing else I can do to help clear up this mystery. You, on the other hand, if you're like most young bucks, probably have a dashed sight more time than money. So let me have my way. Think of it as an investment in law and order."

"When you put it that way, sir, I can't refuse. Thank you." Julian had to admit that the money would come in handy. He was never very flush, and sometimes walked a thin line between merely being in debt and being in Queer Street.

He asked, "Would you be willing to keep Mary's letter and this enquiry confidential for now? If the coroner's jury was right, and I have windmills in my head, it won't have served any purpose to kick up a dust. And if I'm right, and there's been a crime committed, I should rather not put Harcourt or anyone else on his guard. My best weapon is that no one knows I have Mary's letter. The man it came from may have guessed Sally stole it, but he doesn't know if she kept it, or read it, or cares a twopenny damn about it. He surely won't be expecting anyone to track him down on account of it—which is what I intend to do."

"The fact that he had the letter doesn't mean he had anything to do with Mary's death."

"No. But I feel sure he's important. At the very least, if he's the person she wrote to, he should be able tell us who she was. Those three men interest me immensely, Mr. Digby. I've put a name to one of them. Before I'm finished, I mean to identify the others."

"Why not just ask Charles Avondale point-blank if he knows anything about the letter?"

"Suppose he says he doesn't? Since we don't know for a fact that the letter came from him, and we don't know who the other two men are, how can we know if he's telling the truth? I can't but be suspicious of him, especially since you told me about his father's connexion with Harcourt. Still, Harcourt has so many patrons, that could be merely a coincidence. I know Avondale slightly, and he and I have mutual friends. I should rather begin by making discreet enquiries about him, and meanwhile have a try at tracing the other two men. Confronting Avondale directly is a card I can always play. But once I've alerted him to my suspicions, I'll never again have the chance to catch him off his guard, as I can now."

"Well, I'll keep my own counsel about what you're doing for the time being. Lord knows, you'll need every advantage you can get. You seem to have precious little information about those other two men."

"Practically none," said Julian, smiling. "Interesting problem, isn't it?"

Julian came home to find Sally in a fit of temper. Mrs. Mabbitt had hauled her off to the second-hand clothes market in Monmouth Street and made her buy herself some clothes that were fit for decent company. Now she was wearing a plain, dark green merino gown, with a white collar and cuffs. A demure poke bonnet, trimmed with one green bow, projected its broad brim around her face, half-shielding it coyly from view.

"Just look at me!" she stormed. "Nobody at the Cockerel'd even speak to me if they seen me now. They'd take me for an old trout of a parson's wife!"

"I don't think there's much danger of that," said Julian.

"This is a fine rig-out for a game gal! What'll I do with it when I goes back on the grind? Wear it to prayer meetings?"

Dipper, who was just taking Julian's hat, gloves, and stick, shot her a troubled glance. The devil, Julian thought—we still haven't solved the problem of what to do with her. She seems to think she'll simply go back to her old life after her visit here. And I'm damned if I know what to offer her instead, or how to stop her.

He told them about his visit to Digby, and his resolve to get to the bottom of what had happened to Mary. They were eager to help. The first step, said Julian, was for Sally to tell him and Dipper everything she could recall about the three men from whom she might have stolen the letter.

The weather had turned raw and rainy. Dipper mixed some hot punch, and they gathered around the parlour fire like conspirators. Sally racked her brains to remember all she could about Bristles, Blue Eyes, and Blinkers. For the first time, she described in detail what Blinkers had done to her, and she hardly knew if Dip or Mr. Kestrel was angrier. She felt a glow of pleasure, knowing she had two men ready to spring to her defence. She hoped they really would find Blinkers—they would twist him into inches, she felt sure.

When she had finished, Julian sat back, considering. Dipper and Sally gazed at him, like an audience waiting for a conjuring trick.

"Avondale is the least of our worries," he said at length. "I can gather information about him easily enough. Bristles is another matter. What do we know about him? He's middle-aged, timid, and respectable, he's unaccustomed to the sort of entertainment you offered him, he seemed blue-deviled, and he admitted he kept a shop. Have you any idea what kind of shop it was?"

Sally propped her chin on her fists. "I'll take me oath he didn't work with his hands, like a blacksmith or a carpenter. He didn't smell of scent, nor 'bacca, nor grub. He didn't have ink on his forks, like Blinkers." She shook her head. "It's no good. I can tell you what he wasn't, but not what he was."

"Well it's a beginning. It may be an ending, too, for the present. I'm dashed if I know how to get any closer to him."

There was a pause. They surveyed the three handkerchiefs lying in a row on a table, Avondale's blazoned with his initials, the other two maddeningly nondescript.

"Sally met Blinkers at the Cockerel, sir," said Dipper. "If it's a crib he goes to reg'lar, they might know about him there."

"That's a good thought. I'll leave that to you—the people at the Cockerel will talk to you much more readily. What else do we know about Blinkers—other than the fact that he's an infernal scoundrel? He's young and thin, wears spectacles, dresses like a clerk, and has ink on his fingers. And we know one thing more: he has a broken umbrella." He turned to Sally. "How badly damaged would you say it was? I do realize you weren't in any condition to notice."

"Let me have a think. I nobbed him with it once, then he got it away from me. The oil-cloth tore, and a couple of the ribs broke, too, I heard 'em."

"Was it a good umbrella, do you think? Would it have been worth repairing?"

"I s'pose so. It was one of them big stout ones, as coves carries more to keep off thieves than the rain. It had a fine handle, too-carved like a ram's head."

"What would you wager he took it somewhere to be repaired? If we're really lucky, he asked to have it delivered, and the umbrella mender might be able to tell us the address."

"But there's heaps of umbrella menders in London," Sally objected.

"Well, we're not in a hurry." Julian got up and walked about purposefully. "We'll have an advertisement printed up, offering a reward for information leading to the recovery of a black umbrella, of such-and-such a size, with a ram's head handle, damaged in such-and-such a manner this past Monday night. Replies to be sent to the post office, to be left till called for. The reward to be say—ten pounds."

"Ten pounds?" exclaimed Sally. "They'll think you're off your head!"

"Or inordinately fond of umbrellas. Never mind—it will ensure we're taken seriously. We'll send the advertisement to as many makers and menders of umbrellas as we can think of. I expect Stultz or one of my other tailors could help us put together a list. God knows if it will be any use. To begin with, Blinkers may not live in London. For all we know, he got on a coach to Yorkshire directly he left you at the Cockerel. In fact, it might not be amiss to enquire after him at the major coaching inns—and Bristles, too, while we're about it. If either of them had anything to do with Mary's death, he may have found it prudent to put a distance between himself and London."

"Of course," he added, "even if we find the right umbrella mender, he may not remember this particular umbrella. After all, it's been four days—time enough for it to have been mended and returned to the owner. Still, we've nothing to lose but time, and a little of Mr. Digby's money. It's worth a try. I'll draw up the advertisement tonight, and you can take it to the printer's first thing in the morning."

"Yes, sir," said Dipper.

Julian considered. "The other way to attack this problem is to find out more about Harcourt and the Reclamation Society. I can do that by talking to his patrons, and perhaps to some of those adoring women who follow him about. Though I'll lay you odds, if anyone knows what really happened to Mary, it's the inmates at the refuge. And no one can get at them, shut up as they are."

"*I* can," said Sally.

Julian and Dipper looked at her in surprise.

"Don'cha see? I can go to the refuge, like I wants to be reformed. They knows me—I been there once already. If they takes me on, I can twig every nook and cranny in the place. And I can play up to the other gals and find out what they knows. When I seen enough, I'll broom it back."

"It's out of the question," said Julian, "much too dangerous. What if someone at the refuge really did have a hand in Mary's death? If you seem too curious, you may be the next victim. And suppose the man from whom you stole the letter finds out you're at the refuge? If he has an interest in Mary, he may be keeping an eye on it. As matters stand, he has no idea who or where you are, so if he's worried about your having the letter, there's not a mortal thing he can do. By going to the refuge, you may be playing into his hands."

"I ain't afeard of him."

"You ought to be. At best, he's mixed up in something hole-and-corner, and at worst, he's a murderer. Don't you see, once you're inside the refuge, Dipper and I can't do anything to protect you."

"I don't need protection!" she declared, forgetting how sweet the idea had seemed a little while ago. "I can go to the refuge if I likes—you can't stop me. I've as much right to be reformed as any other gal."

"She's made up her mind, sir," said Dipper resignedly "It won't do no good to tug on the reins."

"Won't it?" said Julian. "I can warn Harcourt against you, Sally. And I will, if you cross me in this."

"Then he'll be fly to your game," she retorted. "You wouldn't want that."

"I could tell him you were a lunatic escaped from some hospital. Or I could say you were an egregious thief—I even have proof of that." He held up the handkerchiefs.

"But—but they'd put me in quod!"

"A prison might well be safer for you than the refuge."

"Why, you bloody—"

"Stash your patter, Sal," said Dipper.

"I won't! He may be your master, but he ain't mine! He's got no right to tell me what to do! I can look after meself!"

"It isn't a question of rights," said Julian. "If I'd interfered sooner to get Mary out of the refuge, I might have saved her. Do you suppose I'm going to let you put yourself in the same danger, knowing what I know now?"

"Well—what if I was to find a way to let you know I was all right?"

"How can you do that? You can't write."

"I can, a little. It ain't my fault I never went to school."

"I didn't mean that," he explained, more gently. "I meant that it's too dangerous. Mary died the night after you stole her letter, and just three nights after it was written. It may be that she had an enemy who was looking for her, and the letter told him where she was. Whether her enemy was the person she wrote to, or the letter fell into someone else's hands, is anyone's guess. But either way, smuggling letters out of the refuge would be far too risky."

"I could make a sign. Wave a handkerchief out a window, maybe, every day at noon. And if one day I didn't, you'd know I was in a pickle, and you could come in and get me. Come on, wha'd'ye say? You wants to find out what the gals in the refuge knows about Mary, don'cha?"

"Yes."

"Well, nobody can find out for you but me. If you don't let me help you, I'll pike off. I ain't going to cool me heels, while you and Dip has all the larks to yourself."

That gave Julian pause. He had been wondering how he and Dipper were to keep Sally off the streets. Now she had offered a solution to that problem, at least temporarily And who knew whether a chance to do something brave and useful might not lead to other opportunities for her? Her ordinary life was at least as dangerous as a sojourn at the refuge—her encounter with Blinkers proved that. And the future she faced was bleak. Everyone knew how girls like Sally ended—assuming disease or childbirth or abuse did not cut them off sooner. Picking up men at night in parks and under bridges, where their ravaged looks would not show, performing the vilest acts for a few coppers—

He looked into her vibrant, upturned face, and came to a decision. "Very well. I'll send Dipper to look for your signal at noon every day. He'll wait a quarter of an hour. If he doesn't see your handkerchief at one of the front windows by then, we'll come in and get you."

"I dunno why you don't just wrap me up in cotton-wool and shut me in a bandbox," she complained.

Julian smiled wryly and shook his head. "Don't think I'm not tempted, Sally."

Scruples

That night, Julian wrote out the advertisement for information about Blinkers's umbrella. Dipper took it to the printer's next morning. While he was out, Julian instructed Sally about what to investigate at the refuge.

"Me head's swimming!" she declared when he was finished. "How do you expect me to remember all that?"

"Because I know how clever you are."

"Now, that's the first pretty speech you ever made to me, and it's only 'coz you wants me to smoke out information at the refuge." She hunched her shoulders, glowering. "I've a good mind not to go at all."

"I hope you won't. I never wanted you to."

"Well, I'm going, and that's flat!"

He shook his head. Such perversity was beyond him. "What have you told Queen Mab?"

"I told the truth, partly. I said I was going into a refuge to try if I could get reformed. And maybe I will. I don't think so, though."

"I don't think Mr. Harcourt's methods would reform anyone with a grain of sense or independence. But Sally, you know, I'd do everything I could to help you, if you wanted to—well, to begin a new life."

"I'm proper grateful to you, I'm sure." She curtsied mockingly.

"I didn't mean to offend you. I only thought, if I could be of use—"

"Well, you can't!" Her face closed up. "I don't want to talk to you no more. I'll be waiting downstairs to say goodbye to Dip, if you'll please to tell him so when he gets home."

"Wait, Sally, I don't want us to part like this."

"Well, maybe you won't get everything you want. Then you'll know what it's like."

"Would you mind telling me what we're quarrelling about? Just so that I can argue my side properly."

"Oh, we've nothing to quarrel about—not us! Just 'coz I been telling you every way I knows how that I fancies you, and you been treating me like dirt under your feet, that ain't nothing for a gal to cut up rough about."

"That isn't fair. I think I've treated you tolerably well."

"I know." She sighed and dropped into a chair. "You been first-rate to me. Any other gentry-cove would've turned me out slap off, if he come home and found me here like you done. You can't help it if you don't fancy me. I thought you did once, but I was wrong. You has to have everything clean and fine and bang up to the mark—and me, I'm common, and I been on the grind or thieving since I was so high. What would the like of you want with the like of me?"

"Are you finished? May I speak now?"

His tone brought her up short. She stared. "You—you don't have to say nothing. I told you, I knows how you feel—"

"If you knew anything whatever about how I feel, you wouldn't talk such utter rubbish as you're talking now. Sally, if I've rebuffed you, it isn't because of anything to do with you or me. It's because of Dipper."

"Dipper?"

"Yes. Don't you see, he and I are more than master and man—we're in some sort friends. For me to make free with his sister would be to throw the difference between us in his face. He would have the right to resent it, but not the power. I won't take advantage of his position. That he's my servant doesn't give me leave to make concubines out of his relatives."

"But—but Dip wouldn't care if we knocked up a lark!"

"I can't be sure of that. So the safe course—the only honourable course—is to show his sister the same respect he would have to show mine, if I had one."

"You're off your head, is what you are."

"Then I'm hardly a loss worth lamenting."

She said slowly, "What you're saying is, you fancy me, but you can't do nothing about it?"

"That isn't precisely the point I was trying to make."

"But you do fancy me?" She came up close to him, searching his face.

"I don't see any point in talking about that. Can't we simply part friends?"

Her wide mouth curved into a smile. "If we're friends, then you won't mind kissing me goodbye, now, will you?"

"No, not in the least." He took her lightly by the shoulders and kissed her cheek.

"That ain't nothing."

"Thank you."

"I mean, it ain't a real kiss. This is a real kiss."

She came up on her toes. Her lips found his, softly teasing and questing. He put her from him, but not quickly enough—not before his lips, his hands, his pulse, had given her a better answer than his words.

There were footsteps in the passage. Julian turned abruptly and went away to the window. Sally gazed after him, dazed, triumphant, bereft.

Dipper came in. After one swift look around him, he fixed his eyes opaquely on the opposite wall. "The advertisement'll be ready by darkmans, sir."

"Good."

"Any place else you'd like me to go, sir?"

"No," said Julian quickly. "Unless you'd like to escort Sally to the refuge. You could stop at the Cockerel on your way back, and ask after Blinkers."

"Yes, sir. You ready to pike off now, Sal?"

She nodded, her eyes still fixed on Mr. Kestrel. "Goodbye, Lightning. Try not to miss me too much."

"I'll endeavour to struggle along in your absence."

She smiled sweetly. "Kiss me arse!"

Dipper shot her a quelling look and led her out. Julian stayed by the window. A few minutes later, he saw them come out at the street door, Dipper carrying a small, neat bundle of Sally's things. They walked off companionably in the direction of the nearest hackney coach stand. When they were out of sight, Julian leaned back against the window and drew a long breath. Could it be that, only a few short days ago, he had complained to MacGregor that he was *bored*?

"Your master's queer in his upper story."

"No, he ain't," Dipper said tranquilly.

"He is, then," she insisted. Fancy him holding her at arm's length on account of Dipper—Dipper, who would not care a bean if his master got up her petticoats! Would he?

She studied him, sitting across from her in the hackney coach. He was looking out through the side-glass at the people in the street, with the lively interest he always took in people and their doings. It was partly an animal watchfulness left over from former days—the need of a hunted thing to know where its enemies are. And, partly, he liked people—pretty much all people, except the real stinkers.

She bit her lip. The truth was that, even if he did not care if she had a brush with Mr. Kestrel, still, she would come between them and change their relationship forever. And she had no right to do that. Dip was happy. He was settled somewhere, with a home and a family of sorts—one that did not spend half its time either in the stone jug or playing least-in-sight with the Bow Street Runners. How could she queer that for him? Mr. Kestrel was right. He had been a better friend to Dip than she had been a sister.

They got out of the hackney at the corner of Stark Street. "You'd best not walk me there," she said. "Somebody might twig you, and ask questions."

"I'll be back at noon tomorrow, to watch for you to wave your handkerchief at the window. You sure you're plump currant now, Sal?"

"'Course I am. Just look at me. You can't hardly see the mouse no more." She pointed to her eye, where the bruise was fading fast.

"Goodbye, then." He handed over her little bundle of clothes. He did not tell her to be careful and not take any risks. He knew he would be wasting his time.

She tucked the bundle under one arm and clasped her other arm around his neck. "Goodbye, Tom."

He hugged her without speaking, No one had used his real Christian name in years.

"Will you tell Mr. Kestrel some'ut for me? Tell him I sees now what he meant to do, and I'm sorry I cut up rusty."

"I will," he said, without asking for explanations.

She winked at him and set off down Stark Street. He turned toward Tottenham Court Road. Neither of them looked back. They would see each other again—or, if they did not, they would face that when it came.

It was a fine, warm day for October. Real sunshine found its way through London's perpetual haze of coal smoke. Dipper decided to save his master a few bob, and himself another jouncing in a hackney. He set off on foot down Tottenham Court Road, glancing at the men he passed to guess where they kept their pocketbooks—old habits died hard—and looking under the bonnets of all the girls. He crossed Oxford Street, then threaded his way through short, narrow lanes to the Haymarket.

He found the Cockerel and went inside. The taproom was quiet at this time of day. A shabby old woman sat in a corner, nursing a quartern of gin and peppermint, and muttering to herself. A draggle-tailed whore was slumped over a table, an empty glass beside her. Three middle-aged men with rakish neckcloths, dirty gloves, and the remains of good looks were putting on a show of ease and joviality. Out-of-work actors, was Dipper's guess.

He went up to the bar. "Fine morning," he greeted the thickset man behind it.

"It'll do."

"You Toby?"

"Who wants to know?"

"Me name's Dipper. Sally Stokes is me sister."

Toby leaned his big, meaty hands on the bar, his eyes hard and measuring. "Well?"

"I come to have a confab with you about what happened to her last time she was here."

"That's ain't my look-out."

"I knows that. I ain't here to blow you up. What I wants is to find the cove as done her. You know, she was rumbled something mortal."

"Happens sometimes."

"It don't happen to Sal—not without I serves out the sod as done it. But I dunno nothing about him. I was hoping you could put down to me who he is."

Toby shook his head. "I remember the cove, but I don't know him. He was never in here before. A bit respectable for the like of this place."

"You can't tell me nothing else?"

"No." As Dipper still looked at him expectantly, he added, "I'll tell you what: I likes Sally all right, but I ain't getting mixed up in trouble—not for her nor anybody else."

Dipper shrugged, took out a crown piece, and spun it on the bar, whistling to himself.

Toby eyed the coin. At last his hand shot out and scooped it up. "Right. There's one thing I can tell you, for what it's worth, but if there's a dust kicked up, you has to keep me out of it."

"I will, s'elp me Bob."

"That night—Monday night, I think it was—Sally come in first with another cove. Pluckless sort, he looked. Respectable, not used to cribs like this, nor gals like Sally. I give 'em the second floor back. So then this cove you're looking for—young, thin, specs on his nose—comes up to the bar. He must've been watching Sally and her flat, 'coz he says, 'You give 'em a room?' I says, 'Maybe.' So he has a bit of a think, then he asks how much I'd charge to let him go up after 'em. Well, I've had peepers before—they don't do no harm, just listen a bit, have a look through the keyhole, and nobody the wiser, I has to make a living, don't I?"

"'Course you do," said Dipper encouragingly.

"I said it'd cost him a bob. So he pays it, and I tells him where they are, and he goes up. A while later he comes down, looking pleased as Punch. Then Sally comes down with her flat, and they morris off, and I thought your cove had gone, too, but he comes back to the bar and orders a pint, and sits down at a table. I wondered what he was staying for. Like I said, he seemed a cut above this place. Thought he might be wanting to peep at somebody else, but another gal come in and took a room, and your cove just stayed where he was.

"Then, maybe half an hour later, Sally come in again. Your cove stood her a drain of pale and took her upstairs. I had an idea he'd been waiting around for her, hoping she'd come back. Liked what he saw when he peeped at her, I expect. I didn't think nothing of it. I won't have him in again, though—not after what he done to her. His kind brings trouble—have the constables in, like as not."

"You see him again after he tracked up the dancers with Sal?"

"He come down afore she did, but I didn't take much notice. I expect he took himself off. I don't know where, and I ain't seen him since."

He folded his lips and began methodically stacking pint pots behind the bar. He had earned his crown piece, and as far as he was concerned, the conversation was over.

Dipper thanked him and went out. He walked back along the Haymarket, deep in thought. This was all very rum. Sally had said she heard a peeper outside the door when she was with Bristles, but Mr. Kestrel and he had not attached much importance to that. They had had no idea who the peeper was, and no reason to think he had anything to do with the Mary mystery.

Now they knew the peeper was Blinkers, and he had apparently been interested enough in Sally to lie in wait for her at the Cockerel till she returned from her bout with Avondale. But what could they make of that? Only that he had taken a fancy to her, and singled her out for his cursed sport. Who knew what drew a man of his kind to a particular victim? And yet—

Dipper shook his head. He had a feeling it meant something—Blinkers's peeping at Sally like that. If only he knew what that something was!

Sally Turns Ferret

Mr. Harcourt interviewed Sally in the bare back parlour of the refuge. With him was Miss Nettleton, the matron on duty today. She was a thin, faded woman, about forty years old, with mouse-brown hair crimped into corkscrews. Sally recognized her from the inquest: she was the matron Mrs. Fiske had sneered at for having hysterics on learning of Mary's death.

Mr. Harcourt asked Sally her age, and whether she had any family. She said she was eighteen, and alone in the world. (It seemed best to keep Dipper out of this.) Mr. Harcourt then questioned her closely about how she fell from grace. She was hard put to answer. She could not remember a moment when she *fell.* She had been born about as low as a girl could get, and simply went on from there. But she knew he would not be satisfied with that. He made clear that, to show she was really repentant, she must make a full confession of her sins. Well, if that was what he wanted, it was easy enough. She spun a long, lurid tale of her transgressions, some real and some invented. Miss Nettleton blushed and shifted about in her chair, but Harcourt listened avidly. Sally felt just as if she were entertaining one of her flats, except that this man wanted nothing but talk. And of course he did not pay her anything—though he ought to have, she told herself, after all the enjoyment she gave him.

When she could think of nothing more to confess, it was Harcourt's turn to talk. He lectured her for a long time about how wicked she had been, and how extraordinarily lucky she was that a lady like Miss Nettleton would condescend to be in the same room with her. That's how he makes slaves of the Mrs. Fiskes and Miss Nettletons, Sally thought: feeds 'em soft sawder, and gives 'em gals like me they can lord it over.

If she wished to stay at the refuge, Harcourt said, she must obey its rules to the letter, be diligent, humble and pious, and show becoming gratitude to those who reached down to lift her out of the pit. If she failed in any of these duties, she would be turned out. But if she worked and prayed, and proved that evil was truly rooted out of her heart, then she would leave the refuge with his blessing, and honest work would be found for her as a servant, seamstress, or the like.

"Do you understand me, Sarah?" His pale, cold blue eyes fixed on her intently.

"Yes, sir."

"Very good. I trust you'll soon learn our routine. If you have questions, ask Margaret Muldoon. She's been here longer than any other inmate. In fact, she has finished her formal rehabilitation, but she wished to stay on and help her erring sisters."

Wideawake Peg—now there was someone Sally would like to know more about. It was no mean feat to put the fun upon Harcourt. Whatever else you could say about him, he was not a fool.

"The matron in charge will assign you particular duties each day, and each week," he went on. "We have no servants here. The inmates are trained to take care of the cleaning, cooking, laundry, and other chores. It fosters habits of industry, and fits you for domestic service, which is the sphere that many of you will enter when you leave us." He rose. "Miss Nettleton, I must go. May I entrust Sarah to your care?"

"Oh, yes, Mr. Harcourt."

"Thank you. I know I could not set her a better example of piety and devotion to duty. Goodbye, Sarah, I hope our efforts on your behalf will not be thrown away."

He took his leave. Miss Nettleton fluttered about, showing Sally to her room and finding her everything she needed to begin her life at the refuge. She gave her a uniform, a Bible, a prayer book, a towel, and two small tallow candles. She must use the candles sparingly, Miss Nettleton warned—they were her week's supply, and if they ran out, she would not get any more.

Miss Nettleton then opened Sally's bundle, without so much as a by-your-leave, and spread out its contents on her bed. "I must see what you've brought," she explained. "It wouldn't do to let you keep anything unsuitable."

"Do you look at all the gals' things when they comes here, ma'am?"

"Mercy, yes. Not only when they arrive, but from time to time while they're here, to make certain they haven't got hold of something they shouldn't. So I just can't think how—oh, dear, I mustn't think of that. It gives me such a turn."

"Think of what, ma'am?" asked Sally innocently.

"It doesn't do to talk of it. Least said, soonest mended. Indeed, yes. Oh, dear." She looked at an old-fashioned watch pinned to her gown. "It's nearly two o'clock. We dine at two, so I'd best leave you to change your clothes and put your things away. There's water to wash with in the jug there. You'll hear a bell five minutes before dinner. One of the girls will show you where the refectory is. Don't be late, mind, or you won't be allowed in, and you'll have to go hungry till supper."

After she had gone, Sally shook her head glumly. Cold Bath Fields Prison's a palace next to this, she thought. She set about folding up her things, which Miss Nettleton had left spilled on her bed. She was glad she had brought few clothes, and none of the gaudy bonnets she loved. She could not have worn them here, and she would not have put it past wax-faced Harcourt and his matrons to take them away.

She took stock of her room. There were four beds, all with plain deal frames, coarse sheets, and woolen blankets. Beside each bed was a small night-table with a cupboard. The only other furnishings were a washstand and a few spindly chairs. There was a raw, almost painful cleanliness and order about the place.

She put her belongings away in the cupboard by her bed, then changed into her uniform: a gown of rough grey wool, a starched white apron, and a white cap. She shivered as she took off her clothes, for there was no fire, and the room was clammy and cold. When she was all hooked-and-eyed, and her hair tucked primly under her cap, she went to the window.

Her room was on the first floor of what was known as the "inmates' house": the house on the left-hand side of the refuge, where all the inmates slept. The window looked out on the back garden, which was surrounded by a high, brick, iron-spiked wall. There were no gravel walks or flower-beds here, as there were behind the right-hand house. A rough-cut path led to a small, squat, yellow-brick structure in the far left corner. No doubt Harcourt thought indoor water-closets too good for the inmates.

Like all the windows of the inmates' house, this one was covered with a thick iron grating. Sally tugged at it experimentally. It was too finely fixed to be removed without leaving tell-tale damage. And the fretwork was too dense to pass a bottle of laudanum inside.

"Here you are!" said a voice.

Sally turned and recognized Florrie Ames. "Hullo!" she exclaimed, delighted to see anyone who seemed at all like a friend. "How'd you know I was here?"

"I saw Miss Nettleton bringing you up here, and thought I'd come on after her, to welcome you and all. I must say, I did wonder if you'd come back, after what happened to Mary."

"That ain't no bread and butter of mine," said Sally carelessly. "There's still a lot of palaver about it, I s'pose?"

"There was at first. But now things is settling down."

"This your room, too?"

"No. I'm in the second floor front—and I do hate stairs so! But there you are, this ain't no place to go if you wants to live easy."

"What did you come here for?" asked Sally curiously.

"What makes a gal go anywhere?" Florrie laughed. "Either she wants to get *to* a man or *away* from one. I was getting away."

"Was he your fancy-man?"

"Not him! Men!—if you don't let 'em poke you, they're nothing but trouble, and if you do let 'em, they're worse!"

"Did he rumble you?" Sally asked, thinking of Blinkers.

"Oh, men can be trouble enough without that! Don't tease me about him no more—I'm sick of the very thought of him. Oh! there's the bell. That's dinner."

She led Sally downstairs to the ground floor. "The dining room's in the other house—the 'office house,' we calls it, 'coz Mr. Harcourt has his office there. The chapel's there, too, and the kitchens, and the room where the matron on duty sleeps. There's nothing in this house but our bedrooms, and the laundry in the basement. See that door there? It's the only way to get back and forth 'twixt the two houses. At night they locks it, so we're penned up here. If you has to visit Sir Harry, you goes out the back door to the boghouse in the garden."

She stopped suddenly, putting a finger to her lips. "Come here," she whispered, "and I'll show you something afore we go to dinner."

She opened a narrow door opposite the stairway, between the front and back rooms. Sally peered inside, screwing up her eyes to see in the dim light. It was a cubby-hole of a room, about ten feet square, with a small bedstead stripped of its covers, a wooden chest, and a night-table with a porcelain basin on it. There were no windows and no fireplace. Damp oozed down the walls.

"The Black Hole!" Sally whispered.

Florrie nodded solemnly. "This is where Mary slept—and where she was found, that morning. Nobody's used it since."

Sally had been looking forward to inspecting Mary's room, but now that she saw it, she could not imagine what she would find that could be any use. The room was so small and scrubbed and bare—not even a hole in the wall or a crack in the floor to hide anything in. Fancy putting a gently bred girl in a dark, dank hole like this—not because she had done anything wrong, but just to break her spirit, and make her tell you who she was!

Well, the tables were turned on Harcourt now, Sally thought. He was the one being spied on. She had come here like a ferret down a rabbit hole, hunting secrets—hunting a murderer, perhaps. So have a care, Wax-face! she thought. I just might find out some'ut as'll knock you off that high horse of yours!

Sally soon learned the routine of the refuge. Housework, needle-work, prayers, a meal—then it all began again. Miss Nettleton flitted about, making sure that every inmate had her task, and that when it was done, she was given another. Fanlights were cleaned, rugs beaten, doorknobs polished, banisters bees-waxed. Bits of stair-carpet were taken up to be mended, then tacked down again. Occasionally half a dozen inmates went out to the back garden of the office house and trudged around the gravel paths for a quarter of an hour. This was called recreation.

It was only at meals and prayers that all two dozen inmates gathered together. Sally watched the serving of meals closely. Miss Nettleton and Wideawake Peg circled the room with large platters, doling out black bread, vegetables, and a little cheese to each inmate. It would have been hard, Sally thought, to slip anything into Mary's food on the night she died. How could you be sure that she and nobody else would eat the poisoned slab of bread, or dollop of cheese? Unless of course the same person who hocussed the food was the one who served it. Sally gathered that it was always Peg and the matron on duty who served the meals. So that meant Peg and Mrs. Fiske were handing out food on the night Mary died.

But how important was that, really? Mr. Kestrel had said that if Mary had been given a fatal dose of opium at supper, she would have shown signs of it by the time she went to bed an hour or two later. So if Mary was poisoned by some hand other than her own, the poison was almost certainly in that cordial she took at bedtime. No wonder one of the principal tasks Mr. Kestrel had given Sally was to find out where that cordial was kept, and who had access to it.

The inmates around her were complaining in hushed tones about the food. Nothing but vegetables—never a morsel of beef, or even mutton. Beef broth, or a watery, floury stew, was the closest to meat they ever got. Mr Harcourt said vegetables were healthier for them—but he had a nice chop sent up to his office whenever he dined at the refuge.

"Why do we get so many greens?" Sally wanted to know.

"'Coz Mrs. Jessop's husband's a greengrocer," whispered Florrie. "She's one of the matrons, and she sees to it that Mr. Harcourt gets all the greens he wants, dirt cheap."

"That's how he gets everything," rasped Bess, an older inmate with a voice like carriage wheels on gravel. "Cogs it out of the matrons, or them other women as dotes on him."

"Cogs it out of their husbands, you mean," said a florid girl known as Red Jane, to distinguish her from another Jane who was dark. "Or their brothers. Miss Nettleton's brother's a mason, and Mr. Harcourt's al'ays after him to do repairs about the place. And Mrs. Fiske's husband's an apothecary, so we gets all our physic from him, and whenever a gal is took sick, he's the one as treats her."

"I wonder he wasn't called in when that gal Mary cocked up her toes," said Sally.

"But he was," they all said in a chorus.

"Bender! He'd have been at the inquest—" Sally broke off, chagrined. How would she explain how she knew who was at the inquest, and who wasn't?

Luckily no one thought to ask. "He's took ill," Florrie explained. "Around the time Mary died, a couple of the gals here had fever, and Mr. Fiske come every day to see how they was. When Mary was found dead, he was called in double-quick, and it was plain as a pikestaff he was took with the fever himself. Mortal bad he was—very shaky, and green about the gills. He had a look at Mary, and he did cut up—he was fond of her, and it give him a turn, her dropping off the perch like that. Mr. Harcourt sent him home—said he wasn't well, and he'd best keep to his bed. Now he's fair raving with fever, and Mrs. Fiske don't know if he'll live or die."

"And don't care, neither," said Bess.

"Poor Mr. Fiske," said Florrie. "If ever a man lived under the cat's foot, it's him. And he ain't a bad sort."

"He's a good soul," Red Jane declared, "and I won't hear nobody say different. Got a soft spot for us gals, if you ask me. It makes his old hag of a missis cut up savage! She'd as lief not let him near us, only Mr. Harcourt won't fork out for physic—not when he can get it so cheap from Mr. Fiske."

"He was fond of Mary, you say?" Sally mused.

"Oh, yes," nodded Florrie. "I don't mean he fancied her, he was old enough to be her father—"

"That don't stop 'em," ground out Bess.

"I know, but that wasn't how Mr. Fiske was with Mary. She was a pretty thing, and down in the mouth, and he was sorry for her. He's got a kind heart. He was called in to physic her when she first come, because she was a bit weak and howish. He said she was to take that cordial, and after that he looked in on her whenever he come here, to see if she was mending."

"Did she cotton to him?" Sally asked.

"She did, a bit. 'Course, it was hard to tell with Mary. She didn't say much. But if she talked to anybody, I expect it was to him. She seemed to trust him more nor anybody else."

"You think she told him who she was?" asked Sally eagerly.

"Who knows?" shrugged Red Jane. "Nobody told me about it if she did."

Nobody told the coroner, either, thought Sally. Mr. Fiske's name had never come up at the inquest—even though he had treated Mary while she was at the refuge, and it was he who had prescribed the cordial for her. More important, he had been the first medical man to examine her body. That would explain the three-hour delay between the discovery of Mary's death and the Great Doctor's examination of her body. It would also explain where Mrs. Fiske had gone in such a hurry, directly Mary's death was discovered. Harcourt must have sent her to fetch her husband—then changed his mind, bundled Fiske off, and summoned the Great Doctor in his place.

It was nothing short of a conspiracy. Harcourt, Mrs. Fiske, and the Great Doctor had suppressed Fiske's role completely. Was that just because Fiske was too ill to attend the inquest, and Harcourt did not want it delayed? Or did Fiske know something that Harcourt was anxious to keep dark?

She must see Fiske, talk to him, find out what he knew. When he was well, surely he would come back to the refuge? There was always some inmate or other in need of physic. But suppose Harcourt no longer wanted him here? Or worse—suppose Fiske did not get well, but died and took his secrets with him?

Trio of Suspects

At noon on Saturday, Sally contrived to be cleaning a front window of the refuge. She could see Dipper down the street, peering into the window of the stationer's shop. When no one was watching her, she held up the white cloth she was cleaning with and waved it back and forth. He did not appear to glance toward the refuge, but she knew he had seen her signal, because he thrust his hands in his pockets and walked jauntily away.

Sunday marked a change in the routine of the refuge. "No work to be done," said Red Jane, one of the three inmates who shared Sally's room. "'Cept cooking and tidying up after meals."

"What do we do all day?" asked Sally.

"Listen to Mr. Harcourt preachify, mostly," said a ginger-haired girl, who was known as Spots on account of her freckles.

"At least it's warm in the chapel," said Red Jane. "Mr. Harcourt always sees to it there's a good fire wherever *he* is."

"That's a wicked thing to say," chided a young girl named Nancy, who was taking her reformation seriously.

"All I knows is, it's cold and damp as the grave in here," Red Jane retorted. "And it ain't never cold where Mr. Harcourt is."

The others nodded, shivering. They were washing and dressing by the grey dawn light, and the cold made their fingers stiffen and their shoulders hunch. They moved like rheumatic old women.

"I expect there ain't a coal merchant's wife in the Reclamation Society," said Sally.

"You're a knowing 'un," Red Jane nodded approvingly.

Sally got them talking about Harcourt's patrons. "I heard one of the trustees was a reg'lar swell, with a handle to his name."

"That's Lord Carbury," said Spots.

"Oh, him. I knows who he is," said Sally. "I seen his son once—Mr. Charles Avondale. Cor, he's a dimber cove! Hair like gold, and eyes as'd put blue violets to shame. He ever come here?"

"No such luck!" laughed Red Jane.

"Lord Carbury's been here, though," said Spots. "I seen him. A few of us was brought in to curtsey to the trustees, and I stood as close to him as I am to you. He smiled at me particular."

"He probably thought you was a monkey brought in to dance for him," said Red Jane.

"Go and be hanged!" cried Spots.

"You go to the devil, and say I sent you!"

They made a dash at each other. Sally and Nancy tried to pull them apart.

"What's all this rumpus?" Wideawake Peg put her head in at the door. "Draw in your horns, you scabby sluts, or you'll be late to chapel, and isn't it me that's supposed to see we're all there on time? If Himself takes me to task, I'll be quick to put the blame where it belongs. So look sharp, and come along!"

Red Jane and Spots glared at each other, but they drew apart and finished dressing. It was not the first time Sally had seen Peg bring unruly inmates to heel. Everyone knew she would tell Harcourt of any misconduct by an inmate—or, at all events, any misconduct he might find out about some other way.

Having Harcourt's ear gave her a good deal of power. Inmates who crossed her seldom stayed long at the refuge. But she could also use her influence in an inmate's favour, to lessen her punishment or save her from expulsion. That was why the inmates submitted to her tyranny, and never dreamed of exposing her double-dealing to Harcourt and the matrons. They needed her. She made herself useful in myriad ways. She had all sorts of dodges for getting hold of things forbidden to the inmates. Her task of waiting at table gave her access to the larder, and she was ingenious at trimming off bits of cold meat left over from the matron's dinner, or hollowing out the bottom of a pudding without disturbing the top.

She stole candles, too, for inmates whose weekly ration had run out. The candles were kept in a little storeroom known as the matrons' closet, between Harcourt's office and the matrons' private room, on the first floor of the office house. Peg dusted the matrons' closet every day, and was often sent to fetch things from it. The candles were counted, but Peg knew a trick worth two of that. She simply shaved thin pieces of tallow off the bottoms of a number of candles and stuck the slivers together.

Sally had to admire a talent like that. But Peg made the inmates pay dearly for any favours she did them. She gradually extorted the few possessions of any value they brought to the refuge. When those were exhausted, she made them do her work or wait on her like lady's maids. She was turning a tidy profit from her sojourn here. Was that why she stayed so long, or did she have some other reason best known to herself?

Sally sometimes wondered why any of the inmates would stick a place like this. But many of them were getting on in years—Bess must be thirty at least. For a game girl past her prime, it might be worth submitting to reformation on Harcourt's terms, in order to get her character back and find honest work. Some inmates, to do them justice, were genuinely repentant. Seduced maidservants and milliners, mostly—the kind who were forced into tail-trading out of necessity, or despair.

A few inmates were harder to account for—Florrie, for instance. She would not tell Sally anything more about why she had come to the refuge, or about the man she had been trying to escape. She was too indolent and fond of ease for a life like this, but she seemed content enough. She was a sunny soul, candid and good-natured. Sally found it hard to believe she had anything to hide.

On her way to the chapel, her thoughts took another turn. She came up beside Florrie and asked abruptly, "That cordial Mary was taking—where is it now?"

"Good morning to you, too!" Florrie dug her playfully in the ribs.

Sally shoved back, laughing. Peg shot them a warning look, and they came to order hastily. Sally went on in a whisper, "We was just chopping about Mary in our room, and I got to thinking about that cordial. Who'd want to drink any of it now, I says to meself, seeing as how it was give to a gal as clipped her own wick like that? Seems to me it's cursed. I wouldn't swallow none of it—not for a yellow George, I wouldn't. What've they done with it?"

"I don't know," said Florrie. "It used to be kept in the matrons' closet, but I ain't heard nothing about it since Mary died."

They reached the chapel, filed in, and took their seats. Sally stationed herself by a window, so that she could make her signal unobtrusively at noon. They were to listen to sermons all morning, and Bible readings all afternoon. Oh, well, Sally told herself, it would be a good opportunity to sort out her thoughts. While Harcourt ran on about sin and repentance—really, the man had tongue enough for two sets of teeth—she marshalled every fact she knew about how Mary might have been poisoned. Assuming, of course, that her death was murder, and the bottle of laudanum was only a blind.

Three people had been in a good position to hocus her dose of cordial. First there was Mrs. Fiske. It was she who had poured out the cordial that night. Her husband was an apothecary, so she could easily get her hands on opium in all sorts of forms and strengths. Of course, anyone could buy opium, compounds, and not only from apothecaries, but from chandlers, grocers, even outdoor stalls. Still, Mrs. Fiske must know more than most people about mixing drugs, and about the amount of opium needed for a fatal dose. And she seemed to have hated Mary—perhaps because Mr. Fiske was fond of her. The inmates said she had little love for her husband, but that did not mean she would not feel slighted by his attentions to a pretty girl.

She also had a good opportunity to plant the empty laudanum bottle in Mary's room. She admitted she had gone to inspect the inmates' house during the night, and had actually looked in on Mary. What could be simpler than to bring the bottle with her, and put it on the night-table by Mary's bed? Mary would either be dead by then, or too heavily drugged to awaken. To make the illusion of suicide complete, Mrs. Fiske need merely add a few drops of laudanum and water to the empty cordial glass, so that Mary would appear to have mixed her own fatal dose before she went to bed.

But there was also Wideawake Peg to consider. She had no known reason to want Mary dead, but she was sharp enough to plan the murder, and had an opportunity to carry it out. Mr. Kestrel had suggested that, since no one but Mary was taking the cordial, the murderer could have killed her by poisoning the entire bottle. The cordial was kept in the matrons' closet, and Peg was the only inmate allowed in there. She could have laced the cordial with opium at any time during the day on Tuesday and been nowhere near when Mrs. Fiske poured out the dose that night.

It would be easy enough for Peg to leave the laudanum bottle in Mary's room. The ground-floor front room, where Peg slept, was next door to the Black Hole. It would take her only half a minute to dart into Mary's room, then back to her own. If someone should catch her outside her room, she could simply say she was on her way to the boghouse in the back garden. That was always a good excuse for an inmate to leave her room at night.

She might also have planted the bottle in Mary's room when she was sent to fetch her next morning. But in that case, Florrie must have been lying when she said she had seen the bottle on Mary's night-table on her way to breakfast.

There was one serious problem with the case against Peg. Mr. Kestrel had put his finger on it when he was giving Sally instructions before she left for the refuge: "Of course, you realize, if one of the inmates killed Mary, she didn't act alone. Shut up in the refuge, how could she have got hold of the laudanum bottle to leave in Mary's room, or the poison actually used to kill her? She would have needed an accomplice: someone outside the refuge, who could smuggle them in to her—"

Sally felt a jab at her elbow. Florrie was nudging her and pointing to her prayer book. The other inmates had theirs open and were reading aloud in a sort of duet with Harcourt. Sally had not been to church often enough to understand what it was all about. It sounded rather grand, though very sombre. There was no point in trying to find the page they were looking at, since she could barely read anyway. So she opened her prayer book at random, moved her lips when the others did, and went on thinking.

The third target of her suspicions was Harcourt. He could easily have laced the bottle of cordial with opium during the day, since his office was right next to the matrons' closet. He could also have planted the laudanum bottle in Mary's room, and the traces of laudanum in her cordial glass. He was working at the refuge the night Mary died, and Mrs. Fiske had left him alone every so often while she went to the kitchen to make tea. That would have given him time to sneak into the inmates' house. True, he was strict about not going there after the inmates went to bed, but if he were caught, he could have contrived some excuse.

But why should he kill Mary, when he had every reason to keep her alive? Everyone said he wanted to find out who her family was, and return her to them in a blaze of glory. Mr. Kestrel had an answer for that, though, she recalled: "The inmates take it for granted Harcourt was punishing Mary to make her tell him who she was. But suppose that was only an excuse to isolate her, make her murder possible? She couldn't have been poisoned, and the laudanum bottle planted by her bed, if she'd shared a room with three or four other inmates. If nothing else, one of them might have noticed that her sleep was too deep to be natural, and summoned help in time to rouse her from her stupor before it was too late. No, it was essential that she sleep alone, and Harcourt was the only person with authority to bring that about."

Sally wondered what she could do to throw light on these mysteries. She could try to find out more about Wideawake Peg: where she came from, why she was here, and how she got so thick with Harcourt. She could explore possible entrances to the inmates' house, to see how an accomplice to the murder might have gotten in from outside. And finally, she could have a look at that bottle of Summerson's Strengthening Elixir She would have to sneak into the matrons' closet, and might be expelled from the refuge if she were caught. But it would be worth the risk.

Dr. MacGregor called in Clarges Street on Sunday afternoon and found Julian reclining on his parlour sofa. "Don't get up," said MacGregor scathingly. "I wouldn't want to put you to any trouble. Fine way to spend a Sunday afternoon—lying about like a lapdog!"

"I'll have you know I spent the last few hours in a fencing parlour, and I'm quite legitimately fatigued."

"I didn't know you dandies did anything so energetic as fencing."

"We don't as a rule, but I hate to be predictable." He added more seriously, "I studied fencing when I lived on the Continent, and I like to keep my hand in."

"I'd rather hear you'd been in church. Still, I'm glad to see you do something to keep your body in trim, as well as your wits."

"Actually, I contrived to do both today. I went to the fencing parlour hoping to meet Charles Avondale, or at least find out more about him. He belongs to a sporting set who spend a good deal of their time either boxing or fencing. Avondale wasn't there, but I did run into some of his cronies."

"And?"

"And the upshot is, I've realized a man's male friends know nothing about him. In three hours, I gathered that Avondale is a thundering good fellow, sports a first-rate carriage, pays his gambling debts like a gentleman, and has the devil's own luck with women—all of which I knew already, and none of which tells me anything to the purpose. A woman, by contrast, takes a wonderful, minute interest in a man. She can uncover the state of his health, his heart, and his pocketbook on half an hour's acquaintance."

"Well, why don't you talk to Avondale's women friends?"

"That would be easy enough during the season. I could simply hang about drawing rooms and ballrooms, dropping Avondale's name and letting the gossips sharpen their claws on it. But at this time of year, hardly any of the *ton* is left in London. With one important exception: I heard today that Avondale's sister, Lady Gayheart, is still here. I don't think she and Avondale are close—she's not the sort of woman to waste her charms on a mere brother—but she must know a good deal about him all the same."

"Are you going to call on her?"

Julian grimaced. "Not if I can avoid it. I don't know her well, and a sudden visit would signal I meant to join her court of admirers—a difficult position to resign from, once assumed. Lady Gayheart is a famous beauty, and demands a constant tribute of flattery and flirtation. Last year a certain duke nearly caused a scandal by kissing her at Brighton, but I suspect the poor devil was only trying to rest his voice."

"She's not much use to you if you can't talk to her."

"True. Perhaps I can contrive to run into her in some public place. If not, I'll just have to call on her, and damn the consequences."

"How are you coming with those other two men—Bristles and Blinkers?"

"We haven't got any further with Bristles. Dipper and I made enquiries at coaching inns, on the chance he might have left London, but it's like looking for a needle in a haystack—too many inns, too many travellers rushing about in anonymous greatcoats and hats. Blinkers is another matter. We've had the umbrella advertisement printed and sent round to likely shops. Dipper is handling the responses, and I expect he'll be led quite a dance. But he and I have a rather strong incentive to lay hands on Blinkers. Apart from anything to do with the investigation, we'd both get a good deal of satisfaction out of tapping that man's claret."

"Taking a bit of a personal interest, aren't you?"

"I don't approve of young women being knocked about like ninepins, if that's what you mean."

"Especially one particular young woman."

"Especially Dipper's sister."

"Hmph! That's all there is to it, then?"

The fight went out of Julian suddenly. He lay back, his head resting on his arm. "Don't gloat, my dear fellow."

MacGregor gave him one brief, penetrating glance, and tactfully changed the subject.

A Midnight Encounter

Sally thought Sunday would never end. Even the usual routine of the refuge was better than sitting still all day listening to sermons. By evening her mind was weary, but her body was full of pent-up vigour. She longed to stretch her cramped limbs, run and shout, and throw the house out of the windows.

She went to bed docilely enough, but she did not stay there. As soon as Red Jane, Spots, and Nancy were asleep, she stole out from under the covers. The house was colder and damper than ever. She clenched her teeth to keep them from chattering, put on her shoes, and wrapped herself in a large brown woolen shawl. It was one of the dull but serviceable garments Mrs. Mabbitt had made her buy. She was grateful to her now as she burrowed inside its big, thick folds.

She lit one of her meagre supply of candles and tiptoed out, cupping her hand round the flame. There was no lamp in the hallway—only a wisp of fog-choked moonlight, filtering down from a skylight over the stairs. She moved as silently as she could, but the floors were not carpeted like the ones in the office house, and her lightest footfall made a sharp crack on the bare, uneven boards.

Luckily it did not matter much if anyone caught her outside her room. She could simply say she was on her way to the boghouse in the back garden. In milder weather, the inmates often used this as an excuse to go outdoors at night. Of course, on a chill, clammy evening like this, only the hardiest girl would leave her bed if she did not have to. This meant that Sally stood a good chance of conducting her explorations undisturbed. It helped that the matron on duty tonight was Mrs. Jessop. Sally had heard she was a heavy sleeper, and the least likely of the matrons to come inspecting the inmates' house at night.

Sally wanted to see how an accomplice to the murder might have sneaked into the inmates' house. She remembered Harcourt's testifying at the inquest that no windows or doors at the refuge had been forced. That was probably true—he was too clever to tell a lie that could be so readily disproved. Tampering with doors and windows left unmistakable signs—Sally was a burglar's daughter, and she knew. So, since the inmates' house was always kept locked, an intruder would have needed a key. And he could not have gotten one from any of the inmates. They did not have keys: the locks were as much to keep them in as to keep intruders out.

Who did have keys? No one but Harcourt and the matrons, as far as Sally knew. Mrs. Fiske's husband might have a key, since he often came to the refuge to physic the inmates. Even if he did not, he probably had access to his wife's. It intrigued Sally that Fiske was an apothecary: he must know more about poisons than anyone else connected with the refuge. But everyone said he had been fond of Mary. Why would he have killed her?

Sally shook her head. Useless to speculate about Fiske when she knew so little about him. She forced her attention back to the problem at hand.

If someone wanted to get into the inmates' house on the sly, how would he do it? The front door was out of the question: it was boarded up, since the formal entrance to the refuge was through the office house. There was a connecting door between the two houses, but no sane person would try to sneak into the inmates' house that way. He would first need to get inside the office house, which he could not do in the daytime without being seen. Even at night, he might be caught by the matron on duty; moreover, he would need a second key, since the connecting door between the two houses was locked after bedtime. The whole thing was too complicated, and too risky. No: an intruder would enter the inmates' house directly, through either the front basement door in the area or the back door from the garden.

Sally tiptoed down to the basement. It was even more damp and dismal here. A film like cold sweat clung to the walls and the rough stone floor. She went into the front room, which was the wet laundry. It had large and small washtubs, washboards, soap, and a copper for boiling clothes. There was a grated window looking into the area and a locked door that was used for deliveries of coal, or to bring water in from the cistern.

This door would be a good way to get in on the sly. An intruder could come along late at night, when the street was quiet, and climb over the area railings. A narrow flight of stairs led down to the door. There, below street level, he could slip in without much risk of being seen, assuming he had a key. If he were very quiet and cautious, he could then make his way unnoticed up the stairs to the ground floor.

And that would put him right outside the Black Hole. Easy enough to steal into Mary's room, knowing he would find her drugged, or already dead, and plant the laudanum bottle on her night-table, and the traces of laudanum and water in her glass. That would explain how he had made her death look like suicide, but not how he had committed the murder itself. To poison Mary's cordial—or anything else she ate or drank—he would have needed an ally inside the refuge. But if he had such an ally, why sneak in at all? Why not leave everything to his confederate—someone who knew the place, and was already inside?

She was making it all too complicated, she decided. Much simpler if Mrs. Fiske had killed Mary: she had the best opportunity to poison her cordial, and she was a nasty old cat, whom Sally would not be sorry to see nabbed for murder. The trouble was, there was not a shred of real proof against her.

She decided to move on, if only to keep warm. She crossed to the back basement room, which was the dry laundry, and threaded her way among ironing tables and drying racks to the window. It was heavily grated, like all the others in the inmates' house. No means of access here.

On her way out, she stubbed her toe on the mangle, and while she was hopping about, swearing under her breath, a draught blew out her candle. "Pox on it!" she whispered. "I ain't giving up! I won't go back to bed—not as long as there's a hint of a glim to see me way!"

She felt her way upstairs in the near darkness. Hearing no one about, she crept down the hall to the back door and groped for the latch. At last she found it and stepped outsides clutching her shawl around her and lifting her nightdress to keep it out of the mud. The rain had stopped, but there was a heavy mist, milky with moonlight. She could just make out where the brick wall round the garden met the sky.

An intruder could get into the inmates' house through the back door, too, but it would be harder. The door was not locked, but the gate in the garden wall was secured by a thick padlock. There was no way to get through, short of breaking it open. And the wall was high, though an agile man could probably scale it, in spite of those nasty spikes along the top. Once in the back garden, he could bide his time till he was sure there was no one going to or from the boghouse, then tiptoe up to the back door. Or he could simply leave something in the garden for an accomplice to find—a note, perhaps, or the laudanum bottle.

She began to explore the garden—she hardly knew why, since without a candle, she could barely see six feet in front of her through the mist. But she could orient herself by the boghouse, which was in the rear left-hand corner. Its stench permeated the garden, fanning out on the thick, moist air.

All at once she stopped and sniffed incredulously. Mingled with the privy smell was another odour—impossible, surely, but unmistakeable. Tobacco smoke.

It was coming from the direction of the boghouse. She moved toward the squat brick building, her feet sliding on the muddy ground. The tobacco smell was strongest at the back, where the boghouse met the garden wall. Through the mist she made out a human shape, and a pin-prick of reddish light.

"Good evening to you!" Wideawake Peg said softly. Sally jumped.

Peg laughed. She was seated on a tree stump, her back against the garden wall, smoking a rough-cut pipe. Its faint, ruddy glow played over her long eyes and high, pronounced cheekbones, making her look more than ever like a fox. "Now, why should you be after coming out here on a night like this?"

"Maybe I come to use the privy."

"Why don't you, then?" Peg mocked.

A smart retort sprang to Sally's lips, but she bit it back. There was better use to be made of this meeting than kicking up a row. "I couldn't sleep," she said easily, "so I come out for a tramp. I ain't used to being cooped up. Then I smelled your 'bacca, and come over here to see who was fogging. Where do you get it, and how do you keep it hid from the matrons?"

Peg blew out a leisurely puff of smoke and did not answer.

"Strikes me comical, what you gets away with!" said Sally admiringly. "There ain't nobody else here could put the fun upon Wax-face and the matrons like you does." Seeing Peg preen, she went on coaxingly, "I'd give a yellow George to know how you done it."

"Faith, it's as easy as shelling peas. These walls round the garden are all new-built. But since Himself is too much of a pinchfist to spend a farthing more than he can help, they're none too thick, and the brick and plaster work none too secure. There's plenty of chinks and crannies where I can leave a little something in payment, and me pals on the outside can take it and leave tobacco in its place—or anything else me heart desires."

"Ain't you the downy one!"

"I know a trick or two. Where do you suppose I keep me tobacco, now?"

"I dunno. Where?"

"In the Greek urn in Himself's own office!"

"In Wax-face's office? Won't he spring it?"

"And why should he? He's got no call to be looking inside an urn that's only there for ornament. No, me tobacco's safe enough, and I can get at it whenever I like. Isn't it meself that cleans his office every day?" She stretched complacently. "Oh, yes, there's ways of living as high as you like, even in here. I can get you whatever you want from outside, if you've the means to pay for it."

"S'pose I wanted laudanum. Could you get me that?"

Peg's eyes narrowed. "Now, what might you be meaning?"

"I dunno. I just thought, seeing as how nobody knows how that gal Mary got the laudanum—" Her voice trailed off suggestively.

"It wasn't me that got it for her, at all at all." Peg's eyes were amused and unreadable. "Even if I did, you wouldn't expect me to own up to it, now, would you? It must be a crime of some sort, giving a person the means to put hands on herself like that."

"All the same, you must know more nor anybody here about how Mary died. There ain't nothing goes on here you don't drop down to."

"I might know something."

"Tell me! I'm that curious!"

"Faith, and why should I?"

"Come on, be a trump! I won't blow the gab."

Peg puffed meditatively on her pipe. "I'll think on it."

"Oh, well, I didn't mean to jump down your throat," said Sally kindly. "It ain't your fault if you don't know no more nor anybody else."

"It's none of your sympathy I'm needing! There's plenty I know—though I wasn't so deaf to me own best interests as to cackle about it after Mary died. We had a little talk, Mary and me, a few days before she popped off. She wanted a favour, and gave me her silk stockings in exchange for it."

"What favour?"

"She wanted to send a letter, and she didn't want anyone to know about it. So next time I went to clean Himself's office, I fetched her two sheets of paper and a pencil."

"When was that?"

"The Saturday before she died."

And her letter had been dated Saturday evening. It fit perfectly. The letter had taken up only one sheet, but Mary had mentioned an "outer sheet" bearing the recipient's address. Which was odd, now Sally came to think of it. She had never had much to do with posting letters herself, but she knew most people simply wrote on one sheet, folded it, addressed it, and closed it with a seal. Extra sheets meant extra postage. Of course, Mary did not have a seal, so she probably wanted the outer sheet for added security. What a shame the two sheets had been separated! If only Mr. Kestrel and she knew for whom the letter was meant, they might be able to guess who Mary was.

"What happened then?" she asked.

"Next morning she gave me back the pencil, and I put it back in Himself's office. But she never gave me the letter." She added airily, "Perhaps she never wrote it."

"Why should she give it to you?"

"To post it, of course."

"How?"

"Faith, is it culver-headed you are? The post-bag's kept in Himself's office. I can slip in an extra letter, and no one the wiser. Mary and I agreed I'd post it for her, but she never gave it to me. I can't post a letter that's never put in me hands, now, can I?"

Sally thought back on Mary's letter. It had been read to her so many times that she knew most of it by heart. *Thank heaven, there's someone I think I can trust to post it for me secretly.* Had she meant Peg? To give Peg credit, she was a skillful and effective ally, when she had something to gain. But she was not the kind of person Sally would have expected to win Mary's trust.

"Didn't she never say no more about it?"

"Not to me." Peg stood up, knocked her pipe against the wall to empty it, and slipped it into a fold of her shawl. "We'd best be going in."

Sally could not resist asking, "Ain't you ever afraid Wax-face'll drop down to you one of these days?"

"Himself'll drop down to me in the week of four Fridays! Isn't it me that's his model inmate, his great success? And it's making the most of it I'll be. Tail-trading's well enough for them that haven't the wit to earn their bread any other way. As for me, I'm done with it. There's more blunt to be got, and less trouble and danger, in morality than immorality. I was born and bred a Papist, but there's no future for an enterprising woman in that. She can't rise to anything but sainthood, and that's no good to her till after she's dead. Now, in the Church of England, a woman can make herself a fine life as a reformer. Just look at that Hannah More. Himself is setting me on that road, little though he knows it. Every time he trots me out to show off to his patrons, he's helping to make me reputation. A Magdalene, that's me—come to lead me sisters into the light!"

"Maybe Wax-face knows what he's about, right enough. How do you know he ain't using you, same as you're using him?"

"Devil an inch of it! I've got Himself in me pocket. He has no more idea I'm double-dealing than he has of the dark side of the moon. I feed his vanity—and, Mother Mary, what an appetite it's got! I tell him he's a saint upon the earth, and big fool treats it as God's own truth—and everything else I say, too! Here's a bit of advice, and don't be after saying I never taught you anything. If you want to lie to people, tell 'em something they want to believe, and they'll swim right into your net."

Back in her room, Sally lay awake for a long time, thinking about Mary and her letter. Peg's information opened a whole new range of possibilities. Was she telling the truth when she said Mary never gave her the letter to post? Suppose Mary did entrust it to her, but she passed it on to Harcourt or Mrs. Fiske, or some enemy of Mary's outside the refuge? Then again, perhaps she put the letter in the post-bag, but Harcourt or one of the matrons found it there. Yet if Peg had kept her part of the bargain and posted the letter, why would she pretend Mary never gave it to her? On the other hand, if she had done something hole-and-corner with it, why tell Sally about it at all?

Sally wrapped her pillow around her head, to shut out Red Jane's snoring. Very well: suppose Peg was telling the truth, and Mary never gave her the letter. What did Mary do with it, then? How did it end up in the hands of the man from whom Sally had stolen it? Could Mary have found someone else to post it? Or had it been stolen from her before she had a chance to give it to Peg?

She had written the letter on Saturday evening. Maybe she found it hard to catch Peg alone on Sunday, with the inmates gathered in the chapel for most of the day. Perhaps she left the letter in her room, and someone found it there. Sally had learned that Mrs. Fiske was the matron on duty that Sunday, and she was especially zealous about searching the inmates' rooms.

Sally squirmed and clutched the pillow more tightly over her ears. Now it was her own thoughts she was trying to shut out. Curse Mr. Kestrel and his puzzles! Once you started working on them, there was no getting any sleep.

If there were any justice, he was lying awake, too, as baffled and intrigued by this business as she was. She pictured him in bed, his body stripped of those impeccable clothes, his dark brown hair loose and disheveled. She sighed and stretched luxuriously, and was still smiling when she fell asleep.

A Sister, A Mouse, and A Manservant

Julian kept his eyes open for an opportunity to approach Lady Gayheart. On Monday afternoon, he had the luck to see her carriage pull up outside a milliner's in Bond Street. He contrived to stroll by just in time to hand her out, and on learning she was going to try on hats, declared she must have a gentleman's opinion, and he was at her service.

Her dark blue eyes, so like her brother Charles's, widened entrancingly. "Why, Mr. Kestrel, you can't possibly be interested in ladies' bonnets."

"Not in a general way, no. But when they're on ladies' heads, they take on a singular fascination."

"I'm sure you'll find it deadly dull."

"The only deadly feeling you've ever inspired in me is envy of Gayheart."

She rapped him playfully with her sunshade. "You're frightfully impertinent, and you mustn't on any account come in with me." She glided into the milliner's. Her footman, stony-faced, held the door open for Julian to follow. He did.

An unctuous Frenchwoman greeted Lady Gayheart and showed her to a seat before a looking-glass. Assistants ran to and fro, fetching bonnets trimmed with lace and streamers, flowers and ostrich plumes. Lady Gayheart tried the effect of each, frowning prettily at the mirror and turning her head this way and that. Julian drew up a chair close to hers—to see the hats better, he explained—and embarked on the sort of stylized flirtation she would expect, and he could conduct almost in his sleep.

They soon passed to lamenting about how desolate London was at this time of year. It turned out that the Gayhearts, like Julian, had been invited to spend October at Braxton Castle, only to have the entertainment abruptly called off. "I think it's simply horrid of Lord Braxton to promise everyone a party," Lady Gayheart declared, "and then cry off at the last minute, just because his daughter must needs run away and marry a half-pay captain with side-whiskers. Now Gayheart's got involved in some tiresome business matter—one of those South American mines everyone is so nutty upon—and he won't leave London, and you'll hardly believe it, but he won't let me go away without him! Fancy! We shall make such quizzes of ourselves, living in each other's pockets, for all the world as if we weren't married at all!"

"You can't expect me to regret your remaining here, so opportunely bereft of admirers." He added offhandedly, "Town isn't quite empty. Your brother is here, for one."

"Oh, Charles." She lost interest. "I daresay he's afraid the duns will descend on him if he tries to leave London."

"Is he at low tide? I had no idea."

"I don't know how bad it is. But he's always having to ask Papa for money—which of course he gets, because Papa thinks nothing too good for Charles. You can't think how Charles wheedles things out of him. It's too bad, really it is! But he was always Papa's favourite."

"I never thought he lived particularly high."

"I wouldn't have thought so, either, but of course a gentleman has all sorts of expenses he doesn't tell his sister about. Heaven knows how he'll manage if he's such a noodle as to marry Cousin Ada."

"Is that on the cards?"

"I can't say. He and Ada have always paired off, and I believe he's not best pleased to see that stuffy major dancing attendance on her. But I can hardly believe he'd commit such a *niaiserie* as to marry her. She's very sweet, but she hasn't two farthings to rub together, and she's hopelessly without *ton*. Charles would be bored to distraction in a month. Not that Gayheart's powers of fascination are anything out of the common, but at least he had an absolutely staggering fortune."

She smiled charmingly, then turned back to the mirror. "This one is a bit showy, don't you think?"

"I think it's a very game little hat, to get itself noticed at all, with such a face underneath."

"What a shocking great flirt you are. Why do you never come to see me?"

He felt himself getting into deep water and decided to swim for shore. Rising, he took up his hat and stick. "It's been a herculean effort of self-denial, but you see, I hear you have a Pomeranian dog."

"What, you're not afraid of a little dog, surely?"

"No, but on the advice of my tailor, I'm allergic to anything that sheds."

After a little more banter, he got away from her and took himself off to one of his clubs. A servant brought him a newspaper, still hot from being ironed to remove the creases. He screened himself behind it and thought over what he had learned from Lady Gayheart. It intrigued him that Avondale was such a favourite with his father. That gave him a possible hold over the ambitious Mr. Harcourt. Lord Carbury was Harcourt's most exalted patron. What if Avondale offered to further Harcourt's cause with him, or threatened to undermine it? How far would Harcourt go to keep in Carbury's good graces?

Avondale's money troubles were interesting, too, but their implications were less clear. He did not have a reputation for extravagance. In particular, he was not much given to high-stakes gambling, which was how so many young men got themselves smashed up. So where was his money going?

Finally, there was his attachment to his cousin Ada. What that could have to do with the Mary mystery, Julian had no idea. It was certainly a misfortune for Avondale to fall in love with a penniless girl, when he was hard up himself. If he really did mean to marry Miss Grantham, he would have to raise the wind somehow. And there was nothing like urgent financial need for driving a man to desperate measures.

Sally straightened up from scrubbing the floor and listened intently. Hearing nothing, she tiptoed over to the landing and peered through the banisters. Sure enough, no one was approaching from up- or downstairs.

It was the ideal moment. Many of the inmates were out for their daily walk around the back garden. Harcourt was shut up in his office. Mrs. Jessop, who was on duty again today, was the least vigilant of the matrons. She was a tall, officious woman with fat cheeks and red hands, who would rather stand about lecturing the inmates than roam the refuge hunting out misconduct.

Sally crossed the hall to the matrons' closet. It was no more than six feet wide, sandwiched between Harcourt's office and the room where the matron on duty slept. She opened the door and peered in. It would have been safer to go in and shut the door after her, but then she would have been left in darkness.

She scanned the shelves, which were filled with china and linen, candles, soap, and polish. Several bottles stood on a high shelf. She took one down and sounded out the writing on the label: IPECACUANHA. Grimacing, she put it back.

The bottle beside it was the one she wanted. SUMMERSON'S STRENGTHENING ELIXIR, the label proclaimed, and there was the familiar smiling sun in the upper right-hand corner. She had seen that sun often enough: it beamed from shop windows, leaflets, pasteboard signs.

The bottle was still half full. Drawing the cork, she took from her pocket a scrap of black bread she had saved from breakfast. She quickly soaked the bread in the thick, purplish syrup, corked the bottle, and put it back. Wrapping the bread in her handkerchief, she shut the closet door and raced back to her brush and soap-suds.

She was pleased. Not only had she succeeded in getting a sample of the cordial, she had made a useful discovery. From the matrons' closet, you could hear everything that went on next door in Harcourt's office. Not that there was anything worth listening to—just Wax-face walking back and forth and coughing once or twice. But another day she might have a reason to eavesdrop, and now she knew just how.

The dinner bell rang. Sally finished her work and scampered down to the refectory. After the meal, she stole out into the back garden of the office house. Here, all but hidden in a clump of shrubs, she had left an upended sieve, weighed down by a rock on either side.

"How you doing, Barney?" she whispered.

A plaintive squeaking came from under the sieve.

"I knows how you feels. I don't like being cooped up, neither." She looked around to make sure she was not observed, then unfolded her handkerchief and took out the morsel of bread. "I brought you some grub. Your belly must be thinking your throat's cut by now."

She slid the bread under the sieve, taking care not to let the mouse escape. Then she bent down, peering ruefully through the mesh. Barney was sniffing the bread, his whiskers all a-quiver. "It ain't my fault," she appealed to him. "I got to find out if the cordial's hocussed, and you're the only one as can help me. So remember, if you has to croak, it's in a good cause."

She did not see her prisoner again till after supper that night, when she contrived to sneak out to the garden with a candle. She found the bread nearly gone, and Barney capering about inside the sieve, as merry as a cricket.

"Nothing rum about that cordial, anyhow!" she whispered "Thanks, Barney, you been a trump. You can pike off now." She lifted the sieve, and the mouse streaked off into the garden.

At first her discovery seemed momentous. If the *bottle* of cordial was not poisoned, then the *dose* Mary took must have been. Since Mrs. Fiske had poured it out, it must have been she who had hocussed it. But after a little thought, Sally realized the matter was not so simple. Summerson's Strengthening Elixir was widely available, and all the bottles looked alike. What was to stop the murderer from poisoning the bottle on Tuesday, then replacing it with an identical, harmless bottle next day, after Mary was found dead?

It seemed the more she found out, the more questions she had. This investigation was a sharper's game: you could not win it. To make matters worse, she realized that if she could slip into the matron's closet, any of the other inmates could, too, provided they were willing to risk being punished or expelled if they were caught. She knew no inmate had left the refuge since Mary's death. Did that mean she must count all two dozen of them as suspects?

She was focusing too much on who *could* have killed Mary. She must think more about who *would*. Who had a compelling reason to want her dead? Not just dislike or general unscrupulousness, but a real motive?

Tomorrow was Tuesday. Mrs. Fiske would be presiding at the refuge for the first time since Sally arrived. She resolved to watch her like a hawk. Mrs. Fiske was her preferred suspect, partly because she did not like her, and partly because Mrs. Fiske had had such a good opportunity both to poison the cordial and to leave the laudanum bottle in Mary's room. All that was needed was one clue tying her firmly to the murder. And if there were any way to find that clue, Sally would.

It was a little-known fact among gentlemen that their manservants had their own clubs and social engagements, mirroring those of the gentlemen they served. Their prestige depended largely on their masters' rank and position. To be valet to Mr. Julian Kestrel, paragon of dandies, was no mean distinction. Charles Avondale's manservant, Lawrence Birkett, was immensely flattered when Dipper invited him out for a drop of hot flannel on Monday night.

After a few glasses, Birkett grew confidential. It was the very devil serving Mr. Avondale these days. He had always been a good enough master—liberal with wages and cast-off clothes. But lately he was in a fret about something. He went gadding from one engagement to another, without ever seeming to enjoy himself. At night, he kept glancing out of the windows, for all the world as if he thought someone might be lurking about the house. "And that's not the oddest thing," added Birkett portentously.

Dipper poured him another glass. "What could be rummer than that?"

"Well, I'm just going to tell you." Birkett paused to empty his glass. Dipper surreptitiously watered his own drink. He needed his wits about him.

"What was I saying?" Birkett muttered. "Oh, yes! Last week the strangest thing happened. Somebody slashed a whacking great letter *R* in the hood of Mr. Avondale's cabriolet. He was in a great stew about it. It *means* something, that's what I say."

"It was prob'ly just some kids having a lark."

"It *means* something," Birkett insisted. "Because you see, a day or two later, Mr. Avondale came home and found an *R* chalked on his front door."

"That's a queer start," Dipper admitted. "What's the *R* stand for, do you think?"

"I don't know, but I'll wager the master does. He was all of a tremble when he saw it. Of course, he didn't tell me anything about it. He don't trust me, Mr. Dipper, that's what it is."

"That's all your fancy," Dipper said soothingly. "Why shouldn't he trust you?"

"I don't know!" wailed Birkett, who had reached the maudlin stage. "I only know he doesn't. Sometimes he goes away for a week or more at a time, and he doesn't take me with him or even tell me where he's going."

"When was the last time he done that?"

"It was—oh, let me see—I think it was this past July. That was his longest trip yet—about a fortnight. He thought I hadn't an inkling where he was going, but I've got eyes, Mr. Dipper. I know a thing or two."

"You're up to your rigs, and no mistake."

"A-blo-sutely. The fact is, I packed for him He wanted warm woolen clothing—in July! So it's my belief he was travelling north, and pretty far north, too."

"You're a downy one. Your master don't half know your worth."

"Too true! I won't stand for it, Mr. Dipper. I'll find another place, that's what I'll do. Who knows if I'll even be paid next quarter-day?" He sank his voice. "Mr. Avondale's a bit dipped, you know."

"Been studying the history of the four kings, has he?"

"No, he was never much one for cards, nor any kind of gaming. I think he must have a bit of muslin tucked away, though why he's forking out so much for her, and making such a mystery of it, I can't say."

"How mucked out is he?"

"I don't know But he's looking to sell one of his favourite hunters—Delilah, her name is—which he wouldn't do unless he was under the hatches."

Birkett's voice was slurring, his eyes growing heavy. Dipper slipped in one last question before he nodded off. "How long has your governor been like this—looking out the window to see if he's being spied on, and that?"

"I don't know," Birkett mumbled. "I've only noticed it this past fortnight." His head dropped on the table, sending his glass rolling over the edge. Dipper caught it just in time.

He put Birkett in a hackney and gave the driver Avondale's address in Bury Street. Then he went home and recounted their conversation to Mr. Kestrel.

"Do you think we can rely on his information?" Julian asked.

"Oh, yes, sir. He's a square cove, though he looks like some'ut you'd buy off a fishmonger."

"Better useful than beautiful, I suppose. Lady Gayheart managed to be both, but I can't say I found her any great pleasure to question on that account. There's something repellent in beauty like hers—all cold, glossy surface, like a reflection in a glass." He pondered. "So Birkett says Avondale's been in a nervous state for a fortnight? That covers the period just before and just after Mary's death. But what the devil does the letter *R* stand for? *Refuge*? *Reclamation Society*?"

"There's other things it could stand for, sir. *Revenge*, or *reward*—"

"Or it could have nothing to do with Mary at all. That's the damnable thing about this sort of investigation—you need so many facts before you can even begin to say which ones are important."

"Do you want me to keep in with Birkett, sir?"

"That might be useful. But what I most need you to do is to go on sifting through the answers to the umbrella advertisement."

"Yes, sir." Dipper sighed. He had spent the past few days going round to umbrella makers and menders. More than a dozen of them claimed to have repaired black umbrellas with ram's head handles last week, but on closer enquiry their descriptions of the umbrellas, or of the damage done to them, had been wide of the mark. Dipper had gone so far as to trace two umbrellas back to their owners, but neither man fit Sally's portrait of Blinkers.

"For my part," said Julian, "I think it's time I struck up a closer acquaintance with Avondale. Birkett's given me just the pretext I need. Tomorrow I shall take a sudden interest in buying a hunter named Delilah."

If Thy Right Eye Offend Thee

Mrs. Fiske came to relieve Mrs. Jessop early Tuesday morning. A pall seemed to drop on the refuge. If Sally found it dreary and constricting before, it was ten times worse under Mrs. Fiske's sway. The woman was everywhere at once: spying, scolding, disapproving. Sally's only consolation was that she could finally study Mrs. Fiske at close quarters. It tickled her to think that, while Mrs. Fiske was watching the inmates, one of the inmates was watching her.

It soon became clear she was disturbed about something. She could not sit still, kept getting up and pacing about, and kneading her bony fingers. More than once she stopped an inmate to ask if Mr. Harcourt had arrived. Sally resolved to find out why she wanted to see him so badly.

He came at about four in the afternoon. Sally hid under the stairs, pretending to dust, while Mrs. Fiske spoke to him in the hallway. "I've been waiting to see you, sir. I'm in great need of your advice. I would have spoken to you sooner, but I know you've been very busy after—everything that's happened."

"You must never scruple to seek my counsel. You know I'm available to my flock at any hour of the day or night."

"Then will you give me a few minutes, sir? I'm sorely perplexed about something."

"Of course. Will you have the goodness to take tea with me in my office—in about an hour, shall we say?"

An hour later, Sally was shut in the matrons' closet next to Harcourt's office, with her ear glued to the wall. She would catch it royally for being absent from her work, but she did not care. She could not miss the chance to hear Harcourt's conversation with Mrs. Fiske.

"I hope Mr. Fiske isn't any worse?" he was saying.

"Oh, no, he's much better. He'll be up and about in a few days. That isn't what I wanted to talk to you about."

"What is it, then?"

"It all began last Wednesday, just before we all left for the inquest. You were meeting with the trustees, and I'd put Miss Nettleton to bed after she had that attack of the vapours. I went to the front door for a breath of air, and that was when I saw—Caleb."

"Caleb?" Harcourt sounded startled. "Are you certain?"

"I am now. I wasn't then. I'd barely caught sight of him when he turned away and lost himself in the crowd. There were a great many people milling about—the news about Mary had got out, and of course people must needs come poking their noses into anything that smacks of a scandal."

"What was he doing when you saw him?"

"Lurking. Standing off a little by himself and watching the refuge. That was partly what made me recognize him—that way he had of looking all alone in a crowd of people. All the same, I told myself he couldn't be Caleb. He did look like him, though very much changed. But what would Caleb be doing skulking about the refuge? I hadn't seen him or heard a word about him for two years. I thought my eyes must be playing tricks on me. Then when I got home that night, Mr. Fiske was off his head with fever, and I was so taken up with looking after him, I had to put Caleb out of my mind."

"But now you say you're certain it was Caleb you saw?"

"I'm certain, because I saw him again. On Saturday morning, Mr. Fiske was in his right mind for the first time since he was taken ill. Until then, he'd been talking the most complete gibberish. 'Poor little thing,' he'd say. 'Poor little thing. Her hands were so cold, cold as stones.' And then his eyes would fill up with tears, and he'd moan, 'I'm sorry, I'm sorry.' Of course it was Mary's death that was preying on his mind. He had a shameful weakness for that girl. Just because she was pretty and spoke like a lady, he'd have made a heroine of her, instead of what she was."

"We must have patience with our frailer brethren, Mrs. Fiske." Harcourt's voice was a little weary. Sally guessed he had heard many such complaints from her before.

"I try, Mr. Harcourt, but you can't conceive the crosses I have to bear. There's simply no knowing what freakish thing Mr. Fiske may do next. While he was delirious, he suddenly cried out, 'Oh my God, my boots!' I asked him about it afterward, and what do you think he said? He said he'd given away a perfectly good pair of boots to some tramp he saw on the street! Now, that is exactly the kind of bird-witted thing he would do. I don't wonder he was sorry about it afterward. They cost ten and sixpence!"

"*Lay not up for yourselves treasures upon earth, but in heaven*," said Harcourt mechanically. "But I distract you. You were going to tell me about the next time you saw Caleb."

"Yes. As I was saying, Mr. Fiske had a lucid period Saturday morning and wanted very badly to see the post from his shop. I wasn't surprised—he's so devoted to that shop of his, he can never bear to be away from it long. In fact, he spends a deal more time there than he does at home. Anyway, he was in such a pother about the post that finally I said I would go and get it, if only to stop him making such a fuss.

"I was walking up Eastcheap toward the shop, when I saw Caleb again. He was moving away from the shop in the other direction, and disappeared round a corner before I could get a good look at him. But this time I was sure beyond all doubt that it was Caleb. I hurried into the shop and asked Mr. Fiske's apprentice if a young man had just been in, but he said no. I expect Caleb came looking for Mr. Fiske and turned tail when he realized he wasn't there."

"Did he notice you, either that time or the previous time you saw him?"

"I'm sure he didn't. He would have given some sign. The fear of God would have come upon him! He knows what to expect from me, if he ever falls into my hands. *If thy right eye offend thee, pluck it out!* the Bible says.

"I went straight home and told Mr. Fiske I'd seen Caleb for the second time in a week. He had the brazenness to tell me I must be mistaken. Mistaken! 'Do you think I'm a fool?' I said. 'Do you think I don't know my own son?'

"He went on implying I was imagining things. He insisted he hadn't seen Caleb since we came to London, and had no idea where he was. I'm sure he was lying. He's protecting the boy, just as he did two years ago, when he put the constables off the scent long enough to let Caleb get away. He's always denied it, but I knew better. The village knew better, too—that's why we had to move away and come to London, where nobody would know us. Even if Mr. Fiske hadn't been suspected of helping Caleb escape, how could we live with the disgrace of having a son like him?"

"I thought nothing was ever proved against him," said Harcourt.

"Proof—that's all humbug! A game lawyers play. Any fool could see he was guilty. A young, strong girl like that doesn't drown in a shallow stream. Even a drivelling half-wit like her would know enough to get up and come out. Somebody held her down in the water—the surgeon who examined her body said so. And Caleb was the last person seen with her. What more proof could anyone need?

"Of course Mr. Fiske could never bear to think ill of him. Always saying what a meek boy he was, what a proper-behaved lad. Well, he seemed meek enough, but the devil was in him, in spite of all I could do to drive it out. Hardly a day went by that I didn't give him a beating or a box on the ear or lock him in the coalcellar, and still I couldn't make a good, God-fearing Christian out of him. Especially with Mr. Fiske standing about wringing his hands, feeling sorry for him. Taking his part.

"I don't know what to do now, Mr. Harcourt. Ought I to go to the authorities and tell them I've seen Caleb in London? He was suspected of murder and—that other unspeakable crime—in our village. He would have been arrested if he hadn't run away. Surely the London magistrates would want him captured and punished?"

"You mustn't do anything hasty, Mrs. Fiske. Remember how little opportunity you had to observe him. The first time, you caught only the merest glimpse, and the second time he was walking away from you."

"Yes, but I know it was Caleb!"

"And of course I believe you," said Harcourt, with his beautiful, practiced earnestness. "But the authorities might not, especially since your husband says he knows nothing of Caleb's being in London."

"Well, of course he would lie for Caleb—he has before."

"And that was very wrong of him, but he isn't as strong in his principles as you are. The weak are too often apt to mistake condonation for compassion."

"Oh, yes, indeed, Mr. Harcourt! So you think I ought to say nothing about seeing Caleb?"

"I think you would be drawing scandal on yourself to no purpose. I know you would gladly sacrifice your own comfort and worldly position—even give up your only child to disgrace and punishment—for sake of what is right, but surely you ought not to jeopardize your good name and your husband's success in his trade, to pursue what really amounts to a chimera. You have a responsibility to the many people working with us in our cause, who look upon you as an inspiration and an example."

"I never thought of it in that light, sir. I daresay you're right—I won't tell anyone about Caleb for the present. But I'll keep my eyes open. If Mr. Fiske is having aught to do with Caleb behind my back, I'll know of it—and the law will know of it, too! I don't want to pull an old house down on our heads, but Caleb is a grievous sinner. He's flouted all I tried to teach him. He must be caught and punished!"

Harcourt murmured sympathetically. Sally realized he was trying to put an end to the interview, and thought she had better get out of her hiding-place and back to work. She opened the door of the matrons' closet a crack. Finding the coast clear, she slipped out and hastened upstairs to the workroom opposite the chapel, where she was supposed to be helping a group of inmates hem sheets.

"Kind of you to join us," said Wideawake Peg.

Sally curtsied saucily.

"You're in high feather now," Peg retorted, "but Himself'll make you sing 'oh be joyful' on the other side of your mouth when he hears you've been missing from work above half an hour."

Sally itched to grab hold of Peg's black locks and yank for all she was worth. She was out of temper with her already. For the past two days, ever since their conversation near the boghouse, she had been keeping an eye on Peg, and prowling around the back gardens whenever she got the chance, in the hope of learning more about how Peg smuggled things into the refuge. But she had had no luck—Peg was too clever to leave clues behind.

She kept her temper. This was no time to get herself thrown out of the refuge. "All right," she grumbled, "what'll you take not to snitch?"

"A shilling, and cheap at the price, I'm thinking."

"If I wants to get shaved, I'll go to a barber's."

"Suit yourself," Peg shrugged.

"Oh, all right!" Sally plunked herself down in a chair and took up a needle and thread. "I'd take her for a highway robber," she whispered to Florrie, "only she ain't half civil enough."

Florrie giggled. "Where you been all this time?"

"I was meeting Wax-face in his office for a bit of threepenny upright."

"Don't make me laugh so! Peg's looking. Really, now, where were you?"

What's that to you? Sally wondered. "I was having a nap. I don't get no sleep, on account of Red Jane snores fit to bring the house down."

She bent over her sewing, discouraging further conversation. She wanted to think. Till today, she had never heard that the Fiskes had a son, much less that he was wanted for murder. Had he really drowned a girl in his village? And what was the other crime he stood accused of—the one Mrs. Fiske could not bring herself to name? Sally hoped he was not guilty. Mrs. Fiske's account of his upbringing roused her to take his part. Her own father could be free with his hands, especially when he was boozing, but this cold-blooded beating of a boy, day in and day out, to save his soul, seemed much worse to her. All the same, the suspicions about him might be true. And if they were, his hanging about Fiske's shop and the refuge was intriguing. Could he have had a hand in Mary's death?

If anyone knew the truth about Caleb, surely it was Mr. Fiske. Mrs. Fiske had said he was nearly well—perhaps he would soon come to the refuge. If he did, Sally was determined to beard him. He had been fond of Mary—surely he would want to see justice done by her. And he would be a useful ally, if he could be trusted.

But that was a very great "if." Suppose Caleb had had a hand in Mary's death? According to Mrs. Fiske, there was nothing Fiske would not do to protect his son. For that matter, how could Sally be sure Fiske had not killed Mary himself? His affection for her might have been a blind—or the mask for a secret lust that had driven him to violence. He had been at the refuge on the day Mary died and could have poisoned the bottle of cordial. Next morning, when he came to examine her body, he could have brought an identical bottle of cordial and switched it for the poisoned one. When he was delirious, he had moaned, *I'm sorry, I'm sorry*. Was that a confession of guilt?

She did not know, and had no means of finding out till she could talk to Fiske. But while she waited for a chance to waylay him, there was something else she could do: she could keep an eye out for Caleb. He had been seen near the refuge once before—why shouldn't he come back? Of course, it would not be easy to pick him out. Young men often lingered about the refuge, curious to get a look at the inmates. How could she tell if one of them was Caleb? Besides, she was so busy all day, she had little time to look out the windows. It was hard enough to appear at a front window long enough to make her noon signal. At night, though, she might be able to keep watch, at least for an hour or two. There was little chance that anything would come of it. But what did she have to lose?

The morning after Dipper's conversation with Birkett, Julian sent Avondale a note saying that he had heard he was selling his horse Delilah. If so, would he be good enough to show her to him? Avondale wrote back promptly, offering to take him to see the horse tomorrow.

On Wednesday, the two young men went to the mews where Delilah was stabled. She was a beautiful bay. Julian admired but could not afford her; it cost him more than enough to feed and stable the horse he already had. But he walked around her like a serious buyer, asking the appropriate questions.

"She's a fine bit of blood," said Avondale. "I know there was never a fellow selling a horse who didn't say so, but you can see it to look at her."

"You seem in two minds about parting with her."

"No choice! I'm deuced hard-up."

"Indeed?" Julian lifted his brows. To express sympathy would be out of place; young men of fashion did not condole with each other about a misfortune so widespread and uninteresting as being in debt. "That's rather an achievement. Anyone can run aground during the season, but it takes a singular imagination to find anything worth ruining oneself for at this time of year."

Avondale laughed, but wincing a little, as though the movement opened a wound. "There's no imagination involved, I'm afraid. It's just the usual thing—debts of honour, tailors, wine merchants. Well, what do you say about Delilah?"

"I'll have to think it over."

"I'll give you a day or two, but after that I'll have to start showing her to other buyers. You understand."

"Of course."

They came out of the stables, blinking at the sunlight, and taking deep draughts of fresh air. "I heard the most curious rumour the other day," Julian remarked.

"What?" Avondale looked at him quickly

"Someone told me your father was hand in glove with a clergyman, and had taken to rounding up Drury Lane vestals for reformation."

"Oh, you mean the What-do-you-call-it Society. Yes, that's rather a lark, isn't it? You mustn't think the old man's got religious in his dotage. He's just amusing himself. He says that, after doing so much in his youth to support those girls in their chosen calling, he has a mind to rescue some of them, if only to make room for new blood."

Julian regarded him thoughtfully. Avondale was leaning his hand against a post, his dark blue eyes alight with amusement. There was an easy grace about him—the confidence of one who knew his own beauty, and used it as an animal uses its strength or speed, to gain an advantage. Suspicions glanced off his charm, like arrows off armour. If the mention of the Reclamation Society disturbed him, he gave no sign.

"I thought I'd stop at a coffee-house," said Julian, "if you care to come."

"Can't, I'm afraid. I'm dining at Caroline's, and I've got to make myself presentable. You wouldn't understand: you can come out of a stable looking as if you'd spent the day in the bow-window at White's, but the rest of us have to prink to get the same effect. Speaking of Caroline, what the plague have you done to her? She's been talking about you for two days."

"I'm flattered."

"You ought to fly the country."

"Lady Gayheart is a very charming woman. Her brother may not be in the best position to appreciate that."

"Wait till you know her better. She's monstrous vain, and selfish into the bargain. If she weren't such a stunner, no one would touch her with a pair of tongs. Well, let me know when you've made a decision about Delilah. If you've got any other questions, I'll be glad to answer them."

Julian did have several more questions. He had held them in reserve on purpose, so that he would have an excuse to call on Avondale at home in the evening. In his own house, he would not be able to run off just as the conversation got interesting. Then, too, one always learned more about a fellow by looking around his home. And, most important, Birkett had said Avondale seemed skittish at night, as though he thought his house was being watched. If someone was spying on him, Julian meant to find out who, and why.

Miss Grantham's Bridegroom

On Wednesday night, Ada Grantham sat at her dressing-table, combing her hair. After a while she sighed, put down the comb, and propped her chin on her hands.

This morning it had happened at last. Major Thorndike had called and asked her mother for permission to address her. Mrs. Grantham gave him her blessing and summoned Ada to speak with him in the drawing room. Ada went in fully intending to accept him—and at the last moment, her courage failed her. It was no light thing, she realized, to give herself to a man she did not love.

She compromised—told him she was honoured by his proposal, and asked for a day to consider carefully before she gave him her answer. He commended her prudence and agreed to return tomorrow. If it had been Charles, he would have pressed ardently for an answer—but it isn't Charles, she told herself. It never will be Charles.

The rest of the day was dreadful. Mama dithered, longing to see her safely married, but afraid to press her against her will. The younger children knew something was in the wind and trailed after her, asking questions. Then her cousin Caroline called, and Mama *would* tell her about Mayor Thorndike's offer. Caroline gushed with admiration for Ada's cleverness. Such a sly-boots, bringing him up to scratch so gracefully! Why, he had five thousand pounds a year, and his first cousin was a baronet with no sons, and said to be sickly!

Caroline's praise stung Ada more than any criticism could. She saw her project in its ugliest light. She was, quite simply, marrying for money. What was the difference between her and women who sold themselves in the streets?

She summoned all her resolution. This wavering must not go on. Tomorrow she would give Major Thorndike her answer, and that answer would be yes. Once she was bound by her word of honour and could not escape, things would be easier. At least she would be at peace—

The street-door bell rang violently, and kept on ringing. Ada threw a shawl over her nightdress, caught up her candle, and ran out into the hall. Her mother met her at the top of the stairs. They heard Sukey, the maid of all work, answering the door two floors below "Lawks!" she exclaimed. "Mr. Charles!"

Mrs. Grantham started downstairs, clutching an immense shawl around her. Ada followed. Younger Granthams peered over the landing-rails or spilled down the stairs

Charles was in the front hall, pulling off his gloves and stuffing them into his hat. His wild eyes fixed on Mrs. Grantham. "I'm sorry to call at this hour, but I have to see Ada."

"I hardly think, at this time of night—" Mrs. Grantham began.

"Please, Aunt Dot! I'll only keep her for a few minutes."

Ada went down to him, pale and composed. "It's all right, Mama. I won't let Charles stay late."

She brought him into a little back parlour on the ground floor. There was no fire. Charles took off his coat and draped it around her, then kept his hands on her shoulders. "I've just come from Caroline's. She told me Thorndike's come up to scratch."

"Yes."

"Ada, tell me you haven't accepted him! Tell me it's not too late!"

"I told him I would think it over."

"That's just what you won't do. I'll make the decision for you—your answer is no! Ada—darling, wonderful Ada!—did you think I'd let you marry anyone but me?"

She felt the colour rush into her face. "Charles—I—I don't know what to say. I'm so surprised—"

"How can you be? You must know I've been eating my heart out over the idea of your marrying Thorndike."

"I knew you didn't like it. But that isn't the same thing as wanting to—to marry me yourself."

"I know I've been a long time coming to the point—"

"Perhaps you were wise, and knew your mind. This is a sudden impulse, you may think better of it tomorrow—"

"There's nothing sudden about it. I've thought of nothing else for weeks but making you my wife."

"Then—forgive me, Charles—why haven't you spoken sooner?"

"Because I know I'm not half good enough for you. Pray God you never know just how unworthy I am! But no one's ever loved you as I do—no one can, and no one will! Marrying you is the only worthy aspiration I've ever had. To live up to you will bring out the good in me, if anything can."

"I'm not a saint," she faltered. "I can't *save* you."

"Can you love me?"

What could she say? *Yes* would commit her to accept him. *No* would be a flagrant lie.

"Can you look at me and tell me you don't love me?"

"No," she whispered.

"Then you must marry me, Ada! We were meant to be together. Say you'll have me, and I'll labour all my life to make you happy. You'll never be hurt or sorry, I swear it—"

"Yes, Charles," she heard herself answer. "I'll marry you. Yes."

He caught her against his breast. She clung to him, her bridges burned, her future transformed with a single word. She tipped back her head to look at him—see if it was really true. She caught him unawares, and felt chilled to the heart. It was not love or triumph she read in his eyes. It was grief, remorse, despair.

By Thursday, Dipper was sick of the sight of umbrellas. He had listened to some twenty descriptions of them and their owners in the past few days, and he was no closer to finding Blinkers. At least his task was easier now: the responses to the advertisement were dwindling. Today there were only three, and two of them did not fit the timing of Blinkers's encounter with Sally.

The third was from a little shop on the south side of the river, off the High Street. Dipper went there and spoke with the owner, a round, bright-eyed old man named Mr. Tuttle. He described how a young man had brought a black umbrella with a ram's head handle in to be repaired last Tuesday. It was a good one, strong and sturdy. Tuttle was sure it had been used in a fight—no mere rainstorm could inflict that kind of damage.

"I can't tell you much about the owner," he said, scratching his head. "Very ordinary, he was—you'd never look at him twice. But my delivery boy, Ned, as took the umbrella back to him when it was mended, says he remembers him well. Ned! Here, Ned! Where *is* the lad?"

A boy of about fourteen swaggered into the shop. He clearly aspired to cut a figure as a gent. He wore a tailcoat much too long for him, soiled white gloves, and a beaver hat that looked as if it had been kicked around the neighbourhood. "You wants me, old shaver?"

"You be civil, now. This here is the man as sent us that broadsheet—the one with the ten-pound reward for information about the umbrella."

The boy pushed his top-hat back on his head and looked Dipper up and down. "Now, that's a queer start, that is. Who'd give ten quid to know about somebody's broken umbrella?"

"Me master would," said Dipper imperturbably.

Ned tried to stare him out of countenance. Dipper returned the stare with interest. At last Ned acknowledged defeat and told his story. He had delivered the mended umbrella last Wednesday to the address the owner had left. It was an office above a tobacconist's, in a little court a few streets away. There was a glass plate in the office door, with "Smith and Co., Dealers and Importers" printed on it.

"I remember the cove as answered, 'coz he didn't give me nothing for me trouble, the pinch-fist! Just opened the umbrella and looked it over careful-like, as if he'd have been glad to find the work done wrong, then paid for the repairs and sent me about me business. He was quiet, but very toploftical in his ways—like he was Captain Grand, and everybody else was dog's meat."

"What did he look like?" Dipper asked.

"He was thin, and not above five-and-twenty, and, he wore gold rimmed specs. I don't know what his name was. I didn't see nobody else there, so maybe he was Smith, like the sign."

"Did he have a mouse on his dial?"

"He did, now you mentions it! Just here." Ned pointed to his forehead, above his left eye. "And too bad the cove as give it to him aimed too high, and didn't tickle his sneezer."

Dipper thanked Ned and Mr. Tuttle, paid the reward, and asked for directions to Smith and Company. A few minutes' walk brought him to a narrow, dusty court, with a tobacconist's at the far end. He went up to the shop and peered in. A middle-aged man was arranging pipes on a shelf, while a girl of about twenty measured out snuff for a customer at the counter.

Dipper opened the street door and went in. To his left was a door into the shop, while before him a flight of stairs led up to the first floor. Just then a young man came down the stairs. He was thin and nondescript, and wore gold-rimmed spectacles. He brushed past Dipper and went out.

Blinkers!—Dipper was sure of it. He fit Sally's description up to the nines. Dipper watched him cross the little court and disappear round the corner. Then he went upstairs. Here was the door Ned had described, with "Smith and Co., Dealers and Importers" painted on the dingy glass. Dipper tried it, but it was locked. He went downstairs again, and into the tobacconist's.

Here he made himself at home, browsing through the different brands of tobacco, and perusing the theatre playbills tacked on the walls. The shop was evidently a family concern. He gathered from snatches of conversation that the girl was the middle-aged man's daughter. He surveyed her out of the corner of his eye. She was slim and delicate, pale from living out of the sun, with big, light grey eyes that gave great charm to an otherwise plain face. Her father called her Annie.

Dipper smiled at her from time to time. She cast down her eyes and pretended to be busy with some task, but he saw her peek up at him through her lashes when she thought he was not looking. After a while her father went out, leaving her in charge of the shop. Dipper waited till he was out of sight, then went up to the counter. Annie tried to look as if she had had no idea he would come and talk to her, but a blush spread over her pale cheeks, and the eyes she lifted to his were softly bright.

"Morning!" said Dipper

"Good morning, sir."

"Fine day."

"Yes, it is."

"I could say I come in to buy some 'bacca, but it wouldn't be true."

"Then—then I can't help you "

"That don't follow."

She looked away, blushing still more. "I—I don't think Pa would like me talking to a stranger."

"That's settled, easy as winking. Me name's Dipper, and I'm valet to a gentry-cove. How d'ye do?"

"How do you do? My name is Anne Price."

"This your pa's place?" He waved his hand at the shop.

"Yes. That is, we're tenants. We have our shop in the front room here, and live in the back room and the basement."

"What's up the first floor?"

"We let it. There's an office up there—Smith and Company, it's called."

"What's it do?"

She looked troubled. "We don't know, exactly. Mr. Rawdon—that's Mr. Joseph Rawdon, the gentleman who uses the office—don't talk about his work."

"If his name's Rawdon, who's Smith?"

"I don't know. I've never seen anyone from the company except Mr. Rawdon." She added, in a rush of confidence, "It's odd, you know—their sign says they're dealers and importers, but they never seem to deal in or import anything. They don't bring any kind of goods to the office. I saw inside it once—there's nothing there but papers. People call there, though. A few men come quite often, and some women, too—very ladylike, and thirty at least. I don't know what they talk to Mr. Rawdon about."

"What's he like?"

"He's very quiet. We'd never know he was there if we didn't see him go in and out. He comes in every day at about ten o'clock, and leaves by five. He don't have anything to do with us, except when he pays the rent on quarter-day, and when he comes in once in a while to buy a newspaper. He's been there for close to two years now, and he's never given any trouble. Pa says we're lucky to have him."

"But you don't like him?"

"No," she admitted. "He's so quiet, and he watches everything so close, and he always seems to be sneering, even when you can't see it on his face. And there's a way he looks at me—it's not leering, exactly, but it makes me afraid to be alone with him. He—he's not quite real."

"What do you mean?"

"Oh, he never laughs, never shows any feelings, sets himself so apart from people. We don't even know where he lives. He wouldn't give an address, and since he pays his rent so prompt, Pa don't like to press him about it. And there's something else. Once when he was here buying a newspaper, he got a bit of grit in his eye and had to take off his spectacles. He laid them down on the paper for a minute, and the print didn't look any different. They're not real spectacles—they're just plain glass."

"He sounds like a rum customer. I wouldn't have nothing to do with him, if I was you."

"Do you think he—he could be doing something illegal?"

Dipper shrugged. "When a cove keeps himself to himself like that, the odds is he's got some'ut to hide. He could be a fence, or a resurrection-cove, or be drawing the King's picture."

"Drawing—you mean, forging banknotes? Lord, how dreadful! Suppose the constables found out, and thought Pa knew all about it! We could lose the shop, and—"

"Now, don't take on," he said soothingly. "This cove Rawdon may be on the square. I'm only saying—it's possible he ain't."

"I wish I knew for sure."

Dipper cocked his head, considering. "You ever thought of having a look round his office, to try if you can find out what he does?"

"But he always keeps it locked when he's not there."

"Don't your pa have a key?"

"Y-es," she said uncertainly. "But he wouldn't want me going up there while Mr. Rawdon was out. He says it makes no odds how he gets his living, so long as he pays his rent. I think, if there's something hole-and-corner about Mr. Rawdon's business, he'd rather not know. But I don't feel that way. I'd as lief know the worst."

"Mr. Rawdon ever work late, or come to the office at darkmans?"

"No, not as I've ever seen."

"So if you was to get the key and nip up there some night, you could have a look round, and he'd never be the wiser."

"But Pa might find me missing and come looking for me, and if he caught me up there, he'd comb my head—" She broke off.

"You've got an idea," said Dipper.

"Well—Pa's going away on Monday, to visit my aunt in Kent. He'll be gone a whole day and a night. I'm to stay behind and look after the shop."

"There you are, then. You can have a look round the office while he's gone."

"But I'd be afraid. It's true Mr. Rawdon never comes here at night—but what if this one night he came, and caught me?"

"I'd come with you, if you wanted me to."

She blushed. "That's good of you, but I—I couldn't. It ain't proper—and besides, I don't even know you—"

"That's true," he admitted. "I could be meaning to rob the till. But the fact is—I ain't. I'd like to see you get shut of that Rawdon cove. It ain't safe for you as long as he's up there."

Realization dawned in her eyes. "You came here on purpose to ask me about Mr. Rawdon! You know there's something wrong about him."

He nodded candidly.

"What do you know?"

"Not so much as I'd like to. I'll tell you this: he had a brush with me sister, and darkened her daylights."

"Lord! I'm sorry."

"So, you see, I'd like to serve him out. And if I can find out what racket he's in, I can shop him."

"Yes, I see," she said slowly. "We could help each other."

"That's the ticket! Will you trust me?"

"I don't know if I ought to—but I will. Come on Monday night, at midnight. You—you wouldn't mind coming in through the back basement window? People hereabouts talk so, and there's no telling who might be awake."

"I will."

"You know," she said in a low voice, "I'd have agreed at once, if you'd told me what you were about."

"But I didn't know you, did I, any more than you knew me? I had to be a bit peery, till I'd dropped down to you."

"Yes, I see that. Only—you made me think it was because you liked me that you was being so friendly."

He ducked his head, coaxing up her downcast eyes. "I do like you."

"You don't have to say that to be civil."

"I ain't being civil. Do I look as if I was?"

"You—you look as if I ought not to let you in while Pa's away!"

"You've still got time to change your mind."

"What would happen if I did?"

"I'd stay right here till you changed it back."

"That might be nice," she said shyly. "But you'd better go. Pa will be back any minute. Oh, wait, I've thought of something! Pa will take the key to Mr. Rawdon's office with him when he goes away."

"How do you know?"

"He always takes his keys when he goes on a journey. He keeps them on a ring, in the left front pocket of his greatcoat."

"Oh." Dipper broke into a grin. "When's he piking off to Kent?"

"His coach leaves at half past five on Monday morning, from the George."

"That's all right, then."

"What are you going to do?"

"You say it's the left front pocket?"

"Yes."

"Right as a trivet. I'll have the keys with me when I comes on Monday night."

The Letter *R*

On Thursday evening, Julian dined early and alone. Dipper told him all he had learned about Joseph Rawdon. When they had talked the subject out, Julian spent an hour or two at the pianoforte, trying over some Schubert compositions that a Viennese friend had sent him. But his mind wandered; an old ballad ran through his head, and his fingers strayed over the keys, picking out the tune:

Of all the girls that are so smart,
There's none like pretty Sally.
She is the darling of my heart—

He shut up the piano, put on his hat and gloves, and went to call on Charles Avondale.

It was only a few minutes' walk to Avondale's house in Bury Street. But the night was rainy, the cobblestones slick with mud. Julian had no choice but to take a hackney: a gentleman with a sartorial reputation to maintain could not arrive at a friend's house in mud-spattered evening trousers. So he sat in the damp, dingy coach, picking straw from the floor out of his shoes, while the driver negotiated his way inch by inch through the traffic in Piccadilly. A thick fog made things worse: the street was a yellowish grey blur, shot through with light from gaslamps and shop windows.

Julian got out of the hackney at the corner of Bury Street. He had never been to Avondale's house, but he found it easily enough by the number. It was a narrow, elegant bachelor's lodging. He had just set his foot on the front step when the door flew open, and a woman appeared. She wore a threadbare black cloak, with a plaid shawl around her head and shoulders.

She stopped abruptly and stared at him, breathing hard. The shawl around her head fell back, and he saw her clearly by the light from the lantern over the door. She was thin and pale, not above thirty, with gaunt cheeks and eyes ringed with shadows. Her rust-red hair was carelessly done up in back. What might once have been fashionable side-curls hung in an unkempt fringe around her face.

"Are ye a friend of his—of Charles Avondale's?" she whispered.

"We're acquainted, yes."

She came close, her great green eyes boring into him. There was a fetid smell about her of unwashed clothes and skin. Her hand shot out and closed around his arm like a claw. "Ask your friend Charles what he's done wi' Rosemary."

"Who is Rosemary?"

"He'll know." She let go of his arm and flitted past him.

He pursued her. "Wait! I don't understand your message. If you'll stop a moment, let me talk to you—"

"I willna!" She walked faster, slipping and shuffling along the wet pavement.

"How can I help you, if you won't tell me what's wrong?"

"I didna ask for your help! Gang awa', and leave me be!"

"But—"

"No! 'Tis another of his tricks! I'll not be befooled a second time!" She caught sight of a watchman and hurried up to him, practically sliding into his arms. "Tell that man to stop following me!"

The watchman held up his lantern. The woman did not stay to be scrutinized, but darted off, the fog closing in around her. Julian started after her, but the watchman blocked his way. "Now, sir," he said, tapping his truncheon meaningfully against his other hand, "what do you want to go disturbing of the peace for?"

Julian cursed his luck. How had he contrived to run into the one watchman in London who was awake, able-bodied, and inclined to do his duty? "You don't understand. That woman is in trouble—"

"I seen that," the watchman chuckled, "and it's up to me to see she ain't in trouble no more. So you be a sensible young man, and don't make me take you on a visit to the magistrate's court. That's a hunpleasant business, that is. Makes for bad feeling on both sides. And, really, sir, if you don't mind me being a bit personal, you could do a sight better than that nasty bit of bones you was chasing."

"Thank you, Officer. I'm sorry to have troubled you. Good evening."

Julian walked off serenely down Bury Street in the opposite direction from the one the woman had taken. At the first side street, he doubled back, threading his way swiftly through the mass of umbrellas, street-sellers' carts, and young men on their way to gaming hells or fashionable brothels. When he reached the corner of Bury and Jermyn streets, he looked about for the woman and asked bystanders if they had seen her. But he knew already it would be no use. She had had plenty of time to disappear, especially on a foggy night, in a lively neighbourhood like this.

He gave it up and went into a public house for a draught of hot brandy-and-water. Who was she? he wondered. Her speech was Scottish, and to judge by her clothes she had fallen on hard times. What had she to do with Avondale? What did she mean, she would not be befooled a second time? Above all, who was Rosemary?

He could not recall ever hearing that name linked with Avondale or his family. Rosemary, he mused. Rosemary for remembrance. Rosemary—with an *R*.

Could it have been the Scottish woman who had left the *R*s slashed in the hood of Avondale's carriage and chalked on his front door? Why was she there this evening? And did any of this have anything to do with Mary and the refuge?

Perhaps not. And then again, perhaps the girl known as Mary had simply dropped the "Rose" from the beginning of her name. If so, the answer to the Scotswoman's question, what had Charles done with Rosemary, might be grim indeed.

He left the public house and made his way back to Avondale's. His trousers were caked with mud, and worse than mud, but there was no help for it. He scraped off his shoes at the boot-scraper outside Avondale's front door, and rang.

Birkett answered. Julian could see why Dipper had likened him to a fish. He had round, vacant eyes, and his mouth hung open a little, as if his jaw had not been fastened properly.

"I have to see your master," Julian told him. "It's very important."

"He's not at home, sir."

Julian's brows went up. Birkett coughed and looked at the ground.

Julian took out his card-case. "I shall send in my card all the same. I have a message for your master, and I shan't leave until I've delivered it. So I suggest you look about, and see if you can find him."

He wrote on the back of one of his cards: *I must see you about Rosemary*. Birkett let him into the front hall and took the card upstairs.

A minute or two ticked by. Julian walked back and forth unhurriedly, his hands clasped behind him. All at once there was a volley of footsteps on the stairs. Avondale erupted into the hallway, clad in shirt, trousers, and dressing-gown. "What's the meaning of this? What do you know about—about—what you wrote on your card?"

"What have you done with Rosemary?" asked Julian coolly

Avondale gripped the banister-rail. His face was paper-white. "We can't talk here. Come with me."

He led Julian into the front room off the hallway. It was an informal parlour, strewn with riding whips, boxing gloves, cricket bats, and foils. Sporting prints and a racing calendar hung on the walls.

Avondale locked the door, and stirred the fire into life with a few quick stabs of the poker. Then he turned to Julian. "All right. In God's name, what do you know about Rosemary?"

"What have you done with her?" Julian repeated.

"I must be going mad." Avondale clasped his head in his hands "How the plague did Megan get *you* to take up her cause?"

Julian had no intention of revealing how little he really knew. "I came to see you about the horse, and found her just leaving. We—talked."

"What—what are you going to do?"

"I don't know yet. Is Rosemary dead?"

Avondale started violently. "No, of course not! Is that what Megan told you? If she did, she was lying—trying to get your sympathy. Damn her! Oh, damn her soul to hell!"

He flung open a cupboard and pulled out a brandy decanter. With shaking hands, he poured himself a glass and drank it down. His charm began to struggle to the surface. "I beg your pardon. How frightfully rude. Will you have a glass?"

"No, thank you. If Rosemary isn't dead, where is she?"

"If I wouldn't tell Megan, why in God's name should I tell you?"

"To avoid my getting the wrong idea? It's a devilish awkward thing, making young women disappear. It leads to very embarrassing enquiries. If you don't explain, I shall have to tell someone about this. I shall feel a duty to see that something is done."

Avondale stared at him as though stunned. Then he looked away slowly. He picked up the decanter to pour another glass, then changed his mind and set it down again. "You're all wrong about this, Kestrel," he said abruptly. "I haven't made anyone disappear. Surely you can see Megan's off her head?"

"Do you mean Rosemary is a figment of her imagination? She seemed real enough to you a few moments ago."

"Rosemary is real. It's this notion that I—made away with her—that's a delusion." He came closer, all persuasiveness, like a schoolboy sharing secrets. "Come, what did Megan tell you? What maggot has she got in her head now?"

"She said enough to make me curious. I know this wasn't the first time she'd come to your house at night. And I suspect she's been leaving you reminders of Rosemary."

"She has—the devil fly away with her! Look here, Kestrel, we're both men of the world. I'll tell you the truth, but you've got to give me your word as a gentleman you won't let it get about. You see, I'm engaged to be married. My cousin Ada's just accepted me."

He paused to give Julian an opportunity to congratulate him. But Julian only looked at him, his brows raised in cool expectation.

"Well," Avondale resumed, "you can understand. I don't want to fling a scandal in her face directly she's promised to marry me. Rosemary is—she's a relation of Megan's. I—well, it's the usual tale. I got into a scrape with her, and Megan found out about it and followed us to London. But Rosemary's not with me anymore, and I can't tell Megan where she is because, frankly, I don't know. She's probably gone on to some other fellow. Her sort mostly do."

Julian had been debating over how much of his story to believe, but this last part he knew was a lie. Avondale must know what had become of Rosemary, because when Julian had asked him earlier where she was, he had flashed back, *If I wouldn't tell Megan, why in God's name should I tell you?* It was all very well if he chose to hide a mistress somewhere, or pension her off now that he was going to be married. Certainly it was no business of Julian's. But what if he had hidden her in the refuge his father supported? And what if he could not reveal where she was because he knew she was dead?

Julian recalled Mary's letter, abasing herself for an act of folly, putting out a feeler in the hope that some relation would forgive her and take her back. Could her letter have been intended for Megan, and could someone have intercepted it and passed it on to Avondale? Mary was killed on the night after Sally stole the letter. Perhaps Avondale moved swiftly to see that she never made a second appeal.

But questions loomed in Julian's mind. If Avondale had Mary—Rosemary?—killed, it could not have been simply to hide their love affair from his future bride. Miss Grantham would realize he must have had mistresses. Even the most chaste, respectable girl understood that young men-about-town did not live like monks. No, Avondale would have needed a more compelling reason to be rid of Rosemary than that. Julian could think of no such motive that fit with Mary's letter, or her behaviour at the refuge.

"That woman I met tonight," he said, "Miss—?"

"MacGowan," supplied Avondale unwillingly.

"She was obviously Scottish. Was Rosemary Scottish, too?"

"I don't know why you say 'was.' Haven't I told you, Rosemary is alive! Or if she isn't," he added hastily, "I don't know anything about it."

"But is she Scottish?" That was important. There was no indication, either from Mary's letter or from the testimony at the inquest, that she was a Scot.

"She's half Scottish and half English. What does it matter? Look here, I'd as lief not talk about her anymore. It's a painful subject. You won't tell anyone about all this, will you? I'd hate Ada to be hurt."

"I don't think you quite appreciate the quandary I'm in. I don't want to pry into your affairs, but a woman appealed to me for help tonight. At all events, that's how I interpreted her entrusting me with that message for you. She was angry and desperate. She obviously believes you've done Rosemary a mischief—"

"That's rubbish! I told you, Megan is mad. You can't credit anything she says."

"She didn't seem mad to me. In fact, I thought she was rather clever."

"Well, she's crafty. Mad people often are, I believe. They get an idea in their heads, and they act on it sensibly enough, but the idea is crack-brained to begin with—like my great-uncle who thought he was Henry the Eighth."

"My dear fellow, you may be right, and Miss MacGowan may be as mad as a March hare, but I've got to satisfy myself that her fears for Rosemary are groundless. Otherwise, tiresome though it is, I shall have to let Bow Street or some such authority know this young woman is missing."

"No, you mustn't—Hang it, what do you want? What can I do to convince you?"

"Will you answer a few questions?"

Avondale walked back and forth, thinking hard. Julian felt sure he was trying to decide how much of the truth he dared tell. "All right, fire away. But you've got to give me your word you'll keep all this dark."

"If there's no reason to believe Rosemary is in danger, I shall be glad to let the matter drop."

"I suppose I'll have to make do with that. What do you want to know?"

"When did you last see Rosemary?"

"In July."

"Where?"

Avondale hesitated for a moment. "Brighton."

Interesting. Birkett had told Dipper that his master did in fact go away in July. But he said Avondale journeyed north, not south, to judge by the clothes he took with him. And if Avondale had gone to a fashionable spot like Brighton, he would surely have taken his valet.

"How did you and Rosemary part?"

"She left me. I hadn't known her very long—a few weeks. I met her in Brighton. She and Megan were staying there."

"Where, exactly?"

"In a cottage, a little outside the town. I can't describe the place precisely."

Julian did not ask him to try. He felt sure the whole business about Brighton was a blind. But he wanted Avondale to go on talking. The more he said, the better chance there would be of teasing a few strands of truth out of his tissue of lies. "Your acquaintance with Rosemary seems to have begun and ended rather suddenly."

"Well, those sorts of things do, sometimes. You know: you go away for a bit, think you want to be alone, then you get bored and start looking about. And if there happens to be a personable female, you take up with her, but it doesn't amount to anything. One day Rosemary went off, I don't know where, and I went back to London. But the devil of it is, Megan thought I knew where she was and came after me. And when I said I didn't, she went off her head and accused me of hiding her, or—I don't know what."

"How long has Miss MacGowan been hanging about here, chalking *R*s on your door and that sort of thing?"

"A few weeks."

"Since late September, or thereabouts? What was she doing between July and then?"

"How the plague should I know? Looking for Rosemary, I suppose."

"If she thought Rosemary was with you, why didn't she come to you at once?"

"I don't know!" He walked rapidly back and forth. "Perhaps she couldn't find me. Anyway, she doesn't like me—hates me, in fact."

"The feeling seems mutual."

"Well, wouldn't you hate a woman who followed you about, sank her claws into you and wouldn't let go? I didn't want any trouble with Megan. I'd have happily left her where I found her, but she clung on like a leech."

"Why do you let her persecute you this way? At the very least, she's damaged your property—slashed the hood of your carriage You could have her up before a magistrate. You might even have her committed to Bedlam, if she really is mad."

"Don't you see, that would create just the kind of scandal I want to avoid!"

"But if she keeps up these sorts of antics, Miss Grantham is bound to find out sooner or later."

"Then I'll just have to tell her the truth. But I'm hoping Megan will tire of this game before it comes to that."

"How often does she come here?"

"Lord knows. I'm never sure where Megan is, or what she might be doing."

"Where does she live?"

"I don't know. She won't tell me."

That rang true. The frustration in his voice was unmistakeable.

"Did you know Megan before you met Rosemary?"

Avondale looked at him as an animal looks at a boy tormenting it through the bars of its cage. "No."

"You always refer to her by her Christian name. That suggests a certain intimacy."

"You can get very intimate with an enemy. More even than with a friend. You can't always show your true self to a friend—he might not like what he saw! But it doesn't matter what an enemy knows about you."

"So Megan knows more about you than Miss Grantham does?"

"She knows—different things."

"And Rosemary—how much does she know?"

"Not much." Avondale smiled mirthlessly.

"How is she related to Miss MacGowan?"

"Oh, I don't know. Everybody's related to everybody else in Scotland."

"Is her surname MacGowan, too?"

"Yes," he said, after a moment's pause.

Julian was tempted to sound him about Mary and the refuge. If Mary were Rosemary, and Avondale had a hand in her death, the mere mention of the refuge might frighten him into betraying his guilt. But he was clever, and Julian's questions had put him on his guard. He might contrive to hide his shock, and without any real proof, Julian would simply be warning him to cover his tracks. Better to confront him with Mary's letter after Sally had brought back whatever information she could about Mary's life and death.

Avondale seemed rattled by Julian's silence. "I've told you all I can about Megan and Rosemary. Can I count on you to keep it dark, for Ada's sake?"

"Naturally, I shouldn't like to distress Miss Grantham, or put you in a bad light with her."

"Exactly so! It's just a private matter—the sort of scrape any fellow could get into, only in this case it's got a bit out of hand."

"Evidently. But as it seems there's nothing I can do for Miss MacGowan—"

"No, nothing!"

"—and as it's really no affair of mine, I don't see a need to mention it to anyone. I'm sorry I've had to cross-question you like this."

"Oh, I don't mind. To tell you the truth, it's been rather a relief to confide in someone about all this," His smile was engaging, boyish, candid—and Julian did not believe in it for a moment. Avondale had not confided in him. His relief came from thinking he had gotten away with—murder? It was too soon to say.

He talked briefly with Avondale about the hunter, then took his leave. On his way home, he wondered about Megan. Assuming she was not mad, what lay behind her quest for Rosemary? Why was she tormenting Avondale, and why was she so tormented herself? Was Rosemary so dear to her, or Avondale so hateful, that she was driven to savage his property, haunt his doorstep, accost his friends—sleepless, unkempt, a portrait of obsessive love, or hate? I've missed something, Julian told himself. I don't know if Avondale's led me astray, or I've got into a muddle on my own. I only know there's a connexion I haven't made. But where the devil is it?

Vengeance Is Mine

Sally's plan to keep an eye out for Caleb Fiske posed practical problems. The only time she had any leisure or privacy was at night, and her bedroom looked out on the back garden of the inmates' house, rather than the street in front. She supposed that, if Caleb were dexterous enough, he could scale the back garden wall, but that would put him to a good deal of trouble and risk. When Mrs. Fiske had seen him, he was watching the refuge from Stark Street, which would certainly be his easiest, most prudent means of approach. So Sally decided she must keep her nightly vigil at the front of the refuge.

There was only one place in the inmates' house where she could do that without being questioned or disturbed, and that was the area window in the wet laundry. The area was broad enough for her to get a pretty good view of the street, even if she did have to look up at it slantwise. On Tuesday night, she tiptoed down to the wet laundry, her footsteps echoing eerily on the uncarpeted stairs. She pulled up a table to the window and crouched on it, huddled in her big brown shawl. The street was quiet. An occasional drunkard weaved by, the watchman and the baked potato seller made their rounds, a beggar slunk along scrounging for horseshoe nails, but no one lurked about the refuge or seemed to be watching it. After an hour or two, she had to admit defeat and go back upstairs to get some sleep.

The same thing happened on Wednesday and Thursday nights. By Friday, her spirits were a good deal dampened. There was no reason to think Caleb would ever come back. Her joints were aching, she was catching cold, and the inmates who shared her room were beginning to ask where she wandered off to at night. She was getting more kicks than halfpence for her pains.

But she hated giving up. Just one more night, she told herself. Mrs. Fiske was on duty. Did that make it more or less likely Caleb would come? It certainly meant Sally must be especially cautious in creeping downstairs. Mrs. Fiske had the sharpest eyes and ears of anyone at the refuge.

As soon as Red Jane, Spots, and Nancy were asleep, Sally slipped out of bed and felt her way downstairs. She was familiar enough with the refuge by now not to need a light, and she could not afford to use up all her candles. She went into the wet laundry and made for the area window, guided by the smudge of yellowish light that the street-lamps cast on the wall.

But there was not as much light as usual. Midway across the room, she realized why: the window was partly blocked off. Even as she made out a man's shape, it disappeared.

She ran to the window, opened it, and pressed her face against the iron grating. Just enough gaslight filtered into the area for her to have seen the man run up the stairs, if he had escaped. And unless he had a key to the gate, it would have taken him some time to climb over the railings. No, he must still be in the area, and there was only one place he could hide.

Just as she thought: he was crouching behind the big lead cistern. She could see the top of his cap sticking out on one side. It was rather pathetic, really—he must know she would find him at once.

"Come out from behind there," she called softly.

A twitch of his cap was his only answer.

"It ain't no good playing least-in-sight. I can see you plain. So you might as well come out and get acquainted."

His head came up slowly from behind the cistern. He was about two-and-twenty, with a thin face and round, rather bulging eyes. His clothes were worn and patched. His long brown hair was tousled, his cap pushed over one ear. He stared at her in dismay.

"Your napper's on crooked," she advised.

He clutched at his cap and pulled it straight.

"That's better. Now, come over here," she coaxed, "and let's have a confab. I'm all alone. I've got nobody to talk to."

He stood up awkwardly, keeping behind the cistern, even though it hid him only from the knees down. She saw him steal a glance at the area stairs. "You going to cut and run?" she asked. "Now, if you does that, I'll think you don't like me, and I'll howl so loud, I'll have the whole neighbourhood down on us."

He started, and looked about fearfully.

"Now, don't take on," she soothed. "I don't want nobody to come. I want us to have a talk, just you and me. Me name's Sally, by the way." She waited, finally asked, "Can I call you Caleb?"

The boy stared. "If you want to," he faltered.

She supposed she should be glad of the iron grating between them. He was clearly a bit crack-brained, and he was suspected of killing a girl in his old village. But it was hard to believe he would hurt anyone. He seemed completely harmless, timid as a mouse—just the way you'd expect him to be, after years of being harried and beaten by that old cat, his mother.

"I lives here," she told him chattily, "but I don't like it much. You must like it, though—you been here before, ain't you?"

"I—I wasn't doing any harm. You think I was trying to get in, but I wasn't—I know there's wicked women in there. *Pray that ye enter not into temptation. When lust hath conceived, it bringeth forth sin: and sin, when it is finished bringeth forth death.*"

She was taken aback. "I know you wasn't trying to get in. You can't—the doors is locked, and there's gratings on the windows. You can't get in, and I can't get out. So all's right: we can have a confab, and no harm to either of us."

But he was not disposed to converse. He closed his eyes, clasped his hands together, and rapidly moved his lips. He was praying, she realized, in a nervous, compulsive way, as some people might pace or wring their hands.

"Caleb!" she said sharply, to get his attention. "What have you been coming round here for?"

"Because I'm very wicked."

"But you ain't doing nothing wrong here."

"*Lust not after her beauty in thine heart, neither let her take thee with her eyelids. For from within, out of the heart of men, proceed evil thoughts.*"

"It ain't no sin to fancy a woman. Any cove does, that's just nature, and if they didn't there wouldn't be no more people at all."

He shook his head emphatically. "*It is good for a man not to touch a woman. The body is not for fornication, but for the Lord.*"

She tried another tack. "Caleb, have you seen your pa lately? Asked him for help, maybe?"

"I'm always asking my Father for help." He cast up his eyes. "And sometimes He gives it to me, but in strange ways."

"I mean, your pa here on the earth. You went to his shop once. Was you looking for him?"

He was not attending. He crouched down behind the cistern again, curled his feet under him, and went back to praying.

She made you like this, thought Sally. I don't believe you killed nobody—not back in your old village, and not here, neither.

All the same, she had to sound him about Mary. "Caleb, did you start coming round here because you knew somebody inside? A gal—one of the ladybirds here?

He gaped at her.

"A blond gal?" she urged. "A pretty one?"

"God have mercy on my soul," he whispered, turning his face away.

"It ain't nothing to be ashamed of."

He was almost in tears. "*Let not thine heart decline to her ways, go not astray in her paths. Her house is the way to hell, going down to the chambers of death.*"

She tried to put herself in his shoes—to think like a person with a religious mania. After a week in the refuge, that was not so hard. "Caleb, the wicked has to be punished, don't they?"

He nodded, without looking at her.

"Maybe you has to beat 'em, or lock 'em up?"

He nodded again, with something between a hiccough and a sob. "*The wicked shall be cut off from the earth, and the transgressors rooted out of it.*"

"So a wicked gal might have to be killed, so as to save her soul and stop her doing wrong?"

"No!" His face fell. "Well, she might."

"Would you do it, Caleb? Would you kill her yourself?"

He looked up at that, gazing at her with big clear eyes. "*Vengeance is mine*," he said gently. "*I will repay.*"

Suddenly she heard footsteps on the stairs leading down to the basement. "Stash your patter!" she whispered. "Someone's coming!"

She dropped down and hid in the darkness under the window, then looked cautiously around to see who it was. Mrs. Fiske stood in the doorway, holding up a candle. She must be making one of her nightly inspections of the inmates' house. She came in, shining her candle this way and that, and squinting into every corner. Sally held her breath.

Just then there was a scuffle and raised voices from upstairs. Red Jane and Spots must be kicking up another row. Mrs. Fiske's little eyes lit up with zeal, and she raced off to catch them in the act. Sally sighed with relief, jumped up, and looked out the window again.

The boy was gone. He must have clambered over the area railings and run off. She was vexed with herself. She had found out nothing practical about him—where he lived, how he supported himself, or what he had been doing since he escaped from his village. Worst of all, she had not asked him about the crimes he had been accused of there.

Oh, well: least said, soonest mended. She was lucky to have seen him at all. Why had he come? Was there any point in asking? He was obviously queer in his attic. He might not have had a reason—or, at all events, no reason any sensible person could understand.

She looked thoughtfully at the grating on the window. The holes were just big enough to fit two fingers through. That suggested another way Mary might have sent her letter: she could have rolled it up and passed it through the grating to someone on the other side. Caleb? Could Mary have met him in the area and given him her letter to post? He seemed an unlikely messenger—but, then, Mary had not had many choices. He as good as admitted he had known a blond, pretty girl here. But if Mary had given him the letter, how did it get from him to whichever man Sally stole it from?

She all but acquitted him of playing any part in Mary's death. The murder, if it was one, was stealthy and subtle. How could a Tom-noddy like Caleb have committed such a crime? Besides, she did not believe he was vicious or dangerous, whatever he had been accused of in his village. It was just like country people to think a boy must be a murderer merely because he was a bit touched.

Yet there were those ominous last words he spoke: *Vengeance is mine*. Against whom, and for what? If he really thought Mary was evil, would he murder her out of some distorted sense of duty? He seemed like a well-meaning boy, who would not willingly do wrong. But suppose, from his crack-witted point of view, he believed killing Mary was right?

Ada smiled over all the invitations she was suddenly receiving. Ever since her engagement to Charles had been announced, the Quality had been all eagerness to cultivate her. Hostesses who had not known she existed were vying for her to join their country house parties. Everyone took it for granted she would be presented at Court. It was even hinted she had only to crook her little finger to gain admittance to Almacks Assembly Rooms, that inner sanctum of the *beau monde*, where men were still forced into knee breeches, and countless daughters of wealth and power beat on the doors in vain.

Charles must be more of what Caroline would call a "catch" than she had had any idea. Everyone liked and admired him, everyone wanted a chance to laud and lionize—or envy and find fault with—his bride. Ada gazed at him, her eyes brimming over with love. He did not notice; his head was bent over a toy ship he and James were mending. He was so kind—she felt she had not half appreciated him before. She had been trying so hard to keep her feelings for him within bounds that she had dwelt too much on his faults, and not enough on his good nature and generosity. She had thought she loved him, but she had not known what it was to pour out her feelings from a free and open heart. Happiness sang inside her. The reservations she had felt when he first offered for her could not thrive in so much sunshine—they retreated into cover, like the night creatures they were.

"Here's another for you," said Mrs. Grantham. She and Ada were seated at a little table in their drawing room, going through the post. "It smells rather sweet."

Charles looked up in mock indignation. "I don't think I like my bride receiving cologne-scented letters."

"It doesn't smell like cologne, exactly." Ada looked at it in puzzlement. Her name and address were written on it in a spidery hand she did not recognize. She broke the seal. There was no letter inside—only a handful of some dried herb. She held it to her nose. "How strange! It's rosemary."

"Mama, Charles looks so funny," piped up James. "He's gone quite white."

"Not a bit of it!" Charles jumped up, smiling, and came over to look at the envelope. "What do you suppose it means? Is it a new way of wishing brides happy?"

A cloud rose over Ada, blotting out her sun. Don't lie to me now! her eyes entreated. You can hurt me so much more than you ever could before.

He did not meet her gaze. She put the envelope aside for the time being. But later that day, when they were walking in the park with her sisters and brother, she brought up the subject again. James was trying out his little ship on the Serpentine, and Emma and Lydia had moved away to give Charles and Ada some privacy.

"Charles." She laid a hand on his arm. "Do you know anything about that envelope with the rosemary in it that came in the post today?"

"No. What should I know about it?"

"James said you changed colour when I opened it."

"I often change colour around you," he said lightly.

"Be serious for a moment." She stopped walking, and faced him earnestly. "Is there anything you ought to tell me? Please don't be afraid I might be angry or distressed. I'm not so easily shocked as you might think. I can understand more than perhaps you realize—forgive more, if need be."

"I don't have anything to tell you, Ada."

"I trust you, you know. I *must* trust you, or be utterly wretched. When I was little, and you taught me to ride, I knew nothing bad could happen to me, because you would never let me ride a horse I couldn't manage, or do anything dangerous. I had the most perfect confidence in you. Can I have that confidence now? This is the only time I shall ever ask you, and if you say yes, I'll believe in you whatever happens."

He looked at her for a long time, his eyes unreadable. At last he said steadily, "You can trust me, Ada."

She drew a long breath. Her Rubicon was crossed. She prayed he was true and upright, but if he was not, there was nothing she could do. For good or ill, her heart and honour were in his hands.

Sally was furious. Mr. Fiske had finally been to the refuge, and she had known nothing about it. He had come on Saturday afternoon, to replenish the medicine supply and look in on an inmate who had catarrh. Sally heard about his visit that evening, when Florrie mentioned it at supper. Florrie said it was good to see him on his pins again, though he still looked a bit queer about the gills.

This would not do at all, Sally told herself. Of course she was glad to know that Harcourt had not dispensed with Fiske's services, for all his apparent effort to keep Fiske's name out of the inquest. But Fiske could come to the refuge a dozen times in a week, without her ever catching a glimpse of him. How could she possibly speak to him alone?

There was only one thing to do, but she cringed at the prospect. All Sunday, she tried to think of another way, but it was no use. Late Sunday afternoon, when chapel was over, she sneaked into the matrons' closet with a small flask she had stolen from the kitchen. She filled it from the bottle labelled "IPECACUANHA" and took it to bed with her that night.

In the small hours, Red Jane, Spots, and Nancy were awakened by a loud groan. They found Sally doubled up and groping for a basin. Nancy fetched her one, and Sally coughed up her supper—and most of her inner works, or so it seemed to her. She lay back, pale and panting, her brow beaded with sweat. Nancy ran to tell Peg, who rang a bell to summon the matron.

Miss Nettleton was on duty that night. She rushed to the inmates' house, her nightcap askew, and her hair in yellow curlpapers. She fluttered around Sally, wringing her hands, while Peg straightened her bedclothes and mixed her a soothing posset. Sally lay back weakly, making brave speeches, and begging Miss Nettleton not to be too distressed if she should die. Miss Nettleton gave a little shriek, and sent for the apothecary.

By the time Fiske arrived, it was day, and Peg had herded the other inmates off to morning prayers and breakfast. Sally was left alone. She felt much better, but she kept to her bed, ready to assume a death-like pose if anyone should look in. At last she heard a man's boots on the stairs. She lay back, trying to look languid and pathetic, and hoping he would not find the empty flask under her mattress.

A middle-aged man came in, carrying a leather bag. He stopped on the threshold and gasped out, “You!”

Sally sat bolt upright. Then she sank back on her elbow, marvelling. “Hullo, Bristles!” she said softly. “I might’ve knowed it’d be you.”

Mr. Fiske under Siege

"What are you doing here?" Fiske stammered. "What do you want?"

"I come to see if you wants your letter back."

"What?"

"Your letter! The one I pinched."

He looked utterly blank. "I don't know what you're talking about."

"Bender! I done you over while we was snugging—pinched your wipe and the letter with it."

"I know you stole my handkerchief. I missed it later. But you didn't steal anything else from me."

"Come on now, Bristles." She grinned, sweetly reasonable. "I knows it was your letter. It was wrote by that gal Mary before she hopped the twig right here in this refuge. You was the 'pothecary as looked after her. You and her was thick-and-thin pals. She give you the letter, and I pinched it from you, and that's how and about it."

"I tell you, you didn't steal any letter from me. I don't know why you think you did. I didn't have a letter from Mary or anyone else when I—when we met—that night."

He was lying. Of course he was. He must be. If he were not the man she stole the letter from, then her picking him up in the Haymarket that night—Mrs. Fiske's husband, Mary's friend, the medical adviser to the refuge!—would be too outrageous a coincidence to be believed. Granted, he sounded sincere; his astonishment seemed absolutely real. But he must be stringing her on. Perhaps she could catch him out. One thing was certain: she must not tell him about those other two men. That would give him a chance to wash his hands of the letter, saying it must have come from one of them.

She looked him up and down. The effects of his illness were marked and poignant. He had lost so much weight that his clothes looked baggy. Even his skin seemed too large for him, and hung in pouches. His face was chalk-white, his eyes hollow. The stubble on his chin and cheeks looked grotesque, like hair sprouting on a skull.

"I heard you was took ill," she said. "You still ain't plump currant, by the look of you."

"I'm well enough. What about you? I thought you were ill. Miss Nettleton sent for me to see you."

"Oh, that ain't nothing. Miss Nettleton don't know it, but I took ipecac last night a-purpose, so you'd have to come and physic me. That's how bad I wanted to see you."

"Why?"

"'Coz I've got some things to ask you. 'Course, I didn't know then that you was you—I mean, that Mr. Fiske was Bristles. But I knew Mary cottoned to you particular, and it was you as first examined her body after she popped off. So I thought you'd know more nor anybody about why she come to the refuge, and how she died."

"She died of an overdose of laudanum," said Fiske in a low voice. "There's no question about that."

"But how'd she get it? You give it to her?"

"No! Of course not! Why—what makes you think I did?"

"Stands to reason, don't it? You must have laudanum in your shop."

"Well, yes."

"So maybe Mary said as how she was tired of life, and wanted to morris off, and you was sorry for her and helped her."

"I wouldn't do that."

"Well, maybe she just needed the laudanum to help her sleep, and you give it to her on the sly, and she used it to make away with herself. That wouldn't be no fault of yours."

"I didn't give it to her. I don't know how she got it. Why do you care? Why have you come here? What do you want?"

"I've got an idea you ain't happy to see me, Bristles. And I thought you fancied me, last time we met."

A spot of scarlet kindled in his pale cheeks. "I don't say I didn't. But why are you here now? I didn't think I'd ever see you again."

"And it ain't just convenient, me turning up like this." She nodded, grinning. "Here's how it was: I read that letter I pinched from *somebody*, and I got curious. I wanted to know who wrote it. I come here and found out it was Mary, but she'd dropped off the perch the night before. So, seeing as how I was a poor stray lamb in need of reformation, I stopped here meself, to find out who she was, and who might've croaked her."

"Croaked—does that mean *killed*?"

"Right as a trivet."

"What—what makes you say—it—it was murder?"

"I ain't saying it is, and I ain't saying it ain't. That's what I wants to find out."

"But why? Are you working for the Bow Street Runners, or one of the Public Offices?"

"'Course not! I wouldn't give a beak the time of day, nor a constable neither!"

"Then you're doing all this on your own?"

She would have to tread carefully here. She did not want Fiske warned of the other efforts being made to investigate Mary's death. She certainly was not going to reveal who her confederates were. But if she said she was the only one who knew about Mary's letter, she was inviting someone to do her a mischief, in order to scotch her enquiries.

She compromised. "I didn't tell nobody what I was about. But I give the letter to a pal for safe-keeping, and he knows where I am."

"This letter," he said slowly, "what did it say?"

"It was wrote to somebody in Mary's family. She said she was sorry for some'ut she done wrong, and asked to be took back. Said she was shut up in this ken, and folks was spying on her, but she had somebody she thought she could trust to post the letter for her."

"Have—have you ever considered showing the letter to someone? I don't know—a magistrate. You say you don't want anything to do with the law, but still—" His voice trailed off uncertainly.

"The law ain't nothing to me. 'Cept there might be a reward if I was to find out who croaked her, and I wouldn't mind that, not one bit!"

"Oh, dear," Fiske walked up and down, wringing his hands.

"What's to pay, Bristles? You're all of a tremble."

"You shouldn't be here. This—this is a terrible mistake—"

"Why?" she asked quickly.

"Just believe me, trust me, please, and don't ask questions. You must go away—now, quickly, before you leave anybody wondering what's happened to *you*!"

"You know some'ut!"

"I don't. I only know I couldn't protect Mary, and I can't protect you. That's why you have to go. It's too late for her, but you still have a chance. Oh, let me save you! Go, before it's too late!"

She was a little moved. "I can look after meself, Bristles. You don't have to worrit about me. I'd like to know what you're in such a pucker about, though. What do you know about Mary?"

"I don't know anything."

"Now, that's as lame as St. Giles, Cripplegate. You wants to know what I think? I think it was you Mary trusted with her letter. She give it to you and asked you to post it, but I lifted it off you, so you couldn't. And then she took a blinder, and you blamed yourself, thinking as how you let her down."

"You didn't steal that letter from me. I didn't have it, I swear to you."

She was baffled. She *knew* he must be lying, yet she *felt* he was telling the truth. "But Mary cottoned to you—that much is true, ain't it?"

"I think she did like me a little, yes," he said sadly.

"And you liked her?"

"Yes."

"So I'll bet me head to a turnip she told you things she didn't tell no one else. Like who she was, maybe, and why she come to the refuge."

"No, she didn't tell me that."

"Bender!"

"It's true."

"Ain't you ashamed to tell such a reg'lar clanker?"

"I can't make you believe me." He sat down wearily on the bed next to hers, beads of sweat breaking out on his white face.

She was sorry for him, but she could not let him off. Because she was sure he was lying now. He might not be the one she stole the letter from—though no other theory made sense—but he clearly knew more about Mary than he was telling. "Come on now, Bristles. If you was to tell me what you knows, maybe we could smoke out what happened to Mary. If she was croaked, you wants to nail whoever done it, don'cha?"

"I don't want to be involved."

"Oh, show some pluck! We could work it together, you and me. Your missis wouldn't have to know nothing about it, if that's what you was thinking."

"Oh, good Lord! You—you won't say anything to her about any of this, will you?"

"That depends. You going to help me, or not?"

"I can't!" he said piteously. "I don't know anything—or—or, if I do—I can't tell you. You must just do your worst."

"Ain't you the provokingest cove as ever was! I don't want to hurt you, or blow the coals 'twixt you and your missis. All I want is to find out what you knows, and I can't come round you nohow." She decided to try another tack. "You know, I seen Caleb."

"What!"

"That's knocked you, ain't it? Me and him had a confab this past Friday night, at the area window."

"But that can't be. He would have—It's impossible."

"He would've what? Told you? P'raps he forgot. His garrets ain't too well furnished, after all."

"I tell you, this can't be! You didn't see Caleb. He's not in London. I don't know where he is. He certainly wouldn't come here. You're trying to trick me."

"One of us is trying it on, Bristles, and it ain't me. I seen him in the area on Friday night, and called out to him, soft-like. He was struck all of a heap, but he didn't dare hook it, 'coz I said I'd kick up a rumpus to wake the dead if he did. So he stayed, and we talked for a bit. 'Cept I couldn't get much sense out of him, him being such a Tom o' Bedlam. Mostly he just talked Scripture and said prayers. But he let on he's been here before, and I think he might've knowed Mary. Maybe she even give him that letter, and he give it to you."

"He didn't. I didn't have the letter. You didn't get it from me."

"All right, Bristles. No sense going down that road again. But you ain't going to string me on no more about Caleb, are you? You admit he's in London, and I seen him?"

"You say—you say you saw him in the area?"

"Yeh."

"And he's been here before?"

She nodded.

He took a long breath. "If you say you saw him, I suppose you must have. But I haven't seen him for two years."

"Bender! If you hadn't seed him in all that time, you'd be jumping down me throat to know how he was: You was nutty upon him, so your missis says."

"You talked to Ellen about this?" he said in astonishment.

"You don't find out things by talking—you find out by listening." She tapped her ear. "I knows all about you and Caleb—how he was wanted for murder in your old village, but he cut and run, and you was suspected of helping him."

"I told everyone what happened," he said tonelessly, "I sent Caleb to fetch some medicine from the local market town. He was my apprentice—I often sent him on errands of that kind. I didn't know the constables were coming to arrest him. I told them where he'd gone, but they didn't find him. He must have heard there was a hue and cry for him, and run away."

"He worked for you?"

Fiske nodded. "I was training him as an apothecary."

"He must've been more right in the head in them days," she mused.

"He was very clever. He was a good boy, when people were patient with him. His mother—" He hesitated.

"I knows all about that. She blowed him up reg'lar—warmed his hide to save his soul."

"She was too harsh with him. She broke his spirit. That's why the village turned against him. He did act—strange—sometimes, but it wasn't his fault. He was good. He was always good with me."

"Now don't take on. I ain't argufying with you. I liked him meself, spite of his being a bit touched. This gal he's s'posed to have croaked—who was she?"

"She was a poor half-wit creature who worked for a woodcutter and his wife, outside our village. She wasn't a very good servant, but they were too close-fisted to pay for a better."

"And she was drowned? How'd they know it was murder?" When he did not answer, she added, "Come on, Bristles, you might as well blow the gab. I'll only keep at you till you does."

"One day she went missing," he said reluctantly. "She was found face up in a stream. At first it was thought she fell in and hit her head, or something of that sort, but a surgeon came and had a look at her, and found bruises on her neck and shoulders. He said somebody'd held her down in the water. And he also said—he said whoever drowned her had—made free with her—before she died."

"Well, I'll be blowed." So that was the "unspeakable crime" Mrs. Fiske had alluded to. Sally tried to imagine Caleb forcing himself on a girl. It seemed ludicrous—even more unlike him than murder. Yet he had told her he was very wicked, and babbled about lust and temptation. With his fear of God—and perhaps of his mother as well—would he feel the need to kill a girl he'd sinned with, to keep her from telling tales?

"Someone remembered hearing a woman's cries near the stream where she was found," Fiske continued. "And someone else had seen Caleb with her earlier that day. Soon everyone was saying Caleb must have done it. I couldn't convince them they were wrong. They'd been suspicious of him for a long time, on account of his being—different. And it didn't help that his mother believed whole-heartedly in his guilt."

"Must've been hard on you."

"Yes, it was. I was the only one who believed in him. He was all in all to me. When he went, he left—oh, such a great hole in my life! I had nothing, except my work."

But you found him again, Sally thought. She was sure Fiske knew all about Caleb's being in London. That might even be why he had moved here, after he and Mrs. Fiske had had to leave their village. He could well be seeing Caleb frequently, unbeknownst to his wife. Mrs. Fiske said he was always at his shop—perhaps that was where he and Caleb met. Caleb certainly knew where it was; Mrs. Fiske had seen him there the day she went to collect the post, after Fiske came out of his delirium.

That reminded her of something. "When you was in a fever, you said some rum things."

"What things? How do you know?"

"I told you, I keeps me ears open. You said, 'Poor little thing, her hands was as cold as stones.' You was talking about Mary, wasn't you?"

"I don't remember. I might have been. I examined her soon after she died. It was—very sad."

"Another thing you said was that you was sorry. What for?"

"I don't know."

"That's a tarradiddle."

"I don't know," he repeated dully.

She let it go for now. "The queerest thing you said was, 'Oh my God, my boots!' Now, what was you in such a pother about your boots for?"

He stood up slowly. What little colour there was in his face drained away. He stared straight ahead with glazed, horrified eyes.

"What's wrong?" she exclaimed "You look like you seen a ghost!"

He dragged his gaze back to her. His mouth opened, but only a croaking sound came out.

"What is it?" She jumped up, shook his arm. "You has to tell me!"

"I—" He swallowed hard. "I can't tell you here."

"Why not? Nobody's listening."

"I can't take the risk," he said urgently, under his breath. "You'll have to meet me somewhere else."

"I can't. You know the rules. If I pikes off, they won't let me back in."

"I won't talk to you in this place. Anyone could be eavesdropping. It's not safe."

She could see he really meant it. Surely it was worth leaving the refuge, to find out what he knew? "All right. I'll meet you some place outside. Today, mind!"

"Yes. Let's say four o'clock—" He thought a moment. "At Temple Bar."

"Why so far off?" she complained. "If you made it close by, I'd have a chance of getting back before I was missed."

"I want to be well away from here. I told you."

She considered. At least Temple Bar was a public place. If he meant to do her any harm, he had chosen a poor spot for it. "All right. Temple Bar at four."

He nodded, picked up his leather bag, and turned to depart. "Oh—how are you feeling? I never did examine you."

"Not lately," she said mischievously.

He looked down. "Well, I'd better go."

"Goodbye, Bristles. You won't show the white feather?"

"No. I'm quite resolved. Goodbye—er—I think Miss Nettleton said your name is Sarah?"

"Me friends calls me Sally."

"Then, goodbye, Sally." And for the first time, he smiled.

Sally stood at the junction of the Strand and Fleet Street, beside the broad archway of Temple Bar. The City churches were ringing five o'clock in a gay, discordant clangour. Where was Fiske?

Just as well she had taken her belongings with her in a bundle when she sneaked out of the refuge. They would never take her back. She had been gone above an hour and a half—she must have been missed by now. It would have been worth the sacrifice, if Fiske had kept his word. But he was so late, she could only conclude he must have lost his nerve. Well, he would soon see that he could not shake off Sally Stokes so easily!

Someone was plucking at her skirt. It was a small boy—one of those urchins who ran after carriages in the hope of earning a few pence by holding the horses. "Is your name Sally?"

"Why?" she asked eagerly. "You been sent to find me?"

"I've got some'ut for you." He thrust a dirty hand into his pocket. "Here."

He gave her a folded slip of paper. She tossed him a penny—then realized too late that she ought to have questioned him first. He darted through one of the narrow foot posterns of Temple Bar and disappeared.

She did not bother to chase him—she was too impatient to read her note. She squinted at it in the ebbing light, moving her lips to sound out the words:

Forgive me. You wouldn't leave the refuge, so I had to lure you out. For your own sake, I beg you to keep away and

not ask any more questions. You can't help a dead woman.
Let her rest in peace, or you may soon join her.

She crumpled the note, burning with chagrin. I s'pose you think you been mighty clever, Bristles! she thought. But the game ain't over yet!

She smoothed out the note and read it again. Those last words gave her pause. *Let her rest in peace, or you may soon join her.* Was that a warning—or a threat?

Between Friends

Dr. MacGregor was returning to his village in Cambridgeshire on Tuesday morning. Julian took him out to dinner on his last evening in town. In public, they forebore to discuss the investigation. MacGregor inveighed about the rudeness of London waiters, the staleness and unwholesomeness of London food, and the depraved clothing, speech, and habits of the people dining around them. Julian listened, smiled, and injected a dulcet word from time to time.

After dinner, they settled down before a crackling fire in Dr. Greeley's library. The housekeeper had left them a pot of hot coffee. MacGregor added good English cream to his, while Julian took French cream—in other words, brandy.

Julian described his confrontation with Avondale a few nights before. "You seem to have been pretty lenient with him," said MacGregor. "If you thought he was lying or hiding something, why didn't you tax him with it?"

"I'd rather wait till I've heard from Sally. Whatever she's learned at the refuge may make or mar my case against Avondale.

Besides, if I'd called him a liar point-blank, I should have had to stand up with him, which would have been deuced inconvenient, and not at all part of my plans."

"Do you mean to say you'd have exchanged pistol shots with him over a mere matter of words?"

"Not if there were any honourable way to avoid it. But accusing a gentleman of lying is the deadliest of insults. If he'd insisted on receiving satisfaction, I should have had no choice but to give it to him."

"But that's preposterous! It's criminal! I don't understand you at all. One minute you're investigating a possible murder with all the seriousness it deserves—and the next minute you say you'd stand up and shoot at a man because he took offence at something you said!"

"Duelling isn't murder, whatever the press and the pulpit say about it. If one gentleman insults another, he knows what the consequences will be: they'll fight according to the laws of honour, as nations fight according to the laws of war. Killing an unarmed man, or—God forbid!—a woman, is completely different."

"Well, I suppose you can't help these wrong-headed notions. You probably learned them at your father's knee before you were old enough to know better."

"Oddly enough, my father had much the same view of duelling as you do. But, then, my father was too good to live." He added quietly, "And he didn't."

MacGregor regarded him thoughtfully. Not for the first time, he wondered about Kestrel's early life. He knew his father had been a gentleman, whose family had cut him off with a shilling for marrying an actress. That was more than most of Kestrel's acquaintances knew, but it was not much. It did not explain how he had learned so much about clothes, how he had become such a fine musician, why he had lived for years in France and Italy, or where his money came from.

As usual, Kestrel changed the subject before MacGregor could probe any further. "So I've reached rather an impasse in investigating Avondale. I kept watch outside his house the evening after I spoke with him, hoping Miss MacGowan would come back, but the only result was that I was stared at suspiciously by watchmen, spattered with mud by every kind of vehicle imaginable, and subjected to interesting and indecent proposals by what Dipper calls public ledgers."

"Public ledgers?"

"I suppose because any man may make an entry."

"You and Dipper should both be ashamed of yourselves."

"I'll see that he gets your message. At all events, since then I've paid an enterprising link-boy to watch the house at night, and follow Miss MacGowan if she appears. She hasn't as yet. In the meantime, I summoned all my fortitude and called on Lady Gayheart. After dutifully admiring her eyes, her gown, and her abominable dog, I turned the subject to Scotland. She told me her brother John is there shooting, and Charles used to go as well, but a few years ago he conceived a fierce aversion toward the place. Which is interesting, since he told me he'd only met Rosemary and Megan this past July. Then I probed for any scandals she knew about Avondale and women, but she couldn't tell me anything to the purpose."

"What about this young woman he's engaged to? Do you think she knows anything?"

"No. I think he was in earnest when he said he wanted to keep her in the dark. That's just as well, since I haven't the remotest idea how I would go about questioning her. I did have one further thought: I wonder if Avondale is being blackmailed. That would explain where his money's been going, and why he's in such haste to raise more."

"Who do you suppose might be blackmailing him? Not Megan—if she had some way of harming him, wouldn't she use it to make him tell her where Rosemary is?"

"Not necessarily. She may be afraid he would do Rosemary a mischief if she moved against him. On the other hand, if he had that kind of power over Megan, he wouldn't need to pay her off, so you're right, the idea of her as the blackmailer won't wash."

"The blackmailer could be Rosemary."

Julian nodded. "Or someone who knows what's become of Rosemary. Never mind—that's enough of the Honourable Charles. Let's turn to the dishonourable Mr. Rawdon."

He recounted how Dipper had tracked down Rawdon, and what he had learned about him from Annie Price. "I'd give a monkey to know what business Smith and Company is in—if it has any business at all. With luck, I won't have long to wait. Dipper has an assignation with Miss Price tonight to have a look around Rawdon's office. I should have liked to go with them, but I don't want to disturb Dipper's rapport with her—which must be considerable, to judge by the fact that I can't get a straightforward answer out of him about what she's like. And when Dipper won't talk about a woman, it means only one thing—my valet, that most artless and angelic of rakes, has found another victim."

"Hmph. I'd as lief not hear about those sorts of goings-on."

"I'll spare you a catalogue of his conquests—we should be here all night. I do think it's rather hard, seeing that I'm the master and he's the servant, that I should have to play Leporello to his Don Giovanni. At all events, Dipper is meeting Miss Price at midnight tonight. This morning he contrived to brush past her father at the George just before his coach departed, and relieved him of his keys. So he and Miss Price shouldn't have any difficulty getting into Rawdon's office."

"Well, I can't approve his methods, though I know his heart's in the right place."

"He's doing evil in the cause of good, which is one of life's most exquisite pleasures. One has all the enjoyment of getting up to mischief, and none of the guilt."

"You're very clever tonight—all wit and glibness and drawing-room drawl. What's wrong?"

Julian's guard went up—then just as suddenly came down. "I'm worried about Sally. She's been in the refuge more than a week, God knows when she means to come out, and the more I learn about Avondale and Rawdon, the more uneasy I am on her account." He added, "You needn't give me that knowing look. Of course my feelings are personal. I thought that was obvious by now."

"It's nothing to be ashamed of."

"I'm not ashamed. I'm baffled. I don't understand what I see in her. She has none of the traits I admire in women. She's little and brown and has a nose like a pug's, and her voice is like rusty nails scraping on slate. She can barely read, knows no world outside London, thinks Mozart is something you buy at a pastry-cook's. And yet—" He shook his head.

"I'm beginning to think I was wrong about her. I thought she'd make trouble for you, but, the fact is, she's been a good influence. You were too smooth. She's roughening your edges a bit."

"She's rubbing them raw."

"That won't do you any harm."

"I admire your philosophical detachment. It must be wonderfully comforting to your patients."

MacGregor laughed. "All right, I'll have done. Anything else you've found out about this man Rawdon? Where does he live?"

"In Shoreditch. Dipper followed him home from his office on Friday afternoon."

"He lives in Shoreditch and has his office in Southwark?"

"Interesting, isn't it? He obviously prefers to keep his home a discreet distance from his place of work. He moved into the Shoreditch house about six months ago—Dipper found out from talking to servants and tradespeople in the neighbourhood. He bought the house outright, which means he must have had a fair amount of ready money. It's a very respectable neighbourhood, and the house is a good one, though not over-large. The woman who comes in to clean for him says he has quite a set-out inside—good furniture, fine plate, expensive knick-knacks. He lives quite alone, not even a servant, and never entertains. He's not married, has no children—no family anyone's ever seen. No one knows how he gets his living. It's suspected he's in some lucrative but unpopular line of work—a money-lender, perhaps, or an informer to the excise."

"What does Mr. Digby say about all this?"

Julian smiled. "He says so far this investigation seems like a great harvest of a little corn. And he's quite right—we've been rushing about collecting all manner of information, but we don't know that any of it will be any use."

"Well, I'm sorry to be going home just when you're in the thick of this business. I'd like to have seen how it all came out But I've neglected my patients long enough, and Dr. Greeley can get along without me now—though, between you and me, he'll have to give up his practice before long. He's too old and frail to keep it up any longer. I said I'd look out for some young fellow to take it over."

Julian cocked an eyebrow at him. "You wouldn't consider taking it over yourself?"

"What?"

"Dr. Greeley couldn't find a better replacement than you, or one he'd trust more."

"You mean, live here—in London? This filthy, foul-smelling, soot-ridden, rabbit-warren of a place? No, thank you! Why, I'd breathe cleaner air in a peat-bog, and meet with better manners on a convict ship!"

"It's true you've done nothing but complain since you got here. I've never seen you enjoy yourself so much."

MacGregor glared at him. "You've had some crack-brained notions, but this one beats them all to sticks. Why, I'm likely to retire myself in ten years! Well, fifteen—though if my health holds up—oh, dash it, the point is, I'm not going to uproot myself from my home at my time of life!"

"I understand how you feel. But I can't help wondering if living in Alderton, for you, means living in the past: keeping alive the memory of the wife and son you lost years ago, giving the same sorts of treatments and performing the same operations year in and year out. There's nothing wrong with that, if it's what you want. I just thought you might like to have an adventure, start a new life, while you're young and strong enough to relish it."

"Adventure! That's easy enough to say when you're five-and-twenty."

"I do realize I'm being thoroughly selfish. I should like it above all things if you'd stay."

"Bosh! I know how it would be. Half the year you'd be off hunting and shooting, or sailing round Venice in gondolas, and during the season you'd spend all your time gadding in clubs and ballrooms. I wouldn't see you above once in a twelvemonth."

"You really ought to stay and wean me away from this life of dissipation. But, seriously, if you lived in London, of course we should see each other. Most of my friends here are trifling fellows, and all but interchangeable. You must know I'd trade a hundred of them for one of you."

"Hmph—well—I'll think it over. That is to say, I won't dismiss the idea out of hand. That's the most I can promise."

"That's the most I can ask."

They walked out into the hallway. Julian put on his top-hat and his long black evening cloak lined with sky-blue silk. "Goodbye, my dear fellow. Convey my compliments to the Fontclairs—though that seems less than tactful under the circumstances. I daresay I shall always be associated in their minds with violent death. Oh, and please give my warmest regards to Miss Craddock. And if Hugh's not being properly attentive, be sure to give her my message when he's by."

"No fear of Hugh's neglecting the girl. I haven't seen one of those two without the other since they got engaged."

"One more thing." Julian took out a brown-paper parcel from a pocket of his cloak. "This is for Miss Philippa. It's Marco Polo's *Travels*, with illustrations. I thought she might like it, seeing that she's a fledgling historian."

"She'll devour it whole."

"You don't think her family will mind my sending her a present?"

"If I know Pippa, she won't let anything stand in the way of her getting her hands on a new book. But, you know, you're too skittish about the Fontclairs. You don't need to tiptoe round them like this. They think very highly of you."

Julian smiled wryly. "The hanged man's family may have great respect for the judge. But somehow I don't think they like him over much."

As Julian let himself in at the street door of his house, he remembered just in time that Mrs. Mabbitt had succumbed to one of her whitewashing fits. At least twice a year, she had the front hall and stairway repainted, at imminent hazard to anyone going up or down the narrow stairs. He drew his cloak around him as he ascended, like a bat folding its wings. Whitewash was one thing Dipper had never had any success getting out of his clothes.

He was surprised to hear Dipper moving about in the parlour as he entered his flat. Surely he ought to have left by now for his rendezvous with Annie Price. The sounds ceased abruptly; then there were light footsteps running toward the parlour door, and it flew open.

"Sally!" He caught her in his arms. "Sally, by all that's marvellous!"

She laughed up at him, glowing with pleasure. "I'd've stayed away longer, if I knowed how much you'd miss me!"

"Where did you spring from? How long have you been back?"

"I come tonight, while you was out. Dip had to go and nose around Blinkers's office, so I said I'd stay here and look after you proper while he was gone. I've got your dressing-gown laid out neat as ninepence, just like I was your slavey."

"You didn't have to do that. I've been known to find my own dressing-gown, and in extreme cases, even to put it on."

"You're in a fair pucker now, ain't you?" she chuckled. "You're afeard I'll start making up to you, now Dip's gone, and most likely won't be back till morning. But I ain't going to do that no more." She drew away from him primly, smoothing out her dress. "You was right: that's no go, and least said, soonest mended. I just wants to talk to you, friendly-like. I've got a lot to tell you."

She bustled around him, taking his hat, cloak, and gloves. He went into his bedroom to put on his dressing-gown. She followed, and held out her hands to help him off with his coat.

His brows went up. "Were you planning to undress me?"

"Why not? Dip does."

"Dipper is my manservant, which is to say, he's both a servant and a man. You fall rather short in both categories."

"I seen a few coves peel before, you know. I won't faint dead away at the sight of your braces." She added mischievously, "Want me to close me eyes?"

He gave her a darkling look and turned his back to let her remove his coat. She put it away in the wardrobe, then came round to unbutton his waistcoat. Her hair hung loose, a little damp, and smelling of soap. Stray tendrils tickled his nose.

He undid the knot in his neckcloth, a bit more forcefully than was necessary. She folded his waistcoat and neckcloth in a neat pile. "Now, ain't this cozy and comf'terble?" she cooed, as she helped him on with his dressing-gown.

"It's charming," he said acidly.

"There's no pleasing some folks. Here I streaks off to see you directly I gets out of the refuge, I takes first-rate care of you, and all you does is growl at me and gnash your ivories. I never seed such a ungrateful cove." She slipped her arm through his. "You come in the parlour now. I have a pot of rum punch on the fire."

"I know exactly how it feels."

Her eyes danced. "I knows you're just joking. Come on now."

He followed her into the parlour. She poured them each a glass of punch, and they sat by the fire, Sally curling up on the rug with her feet tucked under her. She told him all about her sojourn at the refuge: her nightly explorations of the inmates' house, her suspicions of first one person and then another, her experiment to see if the cordial was poisoned, her eavesdropping on Mrs. Fiske and Harcourt, and her finding Caleb in the area. She finished by revealing triumphantly that Mr. Fiske was Bristles, and recounting all she had learned from him.

"Sally, you're a marvel!"

"Go on!" she said, preening. "It was just luck, mostly."

"Luck be hanged. You're devilish clever. You've brought us a wealth of new information—it's just a question of fitting all the pieces together. Did Dipper tell you what he and I found out while you were gone?"

"Some of it."

Julian filled in the details. "Now, let's see if we can't make some order out of this chaos. We'll begin with those three men, Fiske, Avondale, and Rawdon. They've all turned out to be sinister in one way or another. But when it comes to suspicious circumstances, Fiske sweeps the board. He's an apothecary, which means he has easy access to opiates and knows how to use them. He prescribed the cordial, probably knew where it was kept, and was at the refuge treating fever cases on the day Mary died. He could have added a strong opiate to the bottle of cordial, and then the following day, when he was called in to examine Mary's body, he could have switched the poisoned bottle for another with the same amount of cordial left in it. You say he carries a medical bag about with him—he could have hidden the bottle there."

"What about the laudanum bottle in Mary's room?"

"As you pointed out, his wife has keys to all the doors at the refuge. He could have borrowed or stolen one from her, had it copied, and sneaked in during the night."

Sally frowned. "It don't sound like him. It's so—I dunno, coldblooded."

"He played an elaborate trick on you to make you leave the refuge."

"Yeh, but that was for me own good, partly."

"He says it was."

"He meant it," she insisted. "You didn't see him, I did."

Julian shrugged. "The most ominous fact about him is that he denies any knowledge of Mary's letter, and yet the odds are overwhelming that he was the man you stole it from. He's far more closely connected to the refuge than Avondale or Rawdon, as far as we know. Mary may have entrusted the letter to him, or perhaps his wife found it in her room, and he got it from her. But either way, he was surely lying when he said he knew nothing about it."

"That's what I can't make out. It sounded like God's own truth when he swore I didn't pinch the letter from him."

"Could he have had it and not known it?"

"You mean, somebody planted it in his pocket? What for?"

"To get rid of it quickly, perhaps? But that still doesn't explain why your questioning him about Mary threw him into such a panic. He clearly knows more about her death than one would expect of an innocent man."

She shook her head. "I can't see him putting up a job like this, with poison and keys and all kinds of hugger-mugger—and all to make cold meat of a poor gal as trusted him. He ain't that kind. 'Cept—"

"Except what?"

"If it would've helped Caleb someways, he'd've done it. There ain't nothing he wouldn't do for his son."

"How do you fancy Caleb as a suspect? From what you've said of him, it's hard to imagine him planning a stealthy, elaborate crime—unless of course his simpleton manner was a ruse."

"It was real enough. Though he wasn't al'ays such a Tom o' Bedlam. Bristles said he used to be 'prenticed to him in his shop."

"So he must know something about poisons. And he was accused of killing a young woman once before."

"I don't believe he done it, though. He's a poor lamb as couldn't say 'boo' to a goose. Though I must say, them words he spoke just before he run off give me the shivers. I asked him if he'd kill a wicked gal to save her soul, and he said 'Vengeance is mine, I will repay.'"

"In the Bible, those words are spoken by the Lord. Caleb may have meant that it was up to God to punish him."

"I didn't think of that. My eye, you're a downy one! Let's see if you can make any outs of this: why did Bristles shout, 'Oh my

God, my boots!' when he was in a fever, and why did he come over queer when I asked him about it?"

"I have an idea about that. You said that when you surprised Caleb in the area, he wouldn't come out from behind the cistern, even though it only hid him from the knees down. Perhaps that wasn't so irrational as it seemed. Perhaps he was the 'tramp' to whom Fiske gave away his boots, and he didn't want you to see them."

"Well, I'll be blowed! It's true his duds was shabby—he probably could've used new boots. But why shouldn't Bristles give his boots to his son if he wants to?"

"His son is wanted for rape and murder. If the boots were recognized as Fiske's, that might reveal the connexion between them, and lead to Caleb's being identified and apprehended."

"But I already knowed he was Caleb, so he had no call to hide the boots from me. Besides, if he was so afraid they'd give him away, why would he wear 'em at all?"

"That's a poser." He got up and poked the fire. The coals spat out sparks, then subsided into a ruddy glow.

Sally sat back, her arms clasped around her knees. "I don't see how Caleb could've done the murder. He'd have had to break in the refuge, find Mary's room, tip her the poison—"

"I grant you, if he was involved in the murder, he didn't act alone. The devil of it is, any two of these people may have carried out the murder together. There are all sorts of plausible alliances: Fiske and Caleb, Avondale and Harcourt—Wideawake Peg and anyone who paid her handsomely enough."

"She's a deep 'un," nodded Sally. "Sharp's the word and quick's the motion. She was in good trim to kill Mary: she had the run of the refuge more than any other inmate, and she was thick as two peas in a shell with Wax-face. She told me she had pals on the outside as could get her whatever she wanted—like poison, maybe. And she knowed Mary was writing a letter—she give her the paper and pencil, and offered to sneak it into the postbag for her. Maybe Mary give it to her, and she passed it on to one of them three men."

"But, don't you see, her telling you all that is the strongest argument for her innocence. If she'd had a hand in Mary's death, she would have been at pains to cover her tracks. Instead, she blazed a trail straight to herself." He considered. "What about the other inmates? Do you suspect any of them?"

"No. 'Cept I wonder about Florrie. She said she come to the refuge to get away from a cove, but she wouldn't tell me nothing about him."

"And we have no way of knowing if that's significant or not."

"Well, *I* hopes it was Mrs. Fiske as croaked Mary. She's one I wouldn't mind seeing dangle in the sheriff's picture frame."

"I'm not over fond of her myself. Unfortunately, murderers can't be counted on to be the people one likes least. Still, the circumstantial evidence implicates her more strongly than anyone else. She could have put the poison directly into Mary's glass of cordial, without needing to tamper with the bottle. And she could have planted the empty laudanum bottle in Mary's room when she went on her round of inspection that night."

"I dunno about you, but I needs to moisten me clay." She got up and refilled their glasses from the pot on the hob.

"Thank you. Let's turn to Avondale. Is there any reason to think Mary was Scottish?"

"Nobody knowed where she come from. But if she sounded Scotch, somebody would've said so."

"Avondale told me she was only half Scottish. But I don't think we can put much faith in anything he says. The case against him is straightforward, though highly speculative. Mary was his mysterious Rosemary. He hid her in the refuge, for some reason not yet clear, then contrived with someone there to put her out of the way more permanently."

"If Mary was Rosemary, why'd she keep mum about it?"

"She said in her letter that she didn't want to disgrace her family by revealing who she was. It's also possible that Avondale threatened her, or simply persuaded her to hold her tongue. I imagine he's a great hand at getting women to do what he wants."

"Oh, he is that!" She smiled to herself.

"If you've finished reminiscing, perhaps we could return to the subject."

She came up on her knees on the hearth-rug and leaned on the arm of his chair. "You ain't jealous, are you?"

"No, I gnash my teeth for exercise. Would you mind moving a little away, before I lose my train of thought completely?"

"We can't have that, now, can we?" She grinned and curled up on the rug again. "You was saying Blue Eyes might've put Mary up to keeping mum about who she was. But maybe he didn't even know she was at the refuge. Maybe she hid there, and he didn't find out where she was till somebody tipped him her letter."

Julian shook his head. "That cock won't fight. If Mary was Rosemary, Avondale must have known where she was and arranged with someone at the refuge to watch her—otherwise, how did he get hold of her letter in the first place? It can't have been intended for him. It may have been meant for Megan, but obviously she never got it, or she would have known where to look for Rosemary. Someone at the refuge must have intercepted it and given it to Avondale. And since there's nothing in the letter to connect Mary with him, that person must have known already that he had an interest in her."

"Who do you think give him the letter? Wax-face?"

"Very likely. But, you know, Mr. Harcourt's vanity and ambition go some way toward exonerating him. It's hard to imagine him allowing a suspicious death—let alone a murder—to take place at his refuge, and taint its reputation. On the other hand, his efficiency in hushing up Mary's death suggests he may have known in advance it was going to happen. We know how much Lord Carbury's patronage meant to him. Perhaps he weighed the danger of angering Carbury's son against the scandal likely to arise from Mary's death, and decided it was of paramount importance to keep the Carbury connexion.

"Now then: Mr. Rawdon—the most puzzling of the suspects. On the one hand, he has no apparent connexion with the refuge, and not a glimmer of a motive to kill Mary. On the other hand, he has a vile character, and we know he can be vicious toward women."

"But it don't make sense. I know coves like Blinkers. Any game gal sees 'em now and again. They likes to hurt a gal, make her blubber and beg, or maybe fight. A cove like Blinkers wouldn't get no sport out of doing for a gal the way somebody done for Mary—sending her to sleep forever. He'd only kill like that if he had a reason."

"And we have no idea what his reason might be. But Dipper may be able to throw light on that, once he's had a look around Smith and Company. If Rawdon had a hand in Mary's death, I'll lay any odds his motive is linked to this mysterious business of his.

"We haven't talked about alibis, which is usually the key enquiry in a murder investigation. But I don't think that, in the case of our three men, it would be much use. If Avondale or Rawdon was behind Mary's death, he would almost certainly have had an accomplice, and needn't have been anywhere near the refuge while the plot was being carried out. Fiske is another matter—he just might have committed the entire crime himself. It would be interesting to know where he was—or says he was—the night Mary died."

"I ain't done with Bristles—not by half. I got a mind to bing off to his shop tomorrow, and ask him what he means by trying it on with me like he done."

"You said he was trying to protect you."

"Bugger his protection! I can—"

"—take care of yourself. Yes, you've mentioned that once or twice."

She glared at him. Then she smiled insinuatingly. "You've got a good memory, Lightning. You don't mind if I calls you Lightning, just for old times' sake?"

"We don't have any old times. We met precisely a fortnight ago."

"Didn't know you was counting the days. Cor, you should see yourself, you've got such a furrow 'cross your brow, just there—"

She put up a finger to trace it. He caught her outstretched hand, turned it palm upwards, and pressed it to his lips.

She gazed at his bent head in silence. Then she passed her other hand over his hair. "I been hard on you. I'm sorry. I just wanted to pay you out for being so toploftical before. You wouldn't let on you fancied me—you was al'ays stalling me off. So when I seed how glad you was to have me back, I thought, turn-about's fair play. But I didn't mean nothing by it."

"I suppose I deserved it. I really did make up my mind from the beginning to keep you at arm's length for Dipper's sake. The trouble was, you'd got under my skin more than I realized—after you left, I couldn't stop thinking about you. And the strangest thing is, I was forever asking myself what I saw in you. I don't know how I could have been in doubt. You're clever and courageous and wholly adorable. What I see in you is what any man with eyes, ears, and blood in his veins would see."

Her eyes shone. Then she looked rueful. "We was both wrongheaded. I was just as bad."

"What do you mean?"

"It wasn't just 'coz I fancied you that I was trying to get you up me petticoats. I wanted to prove you was the same as other coves—the mattress-jig was all you cared about. But later on, after I went to the refuge, I seen that wasn't so. They treated me like dirt there—Wax-face and the matrons—but I didn't mind; I'm used to it. 'Coz why, 'coz a game gal's the lowest thing there is, and everybody knows it. You're the only cove as ever treated me—I dunno, polite and respectful. Like I was a *lady*. I'd never've knowed what that was like if it hadn't been for you.

"I'll tell you some'ut else. I used to think a gentleman was a cove with swell togs and carriages, and a handle to his name. Now I knows different. A gentleman is just what it says: a cove as is gentle. Kind to people, treating 'em decent—'specially them as is weaker than you."

He got up abruptly and walked a few paces away. "I don't know how you can say that. I've been snapping at you all evening."

"Well, I been asking for it, ain't I? Tease a dog enough, and it'll bite, no matter how gentle it is." She went up and stood face to face with him, holding his hands. "I want to be with you tonight. But if you think it ain't right, just say so, and I'll never plague you about it no more."

So it was over—the struggle and suspense between them. But it was not ending as he had expected, or resolved. Because in that moment, his perspective shifted. He had often tried to fathom what she meant to him; he had never once asked himself what he meant to her. Looking into her upturned face, he saw her for the first time, not as a seductress, but as offering him the only thing in the world she had to give. And, all at once, it no longer seemed wrong to accept, but churlish to refuse.

He took her in his arms. She blinked at him in surprise. He saw then how little she had expected from her appeal.

"You mean it?" she said. "You ain't trying it on with me?"

For answer, he drew her closer, cupping her head in his hand so that her hair streamed through his fingers. His lips came down on hers, urging them sweetly open. He kissed her deeply, intoxicatingly.

"Last time I kissed you," he murmured, against her lips, "you said it wasn't a real kiss. Was that any nearer the mark?"

"I ain't made up me mind," she breathed, her wide grin teasing but tender. "You'll have to do it again."

Smith and Company by Night

At midnight, Dipper tapped softly on the back basement window of the Prices' shop. Annie hurried over with a candle and opened the window. He slipped through in the wink of an eye, having been trained from childhood to get inside houses by every means but the door. She hastened him from the back room to the front. A quick glance told him why: the back room was her bedchamber.

The front room was the kitchen. Annie stood clasping and unclasping her fingers. "Should—should I make some tea, or ought we to go—upstairs?"

"Biz'ness afore pleasure," he said briskly.

She lit a second candle and gave it to him. They went past the shuttered shop on the ground floor to the office above. "Do you have the keys?" she asked.

"Got 'em." He produced a brass ring with several keys on it. "Which one undubs this door?"

Annie touched his arm. "You—you didn't have to hurt Pa, did you?"

"Bless your bright eyes, no!" Dipper laid down his candle and took her reassuringly by the shoulders. "I done him over very gentle, like this." He lifted her apron pocket lightly with his left hand and slipped the fore and middle fingers of his right hand in and out.

"I didn't even feel that."

"You ain't s'posed to. So don't you worrit about your pa. I wouldn't hurt a hair of his head."

"I'm sorry. I do trust you, mostly. But sometimes I'm a bit afeard of you. I never met a thief before."

"I ain't a thief no more. See, I'm giving you back the keys, and you can tell your pa he must've left 'em at home."

He put them in her hand, his fingers closing around hers. She did not draw her hand away. He reminded himself that there was work to be done and let her go. She turned the key in the lock, and they went in.

The office was grubby and impersonal. Its only furnishings were a deal writing-table and chair, two stiff-backed chairs for visitors, and a hat-tree by the door with a man's black coat hanging on it. Annie started on seeing the coat and clung to Dipper's arm.

"That don't means he's here," he whispered soothingly. "It's prob'ly his second-best coat, as he sports in the office to save his best for wearing on the street." Though it seemed strange that Rawdon should practise such economies, when he could afford to buy a fine house in Shoreditch and fill it with costly furnishings.

To be on the safe side, he poked his head into the back room and shone his candle around. There was no one there. This room was even barer than the one in front. All it contained was a washstand, a cabinet, and a large oak chest.

He returned to the front room. "We'll start here."

There was little to investigate. The room had few bodily comforts, and nothing to throw light on Rawdon's taste or personality. There were no pictures on the walls, the mantelpiece was bare, and the fireplace held only a grimy hob-grate, a poker, and a coalscuttle. On the writing-table were blotting-paper, ink, several pens and pencils, a tinderbox, and a leatherbound ledger-book. It was the book that interested Dipper.

He and Annie went through it together, sitting side by side in the visitors' chairs. The first half was full of entries, all written in the same cramped, clerkly hand. The rest of the book was blank. There were only six kinds of articles listed: tea-pot, tea-chest, tea-urn, coffee-pot, coffee-mill, and coffee-urn.

"Is that what they deal in?" wondered Annie.

"Seems a bit rum," said Dipper, frowning.

Many of the items bore a brief description: porcelain or japan-work, gilded or painted, plain or fancy. A few were identified as having arrived cracked. Most had one or two letters written beside them in the margin, followed by a number between five and thirty. Some items had parentheses around them in pencil; a few had parentheses in ink. Several were crossed out with a bold black line.

"It's a queer sort of ledger," said Annie. "It don't say where the goods come from, nor who they've been sold to. And it don't give any dates or prices."

"Let's have a look next door," said Dipper. "Maybe there's more records in there."

In the cabinet, they found office supplies: candles, foolscap, a few envelopes, a stack of blotting-paper, and a bottle of ink. The chest contained two more ledger-books, with the same kinds of entries as the one on the desk. But these books were full, and obviously older. Many more of the items were in parentheses or crossed out.

There were also several account books listing office expenses, such as rent, coal, paper, and ink. "It must be a much bigger business than it seems," said Annie. "Look at all they pay for dinners and post-chaises and hackney coaches. It can't be Mr. Rawdon who travels so much—he's in his office 'most every day."

"And he leaves by five—ain't that what you told me?"

"Yes."

"Then why does he need so many candles?"

They looked at each other, baffled.

Dipper explored both rooms more closely, tapping on the panels and floorboards and running his hands over the furniture. He could find no secret compartments. The whole place reminded him of Rawdon himself: outwardly nondescript, but when you scratched the surface, sinister and enigmatic.

It was very cold, since they dared not light a fire for fear of leaving traces behind. Dipper saw that Annie was shivering inside her shawl. "We might as well morris off," he said. "There ain't nothing else to smoke out here."

He went about making sure they left everything exactly as they found it. Spying a few drops of tallow on the floor, he carefully scraped them off. They went downstairs, locking the office door behind them.

In the kitchen, Annie hung a kettle over the fire and brought out a flask of gin, a sugar-basin, and two lemons. She set them on a table and cut the lemons in half, squeezing the juice into a large bowl. Dipper offered to help, but she assured him she could manage. He sat down at the table, watching her, his chin propped on his hands.

"We didn't find out much, did we?" she sighed. "We still don't know what business Mr. Rawdon is in."

"Whatever it is, it's on the cross," said Dipper positively. "Maybe he's a fence. That'd account for why his records don't say where the moveables comes from, nor who buys 'em. 'Cept, who ever heard of a fence as only works tea and coffee things? And why keep all them ledgers, if the goods is pinched? He'd want to get shut of 'em double-quick—he wouldn't want to leave any record he ever had 'em, much less what they looked like. You know what? I think it's all some kind of dodge. I think the words in them ledgers means some'ut else."

"What?"

"I dunno. But me master might. He's a rare hand at nobwork." He tapped his head.

She mixed the grog, taking little tastes to see if the proportions were right. "Does he know you've been trying to find out about Mr. Rawdon?"

"Yeh. I told him, and he said he'd help if he could." Dipper thought it best not to tell her about Mr. Kestrel's investigation of Mary's death. She would be even more frightened if she knew they suspected Rawdon of murder.

She poured them each a glass of hot gin-twist, and they sat before the fire, Dipper bringing his chair unobtrusively closer to hers. "You have a young man?" he asked.

"I did have. We was going to be married, but then the landlord of the Bear and Chain died, and John married his widow. She was old enough to be his mother." Resentment flickered in her eyes, then died down to wistfulness. "He'd always wanted to keep a public."

"I'm sorry."

"It happens sometimes." She poked the fire. "I wonder what I ought to do now—about Mr. Rawdon, I mean. I can't tell Pa what we've found out. He wouldn't turn Mr. Rawdon out—after all, there's no proof he's doing anything illegal. He'd only give me the rough side of his tongue for spying on him."

"I'd leave it for a bit, if I was you. We might find out some'ut more."

"Does—does that mean you might come back?"

"Oh, uncommon often." He smiled at her.

She smiled back, her great grey eyes gleaming softly in the firelight.

He cocked his head considering. "If I was to kiss you, and you didn't like it, I wouldn't have to do it again."

She blushed and sat shyly waiting. He kissed her gently, experimentally. It seemed to go off rather well, so he kissed her again. They stood up in order to get closer, then got down on the hearthrug, to be closer still.

"Don't you think I'm very forward?" she said hiding her face in his coat.

"I think you're tip-top, a reg'lar first-rater."

"It's just that I've been so lonely."

"On account of some cove'd rather keep a public than look in them sparklers of yours?" He kissed her closed eyes. "He's a cod's-head, as wouldn't know pure gold if it bit him. He don't bear thinking about no more."

"I'm not thinking about him now," she murmured.

"What you thinking, then?"

She buried her face in his shoulder again. "I'm thinking—I'm thinking we'd be more comfortable in my bed."

Smith and Company by Day

"I can't call you Lightning no more," said Sally, snuggling into Julian's shoulder.

"You don't think I'm flash anymore?" he said, smiling.

"It ain't that." She came up on her elbow, her long brown hair brushing his chest. "But lightning's quick. Which you ain't."

She kissed him lingeringly. He gathered her against him, his hands running along her back and twining in her hair.

She arched like a satisfied cat, then nestled in his shoulder again. "You ain't sorry we done it?"

"Do I seem sorry?"

"No. But now it's over, you might mind about Dip. You know, he don't have to find out. I can make up his bed like I slept in it, and he won't be none the wiser."

"I don't want you to have to lie to him."

"It ain't lying. It's just keeping mum about some'ut as ain't his business anyhow. It's best if he don't know. You and Dip is the two coves I cares about most in the world. I don't want to blow the coals betwixt you."

"Very well. I couldn't refuse you anything at the moment, anyway."

"Have a care, I might ask for diamonds next."

"Then I shall go through the Insolvent Debtors' Court with a smile on my face."

"You're off your head!" she laughed.

"Whose fault do you suppose that is?"

He rolled her over on her back, and kissed her lips, and the fluttering pulse in her throat. She wound her arms around him, stroking the muscles in his shoulders and back. His hands moved over her, his long, strong fingers playing her skillfully. She began to think the piano was very good training for a man.

He sat up suddenly. "Do you know what our problem is?"

"I didn't know we had one," she murmured, nibbling his ear.

"Seriously. Stop that for a moment. And definitely stop *that*." He caught her hand, laughing. "Listen to me. Our problem is that we have too much information."

She gaped at him. Was he really going to talk about the murder—*now?*

He evidently was. "When we began investigating those three men, we expected to find evidence linking one of them to the murder, or at least to the refuge. Instead, we're over head and ears in clues and suspicious circumstances. Fiske turns out to be intimately connected with the refuge, and to have a fugitive son who was accused of killing a woman once before. Avondale's father is Harcourt's patron, and he himself seems to have abducted, or at least mislaid, a girl named Rosemary. Rawdon is engaged in some decidedly rum business, and before we're finished we may find further evidence against him. But only one of those three men had Mary's letter in his pocket. Until we find out who it was, we won't know which facts are important. We shall be conducting three investigations, when we ought to be concentrating on one."

"That's true enough." Sally sat up, interested in spite of herself. Julian drew up the bedclothes around her. The room had grown cold during the night, but neither of them had wanted to leave their nest to put more coals on the fire. They had not even opened the bedcurtains, though a faint light filtering through the gaps showed that dawn must just be breaking.

She clasped her arms around her knees, thinking. "What if we was to write to each of them three coves, and tell 'em we have the letter? We could say, come and meet us at such-and-such a place, and maybe we'll sell it to you. Then we could go there and see which cove shows."

"Do you know, that just might answer the purpose. Whichever man lost that letter probably wants it back very badly. Of course, Fiske claimed to know nothing about it, but you didn't have it with you, so he had nothing to gain by admitting you stole it from him. If he saw the chance of getting it back, he might change his tune. Of course, if our man is Avondale or Rawdon, he'll be taken aback to hear from you—he'll wonder how you identified him. But he probably wouldn't realize you don't know from whom you stole the letter. He'd assume he was the only one you wrote to about it, and wouldn't guess he was giving you a new piece of information by acknowledging it as his.

"All the same," he warned, "we'd have to be very cautious. The man who had that letter in his pocket may be Mary's murderer, and, if he is, he won't be squeamish about killing again."

"If I plays me cards right, he won't think I'm worth killing. I won't let on I knows who wrote the letter, nor anything about it. I'll just say I guessed there was some'ut rum about it and thought he might fork out a quid or two to get it back. Which he most likely will, and then he'll think he's safe."

"But you'd have to give him the letter, and we don't want to part with it. And what do you mean by *I*? You can't seriously think I'd let you meet this man alone?"

"Why not?"

"If you tell me once more that you can take care of yourself, I'll lock you in the hall cupboard till the investigation is over."

"That's how it al'ays is with coves," she complained. "Lift your heels for 'em, and they thinks they owns you."

"I'm not going to argue with you about this. You're not going to confront that man without me, and there's an end of it." He drew her against him. "Do you think I could let anything happen to you, after last night?"

She was mollified, but wanted a little revenge. "Cor, look how light it is! Time we got up."

"Not yet."

"Dip'll be back any minute."

"Then we'd best make the most of the time we have."

She tried to slip out through the bedcurtains, but he pulled her back. There was a scuffle, ending in a joyous surrender.

They got up about half an hour later. Sally played valet to Julian, tidying his bedroom, preparing his bath, and laying out his clothes. She even insisted on shaving him. He looked doubtfully at her as she hovered over him with a razor. "Are you quite sure you know what to do with that?"

"'Course I does! Me sailor taught me." She tweaked his hair reproachfully. "Last night you said me hands was mi-ra-culous."

"The context was somewhat different."

"You stash your patter, or you just might lose your nose."

It turned out she handled the razor very deftly. Julian gave himself up to the pleasure of being shaved. But when she would have helped him on with his clothes, he shooed her out, saying her presence was highly detrimental to his ever getting dressed at all. She went into the parlour, where she put coffee on to boil and speared bread on toasting-forks. Seeing an apple-seller in the street, she ran out and bought half a dozen pippins.

By the time Dipper came home, they were breakfasting demurely in the parlour. Dipper reported on what he and Annie had found out at Smith and Company. "Tea-pots and tea-chests?" said Julian. "You're right: it must be some sort of code."

"For what?" asked Sally.

"That's what we have to find out." He considered. "Smith and Company purports to be a business; the sign on the door says 'Dealers and Importers.' I think it's time we provided Mr. Rawdon with a customer."

Sally stared. "What, you mean walk in and ask to buy a tea-chest?"

"It might be as simple as that."

"But you dunno what that means."

"He won't know I don't. He may assume that since I know about the code, I must understand it. And if he's angry or suspicious, the worst he can do is put me over the door."

"It might do the trick at that, sir," said Dipper. "But won't he be took aback to have a gentry-cove like you come asking after his wares?"

"Since we don't know what his business is, how can we know what sort of customers he's expecting? The role of bored young exquisite in search of amusement might make a rather good cover. If worst comes to worst, I can always say I came to see him on a wager. That excuses any sort of odd or asinine behaviour in a gentleman."

Sally broke in, "But what about me idea of setting a trap for the cove I pinched the letter from?"

"It's a good one," said Julian, "but it needs fleshing out. For the moment, I should rather concentrate on Mr. Rawdon."

She hunched down sulkily in her chair.

"I was thinking, sir," said Dipper. "If Mrs. M. was to find out Sally's come back—"

"Good God, I forgot all about Queen Mab. We'll have to ask her to let Sally lodge with her again."

"I don't want to go back there. She ain't a bad sort, but I likes it here."

"There'll be the deuce to pay if she finds out you stayed here again last night, after she told us she didn't approve. I owe her some consideration. She's a first-rate landlady—I don't suppose there are half a dozen like her in London. I'm afraid you'll have to go."

"Come on, Sal." Dipper took her arm. "Let's pack up your traps."

"I'll do it." She jumped up and ran off. She had to disarrange his room a bit before he saw it, to make him think she had slept up there.

Dipper looked after her, puzzled. Then he shrugged and began clearing away the breakfast things. When he had finished, he went into Mr. Kestrel's room. He noted appreciatively that Sally had tried to tidy it. She had made the bed, but clumsily; he would have to do it over.

As he pulled back the covers, something flew out and bounced along the floor. He picked it up. It was a button covered in green wool, with a bit of broken thread hanging from it. He knew it was not his master's. It came from Sally's dress.

He looked more closely at the bed. Clinging to one pillow was a long brown hair that was certainly not Mr. Kestrel's.

He smiled, put the hair in the dustbin, and pocketed the button, whistling softly to himself. So Sally had finally brought Mr. Kestrel up to scratch. Dipper could not but be pleased. It brought him and his master closer, somehow—like being brothers-in-law, wrong side of the blanket. Of course, he would not say anything about it to Mr. Kestrel. It was just the kind of thing he would feel delicate about. Mr. Kestrel could be skittish, like a high-bred horse. You had to be careful how you came at him, or he'd shy.

Later that morning, Julian strolled into Smith and Company. Lifting his quizzing-glass, he surveyed both the office and Mr. Rawdon. Neither appeared to impress him very much. He inspected a chair to see if it was clean and sat down.

Rawdon watched him from behind his desk, appraising and a little wary "Good morning, sir."

"Good morning, Mr. Rawdon." Julian smiled and lounged back in his chair, stretching out his legs.

"You know my name."

"Oh, you're very well known in some circles."

That seemed a safe enough generalization. Rawdon even looked faintly pleased—or as pleased as his pinched countenance would allow.

"What can I do for you?"

"I thought I might make a purchase."

"What did you have in mind?"

"What do you recommend?"

"We don't make recommendations. We supply what our customers ask for. Their tastes are their own affair."

"What can you show me in the way of"—Julian chose at random—"tea-chests?"

Rawdon smiled unpleasantly. Julian thought: I've just signalled something about myself—something dishonourable or embarrassing—and he enjoys being let in on the secret.

"We have a wide variety," said Rawdon. "Some are cracked, but there are some new ones as well. What's your preference?"

"Oh, a new one, I think."

"They don't come cheap."

"My dear sir, I beg you won't plague me with figures. I can't abide them."

"You have to know the price. It's fifty pounds. Have it with you, in cash, when you take delivery of the item. One of our employees will be there to see that the money's paid. I'd advise you not to argue with him. He's been known to do very nasty things to a gentleman's face."

"You have such a charming manner about you, Mr. Rawdon, it's no wonder your business is flourishing." Julian glanced around at the bare, dingy office.

"We're doing very well," Rawdon said tightly. "There's no need to furnish up the office—we don't get many customers calling on us in person. Most of our patrons write, or send for someone to call on them."

"I was—curious."

Rawdon shrugged. "Tell me more about what you're looking for. Do you want the tea-chest gilded? Painted?"

Julian considered the matter, with an epicurean air. "Gilded."

"Hm." Rawdon consulted the leatherbound book on his desk "We can supply you with a tea-chest of plain work, porcelain and gilded. It came in eleven days ago. What do you say?"

"It sounds satisfactory."

"Right." Rawdon shut the book with a snap. "You can pick it up tonight at ten o'clock, in Windmill Street. Here's the number of the house." He wrote it down. "And remember, have the money in cash."

Julian rose and took up his walking-stick.

"One more thing," said Rawdon. "I need a name to call you by. It doesn't matter what it is, so long as you always use the same one."

Julian smiled. "Why not call me Mr. Ketch?"

"After the famous hangman? I don't think much of your sense of humour, sir!"

"Don't you? I'm devastated, Mr. Rawdon. Good afternoon."

He strolled out of the office, down the stairs, and into the narrow court outside the tobacconist's. Only then did he allow his face to express something of his feelings. He had little doubt now what Rawdon's business was. Tonight he would know for sure.

Delivery of a Tea-Chest

Julian arrived in Windmill Street at a quarter after ten that night. Punctuality would not have been in keeping with the character he had assumed. He got out of his hackney coach at the address Rawdon had given him. It was a grey brick house, with shuttered windows that let out no gleam of light. The place was so dark and silent, Julian wondered if anyone was there to meet him.

He rang at the front door. Someone must have been waiting just inside, for it opened at once, though only a little way. A pair of yellowish eyes surveyed him. Then the door opened fully, and the owner of the eyes beckoned him in. "Good evening, monsieur."

She was a woman of about forty, dark-haired, with a pointed nose and chin. Her clothes were fashionable, in a matronly style. Her French accent sounded genuine. With her was a man a whole head taller than Julian, with broad shoulders and arms like tree-trunks. He had thick black brows and side-whiskers, and smelled of tobacco and sweat. A yellow silk kingsman round his neck half hid his grubby shirt-collar. His gloves and boot-tops were yellow, too, and his waistcoat was white with red spangles.

"Good evening." Julian sauntered in, giving the woman his tall silk hat, his evening cloak, and his ebony walking-stick. While she disposed of them at a hat-tree by the door, he took quick note of his surroundings. The front hall was lined with wood panelling, painted to look like mahogany. A stairway wound to the upper floors. The backdoor at the far end of the hall was boarded up.

The Frenchwoman ushered him into a small front parlour, furnished in an elegant, impersonal style. Her hulking companion followed at their heels. "You are late, monsieur," she said. "Bart and I, we were becoming anxious."

"I was otherwise engaged. Where is the—article—I came for?"

"It is upstairs, monsieur. We will wait here until you have finished with it. I hope you have brought the money?"

"Yes, madame, but you really can't expect me to pay for something I haven't seen."

"You pays afterward," said the giant. "I sees to that."

Julian lifted his quizzing-glass and looked him up and down. "My dear fellow, is that a waistcoat, or are you coming out in a rash?"

The giant's eyes narrowed to slits. "I wouldn't mind turning the hands on your dial," he croaked.

And you could probably do it with one hand tied behind you, thought Julian ruefully. If it comes to a rough-and-tumble between us, I've no more chance than a cat without claws.

The Frenchwoman intervened hastily. "Will you have a drink, monsieur—some cognac, perhaps? Or would you like to go upstairs at once?"

"I think I shall go upstairs."

"There is one small formality. A few of our clients bring weapons with them, and you must see, monsieur, that is not *convenable*. I am afraid I must ask you to be so good as to let Bart search you."

Julian's brows shot up, in the manner that made upstart dandies tremble. But realizing that they would not allow him upstairs unless he submitted, he stood with a pained expression on his face and his handkerchief to his nose, while the giant patted him down.

"*Très bien*, thank you, monsieur. Here is the key. The room is the first floor back."

"I hope it's understood that I'm not to be disturbed—that I'm to have complete privacy?"

"Oh, but of course, monsieur! We pride ourselves on our discretion. We have no need to come looking for you. We know you must come back to us in the end. The front door is the only way out of the house."

Smiling, she settled herself on a sofa, from which she could look out into the front hall. Clearly, she meant to make certain he did not leave the house unseen. Picking up an embroidery frame, she began tranquilly stitching. The giant hunkered down in front of the fire with a dice-box.

Julian left them. Taking up a lighted candle from the hall table, he mounted the stairs. The first-floor back room had a thick oak door. He turned the key in the lock and went in. The room was nearly dark; the only light came from the coals gleaming redly in the grate. He held up his candle and looked about.

A small girl, no older than twelve, stood flattened against the opposite wall, staring at him in utter terror. She wore a white muslin party frock, with pink ribbons and lacy pantalettes. Her blond hair hung in curls on either side of her face.

For a moment, he could only stare back. Then he found his voice. "Don't be afraid. I won't hurt you. I won't even touch you."

Her huge frightened eyes remained fixed on him. She was shaking.

"Whatever they told you I might do," he went on steadily, "it isn't true. I won't harm you. I'm going to help you. Look, I'm just locking the door to ensure we're not disturbed, and I'm going to come a little closer, so that we can talk very quietly. But I shall move very slowly, and not come too near."

He sidled round to a chair against the wall and sat down, giving the bed a wide berth. "How do you do? I'm Julian Kestrel. What is your name?"

"Emily," she whispered. "Emily Wickham."

"Where do you come from, Emily?"

"W-Wiltshire."

"How do you come to be so far from home?"

She made a hiccoughing sound. He took out his handkerchief and laid it on a table between them. She clutched it to her face and burst into tears.

He forced himself to stay seated and keep his distance. He must not risk forfeiting whatever trust he had gained. He wished he had some of that brandy the Frenchwoman had offered: Emily could do with a few drops to calm and warm her. But he dared not leave her to go and get it. Besides, he hardly trusted himself not to break the bottle over the woman's head.

Emily's sobs died down at last. She held out his handkerchief gingerly, as though offering a morsel of food to a dog that might bite. "Keep it for a bit," he recommended. "You might need it again. Do you feel well enough to tell me a little about yourself?"

"Y-yes, sir."

"How old are you?"

"Eleven, sir."

Julian recalled that Rawdon had said the "tea-chest" came in eleven days ago. Perhaps that was part of the code. "Gilded" might refer to the colour of Emily's hair, "porcelain" to her fair skin. The meaning of "new" as opposed to "cracked" seemed reasonably clear.

He went on asking questions, till after a while her story flowed of its own accord. She was from a small village near Salisbury. Her father was a tenant farmer, her mother a laundress. They had six children besides Emily to provide for. One day Mme. Leclerc passed through the village, with two other girls about Emily's age. She said she was a dressmaker from London and was looking for young girls to train as apprentices. She made much of Emily, praising her small fine stitches, and assuring her parents she had taste and talent far beyond her years. If they would allow her to go to London and study dressmaking, she would make a good living, and even have a bit of money left over to send home. Madame would provide her with decent clothes and a comfortable place to sleep, and would chaperone her carefully. The city can be a dangerous place for children, said Madame, if they are not properly looked after.

Emily's parents thought it a good opportunity for her. Madame even paid them a small advance on her wages—to thank them, she said, for letting her take their daughter away on such short notice. So Emily bade farewell to her family and left for London.

Madame was very kind to the three girls on the journey. At an inn where they stopped, she ordered them a good supper, and gave them each a paper to sign. It was a contract of apprenticeship, she said. The girls did not understand the words very well, but Madame assured them it was all right, so they signed.

When they reached London, they went to stay at a sort of lodging-house. Emily could not say where it was, except that it was on the other side of the river. Mostly women and girls lived there, but Emily did not see much of them. She and the two girls she came with were locked up together in a bare, shabby room.

Madame was not kind to them anymore. She said they were not to be trained as dressmakers yet. They were to do other work first. They would each be presented to a gentleman, and they must do anything he asked, or Madame would punish them. She would beat them till they were black and blue, and not give them anything to eat. They had to obey her orders, because they had signed a contract of apprenticeship, and if they were naughty or tried to run away, they would be put in gaol.

"That isn't true," said Julian. "No contract could force you to do this kind of work."

"Are you sure?"

"I'm absolutely certain."

"We didn't know that. Madame said we'd be put in a bridewell, and be whipped in front of everyone. We were afeard."

"Of course."

A day or two after they arrived at the lodging-house, a man came and looked at them and said they would do. He was very thin and had brown hair and wore gold-rimmed spectacles. "Then I was put in a room by myself. Madame came once and-looked at my—without my—my—"

"I understand."

"Then she went away. And I think a few more days went by, and nothing happened at all. Then tonight Madame came and woke me up and made me wash myself and put on these clothes.

And then she came with a very tall man with side-whiskers, and they put me in a carriage and brought me here. She s-said I was going to meet the gentleman—the one I—I would have to please. And she told me again what would happen to me if you weren't pleased with me." Her voice rose on a trill of fear. "Are you?"

"My dear girl—" Words failed him. "You mustn't worry about that anymore. I'm going to take you away from here. I'm going to see that you get safely home to your family."

"Home?"

"Yes. But we have to make a plan, and you must try to follow it exactly. Can you do that?"

"Yes, sir."

He thought briefly. "We'll leave this room together. Then you must wait at the top of the stairs, while I go down and speak with Mme. Leclerc and her friend. When you hear me call to you to run, run as fast as you can down the stairs and out the front door. Don't wait for me to follow. Turn right and run down to the end of the street, and wait for me there. If I don't come in—oh, about ten minutes—don't on any account come back here. Stop a hackney—one of those broken-down coaches with a number-plate behind—and tell it to take you to this address." He wrote it down and gave her some coins to pay the fare. "When you get there, ask for Dipper, and tell him what's happened. Do you understand?"

She was concentrating with all her might. "Yes, sir."

"Good. Don't be afraid—we'll manage famously. Now then."

He put a finger to his lips, went to the door, and peered out cautiously. Then he beckoned to her. "Keep behind me," he whispered, and walked down the hall to the stairway, Emily following.

He left her at the top of the stairs. Halfway down, he paused, revolted by the part he had to play. What kind of man would pay fifty pounds for the privilege of debauching a child? And yet there must be scores of such men in London, to judge by Smith and Company's thriving trade. All those ledgers—but he must not think about that now. Gathering his blasé, indolent manner about him, he descended to the front hall. He stopped to retrieve his hat, cloak, and walking-stick, then strolled into the parlour.

Mme. Leclerc rose gracefully, putting aside her embroidery. The giant, who had been warming his trouser-seat at the fire, strode up to Julian purposefully.

"I trust everything was satisfactory, monsieur," the Frenchwoman purred.

"Tolerable," said Julian, with a shrug. "You won't allow me to vowel you, I suppose?"

"I am afraid we cannot take an I.O.U. We must insist on immediate payment."

The giant raised an enormous fist. "If you won't pay one way, I makes you pay another."

"Now, Bart, I am sure monsieur means to be reasonable. Do you not, monsieur?"

Julian looked up at the giant looming over him. "You don't leave me a great deal of choice."

He took out his pocket-book, opened it, and blew. A cloud of snuff flew into the giant's face. The giant clapped his hands over his eyes, sneezing convulsively. In that moment, Julian struck him sharply with his walking-stick: once at the knees to fell him to the floor, and once on the head to stun him.

"Run, Emily!" he cried.

He heard the child's frantic footsteps on the stairs. Mme. Leclerc leaped toward the door, but Julian pulled her back, pinning her arms behind her. She struggled, kicked, and tried to bite him. He pushed her onto the sofa face down and thrust his walking-stick under her nose. "If you move again before I give you leave, I'll serve you in the same manner as I did your friend."

"*Salaud!*" she spat at him. "*Merdeux!*"

"Listen to me, madame. I'm going to leave you now, because I have to find that child and make certain she doesn't run into any more benefactors like you. Otherwise, it would give me great pleasure to turn you over to the law—or pitch you into the river. I advise you to stay here and not attempt to follow me. I'm not in the habit of striking women, but for you, madame, I would make an exception. *Vous comprenez*?"

She shook with rage, but she nodded.

"*Au revoir*, madame." He bowed and left her.

He found Emily waiting for him at the corner of Windmill Street. She was shivering violently in her light muslin frock, and he draped his coat around her.

"Are they coming after us?" she asked, looking fearfully down Windmill Street.

"No. But all the same, we'd best get out of this neighbourhood directly."

He hailed a hackney coach and gave his address in Clarges Street. "I'm taking you to the house where I live. I shall ask my landlady to let you stay with her. She's very kind, and likes children."

"Can't I go home?"

"You will, very soon. But in the meantime we've got to find a place for you to sleep tonight. Tomorrow we'll make arrangements for you to go back to your parents."

"Oh." Tears welled up in her eyes. She had had "arrangements" made for her before.

"Can you trust me this one night, Emily? Can you believe I mean well by you, and I won't let anyone hurt you—not tonight, not ever?"

She lifted beseeching eyes. "I want my mother."

Damnation, he thought. This is preposterous. I can't put her on a coach to Wiltshire and send her off like a parcel after everything she's been through. And I can't simply drop the investigation and go rattling off to the West Country. Besides, she may be needed in London to give evidence. Perhaps her people could come and fetch her—

She was still looking at him with those eyes. Oh, the devil, he thought. He stopped the hackney and told the driver to take them to the Golden Cross.

Emily looked bewildered. He explained, "That's a large coaching inn near Charing Cross."

"Why are we going there?"

He sighed. "Because we should get very tired, walking all the way to Wiltshire."

At the booking-office, Julian debated over whether to take the stagecoach or hire a private chaise. Emily might feel safer in a group of people. But seeing her yawn and rub her eyes, he decided she needed sleep more than anything else, and sleeping on a stagecoach, even for the inside passengers, was anything but easy. Moreover, he and Emily made a curious pair and might attract unwelcome attention. Even the bored booking-office clerks stared at him in his satin-lined black cloak, and at Emily trailing his tailcoat along the floor.

He ordered a post-chaise to be ready in an hour. Fortunately he had plenty of money, having brought the fifty pounds demanded by Smith and Company, in case he needed to pay it. But Emily could not travel some seventy or eighty miles without warm clothes. He wrote a note to Dipper, explaining briefly what had happened and bidding him bring some woolen garments for Emily, and a dressing-case and change of clothes for himself. He did not propose to be away more than a night and a day, but he had no intention of travelling all the way to Wiltshire and back in evening dress.

Even at this hour, there were urchins hanging about the coachyard, eager to run errands for the passengers. Julian gave the note to one of them to deliver. Then he took Emily inside and ordered her a plate of roast beef and a posset of hot milk and treacle. She fell on the food ravenously. Either she had not had much appetite since she came to London, or Mme. Leclerc had starved her to make her more compliant. For himself, he ordered a case-bottle of brandy to take on the journey. It would provide a little relief from the cold and discomfort of long-distance coaching.

Dipper arrived as Emily was finishing her meal. He had everything in hand, as usual. He brought a woolen cloak and stockings for Emily—borrowed from Sally, he explained—together with a carriage rug, a caped greatcoat and portmanteau for Julian, and a small carpet-bag for himself.

"You mean to come with us?" said Julian.

"'Course I do, sir. I has to give you countenance."

Julian's brows went up in amusement. "Really?"

"Yes, sir. On account of at the cribs where you stops along the road, you has to show you're a nob, or they won't tip you the best grub and lodging. And for that, you has to travel with a slavey."

"Of course. I can't think what possessed me. But what about Sally?"

"She'll be all right, sir. She can stay at Mrs. M.'s till we gets back. She don't like it above half, our piking off without her, but I said it don't make sense for us all to go."

"No, hardly. We can't come trooping into Emily's village like a deputation. By the way, that's a very useful trick you taught me, the one you call the sneezing-racket."

"It's a prime dodge, sir," Dipper agreed.

Their carriage was waiting in the coachyard. Like most post-chaises, it only fit two inside, but there was an open seat at the back for servants. Dipper was happy to ride there, since it allowed him to watch for what he called peter-hunters: thieves who slashed through the boots of carriages and stole the luggage. Julian wondered, not for the first time, how other gentlemen muddled through life without a former thief for a servant.

Emily was practically asleep on her feet. Julian handed her into the carriage and climbed in after her. The post-boy sprang on the left-hand horse, the ostler cried, "All right, put 'em along!" and the chaise sped away.

Emily nodded off at once. Julian tucked the carriage rug around her. His thoughts turned to Sally. He had forebodings about leaving her alone. It was hard to see how she could get into trouble in the short time he and Dipper would be gone. But if there were a way, he felt sure she would find it.

The Best-Laid Plans

Sally gave her pillow an exasperated thump and sat up. It was no use trying to sleep. How could they go away and leave her like this? They knew how much good work she had done in the investigation, how intrigued by it she was. Now they had packed her off to Mrs. Mabbitt's like so much unwanted baggage, while they went off adventuring in the country. All very well for Mr. Kestrel! Have his sport with a gal and throw her away.

She folded her arms and tried to sulk, but it was no use. Badly as she wanted a grievance, that last one was too silly. She giggled, and felt much better.

She sat up, arms wrapped around her knees. That was enough feeling sorry for herself, and angry at everyone else. Mr. Kestrel (she could not call him by his Christian name; he was a gentleman, after all) had written that he expected to be back by the end of the day tomorrow. Or, rather, today, for it was past midnight. She ought to think what she could do to speed the investigation along in his absence.

He had said her idea of arranging a meeting with the three men needed fleshing out. To write a note to each man, offering information about Mary's letter, was simple enough. But where should the rendezvous be? Some secluded spot—a park or an alley at dead of night. No, that was too dangerous. The man might really try to do them a mischief, especially when he found they did not intend to give up the letter. There had to be a way to lessen the risk—otherwise Mr. Kestrel would not let her go, and that she could not bear: Whose idea was this, after all?

A dark, deserted spot was all wrong, she decided. A public place would be much safer. What could the man do to them, surrounded by a throng of people? They could parley with him about the letter, and sound him about Mary's life and death. Then, when they had got all they could out of him, they would simply morris off. How could he stop them?

Of course, if it were Avondale who came to the meeting, he would know who Mr. Kestrel was and where he lived, and might make trouble later. And if it were Rawdon, he would recognize Mr. Kestrel as the man who rescued that little girl, which would put him in a savage temper from the start. It would really be much better if Mr. Kestrel kept out of this. But she knew he would be no more willing to miss the rendezvous than she was.

Where could they arrange to meet their man? The Cockerel, of course! Fiske and Rawdon both knew where it was, and Avondale could surely find it. There were always plenty of people in the taproom at night. Their man would have no choice but to behave himself.

She hugged her knees delightedly. They were going to find out, at long last, which man had Mary's letter in his pocket the night before she died. As soon as Mr. Kestrel and Dipper came home, they could put her plan into action.

But why wait so long to take the first step? Why shouldn't she set up the rendezvous while they were gone, and surprise them? She could send a note to each man in the morning, proposing a meeting that night. If she made it late enough, Mr. Kestrel and Dipper would surely be back.

She got up, threw a shawl over her nightdress, and lit a candle. Next door to her room was a back kitchen where Mrs. Mabbitt worked on her household accounts. Sally rummaged through the desk and found three sheets of paper and a pencil. She grimaced at the task before her. The thought of so much writing made her head ache. She sat down, bit hard on the pencil for a while, and finally printed laboriously on the first sheet:

Deer Mr Fisk
If you wants to no about a surtan letter com to the Cockerel tonite at ten oclock.

A frend

She sat back and read it over. It would do. At least she was sure she had spelled "Cockerel" right—she had seen the sign often enough. She copied out two identical notes, one to Avondale and one to Rawdon. Then, tired out from her labours, she crept back to bed and fell asleep.

She was up at dawn, eager to get the notes delivered as soon as possible. The twopenny post would not be quick enough. She could pay a boy to deliver them, but he might dawdle, or even throw the notes away once he got his money. It was not as if she could promise him a tip at the other end. The only way to be sure the notes arrived safely was to deliver them herself.

She set off directly after breakfast. In the front hall, she nearly bumped into the workman Mrs. Mabbitt had hired to do the whitewashing. He ought to have finished by now, but Mrs. M. was always finding bits that needed to be done over.

She went first to Bury Street, where she boldly rang and gave the note to Avondale's servant. Then she walked to Eastcheap, remembering that Fiske's apothecary shop was there. She had a little money, but she scorned to take a hackney. A shilling a mile, when her feet worked perfectly well? Not likely!

She found Fiske's shop easily enough. It was not open yet. A boy of about fifteen—Fiske's 'prentice, no doubt—was taking down the shutters. "Where's your master?" Sally asked him, under her breath.

"In back."

"Give this to him." She handed him the note, with her most winsome smile. He gaped at her, poised to fall in love at the slightest encouragement. But she had no time to spare. Taking to her heels, she lost herself in the morning traffic.

One more note. A cold dread stole over her. What if she ran smack into Blinkers?—Well, she was fly to him now. If he tried to lay a finger on her, she would be ready.

She walked across London Bridge to Southwark. She had no trouble finding the Prices' shop—Dipper had described to her just where it was. She looked up at the windows above it. The blinds were drawn. She frowned. Suppose Rawdon were not there today?

She went to the window of the shop. There was a man helping a customer at the counter, and a girl sitting in a corner, sorting cigars. Sally caught her eye and beckoned vigorously. The girl glanced toward the man at the counter, then came outside.

Sally drew her away from the window. "You must be Annie Price."

"Yes."

"I'm Sally Stokes. Dipper's me brother."

Annie's face flamed.

You rogue, Dip! thought Sally admiringly. "I'd like to stay and get acquainted, but I can't. *He* might see me." She shot a glance at the first-floor windows.

"Is he up there?"

"Yes. There's another man with him."

"Who?"

"I don't know. I hardly got a look at him, he went in so quick I think he was in a pother about something."

Sally could not make anything of this. "I've got a note for him. I think I'll just leave it outside his door, and cut and run before he twigs me. Nice to meet you!" She shook Annie's hand warmly and turned away.

"Oh, Miss Stokes—your brother—how is he?"

Sally's eyes danced. "He had to light out for daisyville with his master, sudden-like. He'll be back tonight. I'll tell him you was asking after him."

"Oh—thank you." Annie blushed again and went back into the shop.

Sally crept upstairs to the door of Smith and Company and poked the note into a gap between two floorboards, where Rawdon would be sure to see it. Summoning all her courage, she knocked loudly. Then she ran down the stairs and did not stop running till she reached the High Street.

She was gleeful. Everything had gone off perfectly. Now there was nothing to do but wait, and see which man answered her summons.

Mud squelched under Julian's boots as he and Dipper set off down the road. A little pool of rain that had gathered in his hatbrim spilled over and ran down his back. He was already so wet, he hardly noticed. He lifted a corner of the short cape attached to his greatcoat, which he had flung over his head to keep off the rain, and looked into the distance. There was nothing to be seen but pelting rain, sodden hedgerows, and the empty road stretching to the horizon, where grey earth met a greyer sky.

The first half of the journey, from London to Emily's village, had gone well. Thanks to the breathless speed and efficiency of posting, they reached Salisbury by mid-morning. There they breakfasted at an inn, and Julian shaved and changed his clothes, while Dipper arranged for Emily to wash and make herself presentable for her parents. They hired a gig to take them the short remaining distance to the village. Emily gazed with glowing eyes on every fence and tree, like a shipwreck victim finally sighting land.

Mrs. Wickham welcomed her daughter with joy and surprise, which turned to consternation when Julian took her aside and explained what had nearly befallen Emily. She sent for her husband, who was working in the fields, and the two of them spent the next hour alternately heaping thanks on Julian, and abuse on Mme. Leclerc and her accomplices. Julian stayed long enough to be courteous, then said he must return to London if he was to put a stop to Smith and Company's trade. The Wickhams sent him on his way with their blessing, and promised to bring Emily back to town if she was needed to make a statement to a magistrate. The last Julian saw of her, she was standing by her mother on the doorstep of their cottage, shyly waving a handkerchief at the gig as it rumbled away.

They hired a chaise in Salisbury, and that was when the trouble began. A rainstorm broke out, and the road to London became a hasty pudding. Their progress slowed to a walk. Then, just ahead of them, a great rattling stagecoach—the inaptly named *Reliant*—skidded and overturned into a ditch, sending the outside passengers flying into hedges, and showering the insides with broken glass. Julian stopped his chaise, and he and Dipper sprang out to help cut the horses free and assist the passengers. Two of the outsides were badly hurt, with broken limbs and bleeding faces. The coachman had been dragged off the box, and was limping about insisting it was not his fault, he never touched a drop when he was handling the ribbons. The horses were terrified; one had been lamed for life, and was no doubt destined for the knacker's yard.

The stagecoach guard rode to the nearest town to hunt up a surgeon and another conveyance. Meanwhile, Julian, Dipper, and the least hurt of the passengers tended to the injured. All the passengers were shaken and bruised, and one young woman kept breaking into hysterics. Her husband, who looked like a minor solicitor or clerk, hovered over her helplessly.

Presently he came up to Julian, doffing his hat in spite of the rain. His wife was in an interesting condition, he confided. They had travelled all the way from Devon, she was exhausted, he was at his wits' end—

There was only one course open to a gentleman. Julian begged they would be good enough to take his chaise and send another back for him when they got to the next posting-house. The young roan thanked him profusely and handed his wife into the carriage. The other stagecoach passengers looked on enviously.

Julian turned to Dipper. "The post-boy said the next stage is six miles ahead. I don't see that we can do any more good here, so why don't we walk on and meet our new chaise on the road?"

They set off, Dipper swinging his master's portmanteau in one hand and his own carpet-bag in the other. "I'll take one of those," said Julian.

"I've got 'em all right, sir."

"It's very evident Nature didn't intend you for a packhorse. In fact, a packhorse could probably swallow you in a mouthful. Give me my portmanteau."

"It don't look right, sir. What if somebody you knows was to see you?"

"If any of the lady patronesses of Almacks should come tooling along in a pony phaeton, I'll smear my face all over with mud and masquerade as a swineherd." He took firm possession of the portmanteau. "You're becoming deuced insubordinate. Remind me to beat you when we get home."

They tramped on companionably, their heads bowed against the wind and rain. "It's a mercy we haven't any urgent business in London," said Julian. "We'll be lucky to reach Charing Cross by midnight. At least we finally have an opportunity to talk about the investigation. Between looking after Emily and catching the odd wink of sleep, we've been giving it rather short shrift. We know now what Smith and Company's business is, and that suggests a whole new range of possibilities. We wondered how a girl of Mary's breeding and education, with such a keen sense of shame and remorse, could have ended up in a refuge for prostitutes. Now I keep remembering what she wrote in her letter: *My ruin has not been all my fault... I never knew there was such evil in the world as I've known since I left you.*"

"You think she was trepanned, sir?"

"Trepanned?"

"That's what it's called, sir. Trepanners, they brings gals in from the country, or nabs 'em off the streets in town. Then they either sells 'em to knocking-houses or ships 'em across the water. It's a bang-up trade, sir. There's many as follows it."

"It's hard to believe there could be a demand for yet more prostitutes in London. It's a devilish high price to pay for keeping our wives and sisters virtuous.—Damnation. Stop a moment, I've got a nail in my boot. What have we done with the case-bottle?"

"I've got it here, sir,"

"Is there any brandy left in it?"

"A bit, sir." Dipper handed him the bottle.

"We'll share it. Don't make that face again. There's no point in trying to martyr yourself in this weather—we should never find enough dry tinder to burn you with." He took a few warming swallows of the brandy, then gave the bottle back to Dipper, who followed suit. "At all events," he resumed, "it would be a worthy achievement to clean out this one rats' nest, however many other rats may come to take their places. God knows how many girls like Emily vanish into that sink-hole, Smith and Company, leaving their relatives wondering what's become of them, and losing hope as the months go by, and they never get any word. Mary could well have been one of them, even though she wasn't so young as Emily. Those items in Rawdon's ledgers—tea-chests, tea-pots, tea-urns—may mean different types of human inventory. Little girls, young women—"

"Boys," said Dipper matter-of-factly.

Julian shuddered.

"The thing is, sir, trepanners ain't easy to shop. They hardly ever gets took up by the law, on account of they greases the nabsmen." He made a gesture eloquent of bribery. "And if they does get pulled in, oftentimes there ain't much proof against 'em, so they gets acquitted, and they're back on the streets again. Once in a way they fetches a lagging, but it ain't for more than a month."

"A month's imprisonment? For making a slave and light-o'-love out of an eleven-year-old girl? Eleven years old—that's the same age as Philippa Fontclair!"

Dipper nodded, remembering the precocious little girl who had been Mr. Kestrel's friend and ally at the time of the Bellegarde murder. "But it don't happen to her sort, sir—gentry-morts with plenty of blunt, and a father with a handle to his name. Them as gets trepanned is orphans, or comes of families like the Wickhams, as hasn't the means nor the h'influence to buy 'emselves any justice."

"That's as formidable an indictment of our so-called English liberties as I've ever heard." Julian pondered. "Suppose Mary was trepanned, but she escaped from her captors and hid at the refuge. Rawdon found out where she was, and got some ally in the refuge to kill her, to keep her from revealing what she knew about Smith and Company's trade. Wideawake Peg would be an ideal candidate: she's clever and venal, and has Harcourt's trust. She knew Mary was writing a letter, so she could have intercepted it and passed it on to Rawdon. Though I still think her frankness to Sally about the letter suggests she had nothing to hide."

"But sir, there must be heaps of folks as knows about Mr. Rawdon's business. Supposing Mary was trepanned, and piked off to the refuge—well, she can't be the first mort as ever tipped Mr. Rawdon the double."

That was true, thought Julian. Victims must have escaped from Smith and Company before. What would be done with a girl like Emily, once some customer had paid fifty pounds to ruin her? Most likely she would be consigned to a brothel. There were probably women in houses all over Covent Garden and the Haymarket who owed their careers to Smith and Company. And some of them must surely drift away in time—some upward, into marriage or respectable work, some downward, to sell themselves for sixpence in the parks and the East End rookeries. It could not be that Rawdon set out to kill every girl who slipped through his fingers.

He suggested, "Perhaps Mary knew something out of the common about the trepanners. The identity of one of their customers, for instance—some eminent, outwardly respectable person. Or Rawdon might have a partner in high places who's anxious to preserve his anonymity. In that case, Rawdon may be only an instrument—there may be a powerful but unseen hand behind the murder.

"And then again—remember what you said a moment ago? You said a girl like Philippa Fontclair would never be trepanned, because Mr. Rawdon's kind don't prey on women with money and connexions. But suppose they made a mistake? Suppose they netted a person of consequence—one whose family has enough wealth and political influence to hunt them down, and bring the full might of the law to bear on them? In that case, the key question wouldn't be what Mary knew, but who she was."

"If she was a great gun, sir, why didn't she say so?"

"Perhaps precisely because she was a great gun. She would have had a sense of pride and shame in proportion to her position. Her letter suggests she was anxious to hide her identity for her family's sake, and the more exalted they were, the more she would feel the need to protect them from scandal. She was obviously a lady—the question is, was she merely some impoverished curate's daughter, or was she a person of rank and importance? If we only knew to whom she wrote that letter, we'd have the answer. It's maddening that the letter was preserved, but not the outer sheet with the address—Good God—"

He stopped walking. "How could I have overlooked anything so obvious?"

"Sir?"

Julian turned to him, his eyes alight. "Is that man still whitewashing the hallway at home?"

"I think so, sir."

"Good. I have an idea."

Sally could hardly eat a bite of supper. Mrs. Mabbitt declared she was making her giddy, jumping up to look out the window every moment. "You know what they say about a watched pot," she warned.

"They'll be back any time now, won't they?" asked Sally eagerly. "It's nigh to seven o'clock."

"Oh, you know what coach travel's like. So many things can go wrong on the road—horses casting a shoe, poles splintering, wheels coming off. It wouldn't surprise me if they didn't get home till the small hours."

Sally stared in dismay.

Mrs. Mabbitt smiled. "You've never coached any great distance, I can see."

"No," mourned Sally, dropping into her chair.

"There's nothing to worrit yourself about. They'll come back safe and sound. It just might take a bit of time, that's all."

But I've no time to spare! thought Sally.

All evening she hovered at the kitchen window, pressing her face to the glass whenever she heard carriage wheels. Eight o'clock went by, then nine, and still the travellers had not returned.

Mrs. Mabbitt put her sewing away, saying she was feeling peepy and wanted her bed. The hands of the clock crept round to half past nine. Sally got up purposefully and went to her room to change her clothes. Mr. Kestrel and Dipper were not back—so be it. The rendezvous was all arranged; she could not throw away this chance to find out from which man she had gotten the letter. She would just have to go alone.

Whitewash

Sally dug out one of her old gowns, made of pink silk, with green bows at the neck and a big green flounce around the bottom. She could not go to the Cockerel in the prim, poky clothes Mrs. Mabbitt made her wear. Her old friends there would hardly recognize her, and the man she was meeting might be suspicious. She bound up her back hair more securely, then spat on her fingers and slicked her front hair into tighter curls. Tying on her widebrimmed, red-feathered bonnet, she beamed at herself in the glass. Now, that was something like!

She struggled through yet another note, explaining where she had gone, and why. Hastening upstairs, she propped it on the mantelpiece in Mr. Kestrel's front parlour. Glancing at the clock, she saw that it was a quarter to ten. She flung on her cloak and ran out.

Piccadilly was clogged with traffic, as always. She would move fastest on foot. She wove, edged, and shoved her way along the pavement, till at last she reached the Haymarket. Leaving the gaslit thoroughfare behind her, she darted down the little dark street where the Cockerel was.

The taproom was crowded tonight. She was glad—the more people around her, the safer she would feel. She scanned the room, her heart thumping fast. The customers were the usual types: broken-down boxers, decaying actors, bawdy-house bullies, and whores. She had no trouble picking out the man she had come to meet. He looked as out of place among this lot as a peacock in a chicken-yard. Charles Avondale.

He was pacing restlessly back and forth, as well as he could in such a small, crowded space. When he caught sight of Sally, he frowned as if trying to place her. She grinned and dropped a curtsy.

Recognition dawned in his eyes. He made his way toward her, staring in amazement. "You!"

"'Course it's me! Who'd you expect?"

"I didn't know who or what the plague to expect!"

"Well, you must've knowed it was me as pinched your letter."

A feverish light sprang up in his eyes. He caught her arm. "Have you got it with you?"

"No." For the first time, she was a little frightened. She had told herself no man in his right senses would harm her in a public place like this. But was Avondale in his right senses? "You're hurting me arm," she complained.

He let her go and took a few long, struggling breaths. "You want money. Of course. Come, we'll sit down there and talk." He pointed to a table in the corner.

"You has to stand us a drop, or Toby'll cut up rusty."

"All right. What will you have?"

"White satin."

She secured the corner table while he went to the bar. He brought back a glass of gin for her and a pint-pot for himself. She lifted her glass convivially, but he did not notice. He was glancing uneasily around the taproom.

"What you looking for?" she asked.

"I have a feeling I was followed here. But it's probably all my fancy." He laughed mirthlessly. "I often have that feeling these days."

He took a few gulps of ale. She watched him, thinking: So it's him I pinched the letter from. So Mary must've been this Rosemary of his, and most likely it was him as croaked her. But why? And who's that gal Megan MacGowan?

"All right," he said. "Let's talk business. How much do you want for the letter?"

"I ain't made up me mind," she stalled. "I'd like to know a bit more about it first. Otherwise, how'll I know how much to ask for it?"

"You can't think I'm going to tell you about the letter? As far as I'm concerned, the less you know about it, the better."

"Oh, if that's how you feel—" She shrugged and stood up.

His left hand shot out and grabbed her wrist.

"Sit down!" he hissed.

"Why should I?"

"Because I'm pointing a pistol straight at your heart, and if you don't sit down, I'll kill you."

Her eyes dropped to his right hand, which was thrust into his greatcoat pocket. He drew it out for a moment, showing her a wicked little pocket pistol. It was double-barrelled, which meant he could even afford to miss her once.

"You're faking," she stammered. "You'd never pop me in front of all these people."

"Wouldn't I?" His grip on her wrist tightened painfully. The skull ring he wore on his little finger glinted in the candlelight. "I've been through hell on account of that letter and everything it signifies. That it's a hell partly of my own making doesn't make it any easier! A few years ago, I trifled with a woman—I made a rash promise I never meant to keep. God knows, it was wrong, but hundreds of fellows like me have done the same, and they haven't been cursed with the consequences I have. There's nothing I wouldn't do to get that letter back. I've dug myself so deep into the pit that I don't care a damn what I do now, or how far I go, or whether I drag you down with me. So for the last time, sit down, and name your price!"

She sank slowly into her chair. She could not doubt he was in deadly earnest. What should she do? To give up the letter to him was out of the question. She and Mr. Kestrel had agreed they would not part with it. Even if she were willing to hand it over, they would have to go to Clarges Street to get it, and that would alert Avondale that Mr. Kestrel and Dipper were involved in this. She could not split on her friends. No, she would have to find her own way out of this coil.

She looked around wildly for someone or something to assist her. What she saw, incredibly, was Matthew Fiske coming toward them, kneading his hat between his hands. What was he doing here? Did he know something about the letter, after all? Or was he still trying to warn her off?

"What do you want?" said Avondale sharply, keeping a firm grip on Sally's wrist.

Fiske looked from him to Sally. "I came in answer to your note."

"What note?" Avondale rounded on her. "Is this fellow in league with you? Shall I have to pay him, too?"

"Pay me?" said Fiske. "I don't understand you, sir. I came to see this young woman about—about a private matter."

"Well, you can't see her now. She's with me at the moment. So have the goodness to take yourself off."

"You'd best do like he says, Bristles," Sally sighed. "He ain't one to take no for an answer."

"But—but what about the letter?" faltered Fiske.

"What the plague does *he* know about my letter?" Avondale demanded.

"He don't know nothing about it," said Sally. After all, why should poor Bristles get mixed up in this? "I thought he did at first, but now I knows it was you I pinched it from."

Avondale stared. "What in God's name are you talking about?"

"The letter!" she said impatiently. "The one I pinched from your pocket while we was having a ride that night."

"From *my* pocket! My God, do you think if I'd had the letter I'd be carrying it about for you to lay hands on? Don't you think I'd have destroyed it the moment I had the chance?"

"But—" She broke off. Light began to dawn. "This letter you're after, was it wrote by a gal as lost her character, and was asking somebody in her family to take her back?"

"The devil it was! It was *my* letter, I wrote it! You're trying to confuse me, but it won't work. I won't be led a dance!" The nose of the pistol rose warningly.

"Don't you understand?" she urged. "It's two different letters! The one I have ain't the one you want. The night I picked you up, I picked him up afore you"—she nodded at Fiske—"and another cove after. I pinched a letter from one of you, but I didn't know which, so I wrote to all three of you asking you to meet me here, to see which one would show. And two of you did, but *you've* found a mare's nest. It ain't your letter. You understand?"

It was nearly midnight by the time Julian and Dipper got home. Julian sent Dipper downstairs to fetch a container of whitewash and a brush from the hall cupboard. He himself went to the pianoforte and pressed a hidden spring. A panel flew open, revealing a small compartment. He took out Mary's letter. Spreading out an old *Morning Chronicle* on a table, he laid the letter on it, face down. Then he lit an Argand lamp, turning up the wick to make it burn as brightly as possible.

When Dipper returned with the whitewash, Julian opened the container and dipped the brush in. "I wonder I didn't think of this before. We knew Mary had used a second sheet of paper as a makeshift envelope. And we knew her pencil-point had grown dull as she wrote, till she had to bear down very hard. If the address was the last thing she wrote—which stands to reason, since she had to finish the letter before she could wrap it in the outer sheet—perhaps we can conjure up the ghost of the address."

He painted a gossamer-thin coat of whitewash across the back of the letter. Then he held it up to the light, slanting it to see its surface in relief. In the middle of the sheet were faint impressions of written words, the whitewash coating the indentations: *Lord Braxton, Braxton Castle, Shropshire.*

Julian put the letter down slowly. "And to think we joked about it as the Braxton disaster. And we had no idea."

"Lord Braxton—he's the cove as invited all the nobs to his castle, then put a stopper on it when his daughter run off to France with a half-pay captain."

"Not *with* him, *to* him. Captain Hartwell was already in France—he'd done a moonlit flit on account of his debts. Lady Lucinda ran away to join him—and we know now she never arrived. She's buried in a pauper's grave, branded a prostitute and a suicide."

"You think she was nabbed by the trepanners, sir?"

"It seems the most likely explanation, doesn't it? She was travelling alone, and almost certainly didn't go by her real name. She may well have seemed like a nobody—genteel but poor, without connexions. She wasn't out yet, so the world didn't know her, and she didn't know the world. She could easily have been entrapped by someone like Mme. Leclerc. She hasn't been missed, because she's presumed to have joined her lover on the Continent, and her father is in too much of a temper to write to her or try to find her. Captain Hartwell may not have known she was coming, and even if he did, he can't return to England to look for her without his creditors arresting him for debt."

He turned the letter over and scanned its contents. "Read in that light, everything she wrote makes sense. *I do not think I could face anyone I know, ever again—not you, nor anyone else in our family, nor him I once thought I loved.* The 'you' is Lord Braxton, and 'him I once thought I loved' is Captain Hartwell. The 'stupid, stubborn ungrateful rashness' she repents is her running away to marry the captain against her father's wishes. And, of course, 'My ruin has not been all my fault' would refer to Smith and Company.

"How she ended up at the refuge is anyone's guess. Perhaps she simply ran away from her captors and sought shelter there. Imagine Rawdon's consternation, if he'd found out by then who she really was! He'd connived at the kidnapping—the rape, very likely—of Lady Lucinda Braxton, the daughter of one of the wealthiest peers in England, with half Parliament in his pocket, and the devil's own temper besides. If she told her father what had happened to her, he'd hunt Rawdon and his cohorts down like dogs. But she didn't tell him—not at once. She was so shocked and ashamed, she hid at the refuge, telling no one who she was. That gave Rawdon a respite, and he's clever and ruthless enough to have made the most of it.

"But how would he have found out she was at the refuge? From her letter, perhaps? Suppose someone—Wideawake Peg, for instance—intercepted the letter and passed it on to him. That would fit the timing: Lady Lucinda wrote it on Saturday evening, it had come into the hands of one of those three men by Monday, and Lady Lucinda died the next night. Which would mean Mr. Rawdon acted with his usual efficiency.

"I think we can absolve Avondale of any role in the murder. Whoever his Rosemary is—or was—she's not the young lady who was killed at the refuge. Fiske's role is more troubling. If he's innocent, then he's ringed by some very improbable coincidences. Of all the places where Lady Lucinda might have sought asylum—churches, workhouses, charitable institutions—she ended up at the refuge where Fiske's wife works, and where he himself serves as apothecary. It was he who prescribed the cordial for her. By all accounts, he was one of the few people at the refuge she trusted, and might have told about the letter. And yet Sally is convinced he was telling the truth when he said she didn't steal it from him. It doesn't make sense—unless—Good God! Is it possible?"

"Sir?"

Julian said slowly, "Dipper, what do you know about thimblerig?"

"It's a game played at fairs, sir, with three cups and a pea. Them as plays it tries to guess which cup the pea's under."

"But they never win, do they?"

"No, sir. 'Coz the sharper—him as moves the cups around—palms the pea, so it turns up under a different cup from the one the player chose."

"Exactly! And I was thinking—What's that?"

Dipper followed his gaze to the mantelpiece and saw a note propped there. Julian went over and picked it up. He ran his eyes over it, and his face changed. He thrust it at Dipper, who read it, then looked up in consternation.

Julian caught up his hat and gloves. "Fetch my pistols. We'll load them on the way."

Blood Will Tell

To Sally's relief, Avondale drew his right hand out of his greatcoat pocket, without the pistol. "I'm back where I started," he said wretchedly. "You were my last hope. When I read your note, I didn't know who you were or anything about you, but I naturally assumed the letter you spoke of was the one I wanted—the one I've been trying to lay hands on for years."

"No wonder you was surprised to see me," she grinned. "You couldn't think how I knowed a thing about your letter."

Fiske tapped her timidly on the shoulder. "Now may I speak to you? I was thinking we might go to one of the rooms upstairs—to talk," he added hastily.

"Oh, no! I ain't shifting me bob from this spot. We can talk right here."

"It's too public. I really must speak to you alone."

"Kiss me arse! Last time you said we'd talk alone, you tipped me the Dublin packet."

"I'm sorry about that. It seemed the best thing to do at the time." He sank his voice to a whisper. "You'll be paid for the letter, and paid well, only you must come upstairs where we can talk privately. Please believe me! Why would I have come at all, if I hadn't meant to have it out with you about the letter?"

"So it was you I pinched it from?"

He hesitated. "I'll tell you about that upstairs. Please come with me now!"

She considered. Then she rose and turned from him to Avondale. "You'll have to morris off now, Blue Eyes. I got business with this gentleman."

Avondale came to his feet heavily. Sally slipped an arm around his neck. "Cheer up. A dimber cove like you shouldn't hang his gib so." She smoothed his brow playfully. "It'll all come right, you'll see."

"Look here," he said impulsively, "I'm sorry I frightened you. I didn't know what sort of people I might run into in a place like this—what sort of rogues you might be in league with—"

"Now don't get in a pucker," she soothed. "It's all over, and no harm done." She came up on her toes and kissed him lightly on the lips. "Push off now."

He took his hat from its peg, bowed slightly to Fiske, and departed. Sally looked after him, grinning. Then she turned to Fiske. "All right. Let's go upstairs."

They went up to the bar. In some embarrassment, Fiske asked Toby if he had a room free. "Second floor back," Toby grunted. Fiske paid his shilling, and Toby plunked the key down on the counter. Fiske reached for it, but Sally was too quick for him. She scooped it up, lit a tallow candle, and led the way out of the taproom.

They entered the back passage, with its peeling paint and tapestry of cobwebs. The back door, leading to the alley behind the Cockerel, was barred as always. They climbed the stairs, Sally reminding Fiske not to lean on the rotting banisters. When they got to the room—the same bleak little bedroom they had used a few weeks before—Sally put her candle on the washstand and turned to Fiske. "Well? What've you got to say to me?"

"We can't talk yet. I have to leave you for a moment. I'll be back directly."

"Here now, what kind of take-in is this? Where you going?"

"There's someone else who wants to see you. We're prepared to pay you a great deal for the letter, but you must wait here a moment while I fetch him. You won't go away, will you?"

"No." She leaned back against the wall opposite the door, her hands thrust into the pockets of her cloak. "I'll wait right here, Bristles. I want to have a look at this friend of yours."

He slipped away, closing the door behind him. Sally waited tensely, her eyes trained on the door. At last it opened. Fiske came in, rubbing his hands nervously. Behind him, silent and deliberate, came Joseph Rawdon. He closed the door behind him and looked across at Sally. His lips curved into the predatory smile she remembered all too well. He lifted his arm, and the candlelight glinted on the long, sharp knife in his hand.

"No!" cried Fiske. "You promised we wouldn't hurt her!"

Rawdon sprang toward Sally. The next moment, he halted and jumped back, choking with baffled rage. Sally stood silently pointing the little double-barrelled pistol that she had stolen from Avondale's pocket when she kissed him goodbye.

Rawdon started backing toward the door. "What's your hurry, Blinkers?" she said. "You ain't going no place. Put that down." She jerked her head at the knife.

Teeth clenched, he started to obey. Suddenly the door swung open behind him, and a woman rushed in. She had a gaunt face and long, unkempt red hair, and wore a shabby black cloak and a plaid shawl.

Rawdon seized her with a cry of triumph and held the knife tight to her throat. "I'm leaving," he told Sally, "and I'm taking this woman with me. If you try to stop me, or send anyone after me, I'll slit her throat from ear to ear."

The woman gasped for breath. Her staring eyes fixed on

Sally. "I saw ye with him," she panted, "with Avondale! I followed him here. Tell me, tell me! Ye must ken! Where is Rosemary?"

"You're Megan MacGowan!" Sally started toward her.

"Stay back!" Rawdon warned.

"Tell me!" Megan's voice rose to a hoarse scream. "Where is—"

"Hold your tongue!" Rawdon pressed the blade harder against her throat. A trickle of blood ran down into her collar.

"I dunno where she is," said Sally, anxious to quiet Megan for her own sake. "I swear, I dunno nothing about her at all. Leave her alone, you bastard! She ain't done nothing to you!"

Fiske stood hunched in a comer, wringing his hands. "You promised we wouldn't hurt anyone," he whimpered.

"And you believed him?" Sally cried scornfully. "You poor old spoony, he's as curst a cove as the hemp ever growed for!" She rounded on Rawdon. "It was you as croaked Mary!"

"No, as a matter of fact, it wasn't," he purred. "Mr. Matthew Fiske had the honour of sending that plaguesome bitch to her final reward."

"You?" Sally gaped at Fiske. He covered his face with his hands.

"Look at him!" said Rawdon. "What a nuisance he's been, with his fears and his megrims, and his damned ill-convenient conscience. You'd hardly credit what I've been through to keep him up to the mark. Well, I'm finished with you now, old man. I'll leave you to swing for the murder of—we'll just keep calling her Mary, shall we?"

"How can you?" Fiske pleaded brokenly. "Everything I've done—every sin I've committed, God have mercy on my soul!—was for you, only for you! And to have you turn on me—I can't bear it! You were all I ever loved in the world!"

"Was I?" Rawdon sneered. "What a pity. Because I never had anything but contempt for *you*, my dear, dear father!"

Fiske let out a groan and collapsed, racked with sobs.

"He's your *father*?" exclaimed Sally. "But—but you ain't Caleb—"

"Not anymore. I sloughed Caleb like a snake's skin, back in the village where this blubbering wreck and my hell-hag of a mother brought me up."

But I seen Caleb, Sally thought dazedly. That Tom o' Bedlam I talked to at the refuge, *he* told me he was Caleb—

Or had he? She ransacked her memory. No, he had never said anything of the kind. She had asked, *Can I call you Caleb?* and the terrified boy had said, *If you want to.* And looked bewildered, as well he might!

"Well, even if your pa done the murder," she said, "it was you as put him up to it."

"Of course it was," said Rawdon. "Do you suppose he'd have had the pluck to carry it out on his own? He can't even stand up to that great bitch, my mother—he never could. He left me at her mercy till I was old enough to look after myself. But now it's *I* who calls the tune!"

"And him as pays the piper!" she retorted. "He took all the risks when you hushed Mary. It must've been him as hocussed the cordial—him as put the laudanum bottle in her room—"

"You *have* figured out a bloody great deal, haven't you? How do you know all that?"

"I've got me ways." Get him talking, that's the ticket, she thought. He thinks he's so frigging clever. Maybe he'll forget to hang on so tight to Megan, and she can cut and run.

"It was a good plan," Rawdon was saying, "It would have gone off like clockwork, if it hadn't been for you. Though I had the devil's own time screwing up Pa's courage to do it. I never could tell him the real reason the little bitch had to be put down. Even he might have bucked if he'd known that."

"What was the real reason?" asked Sally.

"Suffice to say, she might have interfered with my business. I never told my beloved father precisely what that was. Importing—that was all I said."

"Well, I'm flash to it. You're trepanners—you and your dolly pals." She had gathered that much from the note Mr. Kestrel sent Dipper after he rescued Emily.

"There's nothing you don't know, is there?—damn your eyes! Well, my little business would have gone all to hell if the girl known as Mary had been allowed to cackle to her big-wig papa, and he started asking questions and clamouring for revenge."

"Who is he?" asked Sally eagerly.

"Oh, no! You won't tease that out of me. We'll keep that just between us, won't we, Pa?"

Fiske did not answer. He sat back against the wall, his eyes closed, his face puffy and blotched with weeping.

Rawdon went on, "I had to give Pa another reason for putting her out of the way. So I made up a story about her—I let on she wasn't the injured innocent she seemed to be—she was vicious, she'd run away from her fine family and gone on the town out of sheer depravity. I said I'd fallen in with her, succumbed to her charms, and told her all about who I really was, and how I'd been accused of murder in my old village."

"I s'pose you done it, too—killed that half-wit gal."

"Of course. It was a clumsy killing. I was younger then. I thought I could make it look as if she'd drowned, but they found bruises where I'd held her down in the water, and someone saw me with her earlier, headed toward the stream. I've never been so careless again. It's exciting—nothing more so!—blowing out a life like a candle, like that, but usually it's not worth the risk. There are ways and means of taking one's pleasure, short of murder."

Sally was sickened. But she wanted to know the rest of the story, and she had to keep him talking. Megan looked too white and faint to break away from him, but she might yet rally. Above all, Rawdon must be detained, to keep him from getting away. "Did he know you croaked that gal in your village?" she asked, glancing at Fiske.

"I told him some of the truth. I said I'd had her, down by the stream—that was true enough, she was too stupid to put up much of a fight. I said she'd had hysterics afterward, and I was trying to quiet her, and killed her by mistake. Pretty much all that was true, except that I knew from the beginning I'd have to kill her. What else could I do—let her tell everyone what I did to her? Let her tell my mother?" He flushed painfully.

"And he believed you?"

"Don't I tell you, there are no limits to what I can make him believe! He helped me escape. Made himself very unpopular in our village, I'm afraid! That's why he and my mother moved to London, soon after I came here. He found me again by putting discreet advertisements in the newspapers. 'W.F. would be glad to hear from C.F.'—that sort of thing. I met with him from time to time. I didn't see any point in cutting the connexion. Who knew when it might not be useful? Of course he kept it a secret from my mother that he'd found me. I was still wanted for murder in our village, and she would have thought it her pious duty to turn me over to the authorities, if she found out where I was.

"That was what he was most afraid of—that I'd be found and arrested for killing that girl. I played on those fears to persuade him to kill Mary. I told him I'd confided my story to her, and now she was going to blow the gab—reveal I was Caleb Fiske, and set the authorities on me for murder and rape. Day by day, I fed him lies, made him think I was in deadly danger, that I'd have to run away, give up my life in London, my business, and he'd never see me again. And if I were caught—the gallows. He believed me, as always. He wanted to protect me. He's always moved heaven and earth to protect me from everything—except my mother! He was so bloody terrified of her, he'd stand by and let her do anything she liked to me—beat me, scald me, starve me—punish me for anything, or nothing! Driving the devil out of me, she called it. But all she accomplished was to make me dead set on inviting the devil in!"

Sally shook her head. "I ought to've knowed you was her son. You're just like her—you've both got no heart in you, and you likes to grinds your heels in folks and watch 'em squirm."

"*Her young ones also suck up blood: and where the slain are, there is she.* See how well I remember my Bible." He scowled suddenly. "I'd rather have no heart than no backbone, like that lump of jelly who sired me! And he weeps because I say I despise him! What else could he expect?"

Sally glanced at Fiske. He still sat slumped on the floor, his face drawn and his eyes tightly shut. All his energies seemed trained on hearing his son out without running mad.

"At all events, he made a first-rate cat's paw," Rawdon resumed. "He agreed to do Mary's business for her. I made the plan, and he was to carry it out. He had access to the refuge—I didn't. And if he were caught, I could always disappear and leave him to twist for it."

"Lucky for you Mary turned up at the refuge, where you and him could get your hands on her."

"It wasn't luck at all—it was a cursed piece of folly!" His tongue was loosened now with a vengeance, Sally realized. He passed so much of his life imprisoned in silence and deception. The chance to talk frankly, to boast of his triumphs and air his grievances, was more than he could resist. "Mary was caught in our net in the usual way. One of my employees happened on her at an inn outside London. The poor little thing hadn't anywhere to go. They wouldn't let her stay at the inn—she was travelling alone, without a companion or servant, and they smelled something rum and turned her away. She could have brought them to heel by telling them who she was, but she was running away from her family—eloping or some such foolery—and she wanted to keep it dark. This employee of mine—a kind, matronly sort of woman—invited her to pass the night at her house. It's one of the houses we keep in London especially for new recruits.

"To make a long story short, the lamb was led to the slaughter—drugged and turned over to a client of ours who makes a hobby of cracking dainty little pitchers like her. The next day, while she was too sick to talk or put up a fight, she was sold to a mother abbess who keeps a house near Covent Garden. That was where the trouble started. She woke up in the company of the old bawd and started raving. When she let on who she really was, the stupid woman panicked. All she could think of was to get shut of the girl as soon as possible. So she dumped her at the refuge." He added grimly, "She'd heard about the place from me, damn her! Pa had told me my mother was smitten with the canting clergyman who ran it, and later I joked to the old bawd about there being a refuge for whores up near Russell Square. I said they ought to thank us for keeping them supplied with fodder for reformation.

"When I found out who Mary was and what had become of her, I wrote to my father at his shop and asked to meet him. I sounded him about Mary. He knew her. He'd been sent for to treat her at the refuge, and he'd prescribed a cordial for her. I could hardly believe my luck when I found out she hadn't squeaked. But she'd talk eventually. She'd crawl back to her fine family, and then I'd be for it, along with my employees, my whole business. So I put my father up to stoppering her jaw forever."

"That letter I pinched—how does that come into it?"

"Pa was supposed to have doctored the cordial on a Monday, so Mary'd be dosed with it that night. He made up a compound to do the job—a strong opiate, laced with hemlock. I'd arranged to meet with him that same evening in the Haymarket—a nice crowded place, full of drunkards and pleasure-seekers, where we'd never be noticed. I wanted to make sure he'd carried out the first step of the plan. I knew he couldn't lie to me—I'd have seen through him. I always did. But as it turned out, that very afternoon the little slut had given him that damned letter to post. Told him he seemed like a kind man, he was the only one she could trust, and more of the same sickening pap.

"Of course his heart was touched. He pleaded for her. He said, let's just destroy the letter. She'll think her father chose to cast her off, and she'll go away and not make any more trouble. She'd promised as much in the letter. But *I* knew better! She'd never give up till she wormed her way back into her father's good graces. So I made him give me the letter, and I went to work on him all over again, with lies and encouragement and reminders of the danger I was in, till I'd steeled him to carry out the plan. In the end, he promised to doctor the cordial next day.

"I kept the letter—that was my one mistake. I shredded the paper it was wrapped in, that had her father's name and direction on it, but I wanted to read the letter at my leisure—just for my private amusement. So I put it in my pocket for the time being.

"My father and I parted, but I didn't like the look of him. I followed him for a bit, from a distance, and I saw you pick him up. Poor old sod, he probably hadn't had a woman in the devil knows how long. I followed the two of you here. I was still worried. I had an idea he might get confiding in bed and start wagging his tongue. So after you brought him upstairs, I greased the landlord's palm, and he turned a blind eye while I went up and had a look through the keyhole. He wasn't much of a lapful for you, was he? —a lusty little piece like you!"

Words failed Sally. She spat at him.

"Spit and scratch all you want to! I like it, you know. But you'd remember that, wouldn't you? I made up my mind to have you after my father. It was what you'd call piquant, don't you think? I waited in the taproom for the two of you to come down and for Pa to troop off, but before I could get near you, you got into a hack with some man. I hung about the taproom, hoping you'd come back. You did."

"And you still had the letter! So it was you I pinched it from!"

"It was a high price to pay, wasn't it, for a rub-off with a whore? You were a good poke, but hardly worth the trouble you've caused."

Megan suddenly twisted in his arms, trying to squirm out from under the knife. "Oh, no!" he snarled. He gripped her harder, prodding the point against her chin. She strained to hold her head back, her eyes starting from their sockets. "I see how you've been stringing me on!" he hissed at Sally. "I've said more than enough. Now I'm finished with you all, and be damned to you!"

He backed through the door, dragging Megan with him. Sally rushed out after them. At the top of the stairs, Rawdon skidded to a halt. There were footsteps beneath them—men racing up the stairs.

Rawdon cursed, caught between the men speeding toward him from below and Sally coming at him with the pistol. He looked frantically one way and then the other. At last, with a howl of rage, he shoved Megan from him and plunged downstairs, his knife upraised. Megan crashed into the stair-rail, and the rotten wood gave way. In a burst of flying splinters, she pitched over the side of the stairs.

Sally ran forward and looked over what was left of the banisters. Rawdon stood frozen on the stairs, facing Julian Kestrel, who was pointing a slim, sleek duelling pistol at his chest. Dipper hovered just behind him. Toby stared up at them from the flight below. At the bottom of the stair-well, two stories down, Megan lay broken and still.

A Matter for Bow Street

The tableau broke apart. Sally ran downstairs to see if anything could be done for Megan. Julian took the knife from Rawdon and drove him, spitting curses all the way, back up the stairs. Toby locked him in the front room on the second floor, Julian first checking to make sure he could not get out by the window. Dipper discovered Fiske in the back room across the hall, and Toby locked him in as well. It seemed best to confine them separately; Rawdon was in such a savage temper, there was no telling what he might do.

Meanwhile, Sally dropped down beside Megan. "Fetch some blankets," she told the pot-boy, who stood by gawking. "And some brandy, the strongest you've got. And send for a surgeon. Go on! What you hanging an arse for?" The boy ran off.

Megan was alive, but only just. She was white, and barely breathing, and her eyes were misted over. When Sally took her hand, she did not seem to feel it, and she could not swallow any of the brandy when it came. Sally could only cover her with the blankets, and wait.

Julian, Dipper, and Toby came downstairs. Toby looked Megan over. After ten years as a boxer, there was not much he did not know about bodily injuries.

"She don't seem to feel nothing," said Sally, under her breath.

"Her back's broke," Toby muttered, shaking his head. "She'll die in a minute or two."

Megan's dull eyes moved from them to Julian, who was kneeling on her other side. "Charles's friend," she whispered.

"Is there anything I can do for you?" he asked.

"Tell Charles—" Her voice died away. When she spoke again, Julian had to bend close to hear her. "Tell him he's won. There's a letter—in the pocket of my cloak. Give it to him. I was bringing it to give to him tonight, but when I saw him gang awa' from his house all alone, as if in secret—I couldna resist following after him. I thought—he might be ganging—to see Rosemary. Tell him—"

Her voice caught. Her face jerked and quivered with the effort to force her lips to move again. "Tell him to have mercy on her. What I did is none of her fault. Tell him to pity her, if he canna love her. Tell him—"

A spasm convulsed her face. Then the tension drained away, leaving it white and remote, as a statue's. She would not need the surgeon now.

Julian and Toby carried her body into the small, soot-stained parlour behind the taproom, Sally going first to clear out the few customers who were there. They laid Megan on a long deal table, a candle burning by her head. Julian turned to Dipper. "Go to the Magistrate's Court at Bow Street. Tell them to send an officer, and as many men as they think fit, to deal with Rawdon and Fiske. Don't attempt to explain everything that's happened—just tell them it's a matter of murder, and there are people of rank and wealth involved. That should speed them along."

Dipper obeyed. Toby looked very grim at the prospect of Bow Street Runners invading the Cockerel. He went off to assure his patrons that Bow Street's business was not with any of them.

"Let's see what this letter's all about," said Sally, feeling through Megan's cloak. In one pocket, she found a few coins and a grubby latchkey; the other pocket was sewn shut. She broke the stitches' and drew out an old, yellowed paper with a broken seal.

She unfolded it. It was grimy from handling, and the ink was faded, but the writing was still legible. She held it out to Julian eagerly. "What's it say?"

"She asked us to give this to Avondale," he pointed out, "not to read it ourselves."

"I almost had daylight let into me on account of this here letter, and I'm blowed if I'll hand it over without finding out what it says!" She explained quickly how Avondale had come to the Cockerel and threatened her with a gun, only to find that the letter he was seeking was not the one she had.

Julian agreed she had earned the right to know what was in the letter. Holding it close to the candle, he read aloud:

November 1821
Saturday

My dearest Megan,
For God's sake, be sensible and don't come here tonight. The Lauders are having a dinner party for a lot of great guns, and there'll be the deuce to pay if you make a row. You know I love you, and yes, I promise to marry you, anything you like, only please don't come here and kick up a dust in front of my friends. I'll meet you tomorrow in the usual place. Don't worry anymore. Believe me ever your own
Charles

"Well, I'll be blowed!" exclaimed Sally. "What's it mean? Was Megan his fancy woman? And did he get shut of her so he could take up with Rosemary? Then what did Megan want to find Rosemary so badly for? You'd think she would've have hated her like poison."

Julian was only half attending. "What a devil of a muddle I've made of all this!" he said softly. "I was so dead set on connecting Avondale to Mary and the refuge, I looked at everything the wrong way around. No wonder he wanted this back so desperately—"

Toby poked his head in to say that the surgeon had arrived. The surgeon examined Megan briefly, confirmed that her fall into the stair-well had caused her death, and agreed to testify at an inquest if required.

Soon after, Dipper returned with two men. One was a big, jovial man in his forties, with a bulbous red nose. The other was a young man of about five-and-twenty, who wore the uniform of a Bow Street patrol: blue coat with gilt buttons, blue trousers, and scarlet waistcoat. He was armed with a cutlass, a pistol, and a gaudily painted truncheon. A pair of handcuffs dangled from his belt.

The red-nosed man shook hands all around. "How d'ye do? I'm Peter Vance."

He did not need to identify himself any further. Everyone knew the names of Bow Street's elite officers, the Runners. They figured in newspaper stories, street ballads, crime novels; they guarded banks, theatres, even the King himself. They wore no uniform: the sole insignia of their office was a tipstaff, a wooden baton about nine inches long, with a gilt crown at the end. Vance took his out of a leather case on his belt, ready to brandish at need.

Julian introduced himself and Sally. "I'm afraid all this will take a good deal of explaining."

"Explain away," said Vance. "I have time. I knew from the beginning this must be serious. Nothing short of all hell broken loose would have brought this one to Bow Street of his own free will." He clapped Dipper on the shoulder.

"Do you two know each other?"

"Know Dipper? I should say I do! Why, we've been talking over old times all the way here I used to run into him often enough among the cross-coves. Pulled him in once. Bit of an achievement, that. He was a rum diver, was Dipper—damned hard to catch out."

"Thank you, sir," said Dipper.

"Not at all, lad, not at all. Didn't have him up before the magistrates, though—not worth it, only a matter of a handkerchief. So, no need for bad blood betwixt us."

He meant, Julian realized, that the reward for apprehending Dipper for such a minor theft would have been too small. The Runners were brave, determined men, but no one had any illusions about their motives. They worked for rewards; they were expected to. Bow Street did not pay them nearly enough to live on their salaries alone.

"That the victim?" asked Vance, going over to Megan.

"One of the victims." Julian followed him and recounted briefly how she had died.

"Who is she?" asked Vance.

"I've heard her called Megan MacGowan, but I don't believe that was really her name. One man would know for sure: Charles Avondale, Lord Carbury's younger son."

Vance whistled. "So there really are nobs mixed up in this."

"That's only the beginning. I suggest we send Dipper for Avondale, and in the meantime Sally and I will tell you what we know about this business."

Vance nodded. Dipper set off, and Julian and Sally embarked on the story of the refuge, the trepanners, and the murder. Sally repeated what Rawdon had told her about his crimes, and Julian revealed that the murdered girl was Lady Lucinda Braxton. The officers were astonished and a little giddy at this parade of plots and counterplots, mistaken identities and misplaced trust.

At last Vance got to his feet, taking a large swig of the ale that Toby always provided free of charge to any law officers who happened by. "Seems there's more than enough cause to pull in these two men, Rawdon and Fiske. Or rather, Fiske and Fiske, but it's simpler to go on calling the younger one by his assumed name. We'll lock them up for the night, and tomorrow morning they'll be had up before the magistrates. You'll have to come in, sir, and swear out evidence against them. You, too, my beauty."

He winked at Sally, but she turned up her nose. Flirt with a Bow Street officer? Not likely!

Toby took Vance and his assistant upstairs to collect Rawdon and Fiske. Sally turned to Julian, her brow wrinkled. "I still can't make no outs of some of this. Who was that Tom o' Bedlam I caught nosing around the refuge, if he wasn't Caleb?" She added with a touch of resentment, "It didn't seem to knock you, not by half, to find out Blinkers was Caleb, and him and his pa done the murder together."

"No, because my suspicions were already turning that way. I hadn't worked out that Rawdon was Caleb, but I realized there must be some sort of alliance between them. This whole investigation's been like a game of thimblerig: we had three men and one letter, and we made the same assumption that the dupes who play thimblerig do—they think the pea is under one of the three cups, and they have only to determine which one. But the pea moves: the sharper pretends to put it under one cup, then he palms it and puts it under another. And I saw that that's what must have happened here: Fiske had the letter first and gave it to Rawdon.

"The motive, you see, was Rawdon's. I felt sure he and his colleagues had trepanned Lady Lucinda, and that gave them every reason to want her out of the way, once they knew her true identity. But there was no connexion between Rawdon and the refuge. It was Fiske who had access to Lady Lucinda—Fiske who could easily have got hold of her letter, poisoned the cordial, and sneaked into the refuge at night to plant the laudanum bottle in her room. What he denied so convincingly wasn't that he ever had the letter, but that he was the man from whom you stole it.

"If Fiske got the letter from Lady Lucinda and passed it on to Rawdon, that would explain why they were both in the Haymarket that night. You said you couldn't conceive what Fiske was doing there at that hour—he clearly wasn't looking for the kinds of entertainment the neighbourhood has to offer. Then there was Rawdon's spying on you and Fiske at the Cockerel. We wondered what there was about you to rouse his interest. We never thought to consider that he was watching you because you were with Fiske."

"Watching his own pa!" she said in disgust. "He's a stinker, and no mistake! You know, I didn't think he'd be, like that—Caleb, I mean. When I heard his ma talk about him to Wax-face, I was sorry for him. I thought she'd treated him like dirt. And when I seen that boy at the refuge, as was so addle-paced and afeard of his own shadow, I just naturally thought he was Caleb."

Julian nodded. "You had an image of Caleb in your mind, and that boy obligingly stepped into it. I made exactly the same mistake about Rosemary, and it played the devil with my whole analysis. Because I thought she might be Mary, I kept picturing her in Mary's image—as a beautiful, helpless young girl, a victim. The real Rosemary may be nothing like that—"

He stopped, caught up Avondale's letter again, and stared at it "Good God. *Half English and half Scottish.* How could I have been so blind? Avondale as good as told me who Rosemary was, and I didn't see it!"

Sally gaped at him. But before she could get out a question, the officers brought Rawdon and Fiske downstairs. Fiske was meek, but Rawdon was wild with rage. The officers had had to bind his arms with ropes and stuff a handkerchief in his mouth. "You should have heard the language he was spewing out," chuckled Vance. "Nothing we hadn't heard before, but we got tired of listening to it. Well, we're finished here. If you'll come to the office tomorrow at ten, sir, I expect the magistrates will clear everything else aside for this."

"We'll be there," said Julian. "Thank you for all you've done."

"Thank *you*, sir. You're a rare hand at this kind of thing. If you'd been born in my sphere of life, you could have made a fine career of it. 'Course, being a gentleman as you are—and a pink of St. James Street, as everyone knows—this is all a sort of lark to you. A sport, you might say. Like hunting foxes."

"Rather like that." Julian smiled quizzically. He knew very well what Vance meant. A gentleman does not catch criminals professionally—and certainly would not dream of taking a share in any reward that might be granted.

Toby summoned a hackney to take the officers and their prisoners to Bow Street. Julian and Sally saw them off, then returned to the back parlour to keep a vigil over Megan till Avondale arrived. In a few minutes Dipper joined them and told them Avondale was waiting in the taproom. "I left him there, sir, 'coz I didn't know if you was done with Lighthouse Pete."

"Lighthouse Pete?"

"Oh, that's Mr. Vance, sir. It's a nickname we give him, on account of this." He tapped his nose.

"Very apt." Julian glanced toward the door to the taproom. "What have you told him?"

"Just that you needed to see him slap off, sir—some'ut to do with Miss MacGowan."

"All right. I'll go and speak to him."

He went into the taproom. Most of Toby's customers had cleared out, not liking the reek of Bow Street about the place. Avondale came over to him at once. "What the plague is this? First you're taking messages from Megan in the street, and now you send your servant after me, saying you have to see me about her. I don't understand any of this. Why are you dogging my steps?"

"You got into the thick of something I was looking into—some thing that turned out not to involve you, but seemed at first as if it might. It's a very long story. I have something to tell you I'm afraid it will come as a shock. The young woman you call Miss MacGowan came here tonight. She followed you to your assignation with Sally."

"Sally?—oh, the little Covent Garden nun who sent me the note. He caught his breath. "What do you mean, the woman I *call* Miss MacGowan?"

"She got into the midst of a fight," Julian went on quietly. "There was—an accident. She was killed."

"Killed?"

"I'm sorry."

Avondale groped blindly for the back of a chair and held on to it to steady himself. "Dead. Megan is dead."

"She asked me to give you a message. Again," he added ruefully. "She said to tell you that you've won. She asked me to give you a letter she had with her. And she begged you to have mercy on Rosemary. 'Tell him to pity her, if he can't love her,' she said—"

"Oh, no—" Avondale put out a hand to ward off any more. "You have to believe me, I didn't want to win like this. I hated Megan; there wasn't much I wouldn't have done to tear her out of my life. But this—this wasn't what I wanted."

"Would you like to see her?"

"Yes. Yes, I think I owe her that."

They went into the parlour. Avondale went over to the table where Megan lay, and stood looking down at her. Dipper regarded him thoughtfully, Sally with unabashed curiosity.

"This is all my fault," he said. "I had a feeling I'd been followed here tonight. She was always following me, or watching me. She thought I might lead her to Rosemary, or to someone who knew where Rosemary was."

"Where is she?" Sally could not resist asking. "And *who* is she?"

Avondale did not answer, only went on looking sadly at Megan's still, unforgiving face.

Julian handed him the letter. "I'm bound in honour to give this to you, because it's what she wished. What you do with it is between you and your conscience."

"You've read it, I suppose?"

"I did, I confess."

"What's it all mean?" Sally persisted. "Who's Rosemary?" She looked at Julian narrowly. "And why'd you say *her* name wasn't really Megan MacGowan?"

Avondale smiled faintly. "So you worked that out."

"Yes," said Julian. "I have a friend who's Scottish by birth, and he and I once had a conversation about the peculiarities of Scottish law."

"Bugger Scottish law!" Sally stamped her foot. "If her bloody name wasn't Megan MacGowan, what was it?"

"Her bloody name," said Avondale quietly, "was Mrs. Charles Avondale."

Scottish Justice

Sally stared. "She was your *wife*?"

"I suppose you're entitled to the whole story," Avondale sighed, "now you've got into the middle of it like this. But in return you have to tell me what all this is about: how you two know each other" —he looked from Sally to Julian—"and how she died."

Julian told the story yet again, but briefly this time, and leaving out Lady Lucinda's name—though, God knew, her fate would be public soon enough. Avondale did not seem to take in more than the basic outline, but listening in silence had a soothing effect on him. It helped that Dipper, ever practical, had ordered a great, steaming bowl of brandy-and-water, which they all partook of gratefully.

At last it was Avondale's turn to explain. He rose and paced up and down for a short time, steeling himself. "All right. Here's where it all began. About three years ago, I went to Scotland on a shooting trip, and afterward I stayed in Edinburgh with some friends, the Lauders. While I was there, I met a young woman, a governess in the neighbourhood. That was Megan.

"She was very fetching in those days. She'd pretty well gone to rack and ruin by the time you saw her, but she used to have a vitality about her—a fire, a kind of animal spirits, I don't know. She was a little older than I was, but that didn't signify. We started meeting in secret, and—well, you can guess the rest.

"But then she got after me to marry her. It wasn't fair, really, because I'd never said anything to make her believe I had marriage in mind, and she'd never brought it up herself until after she was my mistress. Finally it was nearly time for me to leave Scotland, and I was glad to get away, but Megan wasn't going to let me slip through her fingers without a fight. One morning, just before I was due to leave, Megan sent me a letter. She was in a thundering great temper. She said she was my wife in all but name, ran on for pages reminding me of what we'd been to each other, and threatened to come to the Lauders that very night and kick up hell's delight if I didn't write back at once promising to marry her. And I thought, oh the deuce, why not? If she brought a breach of promise suit afterward, she could always be bought off. The Lauders were having a party that night for a lot of English and Scottish big-wigs, and the thought of Megan coming there and blowing me up in front of all those people made my skin crawl. So I wrote her this."

He waved the letter. His lips twisted into a bitter smile. "And there you have me—a victim trussed and bound I never had any idea what was happening to me. Everybody knows it's easy to get married in Scotland—couples are always running off to Gretna Green. But what most people don't realize—what I didn't know, to my cost!—is that Scotland is the only country in the civilised world where a man can get married *by mistake*! The day after I sent Megan that letter, she was all affection for me—couldn't apologise enough for the way she'd been acting. She got me to spend the night with her at an inn—and the next morning, she told me we were married! By giving her a written promise of marriage, then treating her as my wife, I'd married her under

Scottish law. It's called irregular marriage, and it's as legal and binding as if we'd joined hands in St. George's, Hanover Square. The law treats what ought to be done as done—that's how a lawyer in Edinburgh explained it to me afterward. Megan's father'd been a lawyer—a writer, as they say up there—so she knew all about it.

"It was only then—when I knew it was really true, I was married for good and all, as long as Megan and I both lived—it was only then that I read my own heart aright. I realized that I loved my cousin Ada—that I'd always loved her, but like an idiot, like a spoiled, deluded child, I thought I had time enough to sow my wild oats, and come to her when I'd had all the other women who caught my fancy. I didn't expect she'd marry anyone else. She's not what the world calls a beauty—which only shows how little the world knows—and she hasn't any money, which is all anyone cares about on the marriage mart. So I thought she'd be there waiting—and she was, but I couldn't have her now. She'd never have me on any terms but marriage, because she's the soul of honour, the most virtuous girl that ever breathed. And I couldn't offer her marriage, because I already had a wife! Oh, they grind very fine—the wheels of Scottish justice!"

He paused, pale and out of breath. Dipper refilled his glass. He took a pull, and resumed more calmly, "All I could think of to do was to keep the marriage a secret as long as possible. Once Ada knew I was married, it would be all up with me. But if I could somehow get my hands on that letter—the only proof Megan had that I'd promised her marriage—I'd be as good as a bachelor again. There has to be written proof of the promise, you see, or the law won't recognise the marriage. But Megan had it well hidden, and no power on earth would make her give it up. I knew it was no use pleading or arguing with her. So for the time being, secrecy was my only hope.

"I told Megan my family would cut up rough when they found I'd married beneath me—which there was no denying I had, and they would. I said I'd reveal the marriage eventually, but this wasn't a good time. I had a spinster aunt who was partial to me, and she was an invalid, and likely to cut up large when she died. I told Megan she'd cut me off with a shilling if she found out I'd married a Scottish governess. Megan knew the money would come in handy—she was a Scot, when all was said and done—so she agreed to keep our marriage dark until Aunt Charlotte closed her accounts.

"I knew that was only a stop-gap measure. Sooner or later, either Aunt would die, or Megan would get tired of waiting. Meantime, I set her up in a house in the north of England, well away from my own family in Somerset. Sort of a *cottage ornée*, and damned expensive to keep up. I even visited her once in a while, both to keep her happy and to look for the letter. Of course I never found it. We rubbed along well enough at first. Megan didn't realize how determined I was to be rid of her. She had other things on her mind." He smiled wryly. "I suppose by now you've realized who Rosemary is."

"I was misled for a long time," Julian admitted. "I thought she might be the young woman who was murdered at the refuge. I hinted as much to you, the night I first saw Megan, when I remarked on what an awkward thing it is, making young women disappear. You saw your chance to lead me a dance, and you did—letting me think Rosemary was a girl you'd seduced. Now my guess would be that she's too young for that sort of thing—even assuming you weren't her father."

"She's two years old. I found out after Megan had tricked me into marriage that she was in the family way. That was one reason she was so desperate to marry me. Give her credit, she was devoted to Rosemary, even before she was born. She might decide on her own account to be my mistress, but it was quite another thing to bring our child into the world a bastard.

"It was after Rosemary was born that things started to go wrong. Megan had told the people in the village where she lived that I was in the army, and that was why I came to see her so rarely, but they sensed something hole-and-corner was going on. Rumours flew around that she was only my *chère amie*, and respectable people wouldn't receive her anymore. She was furious. She started writing me angry letters, demanding that I reveal our marriage, and threatening to do it herself if I didn't agree. I pleaded Aunt Charlotte, my mother's health, my sister's wedding—anything. I bought short reprieves, but each time it was harder.

"Then, this past spring, a blow came from a different quarter. Major Thorndike turned up and started dancing attendance on Ada. I was burning to cut him out, but what could I do? I tried to play the friend and mentor, I teased her about Thorndike, gave her advice—but it was brutal. It all but tore me apart. I knew she'd accept him if he offered. Her family was too poor for her to refuse a chance like that. And, God knows, *I* showed no sign of coming up to scratch! I used to lie awake at night and think of her with him—my Ada, my only true love! It ate away at me. You have to understand, I was barely in my senses when I—did what I did.

"In June Thorndike was called to Ireland to help put down a revolt there. I hoped with all my heart some Irish rebel would do his business for him, but I couldn't count on that. I knew he was writing to Ada—he might even offer for her by post. I had almost no time left. And then, in July, Megan wrote to me that her nurse-maidservant had given notice. I saw my opportunity. I went to visit Megan and told her I was going to reveal our marriage. But first, I said, we had to improve her household and style of living. I bought her and Rosemary new clothes, new furnishings for the house. We celebrated Rosemary's second birthday. We hadn't got on so well for a long time. Megan was thrilled—which is to say, she was completely taken in. Well, she'd duped *me* once, hadn't she? Turn-about is fair play.

"I also gave Megan a new nurse-maidservant—a London girl, trained in town manners. I said she'd help Megan adjust to her new life. This girl, Selina, was really a Cyprian I'd known rather well at one time—a clever little thing, and a first-rate intriguer. She played her part to perfection. I pretended to go back to London, then I went into hiding a short way off, while Selina got familiar with the routine of Megan's household and won her confidence. Then one evening she gave Megan a sleeping draught at dinner and went off—with Rosemary.

"I'd arranged everything to ensure they couldn't be traced. They changed horses privately, so Megan wouldn't be able to find out where they stopped or what direction they went. I saw to it they got well away, then I went back to London. Selina left Megan a note from me, warning her not to tell anyone I'd taken Rosemary if she ever wanted to see her again. I said she had only to give me a certain letter, and I'd restore Rosemary to her and support them both for the rest of their lives. I would have done it, too. I know that doesn't make what I did any less monstrous. I was desperate, that's all.

"What happened then was stalemate. Megan wrote to me, swearing she'd never give up the letter. She said she wouldn't buy back her child at the price of declaring her a bastard. But she didn't dare tell anyone we were married, or that I had taken Rosemary. You can see what she was afraid of. She was a lawyer's daughter—she understood her position all too well. I understood it, too—I'd learned a good deal about the law myself by then. Since Rosemary was born in wedlock, for all intents and purposes she belonged to me, not Megan. And Megan would have the devil of a time getting me to give her up, once I had nothing to lose by asserting my rights as Rosemary's legal father. I could have Megan declared unfit, insane, anything. And my governor would have stood by me, and what could Megan do against *him*? There are times when it's damned convenient, being an earl's son.

"So there we were. I refused to give her back Rosemary. I also stopped supporting her, so she couldn't keep up the cottage anymore, and had to sell off everything she had, just to pay her debts. What can I say?—I thought it would bring her to heel faster. But she wouldn't give in. She searched the countryside for Rosemary. Meantime, I went to the cottage after she left and searched high and low for the letter. Neither of us found what we were looking for. Stalemate, as I said.

"About a month ago, Megan came to London. She turned up at my house one night, and I was shocked at the change in her.

She was dirty and haggard, and her clothes were soiled. I told you she was mad, and I think she was a little, by then. I think we both were.

"She started by pleading with me to give Rosemary back, but pretty soon she flew into a rage. I'd ruined her, she said, I'd left her penniless, ripped her daughter away, she'd been a respectable woman once, how could I make her live like this? And I said it was all her fault we were in this mess, if she hadn't tricked me into marriage none of it would have happened, and—oh Lord, never mind the rest! No one can torture each other like married people.

"Megan begged me at least to tell her if Rosemary was all right. She was afraid she might be sick, neglected—even dead. I wasn't brute enough to keep her in suspense about that. I said Rosemary was safe; the women I'd sent her to live with were taking good care of her. What kind of women? Megan wanted to know. And, God help me, I said: The kind who don't marry."

"And was that true?" asked Julian.

"Oh, yes, it was true. Rosemary's in a convent in France. But Megan jumped to a different conclusion. I meant her to. She thought Rosemary was in a knocking-shop, and she was livid. But she still wouldn't give in. It all ended with her rushing off into the night, and I was left fearing I'd be tied to her, stuck in this nightmare, for the rest of my life.

"I don't know what she did for the next few weeks, except that she watched me a good deal. I'd look out of the window sometimes at night and see her in the street. And she chalked a letter *R*, for Rosemary, on my door, and slashed another one in the hood of my cab. It wore me down. On top of everything else, I was getting over head and ears in debt. That convent's expensive, and I had Selina to pay off, too. By the time I picked you up" —he turned to Sally—"all I wanted was to rest for a little while and forget about everything.

"The next morning, I ran into Thorndike at my club. That was the first I'd heard he was back from Ireland. I dashed off to see Ada, and she confirmed she meant to have him if he offered for her. He did, the following week. I made up my mind: Megan still had the letter, but Thorndike wouldn't have Ada—not if I could do anything about it. I offered for her myself, and my poor dear love accepted. Not long before, I'd have cut off my right hand sooner than offer it to her, knowing I was already married, and the truth might come out at any time. But it's funny how, once you've done one base thing, it's easier to do another. It's as if your conscience is worn away. I meant to marry Ada, if that was what it took to keep her from Thorndike. Because I loved her, I was prepared to go through a mock wedding with her, make her my mistress—Ada, the purest angel, the sweetest, most trusting—" He swallowed hard. "I'm sorry. Anyway, it was madness, a terrible risk. Megan could have scuttled the whole thing at any time, just by producing my letter.

"I thought she meant to do just that. She came to see me as soon as she heard about my engagement, and we had another row. She said I'd never marry another woman while she lived. I said she'd better give me the letter, or I'd have her locked up as a madwoman. And if she tried to harm Ada, or did anything to frighten her, I'd kill her. She was in a white rage when she left—and ran smack into you in the street. I suppose that was why she left that message—told you to ask me what I'd done with Rosemary. She wanted to make trouble for me, but that was as far as she dared go.

"She played another little trick a few days later—sent Ada an envelope through the post with nothing in it but some dried rosemary. Megan is—was—devilish clever. She knew just how to keep me off balance, without pushing me too far.

"Well, that's the story." He turned to Sally. "You can see why, when I got your note this morning, I thought it was about my letter to Megan. I didn't know who you were, or how you'd got mixed up in my affairs, but I was prepared to pay you heaven and earth to get the letter back. But since I didn't know what I was letting myself in for, coming here tonight, I brought a pistol. Which I didn't have when I got home, by the way."

He looked meaningfully at Sally, who opened her eyes innocently. "Keep it," he told her, with a faint smile. "You may need it—you seem to have a knack for getting into dangerous company."

"Thanks," she grinned. "Say, you're in luck, ain't you? You has everything you wants. You has the letter, you're shut of Megan for good, and your Ada don't have to know nothing about it."

"You don't understand." Avondale smiled sadly. "And neither did Megan, when she said I'd won. I haven't—I've lost. Because, you see, I can't do to Megan dead what I could do to her alive. I always meant to take care of her and Rosemary, if only she'd give in and relinquish her claim to be my wife. That she should die, and Rosemary should be left without a mother—I never intended that. What Megan wanted above all—" He broke off, looking bleakly at her corpse. "She wanted legitimacy for her child. She died striving for that—following me to this place, getting into the middle of your quarrel with those men. I can't deny it to her now. Tomorrow morning—or, rather, today, it must be long past midnight—I'll go to Ada and tell her everything. And I expect I'll lose her. When she finds out how I've deceived her—what I meant to do to her—that will be the end." He paused, then finished steadily, "Then I'll go to the family lawyers and lay this whole business before them, so that they can do whatever has to be done to get my marriage to Megan recognized. This should be all they need to set the wheels in motion." He held up the letter.

Suddenly a look of fear came into his eyes. "Kestrel, you could do me one great favour."

"What is it?"

"Keep this for me, just for tonight. I mean to do right by Megan and Rosemary, but—I know myself. Till I've had a chance to talk to Ada, I don't trust myself with it. It would be too easy to throw it on the fire, and be damned to Megan and her rights. As soon as I've seen Ada—crossed the Rubicon—I'll ask for it back."

"Very well." Julian took the letter.

"Thank you." He departed, exhausted, but strangely peaceful in his resolve. Dipper went out after him, to summon a hackney to take them back to Clarges Street.

Sally took out Avondale's elegant little pistol and held it up to the light. "Ain't it fine? And he never felt a thing when I nicked it from him. I may not be the rum diver Dip is, but I'm handy with me forks. And lucky I am, or I'd never've got out of that kickup with Blinkers."

"You'd never have got into it, either," Julian reminded her. "Your stealing that letter was what started this whole business."

"And a good thing, too, she retorted. "If I hadn't, Blinkers and Bristles'd never have been nabbed for murder, and Blinkers'd still be making game pullets out of kids like Emily. A lot of things might not have happened," she added softly, coming up close to him. "Was you a little bit worried about me?"

"I might have felt a twinge or two of unease."

"I'd like to make you feel a twinge or two of some'ut else." She came up on her toes, her lips seeking his. But then she backed away, remembering Megan's body lying uncovered so close by. She went to her and drew her cloak over her face. A feeling of weakness swept over her. Her legs felt wobbly, as 1f she had just stepped off a boat.

"Sally." He was by her side at once, drawing her against him, stroking her hair. "Don't think of it anymore, sweet. It's over now."

The Price of Weakness

It was not completely over, of course. The next morning, Julian, Dipper, and Sally had to appear in the Bow Street Magistrate's Court to give evidence against Rawdon and Fiske. Julian had some knowledge of the court's proceedings, having come here as a spectator several times since the Bellegarde murder piqued his interest in crime. The daily round of hearings and committals took place in a dirty, soot-blackened room, close and musty despite its large size, with a bench for the magistrates at one end, a dock at the other, and a railed-off space in between for witnesses. Beside the dock, a group of prisoners in irons awaited interrogation, Rawdon and Fiske among them. The usual crowd was milling about: Bow Street patrols in the scarlet waistcoats that earned them the nickname "robin redbreasts," distraught or outraged victims of crime, relatives and friends of accused and accusers, young gentlemen in search of amusement, and tramps in search of shelter. But there were a few signs that something out of the ordinary was brewing. Journalists were here in force, their pens already scratching, their gazes darting about. And the Chief Magistrate himself, Sir Richard Birnie, was presiding.

The magistrates turned their attention at once to Rawdon and Fiske, who were put in the dock. Julian, Sally, and Dipper recounted the case against them. The spectators hung on every word; the reporters scribbled furiously. Peter Vance and Toby contributed what they knew of the final act in the drama. The complicated web of crime and deception took a long time to untangle, and at first Sir Richard seemed half inclined to suspect that Julian was a bored young man about town perpetrating an elaborate hoax. But Samuel Digby, to whom Julian had written, arrived and confirmed that the whole investigation had been carried out under his aegis. Sir Richard could no longer doubt that he was confronting a case of murder, kidnapping, and rape, involving two of England's highest-ranking families.

The magistrates examined Rawdon and Fiske. Rawdon would only snarl defiance, cursing his father, Julian, Sally, the magistrates, and anyone else who came near him. Sir Richard bound him over for trial at the next Old Bailey sessions and ordered him removed. Vance hustled him out of the dock and off to Newgate Prison to await trial.

Fiske looked relieved to see him go. He had said little up to now, but as soon as the door closed behind his son, he lifted a pasty, exhausted face, and announced that he was ready to confess.

He confirmed much of the story that Rawdon had told last night: how Rawdon had made him believe that Lady Lucinda was dangerous to him, and had concocted the plan to poison her and make her death look like suicide. "I took my wife's key to the area door of the inmates' house and had it copied. And I made up a strong poison—opium and hemlock. It would have sent her straight to sleep, so she'd never know—" His voice trailed away.

He was supposed to add the poison to the cordial bottle on a Monday, he explained, while he was at the refuge treating fever cases. But that day, Lady Lucinda confided her identity to him and entreated him to post her letter. "I hoped we needn't go through with it, after all. I met Caleb that evening at an eating house in the Haymarket, and I told him about the letter. I said, 'If we don't post it, her father won't know where she is, and she'll think he doesn't want her back, and then perhaps she'll go away, and not tell anyone who you really are.' Because that was what he kept harping on—that she knew he was wanted for murder in our old village. It seemed so plausible, the whole story, the way he told it."

Sally shook her head. Rawdon's tale seemed utterly ridiculous to her. The idea of making himself out to be that poor girl's victim, instead of the other way around! But then she remembered something Wideawake Peg had said: *If you want to lie to people, tell them something they want to believe.* Fiske could not have rejected Rawdon's story without facing the fact that his son was a cold-blooded, manipulative liar. And that he could not do.

"I suppose I was a fool," Fiske sighed. "But he was my son, my only child. And, you see, we'd always had a sort of alliance—or I thought we did. It was against Ellen, of course, in the beginning. She treated him so badly. I should have stopped her. I tried—but not hard enough. I was afraid of her, you see. I've been so weak, with both of them. And weakness is a terrible thing, worse even than evil, I think."

He had agreed reluctantly to go through with the murder. He and Rawdon had parted, Rawdon pocketing the letter but destroying the outer sheet that bore the address. Soon after, Fiske had run into Sally. He had not realized Rawdon was following him, to make sure he did not do anything rash in a fit of fear or remorse. "It wasn't until after—after Lady Lucinda was dead—that he told me he'd seen me go with Sally to the Cockerel. He had to, to explain how she came to steal the letter. He didn't let on he'd—he'd watched us, or—been with her himself. He said he'd only talked to her, to find out if I'd blurted out anything about what we were planning.

"I mixed the poison into the bottle of cordial the next morning. I did consider putting off the plan till a night when Ellen wouldn't be at the refuge. I knew how strict a watch she kept on everything that went on there. But I also knew she and

Mr. Harcourt were going to be working all night, so perhaps she would be distracted. And I didn't want to delay what I had to do any longer. I wanted it to be over.

"Late that night I went and waited near the inmates' house till there was no one in the street. Then I climbed over the railings and let myself in through the area door. I left my boots outside, because there aren't any carpets in the inmates' house, and footsteps make so much noise. Besides, I didn't want to track in any dirt or leaves.

"I waited in the laundry till I was sure there was no one stirring in the basement or on the stairs. Then I went upstairs. There wasn't much light, but I knew my way about—I'd often been to the refuge to treat the inmates for one ailment or another. I went into Mary's—Lady Lucinda's—room."

"Was she dead?" rapped out Sir Richard.

"I don't know, sir. I didn't want to look at her. But it's such a small room, I couldn't help seeing she was lying on the bed, not moving at all. If she was breathing, it must have been just barely.

"I did what I had to do, as quickly as I could. I'd brought a bottle of laudanum, almost empty—the sort anyone could have bought at a chandler's shop or public house. I poured a few drops of laudanum into the glass she'd drunk the cordial from, added a little water to it, and left the glass and the bottle together on the night-table. I went to the door and listened to be sure there was no one about. Then I tiptoed down to the basement and went out by the area door.

"And then something strange happened. I started to put on my boots, and I realized they weren't mine. They were much older than mine, more cracked and worn away at the heels I was terrified. It seemed as if some devil was playing tricks on me."

"So that's why you said, 'Oh my God, me boots!' when you was took with fever!" exclaimed Sally.

"Don't interrupt!" Sir Richard snapped.

"I don't remember saying it," said Fiske, "but that must have been what I was thinking of. Anyway, I couldn't stay to puzzle it out. I put on the boots and hurried away. When I got home, I hid them, and next day I threw them in the river. But I couldn't stop thinking about them. Someone must have switched boots with me, and that meant someone knew I'd been in the refuge that night. Even if it was just some tramp who didn't know or care who I was, he might tell someone about my boots, and the whole thing might come out. But, you know, in a way I wasn't surprised by any of it. Because I knew I'd done something terrible, and terrible deeds always get found out. At least, the Bible teaches us that, and I believe it.

"I felt very poorly next morning. My head ached, and I was dizzy. I knew I'd caught the fever I was treating at the refuge. But when Mr. Harcourt sent for me, I had to go. I had to know what they were thinking, now they'd found—her body. And I had to substitute another bottle of cordial for the poisoned one, or someone else might take it. I—examined her. I don't know how I got through it, but I did. I thought I looked as guilty as Cain, but no one seemed to see it. I suppose they were all too upset. Mr. Harcourt was already racking his brains for what to say to people. I managed to slip away and switch the cordial bottles, but then I felt so faint I had to go in the parlour and lie down. Mr. Harcourt sent me home. I could see he wanted me out of things. I was so shaken, he was probably afraid I'd lose my head and say something I oughtn't in public. He must have been relieved that I was too ill to come to the inquest.

"Caleb told me afterward that he was very worried when I didn't send him any word about how things had gone. He finally went to Stark Street and hung about the refuge, till he'd satisfied himself from the neighbours' gossip that everything had gone off as planned. He didn't know it, but Ellen caught sight of him there. She saw him again a few days later, near my shop. He was still worried he hadn't heard from me. I thought he was anxious about my health, but of course, now I understand he was just afraid something had gone wrong, and I was going to betray him. Ellen told me she'd seen him, and I braved it out as well as I could, pretending I knew nothing about him—hadn't seen or heard from him in years.

"As soon as I felt well enough, I wrote to Caleb and arranged a meeting with him. That was about ten days after—after Lady Lucinda died—and a day or two before I saw you at the refuge." He turned to Sally. "He told me you'd stolen the letter. I was badly frightened, though it wasn't possible to feel much worse than I did already. He tried to reassure me. He said most likely you didn't read the letter. You probably threw it on the nearest dust heap. But if by any chance you turned up at the refuge asking questions, I wasn't to let on I knew anything about the letter. I was to find out as much as I could about you: where you lived, why you took an interest in the letter, whether you'd showed it to anyone else. And then I was to tell him all about it afterward.

"A few days later, I saw you at the refuge. I was shocked, but I'd had so many shocks by then, I was getting used to that. What really struck me all of a heap was your thinking you'd stolen the letter from me. It never crossed my mind you wouldn't know who you got it from. At least I could tell you the truth about that much.

"It was all so strange. You'd found out a great deal, but you'd got some of it all wrong. You'd mistaken somebody else for Caleb—that man you talked to in the area. I knew he couldn't have been Caleb, because I'd just seen him myself, and he was quite vexed that we had no idea who you were or how to find you. But I couldn't put you right without revealing what I knew about Caleb. Then you gave me a bad scare—you mentioned how I'd raved about my boots. And I suddenly realized, that man you saw in the area—he might be the one who took them. You said he'd hung about there before. And suppose you talked to him again, and he told you he'd found my boots, and switched them for his? It seems like such a little thing, but sometimes just pulling one thread can tear a whole fabric apart. You were dangerous: I had to get rid of you. But most of all, I had to put you out of danger for your own sake." He lowered his eyes. "I didn't want *him* to find out you were at the refuge. There was no telling what he might make me do to you. I—I didn't want to hurt anyone else.

"I didn't hear from you for a day or two, I hoped you'd lost interest. I should have known better. When I got your note yesterday—it wasn't signed, but I felt sure it was from you—I was very uneasy. But I had an idea: perhaps I could go to the meeting you'd arranged, and pay you to give up the letter. Only I couldn't do that without talking to Caleb first. So I rushed off to his office in Southwark.

"He was anything but glad to see me—we'd agreed we'd never meet there—but he didn't seem too disturbed to hear you were taking an interest in the letter. I can understand why now. I was the only one in trouble; there was nothing to implicate him in what we'd done. But while we were talking, there was a knock at the door, and a note was pushed under it. It was another note just like the one I'd received, but addressed to him. He was very shocked to find you knew who he was. He ran out to look for you, but you'd disappeared."

Sally nodded. It all made sense. She remembered how, when she had gone to Rawdon's office to deliver her note, Annie had told her he had another man up there with him. She was not surprised Fiske had arrived before her: he had been in a hurry to see his son, while she had been reluctant to go at all.

Fiske wet his dry lips. He was so weary, he had to lean on the railing of the dock for support. "He made a plan. He said we'd go to the Cockerel that night. He'd wait in the back alleyway, while I went in and persuaded you to come upstairs. Then I was to leave you and come down and unbar the back door, to let him in. We'd both go up and talk you into selling us the letter. Of course he never meant to talk to you at all—he meant to kill you. And I suppose he meant to leave me to take the blame. I was the one who'd been seen to come upstairs with you. That was how he always arranged things. He was never seen or heard from—I took all the risks." He did not sound angry, only sad. "You must believe me, I didn't know what he was going to do. He said we were only going to buy you off."

Sally believed him. But she also thought that if Rawdon had told him the truth, it might not have made much difference. Was there anything Fiske would not have done for his son?

Sir Richard ordered him committed to Newgate till the next Old Bailey sessions, when he would be sentenced. Fiske actually smiled. Sir Richard bridled. "Is it a light thing to you to have the full majesty of the law brought to bear on crimes like yours?"

"No, sir. But, you see, I'm an apothecary. I know about the progress of disease. That fever I had a few weeks ago hasn't left me—it's burrowed deep in my body, to eat away at me from inside. I don't believe I'll live long enough to face a judgement. Not in this world."

Sir Richard sent word of the proceedings to Lord Braxton, who posted to London in a fury. It was all a mistake, he declared—this terrible business had nothing to do with his daughter. She was safe in France with her captain—that twopenny-ha'penny hero she had run away to marry. Blustering to hide his panic, he demanded facts, witnesses, proofs. But the evidence was all too clear. He himself identified the handwriting of "Mary's" letter as his daughter's. And when Peter Vance went to Boulogne to see Captain Hartwell, he learned that the captain had expected Lady Lucinda, but when she did not arrive, he had concluded she must have thought better of their elopement. He had not returned to England to seek her out, because his creditors would have clapped him in prison the moment he set foot on English soil.

Lord Braxton could no longer blink away the truth, and his grief and rage were terrible. Julian, who was summoned to meet with him, recognized that guilt lay at the root of his feelings. If he had not opposed the marriage so strongly—if he had gone to look for Lady Lucinda when she ran away, instead of shutting himself up in his northern castle—

But he was not a man to blame himself long when others could be made to share the guilt. He came down on the trepanners like an avenging angel, hiring the Bow Street Runners to hunt them down, blanketing London with advertisements offering rewards for evidence against them, inducing the government to grant pardons to accomplices willing to turn informer. They were not wanting. To save themselves from being drawn into the net, Rawdon's minions readily revealed how the trepanning operation worked. It rounded up potential prostitutes—willing or unwilling—and sold them to brothels or wealthy individuals. Smith and Company particularly catered to men with exacting or unusual tastes. It owned, through an obscure chain of title, houses like the one in Windmill Street where Julian had met Emily. Rawdon kept the books and records, hired bullies to deal with troublesome clients, and arranged bribes for any watchmen who got too curious.

One of Rawdon's accomplices explained the company's ledgers. The various entries referred to women and children who had been tempted or trapped into prostitution. "Tea-pots" were women, "tea-chests" were little girls, and "tea-urns" were boys. "Coffee" items came from France, which was Smith and Company's other principal hunting-ground. Rawdon had kept a record of each person's description and whereabouts, in case Smith and Company later had a client looking for that particular type. "Porcelain" signified that the woman or child was fair; "japan-work" meant a dark complexion. "Gilded" translated to blond, and "painted" to red-haired. "Fancy," as opposed to "plain," meant a person of relatively genteel background. The letters in the margins identified the brothel that had purchased each item; the numbers recorded the price. Parentheses in pencil around an entry meant that the prostitute was pregnant or otherwise indisposed, while parentheses in ink signified a permanent condition, such as age or disfigurement. If an item was crossed out altogether, it was wholly unavailable, which usually meant dead.

The trepanners were so ready to betray one another that there was no need to drag Emily back from her village and force her to relive her ordeal at Mme. Leclerc's hands. That lady was apprehended at Dover, where she was on the point of embarking for France. Hidden in her baggage was a store of banknotes she had stolen from Smith and Company's office. Rawdon, it turned out, had left them there in readiness for his own planned flight to the Continent, after he had disposed of Sally.

As the news of Rawdon's crimes spread, a reformist furore swept London. The shocking demand for prostitutes, and the atrocities committed to slake it, were on everyone's lips. Julian, to his horror, found himself lionized as a moralist. His role in solving the Bellegarde murder had been kept fairly quiet, but the publicity attending Lady Lucinda's death made it impossible for him to duck celebrity. That he was already widely known as a man of fashion made his foray into hunting down murderers and procurers all the more remarkable. Newspapers wanted to interview him, friends wrote him amused or incredulous letters from their country retreats, the Society for the Suppression of Vice tried to sponsor him in a lecture. A persistent clergyman asked him what should be done about the evils of excessive drinking. Julian recommended soda water and a cold, damp cloth around the head, and began making plans to leave London as soon as Rawdon's trial was over.

Departures

In a climate of such frenzied reformist spirit, the Reverend Mr. Harcourt would have flourished, if his Reformation Society had not been tainted with the scandal of Lady Lucinda's death. Lord Braxton at first threatened to prosecute Harcourt for manslaughter, claiming that his neglect and heartlessness had helped bring about Lady Lucinda's murder. In the end, he contented himself with savaging Harcourt's reputation, and bullying his patrons into abandoning him, if they had not done so already. A fortnight after Rawdon and Fiske were arrested, the refuge closed its doors forever. Sally went to have a last look at the place and see what had become of her old acquaintances Florrie and Wideawake Peg.

She found the front door propped open, and a pair of burly men carrying furniture and boxes outside. They loaded their burdens onto a large cart in the street, then went back inside for more. The door remained open, so she walked in after them.

The hall was dingy and deserted. No matron swooped on her to demand her business. She found two inmates in the front parlour—that sanctum once reserved for Harcourt's patrons—and asked them where Florrie was. They directed her to the kitchen.

In the kitchen doorway, she stopped and stared. Florrie was sitting by the fire, eating toasted cheese. Beside her was a young man with long straggly hair, who jumped to his feet when he saw Sally. "*And, behold,*" he stammered, "*there met him a woman with the attire of an harlot, and subtil of heart. He went the way to her house, in the twilight, in the evening, in the black and dark night*—"

"Stop that, now!" Florrie gave him a good-natured shake. "You said you wouldn't do that no more."

"I'm sorry. But—but it's *her*!" he said in a loud stage whisper. "The one I told you about."

"You been a lot of trouble," Sally told him severely. "Why couldn't you tell me slap off you wasn't Caleb?"

"I was afraid! You said, 'Can I call you Caleb?' and I thought if I said no, you'd make a noise, and someone would come and catch me. *Woe is me! for I am undone; because I am a man of unclean lips*—"

"Nathan!" Florrie rounded on him, hands on hips.

"I'm sorry." He subsided into his chair.

Florrie shook her head in exasperation. "There's no doing noshing with him. Here, you gooseberry." She prodded him with her foot. "Get along now. I want to have a gossip with Sally."

He rose obediently and put on his cap. "Can I come again tomorrow?"

"You would anyhow," Florrie sighed.

She saw him upstairs, then returned to Sally. "He's a curse. There's no getting shut of him."

"He's the cove you come here to get away from!" Sally realized.

Florrie nodded. "Mind, he's a good boy, really. There ain't nothing wrong with him, 'cept his being off at the side." She tapped her head.

"His name's Nathan?"

"Nathan Winters. I met him—oh, few months ago. I was out one night, and he saw me and followed me, and at first I was afeard, on account of his being so queer. He trailed after me all night, till he found out where I lived, and after that he was always coming round to my lodging, jabbering things out of the Bible, and looking at me like a little lost calf. I knowed what he wanted, poor boy, even if he didn't. And I thought, why not? —if I give him a turn in the stubble, happen he'll go away.

"But he only got worse! He was brung up religious, you see. His pa was one of them Dissenting preachers. So he was always ranting at himself for a sinner, and saying we was both doomed to hellfire if we didn't mend our ways. I said, if I'm so wicked, why don't you leave me be? And he tried, but he was so took with me, he couldn't keep away. So I says, well, if you won't shirry off, I will.

"I'd heard about this place, and I knew Nathan couldn't follow me here, 'coz they don't let men visitors in. So I come here. But one night I looked out of the window and saw Nathan creeping about in the street! It turned out some of my friends had told him where I was, just for a lark.

"I didn't tell nobody. Because you know Mr. Harcourt—he might have had him took up by a watchman, maybe even put in a madhouse. And he don't deserve that. He's a good boy. He works for his living—a carpenter took him on, 'coz he's clever with his hands, though his mind's a bit tituppy. Anyhow, I hoped he'd give up and go away. But he didn't, and now that the refuge is all to pieces, he comes round all the time, and I cosset him a bit, 'coz he's been so lonesome without me."

Sally grinned. "You won't never get shut of him, at that rate."

"I won't never get shut of him, nohow," said Florrie fatalistically.

"And I thought I was such a downy one!" mourned Sally. "I asked him if he come here looking for a blond gal, and when he let on he had, I thought it was Mary. And all the time it was you!"

Florrie patted her flaxen curls. She still wore the uniform of the refuge, but now she kept her cap pushed back to show off her hair. "Sit down and have a bit of nuncheon. I want to hear all about how you found out Mr. Fiske had killed poor Mary—Lady Lucinda, I mean. We couldn't hardly believe it when we heard."

Sally basked in her celebrity. Florrie gave her a toasting-fork, with a well-buttered slab of bread and a piece of cheese, and she sat munching and talking, while Florrie gaped at her, and exclaimed, "My eyes!" and "I never did!" at all the right moments.

When her story had been thoroughly told and marvelled over, it was her turn to question Florrie. "What'll you do, now the refuge is gone to pot?"

"I been found a post as maidservant at an inn. I'll try it for a bit and see how I like it. The pay ain't much, but it's regular, and the innkeeper seems like a good sort. It'll be hard work, but maybe not so hard as tail-trading. You know, I don't miss that a bit—walking out every night in scanty clothes, dodging the watchmen. So happen I'll be better off on the square."

"What about Nathan?"

"Oh, I expect he'll find me again. He always does."

Sally asked after the matrons.

"They don't come here no more," said Florrie. "Mrs. Jessop's husband won't let her have nothing more to do with Mr. Harcourt, and Miss Nettleton has the 'sterics at the very thought of him. Mrs. Fiske is selling her house and leaving London, I hear tell she never goes out, not even to church. She ain't been once to see her hubby nor her son."

"Too bad. If there's one thing Blinkers deserves, it's a visit from his ma. I wouldn't wish it on Bristles, though—he's mortal sick. They've had to put him in the infirmary."

"Poor Mr Fiske. Still, it's a lesson, ain't it?"

"I don't want no more lessons. I've had enough to last me all me life." She jumped up. "Come on, let's go upstairs. I want to have a last look round."

They left the kitchen. On their way upstairs, they saw the two workmen inching their way down from the first floor with Harcourt's desk. One of the men had a Greek urn tucked under his arm. As they reached the door, Wideawake Peg came running down the stairs after them. She wore a plain but handsome blue wool gown, with a cameo broach at the neck. "Stop!" she cried sharply.

The men set down the desk and looked around. The one with the urn said nervously, "Is anything wrong, Mrs. Harcourt?"

"Mrs. Harcourt?" Sally gasped.

"Hush!" Florrie drew her into the shadow of the stairs.

"Give that to me!" Peg held out her hands for the urn. "How can you be after carrying it in such a cow-handed fashion?"

"I remember that there urn!" whispered Sally. "It's the one where she hid her—"

"Is anything amiss, Margaret?" Harcourt appeared on the stairs above.

"No, nothing, Gideon. I'm only trying to teach these shabaroons a bit of respect for other people's property."

The man with the urn squinted inside it, frowning. "There's some'ut in here." Turning it upside down, he gave it a shake, and a small pouch fell out. "Why, it's 'bacca!"

Peg snatched the tobacco from him. "Why, you wicked man, you miserable sinner! How could you bring your foul weed into a Christian house—and me husband a man of God!"

"But, Mrs. Harcourt, this ain't my—"

"I'll not be hearing any of your excuses! And to hide it in me husband's own urn!" Her voice broke, dropping from anger to sorrow. "Don't you know the harm you're doing to your soul? Doesn't it pain you to think of the worm of vice eating away at it, till it's all tatters and not fit to be seen on Judgement Day, at all at all?"

"I'm sorry, Mrs. Harcourt. It won't happen again, ma'am." He touched his hat and signalled to his partner to heave up the desk again. They escaped as quickly as they could.

Harcourt joined Peg downstairs. He looked distracted, disheveled, and sleepless. "You're very eloquent, my dear."

"And isn't it all your doing?" she cooed. "Haven't I been a new woman, ever since you took hold of me heartstrings and led me down the path of righteousness?"

"Margaret—" He tried to take her in his arms.

"Shame on you!" She dodged him playfully. "In broad daylight! What would all your fine patrons say?"

His face darkened. "I haven't any to worry about now."

"But you will." She slipped her arm through his. "When we're safe in the country—when the scandal's died down—you'll work your magic again. And this time you can't fail, because you'll have me to help you."

She stroked his cheek lightly and went upstairs. He turned about and hastened after her.

Sally came out of hiding and gazed after them. "Looks like it's her as is leading him—and not by his heartstrings, neither."

"He was very low, after his Reclamation Society went down the wind," said Florrie. "He moped about a good deal, and Peg was the only one as could put him in spirits. And after a while he started looking at her—well, the way he never looked at any of us gals before. He had nothing else to think about, you see."

"So he fell off his high horse, and Peg was there to catch him."

Florrie nodded. "They was married yesterday, and they mean to light out to his rectory in Norfolk straight off, afore the bailiffs comes in. I hear tell the refuge is deep in debt, and Mr. Harcourt hasn't a penny to bless himself with."

"I dunno," said Sally skeptically. "He's such a pinch-fist, I expect he's put a bit away where the catch-club won't find it."

"It's queer, though, ain't it—Peg marrying Mr. Harcourt?"

"It ain't, then. She wanted to get into the morality trade, and this was her chance."

"But she always hated him like poison."

Sally disagreed. Later she told Julian, "I think she al'ays meant to have him. And when a gal really means to have a cove, there ain't much he can do."

"I take your point."

She grinned. "I'd like to take yours again some time."

Fiske's prediction proved true: before the next Old Bailey sessions, he died in the infirmary at Newgate Prison, with only a hastily summoned clergyman for company. Rawdon stood trial alone. There were numerous charges against him, the most serious involving the deaths of Lady Lucinda Braxton and a Scotswoman, first known as Megan MacGowan, but afterward identified as Mrs. Charles Avondale.

The news of Avondale's marriage caused a sensation among the Quality. Everyone was avid to know how Miss Grantham felt about her near brush with bigamy. But she cheated the gossips by leaving London to stay with a school friend in Bath. She had broken off her engagement to Avondale, who had then departed for France—to bring back his daughter, people said. He was expected back in time for Rawdon's trial.

The furore over Lady Lucinda's rape and murder had begun to die down, but Rawdon's trial whipped it up again. Despite a thick, lugubrious November fog, anyone and everyone who could squeeze into the courtroom was there. Among the crowd Julian perceived Avondale and Mr. and Mrs. Digby. Sally pointed out Florrie and other former inmates of the refuge. Lord Braxton sat at the front of the courtroom, bristling with impatience for the trial to begin. Everyone knew that all his wealth and political power were marshalled behind the prosecution. Nothing short of a conviction and sentence of death would satisfy him.

There was a gasp of awe when Rawdon was brought into the dock. Hatred seemed to emanate from him; the spectators felt it like a wave of heat. He looked pale, but otherwise healthy and well-fed. Sally supposed he must have enough money to pay the gaolers well for his food and lodging. He no longer wore his goldrimmed spectacles, but of course he had not needed them anyway. They had merely been a part of his disguise—his mask of ordinariness. Perhaps he had acquired them when he transformed himself from Caleb Fiske into Joseph Rawdon.

He did not take the witness stand, since the law could not compel him to incriminate himself, and would not allow him to testify in his defence. He had no lawyer and presented no evidence—only listened to the parade of witnesses against him with a look almost of satisfaction. Power, thought Sally—it's what he loves best. This whole show is on account of him, and he knows it. So much blunt's been spent to bring him to trial, all the newspapers is writing about him, mothers is using his name to frighten their kids. He's never had so much power as now. Pox take him!—this is just how he would have wanted to die.

The trial lasted all day and into the evening, but the verdict was never in question. Rawdon was convicted as an accessory to the kidnapping and murder of Lady Lucinda Braxton, and as a principal in the attempted murder of Miss Sarah Stokes. He was also found guilty of killing Mrs. Charles Avondale, though that death was held to be manslaughter. He would not be sentenced until the final day of the sessions, when all the prisoners convicted in this round of trials would be herded into court to hear their punishment. But already his fate was sealed. No one could doubt that the judge would don the black cap for him and order that he be hanged by the neck until he was dead.

When the proceedings were over, Samuel Digby shook Julian's hand and invited him to call on him at his earliest convenience, so that they could settle their accounts. He pronounced himself well satisfied with the outcome of the investigation, but Julian suspected he was just a little bit sorry Harcourt had not turned out to be guilty.

As Julian was leaving the courtroom, Avondale fell into step with him. "They'll make a hero of him, of course," Avondale said bitterly, "the way they always do with the worst criminals. There'll be broadsheet-sellers hawking stories about his crimes, ballads about his final days—"

"Last words he spoke," said Julian, "or would have spoken, if he'd had any sense of history."

"Shall you go to the execution?"

"Good God, no! I'm leaving London tomorrow for a shooting trip in the north."

Avondale smiled wryly. "Just remember, if you cross the border, be careful what you promise."

Julian cocked an eyebrow at him. "Would you take it amiss if I asked after Rosemary?"

"No, not at all. I've brought her back from France and set her up at my house, with a nurse-governess my mother engaged.

Between them, they've made it a different place altogether. It's so wholesome and respectable, and so cursed *feminine*, I feel like a visitor. The odd thing is, I don't mind it so much as I would have thought. Rosemary's a taking little thing—I'm devilish fond of her. She'll be a beauty one day—you can see it already. My governor's stumped up to build her a nursery. I'm taking her and her nurse away for a holiday while the work's being done. To Bath," he added casually.

"Indeed?" Julian lifted his brows.

Oh, of course I know what you're thinking. Ada's there. But, you see, Caroline told me Thorndike offered for her again, and she refused him. That means I may still have a chance! I'll call on her in Bath—just a friendly call between cousins. If she won't receive me, I'll lie in wait for her at the Pump Room, the Assembly Rooms—she won't be able to turn around without seeing me. I want to show her Rosemary. She's such a charmer, how could anyone help but fall in love with her? Ada's generous, she won't hold what Megan and I did against our daughter. And in time, she'll see that I've changed. I can be as steady and constant as Thorndike. I'll prove it to her, by God."

Julian had to smile at hearing him vow reformation, while plotting to regain Ada's favour by dangling his motherless daughter under her nose. He had changed, perhaps, but not a great deal. Still, it would not surprise Julian if he won Ada back. Didn't he always manage to get what he wanted in the end?

Sally was still living with Mrs. Mabbitt, keeping her company and helping about the house. Lord Braxton had made her a present of twenty pounds, which seemed like a fortune to her. She did not know what to do with it, or with herself. She and Julian were rarely alone together, and their relationship had subsided for the most part into a friendship. She was restless at first, chafing against the placid life she led. But as the weeks went by, she settled down surprisingly well. She grew thoughtful, talked less, and smiled to herself a good deal. Julian supposed that combating evil and facing death had made her more reflective. Dipper thought she was up to something.

Julian was to leave for his shooting trip on the morning after the trial. He had arranged to stop at MacGregor's along the way, to give him a first-hand account of the solution to the murder. If Dipper was sorry to leave Annie Price for several weeks, he gave no sign. His love affairs were an enigma to Julian—he got in and out of them with a balletic grace, leaving no bitterness behind. It was an extraordinary talent. If it could be bottled, it would knock spots off Summerson's Strengthening Elixir.

Sally came upstairs to Julian's lodging to bid him and Dipper goodbye. She kissed them both in a sisterly fashion, but clung to Julian a fraction longer. "Think of me sometimes," she whispered, and he thought he heard a break in her voice. But when she drew away, she was all smiles and raillery. "I hear tell it's bitter cold up there at darkmans. You'd best find some northern gal to keep you warm."

He had a sudden urge to take her with him.

It was out of the question, of course. He was staying with friends, and would be spending his days out shooting and his nights at cards. What would she do all that time? Be bored and lonely, and get into trouble, which they had all had enough of for the time being.

"We'll be back in a few weeks, you know," he said.

She tossed her head. "Think I can't get on without you?"

"I'll think you'll be into some new scrape before our carriage turns the corner."

"Then you can get me out again, can't you? Give you some'ut to do when you gets home."

"I should rather not have to make it a lifelong habit."

"Go on, you liked it uncommon, finding out who hushed Mary, and all."

"I have to admit," he owned, smiling, "there were some parts I wouldn't have missed."

Julian returned to London early in December. It was a bleak, dreary night; he consoled himself with plans to winter in Italy. The trip had done him good, but he was glad to be back. He was too confirmed a city-dweller to relish the northern wilds for long.

To his surprise, Mrs. Mabbitt was watching for him at the window. While Dipper paid off the hackney coachman, he went to meet her at the door. "You're up very late, Mrs. Mabbitt."

"I wanted to catch you and Dipper, sir, directly you got home. It's about Sally."

Sally! Why had he left her alone? Suppose there were colleagues of Rawdon's still loose on the streets, wanting revenge—!

"What's happened?" he said quickly.

"She's gone away, sir."

"Disappeared?"

"No, sir, just gone. Packed up her things about a week ago and took herself off. She said goodbye and thanked me for everything, just as proper as could be. But she wouldn't breathe a word about where she was going, or what she meant to do. I said to her, Mr. Kestrel and your brother will be back soon—don't you want to say goodbye to them? She asked me to say it for her. I told her on no uncertain terms, it was a very poor return for all you'd done for her, sir, and a most unsisterly way to treat Dipper. But, there!—she *would* go, and go she did. She was good enough to leave me a bit of money for having her here, though I told her there wasn't the least need. Oh, and she sent you both her love."

Julian leaned against the mantelpiece in his bedroom, watching Dipper unpack. "Of course she knew when she said goodbye to us that she wouldn't be here when we got back."

"I think that's so, sir."

"Why should she have gone off like that—in secret, without a word?"

"I expect she thought we'd try to stop her, sir."

"Where do you suppose she's gone?"

"I dunno, sir. But I ain't surprised she piked off. She never was one for a quiet life. She prob'ly thought she'd be turning respectable before long, and she couldn't stick it."

There was a short silence. Then Julian strolled to the window, saying in what MacGregor called his drawing-room drawl, "Well, if she wanted so badly to be gone, I daresay it's just as well she took herself off without any fuss—"

He turned, and found Dipper gazing at him understandingly, with Sally's warm brown eyes. "I shall miss her," he finished quietly.

"She'll be back, sir—you may take your dying oath on it! She was al'ays a gipsy, sir—she never could stick one place for long. But now she knows where to find us, she'll be back—Newgate seize me if she won't!"